BLUE PEARL

T. J. MacGregor

~~~

BLUE PEARL

HYPERION

NEW YORK

BOOK DESIGN BY DOROTHY S. BAKER

Library of Congress Cataloging-in-Publication Data

MacGregor, T. J.

Blue Pearl / by T. J. MacGregor.

p.   cm.

ISBN 0-7868-6061-8

1. Saint James, Quin (Fictitious character)—Fiction.

2. McCleary, Mike (Fictitious character)—Fiction.

3. Private investigators—Florida—Fiction.

4. Women detectives—Florida—Fiction.   I. Title.

PS3563.A31115B58   1994

813'.54—dc20   93-49700

CIP

FIRST EDITION

10 9 8 7 6 5 4 3 2 1

For my daughter, Megan,
and for Mary Ann Eckels

I'm indebted to a number of people who contributed ideas and information about healing: Nancy Pickard for reminding me that Louise Hay and Deepak Chopra are pioneers of a new approach to medicine and healing; Phyllis Vega for telling me about the Seth Network International; Edith Mercier for sharing her personal experiences about alternative medicine; my sister, Mary Anderson, for her medical expertise on the emotional components of disease; and Renie Wiley and Richard Daemian, metaphysicians.

≈

Thanks to my editor, Pat Mulcahy, for her unflinching eye, and to my agent, Diane Cleaver, for her infinite patience and continued faith. Last but never least, my gratitude to Rob, my husband and co-conspirator.

One windy day two monks were arguing about a flapping banner. The first said, "I say the banner is moving, not the wind." The second said, "I say the wind is moving, not the banner." A third monk passed by and said, "The wind is not moving. The banner is not moving. Your minds are moving."

ZEN PARABLE

≈

Healing by the laying on of hands is about as miraculous as radio.

BERNARD GRAD

DECEMBER 5

Jupiter, Florida

The first time I killed it happened in a dream and it was a man, not a woman, and I used a knife, not a gun.

It was one of those stifling, breathless August days when the sky and the sea are bleached of color and the air steams. Barker was on a yacht and everything around him was a surreal milky white, but he was dark, like an oil spill. He was sitting in a beach chair, reading or something, and his back was to me. I had a steak knife in my hand. I don't know why, it was just there, the way things are sometimes in dreams, and I walked up behind him and stared at the hair on the back of his neck.

I remember this part clearly: the tiny strands curling like commas against his tanned neck, the freckles punctuating the skin, the creases like dashes. The longer I stared, the more obvious it became that these commas, punctuation marks, and dashes were a code, a secret language, something intended specifically for me. The message was clear, that I should kill him as he sat there, just push the knife into his back and be done with it. So that's what I did.

In the dream.

This time, though, it wasn't any dream.

Janis was alone in the house. I had seen the Porsche roar out of the gate earlier, her husband and daughter inside. I was sure he and Janis had been arguing. She had probably started drinking as soon as he had left, hard stuff, gin or scotch, and with any luck she would be sucking it down straight from the bottle now.

I crossed the road in front of the ranch, the air warm and still around me. The scent of gardenias and jasmine hung in the air, wildflowers bloomed in clusters as plump as cushions. The melaleuca trees along the driveway stood straight and motionless, like soldiers at attention. Janis's touches. She possessed a certain aesthetic sense about color and shape, the geometry the eye perceives. I admired that about her.

It was everything else about her that I had a problem with.

As I climbed the creaking porch steps, I realized how odd the gun felt inside my jacket. Lumpy, like a piece of wadded-up clothing. I punched the doorbell, waited, punched again. The light from the TV flickered against the Levolors. It was so quiet I could hear a soft burst of canned laughter. When she didn't appear, I rapped sharply, waited again, then called her name. It skipped off my tongue with a disquieting finality.

I finally covered the door handle with my handkerchief, felt no resistance when I turned it, and stepped inside. She was sacked out on the couch, an open bottle of booze on the floor. Next to the bottle was an overturned glass and a puddle of something, melted ice or spilled booze, I couldn't tell. I shut the door and walked over to her.

"Janis," I whispered, but she didn't stir.

She was sprawled on her back, strands of her blond hair curled damply against her forehead. Her mouth was slightly open; the air around her stank of booze. Even in her worst moments she was pretty, no denying that. The pale perfection of her skin, the delicate nose, the high forehead, the silken sheen of her hair. But what struck me most just then was how harmless she seemed, how benign.

My resolve faltered, stuttered like an old engine badly in need of a tune-up. I don't mind admitting that I had my share of second thoughts. But they never lasted long. I knew, after all, what lay beneath that pretty skin, the quick smile, the charm that she turned off and on like a light. And she had made this so much easier by being six sheets to the wind.

I slipped the gun from my jacket, nothing fancy, a standard .38. I picked up a pillow from the other end of the couch, pressed it down against her chest, and fired through it, three quick shots to the heart.

The pillow muffled the sound, but it was a shock nonetheless, a shock that I had actually done it, that it had been this easy. She never knew what hit her.

I stepped back quickly, clutching the pillow and the gun. The spreading stain of blood on the front of her robe possessed a lovely symmetry and I couldn't wrench my eyes from it. It reminded me of something I'd seen on TV, on the Discovery Channel probably, the texture of a rose petal under a microscope. Surprise, the petal isn't smooth at all. It's a vast, complex continent of veins that connect like interstates, of cells that swirl like dervishes. A bit like Janis, I guess.

I became aware, finally, of the voices from the TV, of a clock ticking somewhere in the room. I didn't know how long I'd been standing there, transfixed, and that frightened me. I checked my clothing for blood, jerked the case off the pillow, dropped it on top of her. Then I backed away from the couch, blinking hard and fast, trying to clear my head. I glanced quickly around the room, certain I hadn't touched anything except the door handle and the pillowcase.

I slipped the gun back inside my jacket, wadded up the pillowcase, and used it to open the door. Then I hurried back down the driveway, past the silent, watchful melaleuca trees, a wave of euphoria filling me, lifting me, transporting me.

1

~~~~~~

When Mike McCleary stepped out of the gym that night, a quarter moon hung like a necklace in the February sky. The earlier rain had swept on out to sea and released that deep, humus scent of earth and green and salt, smells that were indigenous to South Florida regardless of the season. The noise of frogs and crickets drifted in the cool air and, more distant, he heard the splash of cars, a squeal of damp brakes.

He had left the windows down in his Miata and the seats were soaked. But on the floor in front of the passenger seat was a shoebox sealed with heavy tape. There was no note with it. The man he had spoken to earlier that evening had said it would be there and it was.

Weeks, he thought. You go along for weeks tracking leads that dead-end, that twist back on themselves, and suddenly the winds change and you have something. What was the catch?

He used his pocketknife to cut along the edge of the tape and went through the contents. A videotape, photographs, printed material. It fit, it all fit, pieces of some vast, complex picture that had eluded him for nearly two months. There were still gaps; he didn't know what was on the videotape, he still wasn't quite sure of some of the connections. But he had enough here to start tightening the noose.

He hadn't told Quin about this investigation, hadn't told his colleagues. It was strictly between him and Fitz Eastman, a senior homicide detective with the Palm Beach County Sheriff's Department who had brought him in on the case. And who was, he thought, out of town until tomorrow afternoon.

What to do with all this until then? If he took it home, Quin might find it and he would have to compromise Eastman's confidence. If he took just the tape to view tonight before he went to bed, the TV might wake Quin or their daughter. Home was out, he decided. The box would probably be secure in the safe at their office, but that was a twenty-minute drive from there, then another twenty minutes home, and he would roll in at midnight. Best to stash the shoebox in one of the lockers in the gym.

He zipped it inside his canvas workout bag, found a roll of masking tape in the glove compartment, and went back into the building. McCleary usually worked out three afternoons a week and at this hour, 10:50 on a Wednesday night, the faces were all different. He didn't recognize the staff or the customers. These were people whose body clocks ticked to another rhythm altogether, the true night owls.

In the men's locker room McCleary went into a stall and looked through the material more slowly. The man he had spoken to, who called himself Blue Pearl, had promised there would be more information. McCleary had no idea who he was or what his interest in this case was. The only thing he knew for sure was that the guy was spooked; they had been playing cat-and-mouse games for weeks. Meet me here, meet me there. But until tonight he had been a no-show.

In early December a woman named Janis Krieger had been shot at her home in Jupiter. Three slugs to the chest and no sign of a struggle because she had been passed out on the couch from the half bottle of scotch she'd consumed sometime before the murder. Her husband and four-year-old daughter had been at a wedding reception at the Breakers Hotel in Palm Beach when it happened and the house-keeper had been out of town.

There were motives, but none strong enough to point the finger at, and all of the suspects had alibis. Eastman had spent a week alone on the case before he had asked for McCleary's help. He was up against Palm Beach money; the state attorney's office was investigating the dead woman's husband, a Chilean healer, for practicing medicine without a license; and the feds had the guy under surveillance. The case had all the markings of a dead end, until now.

Most of the metal lockers along the wall were taken. He finally found an unoccupied locker in the bottom row, slipped the shoebox inside, locked it, pocketed the key. Safe until Eastman returned tomorrow.

His house was three miles west of the gym and he didn't have to drive the interstate to get there. The two-lane road took him past several apartment complexes, a mobile-home park, patches of pasture where half a dozen cows grazed year-round. Six years ago the entire area had still been pasture and the road he was on had ended where there was now a stoplight. Only the newest maps showed that it continued into Walden Lakes, the development where he and Quin lived.

Yes, there were lakes, seven or eight of them, but they had never seemed quite real to McCleary. They weren't comparable to the lakes in upstate New York, where he was from. They were man-made, dug when Walden Lakes was built and filled with rain. They were like optical illusions, quivering in the moonlight as if threatening to vanish.

The black olive trees that fringed the lakes had been planted afterward. They were spaced at precise five-foot intervals from one another and about twenty feet back from the lakes. This same mani-cured look pertained to everything in the development, even the bike path where he and Quin jogged most mornings. The randomness of nature had no place in the South Florida suburbs.

Each of the five subdevelopments within Walden Lakes had a reference to water in its name, RiverBridge, for instance, or Mirror-Bay, and was always spelled as one word. It was par for the cloying tidiness of the place and part of what made Palm Beach County so vastly different from Dade, where he had lived for twenty years. Here, you had mostly developments; in Dade, you had neighborhoods.

Nothing in Walden Lakes was older than five years, and yet within a radius of just a few miles was everything you needed. Two schools, four day-care centers, a mall, grocery stores, a post office, restaurants. At times it all seemed surreal to McCleary, as if he had stumbled into some other man's life and taken up residence.

He turned into RiverBridge, dead at this hour. His house backed up to one of the lakes and beyond the lake was a mango grove. It would probably disappear within the next few years as the demand for expansion seduced longtime owners to get out while the getting was good. It was anyone's guess what would rise where the mango trees now stood.

His home had been custom-built three years ago by an engineer from Pratt and Whitney who had been laid off four months after he'd taken out the mortgage. McCleary and Quin had gotten a good deal, but it had hurt like hell at the time. Saddled with double mortgages because their house in Miami hadn't sold, moving expenses, and the bills from Quin's pregnancy, which hadn't been covered by their health insurance, they'd had some very lean years. Now their PI business in Palm Beach was booming. This county might have less violent crime, he thought, but it didn't lack for people who needed what they could provide.

The house was dark, but Merlin was in the garage when he drove in. He was the oldest of their three cats, Quin's before they were married. He darted through the swinging panel in the utility room and was seated by his bowl when McCleary came into the kitchen. The two other cats, Tracy and Hepburn, wandered in for their share of the can of food McCleary opened. And behind them, tail wagging, was Flats, the sheepdog.

The McCleary menagerie, he thought, and wondered what would be next. Birds? Rabbits? Hamsters? He fed them, changed litter boxes, and balked at the mess in the family room. Michelle's toys and books were scattered across the floor; plastic cups with juice and milk in them stood wherever she had left them; one of Quin's files was open on the breakfast table, the papers probably covering the crumbs from dinner. He turned his back on it, irritated by the sight of it all.

He hadn't bargained for all this when he and Quin had gotten married. An apartment in some funky old neighborhood would have suited him just fine.

McCleary tripped over Michelle's little trike on his way through the dark hall. His shoes crunched over some goddamn thing—a peanut, a plastic toy, he couldn't tell what it was and didn't pause to look. He opened the door to his daughter's room, the night-light glowing behind the toy chest. Such quiet here, he thought, just the softness of her breathing.

She was asleep on her back and had kicked off the sheets. For the longest time she had been nearly bald, just a soft peach fuzz over her head. Now her hair was ear-length, as pale as Quin's had been when she was Michelle's age. Her eyes, when they were open, also belonged to her mother, that same ghostly blue in the center ringed by a darker blue. The mouth and the shape of her face were his and the rest of her was an amalgam of genes from the Irish and German on McCleary's side of the family and the Scots and English on Quin's side.

Her T-shirt was hiked up to her chest and her gray bear, the Fids bear, named after the ex-client who had given it to her, was lying in the crook of her arm. McCleary covered her, kissed her forehead, and she stirred, murmuring in a dream she might share with him in the morning.

A friend of his, a cop, had once told him that the best cops were those who had no families, no ties, and therefore nothing to lose. During his ten years as a homicide detective with Metro-Dade, that had been true for him. There had been women but no wife, kids but not his kids. Even though he was no longer a cop, he understood now what the cop had meant. Michelle, who would be two on the seventeenth of this month, had changed his life and his relationship with Quin in ways both great and small.

His last stop before he hit the sack was the den. He removed the locker key from his pocket, dropped it in an envelope, and tacked it to the wide strip of cork along the edge of the chalkboard where he sometimes plotted cases. He wasn't sure why he did it. Out of guilt maybe that he hadn't confided in Quin about the investigation. They rarely kept professional details like this from each other. They couldn't afford to. In the event that something happened to one of them, the other could always pick up the slack.

But Eastman had been adamant on this point and, considering the contents of the shoebox, probably with good reason.

McCleary showered in the smaller bathroom, surrounded by his daughter's toys. He was forced to use Winnie the Pooh shampoo, the only choice available, and Little Mermaid soap. He stepped on a magnetized letter *E* when he got out and had to use a hand towel to dry himself, the lone towel on the rack. The toothbrush he usually kept in here was gone; he made do with Ninja Turtle toothpaste on his finger, the final violation of his sense of order.

He scooped up his clothes, turned off the light, walked to the bedroom at the back of the house. He jerked open a drawer in his dresser and rummaged for a pair of gym shorts, his concession to Michelle's frequent visits in the middle of the night. As he got into bed, jockeying Merlin for his share of the mattress, Quin woke up enough to ask what time it was. He told her, then said, "I wish to hell someone would pick up around here. I nearly killed myself on the way in."

"Hire a live-in maid," she murmured, and turned over and went back to sleep.

Sure, hire a maid and pay her social security, in the event that he ever ran for public office. A maid to go along with the guy who cut their lawn, the day-care center where Michelle spent at least forty hours a week, the firm's five employees.

It only affirmed his conviction that there was a lot to admire about the times depicted on the covers of the *Saturday Evening Post*.

≈

The black Lincoln appeared suddenly in the dark, as though the night had given birth to it. Alejandro Domingo watched its headlights moving through the gate of the Lazy Quick, past the thickets of pines and rows of melaleucas. The lights vanished briefly beneath the sagging branches of a banyan tree, then reappeared, round and pale, like fading moons.

For a moment the car seemed to drive into his own reflection in the window. The illusion disoriented him and he stepped back, frowning at the face that floated in the glass. His face, changed and yet unchanged. It was thinner than it had been in Chile, the bones sharper, bolder, the black eyes more guarded, the brows thicker, the black hair shorter. The lines and creases of forty-one years had deepened considerably since December 5; his temples had begun to gray.

As he turned away from the window, his gaze paused briefly on the row of photographs that lined the mantel over the fireplace. The faces of the women in his life stared out at him, as if in reproach: his wife, blue eyes, ear-length blond hair, a woman he had loved almost from the moment he'd seen her six years ago; his sister, younger than he by eight years, with eyes and hair as black as his own; and his daughter, a little beauty with wide dark eyes and delicately sculpted features. Of the three, the first was dead and the future of the other two was as uncertain as his own.

His housekeeper, Carmelita, stopped in the doorway, the creases on her face deepening with worry. "Alejandro?"

"*Sí, sí*, I saw it." He zipped up his windbreaker, thrust his hands in the pockets, and looked at her, at Carmelita, aging in her corpulence. He had brought her here from Chile, where she had first been his patient, then his housekeeper. He had also brought his sister here. Now he wished he had left both of them behind.

"It is like the early days under Pinochet," she said softly.

Pinochet's goons had not been part of his world then; the island where he'd lived had been of no interest to them. But they'd been part of Carmelita's world and he'd heard her stories many times. Chile, like Argentina, also had its *desaparecidos*, those who had disappeared. Among them were Carmelita's husband and father.

"I think it is not so bad as that," he replied, and hoped it was true.

"What time will you return?"

"When they tire of me."

Then, whispering, as though she believed the house had ears: "And if you don't return? Who should I call?"

Alejandro kissed her lightly on the cheek. "*No te preocupes.* I'll be back."

Her hand tightened on his arm. "If," she repeated.

"The detective. McCleary. His number is by the phone."

The doorbell rang. He squeezed Carmelita's hand and hurried into the hall. The man on the porch was the same man who had stood there more than a dozen times in recent weeks. He was tall and lanky, with a pleasant but unremarkable face, wire-rim aviator glasses, vibrant blue eyes, a beard several shades darker than his light brown hair. Despite his quick, nervous smile, his manner was smooth, easy, professional. His name was Bob and his greeting never varied. "Ready to split, Alex?"

"Got my passport, Bob?"

Bob laughed and replied, as he always did, "You know how it goes, *amigo.* That's not my department." Then the next question, as inevitable as their greeting: "Did you eat any dairy products today?"

"No. Just fish and fruit. Why is that so important?"

Bob shrugged. "You got me. I'm supposed to ask, so I ask."

As they trotted down the steps, Alejandro said, "How are they?"

"Good, real good." Like a man chatting with a friend over beers. "They aren't mistreated, Alex. We're not monsters." Then the part that Alejandro needed to hear, that he waited to hear, that Bob offered him, an enticement, a promised reward: "That kid of yours is something else, Alex. Sharp as a goddamn tack. Doesn't miss a trick. She and your sister hit the books every morning like clockwork. They've got a regular routine: the books, a walk, lunch, maybe they take a swim, watch a little TV, then it's the books again."

Lies. Miranda wouldn't watch television in the middle of the day and his sister wouldn't swim when the sun was strongest. But perhaps there was a pool where they were and their surroundings were comfortable enough to have a television. In every lie, he thought, there's probably at least a grain of truth.

"Forty days, Alex, you realize that?"

As though he couldn't count. On the calendar in his den he had marked off every long and terrible day since he had driven his sister and daughter to the airport for a flight they had never taken. "What do they want from me?"

Bob touched his hands to his chest, an innocent man just doing his job. "Hey, Alex, they don't tell me shit like that." He opened the back door and Alejandro slid inside.

Leather seats. Tinted windows. Classical music. And Jim sitting on the far side. Jim, with his curly gray hair and his gray mustache and his flat silver eyes. Jim, who had high blood pressure. Alejandro didn't know his last name. He and Bob were the sort of men who never had last names.

The privacy glass between the front seat and the back whirred into place. Bob started the car. Jim reached for the briefcase at his feet, set it on his lap, dialed in a combination. Then he snapped open the lid, removed a minicassette recorder, and popped in a tape.

Miranda's voice was calm, fluid, and filled him with pain. "Hi, Papa. It's the morning of February the third. I had a cold for a while, but I'm doing okay. I've been having bad dreams, but the unicorns in my room chase them away by morning. Please do whatever you have to do, Papa. I want to come home. I love you."

The recorder clicked off. Jim snapped the lid shut on the briefcase and the car sped through the dark.

"Do you write those speeches for her?" Alejandro asked.

Jim lit one of his long, thin cheroots. "Certainly not. We edit, Alejandro, we're entitled to a little editing, but no, she says what she wants. Within limits, of course." He cracked his window to allow the smoke to escape. "I'm sorry about her nightmares. But they'll pass. Kids are resilient and she and your sister are being treated well."

Alejandro felt a surge of hatred for this man, speaking as he did in that soft, arrogant tone, puffing on his stinking cigar. "You need to bring your blood pressure down, Jim."

"What?" *Blink, blink* went those flat silver eyes.

"It's dangerously high."

Jim laughed. "Don't pull your healer shit with me, Alejandro."

But he didn't puff on the cigar again and shortly before Alejandro was blindfolded, Jim slipped the cigar through the crack in the window. Alejandro felt a fierce satisfaction that Jim of the gray hair and silver eyes didn't really know what to make of him.

Since they always blindfolded him before they hit the main road, Alejandro didn't know exactly where they took him. They also removed his watch, so he wouldn't be able to tell how long it took to get there. But even if he had his watch it wouldn't make much difference. He was sure Bob drove around for a while, in and out of neighborhoods, up and down streets, just to confuse him. The machinations of their deceit were endlessly clever.

When they were inside the building, in the room where they would test him, prod him, draw his blood, they removed the blindfold. There were no windows. It could have been day or night, afternoon or morning. He sat in the same chair where he always sat, facing the same pane of one-way glass that he always faced, connected to the same wires, the same machines that monitored his blood pressure, his brain waves, the beats of his heart.

Do this, Alejandro. Do that. A dog with his tricks.

Sometimes they drugged him to study the effects of the drug on the tests, tonight they did not. Tonight they showed him pictures, photographs from the Nazi holocaust, of starving children with swollen bellies and flies in the corners of their eyes. Tonight they showed him tapes of a black man being beaten by cops, of a city in flames, of a Russian citizen who had been at Chernobyl and was now dying of radiation poisoning. Scenes from the world according to network news. And the machines clicked and leaped and ran wild, recording his every reaction.

And tonight they brought him a seagull with a broken wing. Mend its bones, they said. Heal it, they said. Make it fly. But he couldn't, the horror of the photographs and tapes was still with him. They took the gull away, took the gull with its broken wing and probably killed it. They put on soft, pleasant music and showed him photographs and tapes of beaches, mountains, families on horseback. Tranquil scenes, the world according to travel brochures. *Click, click* whispered the machines. *Click, click.*

They drew his blood, four vials that were labeled, marked, pushed out of the room on a cart.

Bark, Alejandro. Jump through the hoop. Sit, roll over, play dead.

More photographs, more tapes, more scenes of war and peace, love and hate, triumph and despair, back and forth, over and over again until his mouth was a desert, his head pounded, and his heart ached. When exhaustion overcame him, they let him sleep, then they took his blood again and brought the gull back into the room, set it on his lap.

Its right wing hung limply, it was losing feathers, pain glazed its eyes. He wondered if they had caught it and broken its wing just for him, to see what he could do. He held it, stroked it, felt its agony, dreamed its dream of sky, sun, heat. His hands grew warm and began to tingle. It was as if bells were chiming deep within his muscles, tendons, and cells, and it was their vibration that he felt.

Click click click spat the machines.

He couldn't make the gull fly, but he banished its pain.

Not good enough, Alejandro. It can't be measured, let's try again.

And again.

And again.

And when its wings finally fluttered and the gull lifted from his hand, its pale form seemed radiant, magnificent. He was allowed to release the gull from a terrace that faced a dark wall of trees. He watched it swooping, soaring, higher and higher until it seemed to brush the moon. Then it was gone. Free.

"Two days ago that bird was on the cosmic shit list, Alex," said Bob, coming over to him. "I found it on the beach with a hook through its wing."

Alejandro heard the awe in his voice and thought, *You fool.* He didn't want to talk to Bob, to anyone. He wanted to go home, but he knew they weren't finished with him yet.

He glanced down at the flowerpots brimming with violet periwinkles. Weeds, he thought. Periwinkles were nothing but weeds that had become fashionable in landscaping because they were hardy. Resistant to the summer heat, to bugs, to just about everything, they were the cockroaches of the South Florida plant kingdom. They had probably been present when the world was formed and they would still be around in ten million years.

And what was he? A throwback? An evolutionary stepping-stone? An alien? What?

When they went back inside, Alejandro noticed that Bob avoided touching him.

2

~~~~~~~

At 6:40 that morning McCleary and Quin ran along their usual route, the bike path, each with a hand on the three-wheeled carriage in which Michelle sat. Flats bounded along in front of them.

Great, menacing storm clouds squatted low in the pale sky and a warm wind gusted off the lake, shaking leaves from the branches. Lightning flashed, briefly altering the dark topography, and was followed seconds later by thunder that echoed like bowling balls in a celestial alley.

"The sky looks ugly," Quin said. "Let's head back."

"Just another half mile, then we'll turn around. Five bucks says it won't rain before we reach the house."

"Ten bucks says it pours while we're still out here."

"Fifteen says you're wrong."

"Aren't we frisky this morning. The loser makes pancakes and also has to clean up."

He laughed. "You're on."

"What time did you get in last night?" she asked.

McCleary glanced at her, dark hair flying behind her in the wind, all five foot ten of her focused on running. Eight years, he thought. He had been married to this woman for eight years and known her for more than a decade and he still couldn't be sure what she was thinking when she asked him a question like that. Was she merely curious? Was she just making conversation? Had she resented pulling child duty last night? What?

He fudged on the truth to avoid any more questions. "I guess it was around eleven. What time did you go to bed?"

"Not too long after you called, nine-thirty, I guess. That's about when Ellie dropped off. So what's the case?"

"Which case?"

"The one that kept you out so late."

"Just what I told you. That domestic surveillance up in Stuart." It wasn't a complete lie; they had such a case.

"Anything new on it?"

"Nope. The husband hasn't slipped up once. If he's screwing around, he's doing it in another dimension."

Michelle clapped her hands and let out a squeal as the wind tossed her hair into her eyes. McCleary heard a car, the morning's first, approaching them from behind. He was vaguely aware that it was slowing and looked back. A dark four-door sedan with tinted windows was pulling to one side of the road. A lost tourist looking for Palm Beach.

But as the window came down, an instinct seized him and he swerved his daughter's carriage to the right, toward Quin, and shouted at her to dive. Thunder swallowed his voice, something struck him in the back, the carriage tilted, the ground surged toward him. He sprawled on the warm cement, in the rain-pungent air, his back on fire. He heard Michelle wailing, Quin shouting, tires shrieking.

As McCleary struggled to his knees, blood streamed out of him. The sight of it shocked him. There was no pain, just a mild discomfort, a burning, the sensation of warmth and wetness rushing from his body. He couldn't catch his breath; he wheezed for air. His head spun; a tide of nausea nearly choked him. He raised his head to look for Quin, for Michelle, and saw the car instead, a dark blur charging toward him, its chrome mouth grinning.

The second shot lit him up with pain. He fell sideways, knew he was falling but was powerless to prevent it. He couldn't control his body: the way his eyes rolled around in their sockets, the horrid strangled noises he made. The sagging sky dropped over him, nearly suffocating him.

He slammed into the sidewalk. The impact vibrated through the bones in his skull, shouts in an underground cavern. Then a black, crippling tide washed over him, shoved him under, and held him there.

≈

Shapes blurred and slid to the right, a crazy kaleidoscope. Quin knuckled her eyes until her vision cleared, then drank in the details of her surroundings, as though something of herself might be recovered in the simple act of identifying the ordinary.

The room, for instance. It was wider than it was long, newly carpeted, with a long picture window smeared with rain and milky light. The chairs were pale gray, comfortable, many of them occupied. She was seated in one of them and Michelle had fallen asleep in the two she'd pushed together. ER, she thought. She was in the lobby outside the emergency room at West Palm General.

According to the clock on the wall, it was one P.M. But of which day? It suddenly seemed possible that she had lost a day, that she'd slept here through the night waiting for some word on McCleary.

She started to get up, to ask someone what the date was, when she saw the cop who had brought her here. She couldn't remember his name, couldn't even remember if he'd given it. He was a rookie, young, eager, somewhat unsure of himself. His dark hair was tousled; he had pimples on his forehead. He reminded her of one of the Hardy boys, a kid barely out of his teens playing detective.

He handed her a cup of coffee. "I hope you like it with cream, Ms. St. James."

"Cream's fine. Thanks." She realized there was a pack of peanut butter crackers on her lap, that she was starved. She shook one out and devoured it.

"I finally got in touch with Detective Eastman," the rookie said. "He's back in town and should be here shortly. Is there anyone else you'd like me to call?"

A dozen names leaped to mind: her sister, her parents, McCleary's family, people at the office. But she shook her head. Later. She would deal with them later. "What time do you have?" she asked, hoping the clock on the wall was wrong.

"One-oh-two."

A precise man, this rookie. 1:02 P.M. She had been here six hours. "Did I give you a statement?"

"Yes, ma'am. We'll get more from you later."

"What's your name?"

"Davidson, Nick Davidson."

"I already asked you that, huh?"

He nodded.

"Has there been any word on my husband?"

"Not that I know of, ma'am."

Six goddamn hours and not a peep from the powers that be. Terrific. She walked over to the double doors of the treatment area, the pack of crackers still in her hand. She willed the doors to open so that she could peer inside. The squares of reflective glass caught her image, a tall, thin woman with wild dark hair and bloodstained clothes. She looked as though she'd stumbled out of the wrong end of a nightmare.

She could feel people in the waiting room staring at her and had a vague memory of gathering McCleary in her arms in the moments before the ambulance and the cops had arrived. Michelle had been kneeling next to her, tugging at her shirt, saying "Daddy 'urt, Daddy 'urt," and then the skies had opened up and it had started to rain.

The rain was coming down hard now, drumming the waiting room's window, running over it in dirty streams. A chilly February rain that, by now, had washed away whatever evidence there might have been.

The ER doors swung open and a perky little woman in a suit, stockings, and dark pumps bounced out and made a beeline for the frail woman seated near the window. As she led the woman toward the double doors, Quin hurried over to her.

"Excuse me."

The woman turned, her smile neatly in place. Her name tag identified her as the director of social services. "I'll be with you in a minute, ma'am."

"I want to know what's going on with my husband. I've been here six hours and no one—"

"In a minute," she said sternly, her smile fading, and ushered the frail woman through the double doors.

Quin went over to the front desk, where a matronly woman in a volunteer's uniform was slouched over a stack of forms. "I'd like answers. And I want them now, not in one minute, not next week, *now.*"

The woman raised her head, double chin quivering, and regarded Quin as though she were an insolent child. "I beg your pardon, ma'am, but—"

"McCleary. The patient's name is Mike McCleary. He's been in surgery and I'd like to talk to someone about his condition."

"The patient's name again?" the woman snapped.

"McCleary."

"Is that M-A-C?"

"M-C."

"Just a minute." She picked up the receiver, punched out an extension number, spoke too softly for Quin to hear. Then she hung up. "Someone from social services is on the way out. Please step aside, there're other people behind you."

Thoroughly humiliated, Quin parked herself in front of the double doors and popped another cracker in her mouth. She glanced at Michelle, asleep on her side now, her legs pulled up against her. Davidson was sitting next to her and eyed Quin with obvious unease.

I'm going to lose it. Make a scene. Get tossed in the psych ward.

So she stood there clenching and unclenching her fists, consuming the crackers one after another as her imagination seized on the worst possibilities. That McCleary was paralyzed. That he was dead. That social services was waiting for the hospital preacher to arrive before they broke the news.

She began to shake and backed up to the wall, arms clutched against her. Please, she thought, please, and the doors yawned open. The woman from social services stood there, one arm straight out at her side, holding the door ajar, the other folded at her waist, as if to contain her potbelly.

"Mrs. McCleary?"

"Gadzilla."

"What?"

"McCleary, yes, I'm Quin McCleary."

"The doctor will speak to you now."

She turned and Quin said, "I can't leave my daughter out here."

The woman looked over at Michelle, at Davidson. "Can't he stay with her?"

"I don't know."

"I'll stay with her. Take your first left. It's the second door on your right."

The moment the double doors shut behind Quin, the odors assaulted her. Disinfectants, cleansers, air fresheners, desperate attempts to mask the stink of sickness and death. She passed an examining room where an elderly man moaned. In another room a child screamed as a nurse inserted an IV needle in his arm. An orderly hurried by, pushing a portable toilet. Two lab technicians came out of a room with trays loaded with vials, syringes, tubes of blood. Business as usual here in the ER.

The office was empty. *Empty.* More waiting, she thought, endless waiting. The moral of ER was triage: if you weren't on the verge of death, you waited. She started counting and at eighty a man in a white lab coat breezed in. Blond hair, Nordic features, someone's heartthrob. Never mind that he looked too young to perform surgery on anyone. Never mind that here at the county hospital he probably saw gunshot wounds every night. Never mind any of that. He was the guy with the answers.

"Is he dead?" she blurted out.

"Who?"

"Mike McCleary. Gunshot wound. Admitted—"

"You're not Mrs. Levine?"

"No, I'm not Mrs. Levine. I'm Quin St. James. Quin McCleary. Whichever. I want to talk to someone about my husband."

"Let me get the right doctor, ma'am."

Ma'am ma'am ma'am. Heartthrob left and she was alone again, alone with a ticking clock, with the hospital smells, waiting just like before. She went over to the tidy, impersonal desk, plucked up the receiver, punched nine for an outside line, and called a local number. Two rings and someone picked up.

"Courthouse, how may I direct your call?" asked an ever-so-courteous male voice.

"Judge Vail's office."

"Just a minute, please."

Then: "Judge Vail's office. How may I help you?"

The judge's secretary. "Hi, it's Quin. Could you put Rita on? It's an emergency."

"You bet."

Rita Vail, county circuit judge, former public defender, and a good friend, knew everyone who was anyone from Key West to Tallahassee. She could move mountains when she set her mind to it. "Quin, what's going on?"

"It's Mac. He's in the ER at the county hospital. He's been shot and I . . . I can't get shit out of anyone." Her voice broke. She bit her lip, blinked back tears.

"My God. How bad?"

"Bad enough for surgery."

"Sit tight, kiddo. Give me ten minutes. Quin? You still there?"

"Yes." She gripped the receiver so tightly her fingers ached. "Ten minutes. Okay."

Rita hung up. Quin replaced the receiver, pressed her fist against her mouth, backed up to a chair, and fell into it. A movie played in her head of the three of them running, McCleary falling, Michelle rolling out of the carriage, the second shot, the blood, her screams, all of it. Then the movie stopped and she thought, Routine. Whoever had done this knew McCleary's routine.

She didn't have a chance to pursue the thought, to follow it up and down whatever twilit paths it might have led her, because a nurse appeared. The moment she smiled, Quin knew Rita had moved a mountain.

"Dr. Hilliard's waiting for you." She led Quin out of the office and three doors down the hall. "I apologize for the mix-up. We're incredibly busy today. It always happens around a full moon."

"Werewolves and vampires and nightmares in the ER," Quin remarked.

"You got it." She accompanied Quin as far as the doorway of the office, then turned without another word. A man Quin assumed was Dr. Hilliard sat at a computer terminal playing with the keys. He was older than his Nordic counterpart, with curly salt-and-pepper hair and a strangely calm demeanor that suggested the chaos in the ER flowed around him.

"The official term for your husband's condition is 'guarded,' Mrs. McCleary." He swiveled on the stool and faced her. "That means he came through surgery and will be in intensive care. It means we don't know whether he'll make it."

She felt herself nodding. She felt the muscles in her neck straining counterpoint to one another. The skin on her face seemed to sag as if beneath an excess weight. Then her mouth moved and she realized she had no idea what she was going to say. It was as though some vital connection between her brain and her mouth had failed, short-circuited.

"You're the experts. You're supposed to do better than 'we don't know.' "

This elicited a sad smile from Hilliard. "You're right. But in a lot of ways the practice of medicine is an archaic science. I wish I could tell you your husband's going to come out of this as good as new, Mrs. McCleary. But the fact is, I just don't know." He paused, giving her the chance to speak. When she didn't, he went on. "He's got a couple of things going for him, though. The bullet he took in the chest entered and exited without touching his heart. He's obviously fit and his pulse suggests his heart will carry him into his hundreds."

She took in everything he said and digested it, breaking it down as if for nutrients. "And the strikes against him?"

"He has a concussion and we won't know how severe it is until he comes out of the anesthesia. He also has a punctured lung; that bullet lodged near his spine. We didn't remove it. Quite frankly, even a specialist would probably have second thoughts about removing it because of the risk involved. At the moment it appears to be immobile. But that doesn't mean it won't move at some point in the future."

"And if it does?"

"He'll be paralyzed."

He made it sound quite simple, really: If A happens, B will follow. Under other conditions Quin might have liked this man. But at the moment he was the harbinger of bad news, which he delivered in such a detached, dispassionate manner that she couldn't stand the sight of him.

"I'd like to see him."

"He isn't out of recovery yet."

"When will he be?"

"Three to four hours."

"I'll wait," she said.

It wasn't what he wanted to hear, but it was obviously the answer he'd expected. "I'll take you to recovery for a few minutes."

"Thanks, I appreciate it."

He waved her gratitude away. "It's got nothing to do with me, Mrs. McCleary. The word came down from the hospital gods that you and your husband get the VIP treatment. Personally, I think going into the recovery room is a bad idea. But then, it's not my wife in there."

"Will the lady from social services stay with my daughter in the waiting room for a few more minutes?"

"Sure. Let me call the front desk."

A few minutes later they passed through a set of double doors and entered a maze of corridors. "Where was your husband when he was shot, Mrs. McCleary?"

"We were jogging in our development."

Hilliard shook his head. "This county is getting as bad as Dade."

"In Dade the shooting probably would have been random. This wasn't."

"How do you know?"

"I just do."

She had been born and raised in Dade County and had met McCleary there nearly a decade ago. They'd lived in Miami through booms and busts, through waves of crime and racial conflicts, through the birth and death of its TV image. She had a certain fondness for the city, the county, the whole complex package. But she hadn't wanted to raise Michelle there, so when she was pregnant they had joined the exodus and moved to Palm Beach County, a hundred miles up the coast.

Where the crime rate was supposedly lower, where car insurance was 30 percent cheaper, where neighborhoods appeared full-blown overnight, ready for habitation. And where, she thought, McCleary had been shot twice in nearly three years. Not exactly a dazzling record.

"Is your husband a police officer?"

"Was. He's a private detective now. We both are. We have an agency in Palm Beach."

They entered a corridor where nearly everyone she saw wore a face mask, gown, and paper booties over their shoes. Hilliard stopped outside the door to the recovery room. "When you see him, just keep in mind that of the six patients in here, he's got the best chance of pulling through."

The remark was supposed to make her feel better, but as soon as Hilliard pushed open the door, her throat closed up and her knees turned to sponge. McCleary was in the bed closest to the nursing station and the only reason she recognized him was because of his beard. Otherwise, he looked like everyone else there, a body suspended in some strange netherworld of catheters and IVs.

She stood by the bed for a beat or two just looking at him, that was all, looking so hard that her eyes burned. He barely seemed to breathe. But she could hear the hiss of the oxygen, the slow *drip drip drip* of the IV, the steady beep of the heart monitor.

Two and a half years ago he had died for twelve seconds during emergency surgery and had been in a coma for more than two days. She had sat at his bedside and willed him to open his eyes, to move his fingers, to communicate, somehow, that he was aware of her. She did the same thing now, her hand tightening over his as she leaned close. She spoke softly, certain he could hear her. But he didn't respond. No twitches, no fluttering in his eyelids, nothing at all.

Hilliard touched her on the shoulder. "The nurse needs to take his blood pressure, Mrs. McCleary."

She nodded but didn't rise. She was afraid to let go of his hand, afraid to leave, afraid he would die as soon as she stepped out into the hall. She wanted to stretch out beside him, slide her arms around him, and infuse him with her strength, her blood, the marrow in her bones.

"Come on," Hilliard said gently.

Quin released his hand: he was still breathing.

She stood: the heart monitor continued its steady beep.

Then she followed Hilliard to the door, stopped, glanced back. He would pull through. He would. He had to.

When they stepped out into the hall, she said, "When may I come back to see him?"

"When he's moved to intensive care. You'll only get thirty minutes with him. That's the limit in ICU."

She balked. "*Thirty* minutes?"

"Look, I'll call you this evening, once he's in ICU. And I'll clear it so you can be here as early as you want tomorrow. How's that?"

"You just earned a bonus from the hospital gods."

He laughed, gave her arm a quick squeeze, and hurried off.

When he vanished around a corner, she poked her head back into the recovery room. The machines were still beeping, the oxygen was still hissing, he hadn't died when she'd left. The nurse glanced up, frowning, and Quin backed out into the hall.

The door whispered shut behind her and she thought, Which case, Mac? Which one?

3

Fitz Eastman was in the lobby when Quin walked out. He was bouncing Michelle on his knee, the two of them laughing like conspirators every time he said, "Giddy-up, horsie, giddy-up."

He was Quin's height, five foot ten, with a chest weight lifters dreamed about, sideburns that were nearly white, and liquid eyes as black as his skin. Born and raised in Miami's Liberty City, he'd been in law enforcement most of his life. He'd spent eight years in internal affairs with the Palm Beach County Sheriff's Department, a position that hadn't endeared him to the men whom he was supposed to keep honest. Now he was a senior detective in the homicide division.

She knew he'd been married and divorced twice and had three children who lived with their respective mothers. She knew he played the dogs or the horses on occasion, that he spent most weekends with his kids, that he was an avid photographer. But that was about all she knew. His nature, like McCleary's, was essentially solitary. Perhaps that was the basis of their friendship, two men comfortable in their silences.

He stood, hoisting Michelle onto his shoulders with a smooth, effortless motion. She laughed and slapped her hands across his forehead, holding on as he loped across the room, playing camel now. He hugged Quin hello, started to say something, but Michelle interrupted.

"Dah? Dah 'ome?"

"He's going to stay here for a while, Ellie. We're going to go home and get something to eat, okay?"

Her head bobbed enthusiastically. "El 'ungry."

"We were going to zip over to the snack bar to grab a bite," Eastman said, "but I wasn't sure how long you'd be in there. I got the scoop from one of the docs who did the surgery." In others words: *I know his status.* "I'll take you home."

She glanced around. "Where's Davidson?"

"Outside."

Rain poured off the awning, a curtain of water that shimmered in the milky light. Eastman picked up an umbrella that stood against the wall and opened it above Michelle's head. They darted across the parking lot to his Caddy, a virtual tank, early fifties vintage, completely lacking in either grace or beauty. But the car, like Eastman himself, was solid and dependable and strictly modern on the inside. Cellular phone, fax, a small computer terminal, quadraphonic sound—everything except a bathroom.

As they swung out of the lot, she saw Davidson in a cruiser behind them. When he followed them west onto Military Trail, then south toward the house, she said, "We have an escort."

Eastman nodded. "He's going to play nanny while we talk."

Michelle squirmed on her lap, trying to reach the dials on the radio. Quin pulled her back and she fussed and started to cry. "Window, Ellie, let's roll the window down." Quin lowered the window halfway and Ellie leaned into the wind and rain, eyes squinted, hair blowing, a big grin on her face.

"So what do you know that I don't, Fitz?"

"Maybe nothing."

Ha, she thought.

"We'll talk when we get to your place," he said.

Their home was a single-story with tiled floors, high ceilings, and huge windows. The living room opened onto a screened porch and beyond that was a tremendous yard, a paradise of color. Crimson bougainvillea, flaming vines, hibiscus that came in three distinct shades of pink, purple blooms of Mexican heather, and beds of impatiens that covered the ground like flocks of butterflies. And there were trees, mangos and papayas, limes and grapefruits, half of which bore fruit.

The back yard sloped down to a small lake shaped like a tube of toothpaste that had been squeezed hard in the middle. Birds loved it. Blue herons waded along the shore, egrets and ibises poked through the shallows, blackbirds skimmed the placid waters. Even seagulls and pelicans dropped by, flocks of them in search of better pickings, and recently a wood stork had been flying in every morning for breakfast.

The birds were an endless source of fascination to the trio of family cats. They spent hours on the porch, watching, their mouths opening and shutting in silent frenzies of feline frustration. Flats, the sheepdog, wasn't interested in the birds or, for that matter, in the cats. His passion lay with the other wildlife that had found the yard: rabbits, snakes, an occasional raccoon, and, just once, a small red fox. In Dade she'd been lucky to spot a common green lizard. It seemed the animals, like the people, had heard life was better to the north.

Until today, Quin had pretty much agreed with them.

While Eastman and his rookie amused Michelle on the porch, Quin attended to herself. She showered, shoved her bloody clothes in the garbage, changed into a T-shirt and jeans, and checked the answering machine in the den. She hoped the half-dozen messages might provide some insight into what case McCleary had actually been investigating, but they were all related to the daily function of the office. She went into the kitchen to fix lunch for everyone.

It appalled her that her appetite was undaunted, that she could move and speak and function as if this were just another day. The shooting already seemed distant, removed from her in time and space, part of the history of the marriage. She almost expected McCleary to stroll in from the garage any second now and say, Hey, remember when . . .

But tonight, in the dark silence of the house, it would be a different story.

The rain had tapered off by the time they finished lunch. Davidson whisked Michelle away in her red wagon, an act that would make him a friend for life, and Eastman began questioning Quin about what had happened. As she talked, she sensed that he had something to tell her and knew she wasn't going to like it.

The occasional notes he jotted down were merely a formality. He would never refer to them again. He didn't need to. Eastman possessed an extraordinary memory, the luck of good genes, training, and a certain compassion that made him a good listener. But like many circumspect people, he didn't offer much feedback in return and she'd learned to be blunt if she wanted answers.

"Your turn," she said when she finished. "And I want it all."

Eastman nodded and she suddenly understood that he was there not only for her version of the events, but because he needed her help. "Since December, Mike has been working on a case for me. The shooting may be connected to that."

There it was, the bottom line. Now he would build on it, exposing the structure, the complexity of layers, what he knew and what he only suspected. It surprised her, though, that McCleary had never mentioned anything about it to her.

Each of them usually had some idea of what the other was working on at any given time. It made it easier to handle each other's cases when the situation called for it. But also, she thought, it was a kind of acknowledgment that they were a team, professional equals, that work was the one area in which they excelled together.

"Quin?"

"I heard you."

"I take it Mike didn't tell you."

"You know he didn't, Fitz. You asked him not to."

"I thought it was better not to involve anyone else."

"So illuminate me, Fitz."

"Six years ago a Palm Beach woman named Janis Krieger was diagnosed with cancer and given less than six months to live. Instead of going through the usual treatment, she flew to Chile and went to a healer named Alejandro Domingo."

"A faith healer?"

"No, this guy's no tent screamer. I guess I'd call him a psychic healer. Anyway, when Janis returned to the States, she and the healer were married, she was pregnant and apparently cured of cancer."

The names were familiar but not in a specific sense. Someone she'd heard about, perhaps, the friend of a friend or a name in the news.

"She wasn't particularly wealthy, not by Palm Beach standards," Eastman went on. "But she was well connected. This town being what it is, word of Janis's cure got around and pretty soon her contacts were coming to Alejandro with their various medical problems.

"Since he wasn't a physician, he couldn't legally be paid for his services. But the grateful made sizable donations to the nonprofit organization Janis had set up. Two years or so ago they purchased a hundred-acre spread at the northern end of the county. By this time Alejandro had so many clients, he was booked solid for a year. Janis handled all the business details."

"If this guy is good enough to heal cancer, how come I've never heard of him?"

"He's real low profile, Quin. We're not talking about a televangelist, okay? This guy's a former fisherman with a tenth-grade education. Bright, but self-educated. He's been written up in small metaphysical publications, but the mainstream press hasn't touched him."

"And he's actually able to heal?"

"That depends on who you listen to. According to the local chapter of a skeptics' organization, he's a fraud who's bilking the public. The state attorney's office had him under investigation for practicing medicine without a license."

"Are his clients mostly Palm Beachers?"

"Some of them were. But they came from all over, all walks of life."

She noticed his use of the past tense but didn't interrupt.

"There seems to be quite a network for this kind of thing. One person hears about a good healer and tells two friends and so on. That's how it's been with him."

"Any celebrities?" she asked.

"A handful. Included among them was Lydia Holden."

"Of Holden Cereals?"

"You got it."

Even though the Holden family had sold their rights to the cereal years ago, the name was up there with Post, synonymous with mega wealth, the social register, the right connections, the right schools, the right skin color, the right everything. They had a mansion on Ocean Drive that was nearly comparable to the old Post place that Donald Trump had bought. And Barker Holden was running for one of the Florida seats in the U.S. Senate this year.

"What was wrong with her?"

"I don't know. Alejandro won't talk about the people he treats. I had to press to get even a list of his patients. Alejandro worked on Lydia half a dozen times, always at his ranch, the Lazy Quick. She arrived at night, alone."

"Tell me about the healer's wife."

"On December fifth, between nine and midnight, someone walked into Janis's home and shot her three times in the chest with a .38 while she was sleeping off nearly half a bottle of scotch. The shots were muffled by a pillow.

"No sign of breaking and entering, the door was probably unlocked. She was supposed to have gone to a wedding reception at the Breakers, but begged off. Alejandro said they'd been arguing about her drinking. He went alone, dropped his daughter at a friend's house for the night, and got home close to one."

"Was he a suspect?"

"Yeah, at first. There were rumors that the marriage was on the rocks. She had expensive tastes and spent most of what was donated. He worked all the time, she drank too much. But his alibi checked out, at least as far as I could tell. There were four hundred people at this reception, so it's possible he could have slipped out for a while without being noticed. But I doubt it. My gut says he didn't kill her, Quin. You'll see what I mean when you meet him.

"This happened about a week before Alejandro was scheduled to meet with a group of local physicians who were going to observe him then report to the state attorney's office about whether charges should be leveled against him."

"Did he go through with it?"

Eastman shook his head. "He hasn't worked since Janis's death. He's gone into seclusion. The state attorney's office has temporarily suspended their investigation, the skeptics are probably as happy as pigs in shit, the AMA has dismissed him as a quack, Lydia Holden has distanced herself from the whole mess, and the case on Janis is still wide open."

And Mac was investigating her murder. "What about other suspects?"

"She had her share of enemies. She was supposedly a difficult, temperamental woman who ran their business affairs with all the subtlety of Quasimodo. But whether any of that is enough for someone to kill her is open to debate. According to the IRS, she may have been a thief. They claim there're some irregularities about this nonprofit organization, like maybe two million that's unaccounted for. As a result, the U.S. marshal's office has had Alejandro under surveillance."

"Where's the two million supposed to be?"

"They don't know for sure but are figuring an offshore account somewhere."

"What about Alejandro's critics?"

"The two loudest have alibis. The guy who's head of the skeptics' organization was on vacation in Mexico. A researcher who had tested Alejandro was at the wedding reception. But then again these aren't the kind of people who would get their hands dirty, either."

"What leads did Mac have?"

"Not many. A few days after Janis's death Alejandro started getting calls warning him to back off on the demonstration with the physicians or his sister and daughter would be next. So he backed off and sent Francesca and Miranda to Chile the day after Christmas. But he didn't tell me this until after the calls had stopped and his family had left. Then, ten days ago, Mike comes out of the courthouse and finds a note tucked under the wipers on his car."

Eastman slipped an envelope out of his windbreaker pocket, opened it, handed her the note. The type was bold and crisp.

> *Boynton boat launch, 9 a.m., 2/4,*
> *for info on Krieger murder.*
>   *Blue Pearl*

"Today," she said.

"Yeah. I've been out of town the past week, but Mike and I had been in touch about this. I called this morning, I was going to back him up, but you must've been out running."

"Any ideas on who Blue Pearl might be?"

"None. But I think Mike may have talked to him within the last few days. Maybe they changed the date when they were going to meet. Maybe they already met. I don't know. What time did Mike get home last night?"

"Around eleven. He was up in Stuart working on a domestic surveillance case."

"Whoever shot him obviously knew he was investigating the homicide and that he was on to something."

"They also knew his routine. We run every morning at the same time, six days a week." She folded the note, creased it with her finger. "How can I help, Fitz?"

Eastman shook his head. "That's not why I'm telling you all this."

"Answer my question."

"I don't want you involved, Quin. It's bad enough that Mike's been injured."

"Get off it. I *am* involved. They could've shot Ellie and me just as easily."

"They? There was more than one person?"

"There must've been. The car was headed west on the first shot, so the passenger side was closest to us. There had to be at least two— the driver and the bastard who did the shooting."

"A driver could lower the passenger window and shoot through it."

"I don't think that's what happened."

"What'd you see?"

"A dark blur."

"That's it?"

"That's all I remember."

"But you feel pretty sure there were two people in the car."

"Yes."

"Why?"

She shrugged, unable to pinpoint it. "I don't know."

"You might remember more than you think you do."

"Everything happened too fast, Fitz. I mean, one minute we were jogging, then I heard what I thought was thunder and Mac suddenly stumbled and fell into Ellie's carriage, knocking it over. I ran over to Ellie and picked her up. I didn't even realize he'd been shot until I turned around."

"And you saw the car then?"

She started to say yes but realized she couldn't really remember, that there were, in fact, gaping holes in her memory. "I don't know." Then crossly: "You changed the subject on me, Fitz."

"Sorry, sorry." He patted the air with his hands, smiling. "Just so you know, there'll be two men outside of Mike's room around the clock. The hospital administrator will advise the ICU staff about what's going on. No one will enter his room without proper ID and a backup ID by the shift supervisor. We want him in a private room and we'll pick up the difference your health insurance won't pay. Just to play it safe, his condition will be listed as critical as long as he's in the hospital."

Now, Quin thought, she and Eastman would have to bargain. "I don't want Davidson or anyone else hanging around here, Fitz." He started to protest, as she'd known he would, but she rushed on. "If I'm under surveillance because of what someone thinks Mac may have told me and a cop is seen around here, it's just going to make me look guilty. So, please, no Davidson."

Eastman didn't like it, but he couldn't argue with her logic. "Business as usual."

As usual as you could get with your husband in intensive care and your life turned inside out like a dirty slipper, Quin thought. "Right."

"Then Davidson will be pulling day-care duty at Tot Stop. Discreetly. I just want to be cautious, Quin."

Okay, that's fair. "I'd like to see your file on Janis Krieger's murder."

"It's in the car."

"And I want access to Alejandro."

"No problem."

"Can I get in to see the Holdens?"

"Shit, this is a murder investigation. You can get in to see whoever you want. I'll notify them that you'll be getting in touch with them." His brows lifted, asking if that was it.

"For the moment," she replied.

Eastman smiled just to show her there were no hard feelings, but she could tell he wasn't thrilled about their arrangement. "And it's all subject to change, just so we're clear on that."

"You got it." *And it works both ways, Fitz.*

He left a short while later and, true to the bargain, Davidson was in tow. For Quin, alone in the house with Michelle and the animals, time assumed a weird, languid quality. This was how she used to feel when she played hooky from school, forsaking her hormonal seventh-graders for a burnout day. But back then she had been a single woman with a cat and had pampered herself. Now she pampered her daughter.

They played dolls.

They baked cookies.

They colored.

They entered that magical world of pretend where anything was possible. When the phone rang, she let the answering machine get it. She didn't go outside to pick up the mail. They didn't leave the house at all. She felt safe and protected within these rooms, sealed up inside the walls. Tomorrow she would cope, make decisions, do what had to be done. But not now.

At one point Michelle held out her red crayon and said, "Byood, byood," and Quin nodded yes, red was the color of blood. Then Michelle gazed at her with those huge blue eyes and asked where her daddy was and Quin started to cry.

Later that evening, with Michelle tucked in bed and the silence gnawing at her, Quin went into the den. It was supposed to be *their* den, but it was actually McCleary's.

His sense of order dominated the room. The books arranged just so on the shelves. The clutter-free desk. The phone there, the fax here, the computer in the center, not so much as a strand of kitty hair in the disk drive. The chalkboard where they often plotted the elements of a particular case was up against the wall, between the bookcase and a filing cabinet, out of sight. McCleary used it less than she did. He was one of those right-brain people capable of retaining a lot of information that he distilled as he obtained it.

The chalkboard was empty, but pinned to the corkboard along the top was a white envelope that had not been there yesterday. Which she hadn't noticed earlier. Quin tore it open. Inside was a silver key. A key, that was all.

C'mon, Mac, you could've left me something more. A clue, a hint, some small goddamn thing to chew on. She would have done it for him. That he hadn't done it for her hinted at many things, both personal and general. But the bonds between men and the inequities of marriage were the two that came most immediately to mind. Her anger at him, at herself for not being more observant, was sudden, savage, and mercifully brief.

When it had passed, she picked up the phone and called John Tark, a detective with their firm, a man she trusted, the only person she felt like talking to.

At first the signs used to come to me in dreams, as they did in that dream about Barker. But as I became more conscious of them and grew more adept at interpreting them, they began to bleed over into my waking life.

I recognized messages in the random arrangement of shells on a beach, the particular way clouds bump and drift across a sky, even a scattering of ashes on a tabletop. One could argue that the very notion is idiotic, symptomatic of a deranged mind. But it's not as if my life was directed by these messages. It was more of a gentle guidance, a nudge. These were signposts, the internal made manifest.

Some weeks after I killed Janis, for instance, I was on my way to Palm Beach and got stuck in traffic when the bridge over the intracoastal went up. Yachts and fishing boats chugged through, some so

large their names were clearly visible on the back. A Chris-Craft
named Mr. Mike *went by and it hailed from Syracuse, New York.*

Mike McCleary's hometown. And that's when I realized he was
dangerous to me.

You see how it works? The seemingly random patterns, the synchronous junctures, force me to sit up and take notice, to act. I'm
not sure whether I intended to kill him or just put him out of commis-
sion for a while. At any rate, he definitely wasn't going to be sleuthing
anytime soon and for the moment I felt quite safe. I knew that if I
was in danger again, I would discover another sign that would alert
me to it and guide me toward the decision that would be best for me.

Life is easier when you take your cues.

Alejandro suspected that they didn't watch him all the time. Maybe they had in the beginning, but not now. Even so, as he nosed the Porsche out of the gate Sunday morning, his eyes swept left, then right, checking for cars. A car parked where it wasn't supposed to be, a car that looked abandoned. But the dirt road outside the Lazy Quick was deserted, as it usually was.

He turned right and drove for two miles along the fence that surrounded the western pasture. Nothing grazed there anymore. He had sold off three hundred head of cattle and five horses less than a month after Janis's death, when the IRS had frozen his assets and he needed the cash.

They claimed he owed half a million in back taxes. Janis's accountant insisted it was absurd, that the nonprofit organization Janis had set up was perfectly legal. He didn't know whether it was or not. She had handled the business end of things, he had merely signed where he was supposed to sign. And in the meantime his appeal was still pending and his cash reserves, which were in Carmelita's name, were dwindling.

The Porsche, like the swimming pool, had been one of Janis's luxuries, a sixty-thousand-dollar toy with a metallic silver finish that flew like a bullet. The only reason the IRS hadn't impounded it was because he had given it to his sister after Janis's murder. Given it to Francesca because he couldn't bear looking at it. Now it was the only vehicle left to drive. The IRS had impounded everything else, the Range Rover, a pickup, the trucks for hauling cattle.

The irony was that until he had come to the United States, he had never driven a car, much less owned one.

He took U.S. 1, ambling south through the relatively sparse traffic. He checked the rearview mirror every few minutes, but he was pretty sure only Carmelita was aware of his departure. He turned east onto the beach road, where he passed grand and magnificent homes. Mansions. Estates. Virtual palaces.

His wife had spent the first fifteen years of her life in such a home, tended to by maids and nannies, cooks and butlers. Then one of her father's investments had failed and forced them to a smaller house, minus the servants.

Her old man had made and lost several fortunes in his lifetime and when he'd died his assets were a trifle by Palm Beach standards. Much of the money had gone to the nursing home where Janis's mother had ended up. By the time Janis was diagnosed with cancer, she couldn't scrape together the plane fare to Chile. Lydia Holden had lent it to her.

Janis and Lydia had met because of Barker Holden, who had been one of Janis's classmates in high school. In that way that seemed so commonplace for women, they had become friends rather quickly. Tennis partners, shopping buddies, partygoers, the jewels of the social set.

Janis had owned a lucrative boutique on Worth Avenue at the time, a business she had bought with the money her father had left her. But after her mother died, she'd been forced to sell it to settle the nursing-home debts. Not long afterward she'd contracted cancer and headed to Chile and into his life.

When they returned, word of Janis's cure had gotten around and Lydia was the first person in Palm Beach's social set to seek him out. She had female problems: irregular periods, PMS, fibroid breast tumors, scar tissue from an ectopic pregnancy. He had treated her for the tumors and a hormonal imbalance that caused her irregular periods, and she had become his most avid supporter, recommending him to her wealthy friends.

They had run the gamut from aging matrons with arthritis and high blood pressure to men with melanoma from decades of golfing in the brutal Florida sun. He had treated their children and grandchildren for ear infections, eating disorders, tonsillitis. He had succeeded with some, failed with others. With Lydia, for instance, he had never been able to reverse the scar tissue that prevented her from conceiving. He didn't know why, it was simply one of the vagaries of his ability. Sometimes it worked, sometimes it didn't.

His talent discriminated in the cruelest of ways, rendering him helpless when it came to his family or to himself. Last year when his sister had broken her wrist in a fall from a horse, he had stood by in the emergency room while a doctor had set it. If Janis had been alive when he'd found her, he wouldn't have been able to save her.

And now he was just as powerless to do anything for his sister or daughter.

He finally turned into the parking lot of a Latin eatery on Old Dixie Highway in downtown West Palm Beach. It was noisy inside, salsa music blaring from the jukebox, the TV tuned to a Spanish talk show, the pool balls clattering.

Carlos Cardenas waited in a corner booth. He wasn't wearing his clerical collar and was dressed in faded jeans and an old shirt, like the *campesinos* who ate here. His straw hat was on the table to his right, there was dirt under his nails, his thinning gray hair was uncombed.

"I did not think you would come, my friend," he said in Spanish.

"You're the exception to all my rules, Carlos."

A plump man with a dimple in his chin brought over two Cuban coffees, a basket of hot rolls, and two bowls of black bean soup. When they were alone again, Cardenas switched to English, the language of the minority here. "Tell me truthfully, Alejandro. How're you doing?"

He shrugged, sipped at his coffee. "I manage."

"Last week Bishop Joaquín came to the rectory. He had heard about your work with the migrants and asked if it was true. He would like to see for himself."

"I don't perform, Carlos. Not for anyone."

"That isn't what he meant." Cardenas's fingers worried the brim of his hat. "He would like to watch you work, talk to the patients before and after."

"I can't. Not as long as Francesca and Miranda are being held."

"Please, let me finish. Bishop Joaquín isn't just any bishop, all right? He's part of a group within the church that investigates incidents that might be miraculous. The sighting of the Virgin before Yugoslavia fell, the weeping Madonnas in Virginia, things like that."

"I've never heard about the Madonnas."

"Religious statues supposedly weep in the presence of a young American priest. A number of healings have also been attributed to him. The skeptics' organizations stirred up so much negative publicity about him, the church ordered him to stop talking to the press and is now conducting a secret investigation.

"This miracle business has given the church much trouble in recent years, so it's an honor that the bishop has taken such an interest in you, Alejandro."

Alejandro didn't agree but kept his opinion to himself. "Why is that?"

"Because if a bishop gives his blessing to what looks like a miracle and it's proven to be a hoax, the church looks ridiculous. So they're very careful about what they investigate. The fact that I know you, that I've seen you work, is—"

"Statues don't weep in my presence, Carlos, and God doesn't whisper in my ear. This doesn't have anything to do with God and the bishop shouldn't be led to believe otherwise."

"I haven't led him to believe anything," Cardenas replied hotly. "I've merely supported the stories he's already heard."

The air in the eatery was suddenly too warm, the noise too loud. Alejandro wished he hadn't come.

"Look," the priest went on. "I know that if you told Bishop Joaquín the truth about Francesca and Miranda, he could help. He has many connections, political connections."

"No." They'd had this conversation before.

"It might save them."

"No, Carlos. I mean it. These people may be responsible for Janis's murder. Last night I found out that the detective who was investigating the case for the police department has been shot and it wouldn't surprise me if these people are responsible for that. And they are definitely responsible for the abduction of my family. I won't jeopardize them."

"What do you intend to do about it, then?"

Don't ask me. "Whatever they ask until they tire of me."

"Tire of you?" Cardenas snorted. "They're not going to tire of you, Alejandro. People like that just keep on until they suck you dry."

"When I've done whatever it is they intend for me to do it'll be over."

"And just who the hell are we talking about?"

"A man named Jim and another man named Bob. That's all I know."

Cardenas shook his head. "You appall me sometimes, Alejandro. Forgive me for saying it, but you do. You don't see the evil in people."

This, too, was old ground between them, philosophical arguments about the nature of man, of God, of good and evil. But all that aside, Cardenas's statement wasn't even true.

"Jim and Bob are irrelevant," Cardenas said when Alejandro didn't comment. "They aren't the ones who designed these abominations they call experiments. Dr. White did."

"You don't know what you're talking about," Alejandro replied crossly. "Those early experiments were Janis's doing. Dr. White hasn't tested me for nearly two years."

"Then you're just going to continue like this," Cardenas said flatly.

"Yes."

"Their guinea pig."

"That's right."

"Their prostitute."

"You don't have a daughter, Carlos, or a sister. You can't possibly understand."

"What I understand," he said softly, his fingers now clutching his mug of coffee, "is that others need you."

"Send them to the free clinic. Send them to the health department. Send them to HRS. There are agencies in this country to deal with these things, Carlos. Use them."

Blood rushed into his cheeks. "What do you think I do six days a week?"

"I'm sorry, I know you—"

"You *don't* know." A biting sharpness had entered Cardenas's voice. "The system is overburdened and my people are beaten down by it. Only two days ago a young woman who was new to my church died of breast cancer. For two years the cancer consumed her, Alejandro. It ate her up inside; she rotted. And all because this system that's supposed to help the poor couldn't qualify her for Medicaid. There are hundreds like her, maybe thousands, and meanwhile you're up there at your ranch healing the rich because they can pay."

"You forget, Carlos. The rich paid so that I could work for free on people like those in your parish."

The priest drew back, his dark eyes softened, and he shook his head. "I'm an idiot. Forgive me."

"There's nothing to forgive. Eat your soup, *amigo*."

They didn't speak of it again. But Alejandro worried that Cardenas would tell the bishop the truth for the greater good of his parishioners. He worried as he left the restaurant, worried and knew there was nothing he could do about it now. Nothing but wait.

And waiting, he thought bitterly, was the one thing he did very well.

He had no destination, no appointment to keep. So he drove north on the interstate, mesmerized by the forward motion, by the illusion that he was going someplace.

"*You're just going to continue like this . . . their guinea pig . . . their prostitute.*" The priest's voice kept intruding in his thoughts, demanding his attention, and he drove faster. Faster. The landscape blurred past; warm air blew through the windows. His daughter's face sometimes floated in the windshield like a computer image. He saw her as an infant. He saw her at two. At three. He saw her as she'd looked the last time he'd seen her, a four-year-old in a yellow print dress, white tights, her best shoes. She'd had her Little Mermaid suitcase with her, jammed with books and puzzles and dolls, things to keep her occupied on the long flight to Chile.

"Papa, why can't you come to the gate with us?"

Since it had been the Christmas traveling season, when thousands of tourists passed through the Palm Beach airport, only paying passengers had been allowed onto the concourses. He had gone as far as the metal detectors with them, then stood there watching, waving, his heart breaking bit by pathetic bit until they were lost in the crowd.

Somewhere between that moment and their gate, they had vanished. He hadn't known about it until the next morning, when the dark Lincoln had driven through the gate of the Lazy Quick and Jim had played that very first tape.

He suddenly realized that he was weeping, that he was parked in front of the passenger pick-up area at the Palm Beach airport. He rubbed his eyes and stared at the glass doors, at the baggage carousels beyond it. Any second now something in time and space would shift and his sister and daughter would walk through those doors.

But a policeman appeared first. His round face and helmet nearly filled the window, his mouth was moving, but Alejandro didn't have any idea what he was saying. It was as if the air around him had stalled, breaking the connection between his ears and his brain.

Alejandro nodded just to get rid of him, then started the Porsche and pulled away from the curb. He parked in the metered parking area across from the terminal, went inside the building, and rode the escalator to the main floor. Then he passed through the metal detector to concourse C and walked where Miranda and Francesca had walked. Saw what they had seen. Heard what they had heard.

When he reached gate 10, the gate they were supposed to leave from that night, he stopped at one of the picture windows. Planes landed and took off, sunlight poured over the runways, the PA system crackled. He pressed his fingers to the glass and squeezed his eyes shut. How many times had he paced this concourse since December

26? How many times had he stopped in the shops and showed their pictures to the bored clerks?

"Do you remember seeing this woman around Christmas? She was with this little girl."

But of course they shook their heads. And when he returned again and again, they looked away as soon as they saw him coming. He no longer bothered with the pictures, the shops. He was here simply because this was where he felt closest to Francesca and Miranda and he didn't know where else to go. His despair sat in the pit of his stomach like an undigested steak.

"Wow, how'd you do that?"

Alejandro's eyes flew open, his arms dropped to his sides, and he glanced down at the boy who had spoken. He was seven or eight, well dressed, well groomed, and was staring at the picture window: at the spiderweb cracks in the glass where Alejandro's fingers had been.

Alejandro stepped back, rubbing his hands against his jeans, unable to wrench his eyes from the fissures. He was drenched in sweat.

"That's a cool trick, mister," the boy said, pushing his own fingers against the glass, smearing it with his prints. "Can you teach me how to do it?"

"I didn't do it." Alejandro stepped back again, hands now jammed in his pockets. "It was already there."

"Was not. I saw it doing that while you were touching it. I saw it. My mom says hardly anything can break this glass, but I saw you break it. I saw it and I'm going to tell."

With that the boy spun around and ran off toward a woman seated near the gate. Alejandro turned quickly away from the window and hurried back up the concourse, alarmed and terrified that his hands had betrayed him.

5

McCleary drifts in a dark sea as smooth and perfect as chocolate. It is noisy with sounds, beeps, hums, clicks, wheezes, a Morse code of the insect world. Now and then he hears voices, distant and muted, like music turned down low.

The voices gradually grow more distinct, more specific, this one male, that one female. They tug at him, urging him up through the blackness toward the promise of light. But he senses the pain crouched somewhere nearby, a dull, stupid beast that will swallow him whole when it finds him. And it will find him, it always does, despite his best efforts to remain hidden.

Sometimes the pain beats the darkness like a boy with a stick, startling him into the open. Other times it sniffs him out, a relentless bloodhound. Then there are moments like now, when he seems to be rising inside a long, narrow pipe and the pain is outside, pressing in *against the pipe but unable to penetrate or crush it. He feels a terrible urgency to surface before the pipe's metal weakens and the pain washes over him. Quick, quick, head for the voices, go for the light, run with your secret.*

His eyelids separate from each other. A thin band of light appears. Shadows move over it, through it. And suddenly he is jogging past the lake in his neighborhood, one hand on his daughter's carriage. The mushroom-colored sky sags with rain. He hears thunder, the deep, menacing rumbles of a discontented god. He hears the slap of their shoes against the sidewalk and Michelle's excited trill of laughter as a gust of wind whips her hair around.

Then the car. The car that sneaks up on them. The car where the window descends and the gun pokes out.

Hide, quick, hide, and he shoots back down the pipe before the pain can find him.

"Mac?"

Her voice. But her face was blurred, bloated, discolored, a stain against the milky air. He tried to speak, but his mouth was too parched, his tongue thick, cold, a piece of dead meat.

"No, don't try to talk." Her hand on his, cool, light. Now her face swam into focus, the ghost blue eyes, the mouth that he had sketched, that he had painted, that he had paid homage to. Her hair fell to her shoulders in wild curls; he wanted to touch it, stroke it, but didn't have the energy to lift his arm. "I can only stay a few minutes. Rules, they've got so many rules. It's Monday, February eighth, Mac. You were shot on the fourth, okay? Ellie's fine, we're both fine. Just get well."

The blue of her eyes turned liquid. His fingers tightened over her hand, urging her closer, but she didn't understand. She didn't get it. *Listen to me*, he wanted to shout. *Be careful, you don't know about . . . What? What was the secret?* Eastman, the healer, yes, he could almost put it together in his mind, but pieces were missing. The drugs that had dulled the pain had also dulled his capacity to make connections, to form words.

"What?" she asked, leaning closer now. "What is it?"

"Blue birds for Mother." *Sweet Christ.* "Pancakes . . ." *Wrong wrong.* He squeezed his eyes shut, forming the words in his mind: *Talk to Eastman. Be careful. Use the key.* But when he opened his mouth, he said: "Men talk, dolphins have funny noses." *Jesus.*

"They've got you drugged up, but you're going to be fine."

"Time's up, Mrs. McCleary," said a nurse who stepped into the room.

"I'll be back later today."

Don't go. "Quiet the rain." *Help me speak.* "Get the hay." *Dear God.* "Wash the dirty windows." Frustration swelled inside of him; he struggled to sit up. But the pain found him, shoved him back into the pillows, and he opened his mouth and the dark sea rushed in, suffocating him.

≈

"I'd like to speak to someone about my husband," Quin said to the nurse at the intensive care station.

The woman raised her head and peered at Quin over the rims of her bifocals. "His name? Room number?"

"Mike McCleary. Room—"

"Room four. Yes, I know. He's the only patient on the floor with a police guard outside his door. Who would you like to speak to, Mrs. McCleary?"

"His doctor."

"That'd be Dr. Brattleboro."

"No, Hilliard. Dr. Hilliard. He admitted him in the ER and I spoke to him just yesterday."

"Your husband's doctor now is Dr. Brattleboro."

"Fine, then I'd like to speak to him."

"I'll give you his office number."

"Has he made his rounds yet today?"

"I'm not sure."

"My husband's in there babbling and you're not *sure*?" Quin's voice lifted sharply. "Then find me someone who *is* sure."

The nurse regarded her with a wariness that suggested she might be dangerous, an escaped mental patient. "I'll, uh, find someone who can answer your questions."

She punched out an extension number and turned in her chair, so her back was to Quin. Quin stared at the big round clock on the far wall: 8:58 A.M., Monday, February 8. It seemed important to ground herself this way, as though the date and time fixed her in the universe, made her real.

"Blue birds for Mother, quiet the rain . . ." Painkillers. Blame the painkillers for that. The important thing was that he'd gotten through four nights that, for her, had passed in fits and starts, wrought with nightmares and insomnia.

Every night she had started out in the king-size bed with Michelle, the cats, and the dog and had ended up on the couch, alternately reading the file on the Krieger murder and staring at the ceiling. She'd spent most of the last three days at the hospital, long, endless hours of just sitting, waiting. At some point she'd realized her time would be better spent trying to track down whoever had shot McCleary. So this morning she had dropped Michelle at preschool by eight, eager to get to work.

"Okay, Mrs. McCleary," the nurse said. "Dr. Brattleboro is still in the hospital and will be right up."

"Thanks."

"You can wait in the sun room." She pointed off to her right.

The sun room was the favored destination for the ambulatory patients who strolled through the corridors, their IV poles clattering along beside them like chained pets. Quin stood in the doorway, watching the hands on another big round clock make their lazy journey from one black mark to the next. At 9:15 Fitz Eastman stepped off the elevator with a short, chunky man who didn't look more than thirty-five. Eastman saw her and they came over.

"Quin McCleary, Dr. Brattleboro."

He was several inches shorter than she and had to look up at her. It made some men uncomfortable but didn't seem to daunt the doctor in the least. His handshake was firm and quick, that of a busy man.

"Your husband's responding remarkably well, Mrs. McCleary. I don't anticipate any problem with the gunshot injuries. The bullet in his back worries me somewhat, but I looked at the X rays again this morning and it's not as close to the spinal column as we originally thought."

We. The brotherhood of doctors. The good ol' boys. Yeah, she got the picture. Hilliard had called it incorrectly and Brattleboro was glossing it over.

"Once he's really on the mend, we'll do an MRI and have a much clearer idea about the bullet."

"What about the way he talks?"

His expression remained unchanged, but she detected a certain caution in his voice. He obviously didn't intend to make Hilliard's mistake. "He's heavily sedated, Mrs. McCleary."

"He didn't make any sense."

He flashed a mouth filled with capped teeth. "You'd be surprised at the things I've heard patients say when they're on morphine. As he heals, we'll reduce the amount of morphine. Give him a few days."

Too smooth. Too pat. Too goddamn easy. "Suppose it's not just the morphine? He's got a concussion and I thought maybe—"

"We won't know anything more for a few days."

It wasn't his wife in there babbling about pancakes and dolphins with funny noses. "I'd like to visit for longer periods of time."

"I don't see any problem with that. But let's start tomorrow. And if you have any more questions, please give me a call." He handed her a card, gave Eastman a friendly pat on the back, said it was great to see him again, and hurried off.

"How do you know him, Fitz?"

"The department uses him and his partners for physicals, shit like that. He's good, Quin. If he doesn't know the answer, he refers you to someone who does and who probably knows it better than anyone else." He guided her toward the elevators. "I saw Mike for a few minutes earlier. He was still gone. What'd he say to you?"

She told him as they rode down in the elevator. "It wasn't just that he was out of it, Fitz. He seemed panicked, like he knew the words were coming out wrong but couldn't do anything about it."

"Got to be the morphine."

When they stepped out into the lobby, she saw John Tark pacing in front of the information desk, his hands jammed in the pockets of his khaki-colored chinos. He stood six foot four and moved with the disturbing quickness of a criminal on the run. The white scar that snaked from his left eye into his brow endowed his face with a quality that was either sinister or tragic, she hadn't decided which. He was the newest addition to their firm, a former tracker with a dubious and questionable past and a man to whom she probably owed her life.

"They wouldn't give me a goddamn pass," he grumbled when he reached them. He rubbed a hand over his curly black hair, a nervous gesture, the only one he had. "How is he?"

"Doped up and iffy," she said.

"Doing okay," Eastman said.

Tark looked from one to the other. "Which?"

"All of the above," Eastman replied, and herded them out the door.

The sky was utterly blue and cloudless. The cool February air smelled of sea, of freshly mown grass, of all the reasons tourists flocked here by the droves from October to Easter. They crowded the roads, the motels, the beaches, and took up space in the hospitals, she thought.

"Was he conscious?" Tark asked, touching her elbow.

"Sort of. He babbled."

"The drugs," Tark said.

"Of course it's the drugs," said Eastman. "What the hell else would it be?"

"The concussion," she said, but neither man seemed to hear her.

Eastman aimed a remote control device at his Caddy as they approached it. The locks clicked and he opened the door. "Let's do our business inside."

They piled into the front seat, Quin in the middle. Eastman grabbed a briefcase out of the back and removed two sets of papers from it, one for each of them.

"This is everything the press has written on Alejandro Domingo since he came to this country nearly five years ago. Like I told you the other day, Quin, most of the mainstream publications have stayed clear of him. But there's enough from newspapers and the smaller magazines to get a sense of who he is and what he's about. I've also included whatever articles have appeared in medical and scientific journals about him."

Quin paged through the packet. The clippings ranged from *Lancet* to the *Journal of Parapsychological Research* to a short piece in *Omni* and a feature article in *Fate*. "I didn't realize he'd been tested extensively." She wondered how much else Eastman had neglected to tell her the other day.

"It was Janis's doing. I think she felt an official stamp of approval would make him more acceptable to the clientele she was hoping to attract. The real heavy hitters, big-time celebrities, stars."

"Only if the talent didn't speak for itself," Tark said. "Is the guy for real or not, Fitz?"

Eastman shrugged. "His patients, at least the ones who were willing to make statements, swear by him. But the medical and scientific evidence is erratic at best. I don't know whether he's for real. I don't give a shit. It's not my job to judge him. I just want to find out who killed his wife and who shot Mike. Alejandro is central to both questions."

Leave it to Eastman to set the record straight right off. "If I remember correctly, Fitz, the other day you told me you didn't want me involved. Why the change of heart?"

"Shit." He laughed. "Who're you kidding? I tell you one thing, you go and do another. I figure I might as well be on top of things from the start."

Tark looked bemused by this exchange. "He's got your number, Quin."

"Very funny. C'mon, Fitz. The truth. Let's hear it."

Another shrug, then: "Part of my agreement with IAD about transferring to homicide was to teach a three-week class to new recruits when they needed me. The class starts tomorrow. I pick who takes on my toughest cases and I figure you two are right for this one."

"Well, goddamn," she murmured.

"But I'm still in charge," Eastman added hastily.

Tark looked at her. "A control freak."

"For sure."

Eastman ignored the comments and slipped two more packets from his briefcase. "That's what I've got on Domingo's two worst critics."

"Any supporters we should know about?" Tark asked.

"Initially there was a physicist. But he's pretty much backed off. His name's in there, too."

Quin recalled something she'd read in the file on Janis Krieger. "You said he sent his sister and daughter back to Chile, right?"

"Right after Christmas."

"So he lives alone?"

"No, his housekeeper lives in the garage apartment."

"Any other family?" Tark asked.

"Not here. There're two brothers who still live in the town where he was born, assorted nephews and nieces and in-laws."

"In Santiago?" Tark asked.

"No, a place in southern Chile called Ancud. It's on the island of Chiloé."

"Hell, that explains it," Tark said.

"Explains what?" Eastman asked.

"The healing shit. Chiloé is an island of maybe two thousand people and most of them believe in mermaids and ghost ships and witches."

"You've been there?"

"Several times."

It figured, Quin thought. Tark had spent much of his life in South America and for the last ten years had lived in Iquitos, Peru. It was a city near the mouth of the Amazon that was surrounded entirely by jungle, the site of the movie *Fitzcarraldo* and a place where the general beliefs tended toward the mystical and the strange. Pink dolphins as shape shifters, for instance. But Eastman wasn't as familiar with Tark's background as she was.

Eastman shut his briefcase and dropped it onto the backseat. "Two rules on this job. You carry at all times and when you talk to these people, you do it together. We've already had one casualty. I don't want any more. Since Quin's days will probably begin and end here until Mike's sprung, you might as well meet here in the parking lot."

"We'll decide where we meet, Fitz," said Quin, chafing at his rules, at the regulations.

"Whatever. If you do anything that isn't above board, I don't want to know about it. You get into deep shit and it's not above board, you're on your own. Any questions? No? Then get moving and one of you give me a call tonight."

Tark saluted, then ducked out of the car with Quin right behind him. "Your wheels or mine?" he asked as Eastman swung out of the lot.

"Mine." They walked toward her Explorer, purchased recently with insurance money. Hurricane Alfred had flattened her old one six months ago on Miami Beach. Considering what their personal casualties could have been, they'd been lucky they'd lost only a car. "Where do you want to start?"

"With this." Tark held up his packet of papers. "Let's head over to the Hungry Pelican for coffee."

She glanced up and searched for McCleary's window on the third floor. *Blue birds for Mother, quiet the rain, wash the dirty windows.* That wasn't just morphine.

Please come back to me, Mac, she thought, then slipped behind the wheel and headed for the Pelican.

≈

The Hungry Pelican was an icon of old Florida, a reminder of what life had been like before tourists had discovered the state.

It stood at the end of the Lake Worth pier like a punctuation mark, a lopsided structure that looked as if it had been slapped together with glue and pieces of driftwood. Its wide porch extended out over the water on three sides and to the east it was completely open to the Atlantic. It had survived hurricanes in its time, but Tark doubted that even the Pelican could withstand a category-four storm like the one that had flattened so much of Dade County six months ago.

The furnishings were an eclectic mix of faded wicker and weathered Florida pine. The menu was strictly down-home Florida cooking and the prices were right. Tourists and locals flocked here as readily as the hungry pelicans the place was named after. Scattered among them were the people Tark came here for, South Florida's information brokers.

They were a peculiar breed of men and women who seemed indigenous to the tropics, people camouflaged by their surroundings. They waited tables, tended bar, peddled T-shirts and tourist trinkets. They worked as maids and butlers and cooks in the homes of Palm Beach's elite. They were clerks and secretaries in law offices and government buildings, boat captains on cabin cruisers, mechanics, nannies, and au pairs. He thought of them as the unsung heroes of a largely invisible society.

His main contact among them was a woman named Estelle Pana-takos, who showed them to a table on the porch. She was part Greek, with short black hair, brows like thick brush strokes over lovely black eyes, skin as smooth and brown as chocolate. She wore very short shorts, a halter top with a shirt thrown over it and tied at the waist, and sandals.

Tark had met her in the Keys, during the same case that had brought the McClearys into his life. She asked about McCleary's condition, sent him her best wishes, then got on with it. "So what's it going to be, you two? Just coffee or a full-blown breakfast?"

"The works for me," Quin said. She scanned the menu and then ticked off an order fit for two men.

"Just coffee," Tark replied.

"Be back in a jiffy with the coffee."

When she returned, he was alone at the table; Quin had gone off in search of a phone to call the office. Estelle set down the pot, fresh cream, a basket of warm rolls. "They got any idea who shot him, Gabby?" she asked.

Gabby was short for Gabriel, his middle name, the name he'd been using when they'd met. "No. Just a few leads. You heard anything?"

"Too soon. If there's anything to hear, it'd be while I was tending bar. I start back on nights this week. The tips are better. Want me to ask around?"

"Discreetly. I'm particularly interested in anything you hear on Barker Holden and his wife. They've got a place on Ocean Drive."

"The cereal snobs, sure, I know where they live. It's not too far from the Kennedy compound." She leaned toward him with a conspiratorial grin. "Come clean, Gabby. Is it major scandal time again? Should I call my source at the *National Enquirer* and promise a scoop in return for some tidbits?"

Tark laughed. "Not yet. Just nose around."

"Righto."

Her eyes held his for a moment, open and unapologetic in their scrutiny. He knew that look. He had seen it the day she'd moved in with him six months ago and the day she'd moved out six weeks later. He saw it sometimes when they were lovers, occasions that had grown increasingly rarer. But he hadn't known what it meant until she said, "You're still hung up on her, aren't you, Gabby."

"On who?"

She rolled her eyes in mock exasperation. "On who do you think? Quin."

"Sure. And I shot Mike."

"Hey, it doesn't make any difference with you and me, okay? You know how it is with us. But I've seen the way you look at her. It's like everything else in your life is just filler."

"You're not."

"You're a sweetie." She cupped his chin and squeezed. "But you can't lie worth a damn. Check in with me later in the week and I might have something."

He watched her as she strolled off and hated the fact that she read him like the Sunday funnies.

Quin ate enough in a single breakfast to last him two days. And this meal wasn't the exception. She consumed food, as McCleary often remarked, as though every meal might be her last. The mystery was where it went. She didn't weigh more than a hundred and twenty-five pounds, if that.

She polished off the last of the grits, dabbed at her mouth, and set aside the articles she'd been perusing. "You and Estelle on now or off?"

"Neither."

"Neither?" She smiled. "C'mon, it's got to be one or the other."

"Why?"

She seemed genuinely puzzled. "You either have a relationship or you don't."

"No gray areas?"

"Someone's either your friend or not your friend. You're either married or you're not married, it can't be both ways."

She clearly wasn't a candidate for an extramarital affair. But he'd already known that. And given his friendship with McCleary, as well as the man's present condition, it was ludicrous to even dwell on it. But he did. It had become as inevitable as breathing.

When he was around Quin for any length of time, he absorbed everything about her: the way she moved, the way she spoke, the way she laughed. When he couldn't sleep at night, he imagined that she was beside him, imagined himself in McCleary's place, turning to her, rousing her, making love to her. Sometimes she followed him into his dreams, erotic landscapes that left him wasted by his desire.

Once, just once, she'd appeared in the old nightmare about the explosion that had killed his wife and daughter more than eleven years ago. She had been his wife, bleeding on the floor of that restaurant in Little Havana that his father-in-law had owned, shattered glass strewn around her. It had terrified him, Quin in that surreal place where she didn't belong. The next day he had avoided the office, certain that if he went in she or McCleary would read the truth in his face.

Some part of himself seemed to be sending a loud, clear message that he was cursed, that the people he loved were doomed to horrifying deaths. His wife, his daughter, his father-in-law. But his desire continued, impelled by its own momentum.

"Earth to John," Quin said.

"Let's get moving." He pulled a twenty from his wallet to cover the bill and a tip for Estelle and pushed up from his chair.

"I didn't mean to pry," she said as they crossed the restaurant. "Next time just tell me to shut up."

"You weren't prying."

"Something pissed you off."

"I'm not pissed off. Who do you want to see first?"

"The researcher, White."

Quin stepped through the door just as Estelle called out, "Later, guys," and winked at Tark.

He followed Quin down the pier.

6

~~~~~

Palm Beach County was the largest in size in the state, more than twenty-five hundred square miles. It lacked the diversity of Dade's population, but it possessed its own peculiar extremes. To the east, for instance, were the cities, the tourists, the crime, and most of the wealth. To the west, the closer you got to Lake Okeechobee, lay farms tilled by migrant workers.

They were real farms in the sense that they produced everything from papayas, mangos, and cherries to grapes and pecans. But to Quin, they weren't like the farm in upstate New York where McCleary had been raised: They were huge corporations.

The town of Jupiter, where she and Tark were headed, was at the northern end of the county. It was Burt Reynolds country, site of his ranch, his dinner theater, a park that bore his name. The bitch of progress that had turned much of the state into asphalt seemed to have skipped Jupiter, which was surprisingly rural. An ideal spot for a think tank.

The Link Research & Development compound covered twenty-five acres of pines and banyan trees and was entirely surrounded by an eight-foot-high chain-link fence. There was a guardhouse at the front gate.

"I get the feeling we should've called ahead," Quin said.

"There was nothing in Fitz's report about a goddamn fence."

"Fitz sometimes neglects to include the little details." She pulled up to the gate. The aging security guard peeked out of his two-by-four prison, then walked over to the Explorer.

"Hi," Quin said in a voice filled with bravado. "We have an appointment with Dr. White."

"Name?"

"Palm Beach County Sheriff's Department."

"Your name, ma'am, and the gentleman's."

She handed over their driver's licenses. The guard jotted something on a clipboard, then walked around to the back of the Explorer and took down the license-plate number. He returned their licenses and waved them on through.

"Not even a phone call," Tark said. "So the fence is for show."

"Those dogs aren't for show." She motioned toward the trio of Rottweilers in a fenced run to her left.

Quin followed a road that wound lazily through the grounds, past benches, a stone fountain, a bike path where several men in warm-up suits were jogging. Three prefab units stood in the thick shade to the right, separated from one another by swollen clusters of impatiens and hibiscus hedges trimmed to perfect geometric shapes. Small landscaped mounds appeared here and there, breaking up the shadows and the flatness.

According to the material Eastman had supplied, Link specialized in the development of high-tech oddities. They had designed, for instance, a specific kind of laser for a Colorado mining company and a prototype toilet for NASA that would be used on future space flights. There were three facilities nationwide, but this was the largest. They were obviously doing well; the monthly maintenance on the grounds probably cost a small fortune.

The road ended at an L-shaped building of pine and dark glass. Quin pulled into the parking lot off to the left.

"How do you want to play this?" Tark asked.

"By ear."

"Are you St. James or McCleary today?"

"St. James." Unless it behooved her to be otherwise.

The lobby looked like a travel ad for the Southwest: Mexican tile floors, furniture in soft blues and vibrant yellows, cactuses in huge clay pots that basked in the filtered sunlight spilling through the darkened glass. Music drifted in the still, quiet air, a haunting melody of wind instruments that conjured images of towering, mystical canyons and vast blue skies.

The receptionist was one of those young women who populated Florida's beaches on weekends, slender, sun-blond, magnificently tanned, a California clone.

She took their names, punched out an extension number, spoke to someone. When she hung up, she said. "Dr. White can you see you now." Her smile was aimed at Tark. "I'll take you upstairs."

She insinuated herself between them and flirted outrageously with Tark as she led them down a hall and up an escalator. Quin found it vaguely irritating: the woman's phony laugh, the way she kept touching Tark's arm. And he acted like a guy in a singles bar who knew that his search for a hot little number for the night had just ended.

They stopped at a set of double doors. The receptionist, whose name was Zelda, inserted her hand into a slot to the right, where it was scanned, and the doors clicked open.

Star Trek, Quin thought.

"Thumbprint," Zelda said as they entered another hall. "In one area of the complex access is by retinal scan."

Quin marveled at how quickly the blonde-on-the-make routine vanished. "The perimeter security doesn't seem tight at all."

"During the day it isn't. At night, though, the fence is electrified, a dozen Rottweilers roam the grounds, and there's an armed security guard. We had problems a few years ago with vandalism and break-ins. Teenagers, mostly, looking for kicks." Her grin lit up her denim eyes. "Now they look elsewhere for their kicks. News got around."

"How long have you worked here?" Tark asked.

"Six months."

And in another six months, Quin thought, she would move on like a weather front.

Zelda rapped at a door midway down the hall, opened it. "Dr. White?"

A woman was hunched over a desk fiddling with parts of a disassembled coffeemaker. "Brand new and it leaks like a sieve," she grumbled. "And all because of this." She pinched the end of a screw; it poked up between nails painted the same soft peach as her silk blouse. "It's not just rusted, it's stripped bare. And then people seem amazed when something like the *Challenger* happens."

She tossed the screw toward Zelda, who didn't catch it. "See if you can find a screw like this in the supply room, Zelda."

Zelda disappeared and White came out from behind her desk. She was taller than Quin had thought, just under six feet, and large-boned, older than she looked, midforties or so. Her features were exquisite: exotic topaz eyes that were bright with a sly intelligence, a moody, expressive mouth, the skin tone of a Gypsy. But she was no beauty. Her face was flawed by excess: a chin that was too angular, a forehead that was too broad. She wore her hair in a way that accentuated the flaws, pulled back from her face in a single thick braid, dark and threaded with gray.

Like the decor in the lobby, she was a walking testament to the Southwest, all of it in jewelry. Two earrings graced each ear, a pair of dangling pink quartz crystals set in silver and a pair of silver posts inlaid with turquoise. Four silver and turquoise bracelets climbed her left arm, a silver and turquoise necklace shaped like a quarter moon hung from her neck. The belt on her black, tailored slacks was also silver.

"Eden White," she said, extending her hand. "What can I do for the sheriff's department this time?"

She said it with a smile, but it was apparent that she resented the imposition on her time. "We'd like to ask you a few questions about Janis Krieger and Alejandro Domingo," Quin replied. "It won't take long."

"I talked at length with Detective Eastman and Mike McCleary about Alejandro and Janis. I don't know what else I can tell you. But let's sit over here, we'll be more comfortable."

They settled in a sitting area on the other side of the room, where Eden White's degrees decorated the wall. Harvard for medical school, Dartmouth for her undergraduate work, citations from Walter Reed and several other research centers for her "contributions to the advancement of scientific inquiry."

Tark asked how she had come to test Alejandro. She and Janis, she said, had met through mutual friends shortly after her return to the States. "I'd heard about her alleged cure, of course, and I was curious. I was also somewhat skeptical. I was trained as a physician and did a stint in oncology for a while. Spontaneous remission among cancer patients isn't common by any means, but it's not unheard of.

"Something triggers the immune system—a powerful will to live, our emotions, our beliefs about a doctor or a particular treatment. I think Janis's immune system was triggered by her falling in love with Alejandro."

"That doesn't sound very scientific," Tark remarked.

"On the contrary, Mr. Tark. The whole field of psychoneuroimmunology is causing even the most rigid Western physicians to rethink the role of emotion in health and disease. Touch changes the immune system. That's a fact.

"In one study lab rats were injected with tumors. They were housed in the same place, fed the same diet, treated the same. But some of the rats began to die within weeks while others lived on for months. The only variable was that the person feeding the rats was short, so that when he fed the rats in the lower cages he handled them. The rats in the upper cages weren't touched at all and died more quickly."

"So that may be what Alejandro does?" Quin asked.

"Very likely. He's good with people but doesn't do well under laboratory conditions. We tested him extensively over a period of two years, but I actually got more out of observing him in his own environment than I did out of anything we did in the lab."

"What kinds of tests did you do?" Quin asked.

"Tests that measured the autonomic changes in his body when he heals, tests for ESP, clairvoyance, precognition. Healers sometimes show ability in other areas as well."

"And you concluded he's a fraud," Tark said.

"I'm afraid it's not that simple, Mr. Tark. In some instances there was a definite improvement in patients' conditions. But I think that was the placebo effect in action. Those people believed absolutely that he could help. And their ailments weren't organic; they stemmed usually from the autonomic nervous system—ulcers, migraine headaches, high blood pressure.

"The healers I've read about and observed have an impressive success rate with these kinds of problems. They're also good at curing ailments that are emotionally induced, like hysterical paralysis. But when it comes to organic problems, that's tougher.

"There was one man, a Vietnam vet, whose spinal cord was crushed; Alejandro couldn't heal him. I saw him work on two AIDS patients: one is dead and the other is dying. I saw a woman with multiple sclerosis walk, supposedly without pain, but she was still crippled. Anyway, my report was inconclusive. I'd have to observe him over a period of several years and with several thousand patients to be able to arrive at a fair judgment."

"But in some of the newspaper articles I read you implied that Alejandro was a phony," Quin pointed out.

Eden looked miffed. "I was quoted out of context."

"Why did you stop observing him?" Tark asked.

"Janis blamed me for the negative press and wouldn't let me near him. You couldn't get to him without going through her first. She didn't understand that newspaper editors rip apart phenomena like this. If you get misquoted, well, tough, it makes good copy. Since Watergate, nothing is sacred. I guarantee you that if Edgar Cayce were alive today, he'd be ridiculed and maligned in a way that was unheard of in his time."

"What kind of cancer did Janis have?" Quin asked.

"Of the kidneys. It's one type of cancer that has been known to spontaneously regress. If she'd had leukemia, she wouldn't have lived long enough to get to Chile."

If it had been this way, if it had been that way. Even when you investigated the weird and the strange, Quin thought, you got caught up in dogma. "When was the last time you observed him?"

"September sometime, shortly before the first negative article appeared in the *Miami Herald*. About a month later, in early October, the state attorney's office got on his case."

"When was the last time you saw Janis or Alejandro?"

"I haven't seen Alejandro since. But Janis called me several times after that, blasting me for what I'd said to the press and blaming me for their problems with the state attorney's office. I explained that I'd been misquoted, but she'd been drinking and didn't want to hear about it."

"I didn't realize this facility investigated psychic phenomena," Tark remarked.

"We don't as a rule. But anything that concerns medicine and healing is of considerable interest to me personally."

"Were your observations of Alejandro on your own time?"

"Sometimes. But as Link's director, Mr. Tark, I have an obligation to investigate a variety of areas. Our only rule here, really, is that nothing is too odd or esoteric if it furthers the advancement of science."

Oh, please. Quin thought. "Do you study UFOs?"

Eden White wasn't pretty until she laughed and then her face was literally transformed. "That's probably the one thing we've never gotten into."

"Wouldn't a genuine UFO contribute to the advancement of science?"

She offered Quin a patient, patronizing smile. "We research areas within reasonable limits."

Reasonable. A legal term. *Reasonable* cause, *reasonable* requests, *reasonable* justice.

"Isn't your research geared toward the development of products?" Tark asked.

"Products pay the rent."

"What kind of products could possibly evolve from your observations of a psychic healer?"

"None that I know of. Like I said, Mr. Tark, we're researchers first."

She glanced at the clock on the wall. "I've got an appointment soon. Is there anything else you'd like to know?"

"Just one other thing," Tark said. "Do you know of anyone who hated Janis Krieger enough to want her dead?"

"Janis had her good points, but frankly she didn't head a lot of popularity lists. Oh, she was social enough, people enjoyed her at parties, but basically she was a complex, difficult woman who was determined to prove that Alejandro's the real thing. She used anyone she thought might further her cause."

"Why was it so important to her?" Quin asked. "I mean, he supposedly healed her, wasn't that enough?"

Bemused, she replied: "I can tell you don't know much about the inner workings of Palm Beach. The island is populated by snobs. And when one of their own leaves the flock and then returns married to a humble fisherman, people snicker, they gossip, they laugh behind your back. Even when some of these same people became Alejandro's patients, they still snickered and gossiped and talked behind her back. So I think she felt that some sort of official validation would vindicate her. Instead it backfired and that was tough for her to swallow." Another glance at the clock, then: "I really have to get going. But if you have any more questions, feel free to call me."

She strode to the door with them, the slipstream of her perfume as sweet and rare as some desert flower, and inserted her thumb in the scanner. Neither Quin nor Tark said anything until the door had shut behind them. "Information qualifies as a product," she said.

Tark grinned. "Great minds obsess about the same things. There'd have to be a potential buyer. I guess what we need first is a list of their customers."

"Zelda might be willing. If it came from you."

"I doubt it. I don't have a tan."

Quin laughed. "All the more reason for her to invite you to the beach, John."

At the bottom of the escalator Quin walked off in search of the restroom and Tark continued on to the desk. She wondered how he would play it, if Zelda would bite.

It occurred to her, and not for the first time, that fifteen years in the business had jaundiced her perception of the world. These days she seemed to view most people in terms of secret agendas, furtive motives, hidden passions, as though humanity were like an iceberg, two-thirds of it invisible to the naked eye.

There was a pay phone in the restroom and she started to call the hospital to check on McCleary, then changed her mind. For all she knew, the phones in this complex were bugged and video cameras and directional mikes were hidden in the ceiling. You couldn't have an employee running off at the mouth when the stakes were a two-million-dollar space toilet or a fisherman who might actually cure cancer with nothing more than the touch of his hands.

≈

Evening light painted the front yard in shades of violet and indigo and spilled through the branches of the melaleuca trees along the driveway. Neruda, Miranda's large black cat, stalked something near the gardenia bushes. A mockingbird swooped over him, fussing noisily, and Neruda froze, watching the bird. When it made a second, lower swoop, the cat rolled onto his back, playing dead.

Like me, Alejandro thought. *That's what I've been doing.* Playing dead to buy time for his daughter and sister.

He turned away from the yard, embarrassed for Neruda and disgusted with himself. The wicker porch chair creaked as he sat in it. He looked at the map spread open on the table, a county map that was detailed, easy to read. With a yellow marker he circled the airport and the approximate location of the Lazy Quick. He drew a yellow line between the two, following the route he had driven the night he had taken Miranda and Francesca to the airport.

Their itinerary had been simple: a short flight to Miami to connect with a midnight Ladeco flight to Santiago, a journey of eleven hours. The next night they were supposed to have taken a train to Puerto Montt, a ten-hour trip, where they were to catch the ferry to Chiloé. His brother would have picked them up there and driven them to Ancud.

But the flights had left without them.

In his worst moments he imagined his life would continue like this, suspended in limbo, the Lincoln arriving and departing, the future of his daughter and sister dependent on his cooperation with Jim and Bob. If he knew what they wanted of him, he could at least cling to a hope that it would eventually end. But his speculations were useless.

Contrary to what the priest believed, Alejandro didn't think Eden White was involved in this. Her experiments with him nearly two years ago had involved hardware: machines, computers, compasses, gadgets. Most of the tests in the windowless room focused on living things, like the gull.

Heal this, heal that, take away its pain, Alejandro.

Although they measured his body's responses just as Eden had done, they seemed more interested in manipulating his emotions. They were searching for something in that vast, complex network of neurons and hormones, a trigger of some kind. But he couldn't divine their motives: he was not clairvoyant or telepathic—nothing useful like that.

So he would attempt to use what he had. His hands.

He rubbed them together and shut his eyes. He conjured an image of his daughter: the dark eyes, the smile, the unblemished skin. He kept the image in his mind, looked at the map, and held his hands several inches above it, over the ranch. Then he moved his hands over the route he had driven that night, south to the airport. He felt something, a tingling, a slight warmth in his fingertips, and dropped his hands another inch.

His hands hovered over the airport. He waited for a nudge in a particular direction, but nothing happened. The tingling stopped; his palms grew cold.

He tried it again.

And again.

And again. Each time the tingling and warmth ceased at the airport. His hands dropped to the map. Stupid, useless slabs of flesh and bone, he thought. What good were the goddamn things if they couldn't help the people he loved? In a fit of anger and despair, he bunched up the map and hurled it into the dark.

The screen door squeaked as Carmelita stepped outside. He wondered how long she'd been standing there, watching him. "You might not be able to locate them like that if they were drugged, Alejandro."

Or killed, he thought. "I don't know what my hands can find or not find."

"What does Padre Cardenas think you should do?"

"Perform for a bishop who has connections."

"You have to trust someone, Alejandro. It can't go on like this."

"No, not yet."

She sighed, a soft sound of resignation. "I made seafood soup. Would you like a bowl?"

"In a while."

"You hardly eat anything."

Other men, he thought, were blessed with large families and loving wives; he was blessed with Carmelita. Since she had first come to him as a patient eighteen years ago, she had been his confidante, his closest friend. There were no secrets between them. But even she didn't understand the depth of his fear that if he made the wrong decision his sister and daughter would die.

Headlights appeared in the distance. He and Carmelita watched, locked in a dreadful silence, as the car drew closer. Both of them expected to see the Lincoln swing into the driveway, a black chariot. But it was a sleek red Mercedes, Lydia Holden's sporty convertible.

Carmelita was prepared to run interference. "I'll tell her you're not seeing anyone, that you're ill."

"No, it's okay."

Carmelita nodded but remained where she was, glaring as Lydia paused to scoop up the map he had tossed into the yard. She trotted up the steps, a woman of abundant energy with a compact, sinewy body like a professional runner's. She was carelessly dressed in white shorts, a cotton blouse, and white sandals. The glow of the porch light spilled over her hair, darkening the mass of wheat-colored curls that framed her striking face.

"Hi, Alex, Carmelita."

"*Buenas noches, Señora Holden,*" Carmelita said in an icy voice, then turned and went inside, letting the screen door slam behind her.

"If an employee of mine had an attitude like that, I'd fire her," Lydia said.

"She's not an employee."

"Oh, that's right." She smiled slightly as she sat in the wicker rocker to his left and dropped the wadded-up map on the table. "I forgot. She's a member of the family. I think that always irritated Janis."

"Probably."

She slipped a cigarette from her canvas bag and lit it with a monogrammed gold lighter. "So how've you been, Alex?"

"I've had better days."

"I can imagine."

I doubt it.

"I'm really sorry I haven't called or anything, Alex." She blew smoke out into the dark. "I meant to call, but, I don't know, I felt awkward about it."

Or guilty. She had distanced herself ever since the negative press on him first appeared last fall. He hadn't seen her since Janis's funeral, where she and Barker had stayed long enough to offer their condolences. They had extended a few invitations for dinner in the months since, but he had turned them down and eventually they had stopped asking.

"Does Barker know you're here, Lydia?"

"Of course not." She got up, walked over to the railing, and flicked ashes over the side. Then she sat on the railing and leaned against the post. Light glinted in the four-carat emerald on her finger. "As far as he's concerned, you're a political liability."

"I could say the same thing about him."

"C'mon, Alex, we've been all over that before. He didn't have anything to do with those complaints filed with the state attorney's office. And he sure as hell didn't initiate their investigation."

"Why're you here?" he asked bluntly.

Now that he had asked, she didn't hesitate to say her piece. "Did you tell the police I had been one of your patients?"

"Yes."

"Even though I asked you not to."

"I didn't have any choice. Detective Eastman requested a list of people who had made donations."

She stabbed the end of the cigarette against the railing, quick, violent stabs, then ground it out and flipped it into the dark. "Christ, Alex, you violated a confidence."

Her confidence, *her* world, *her* secrets, *her* marriage. She was the sun around which other people revolved like planets. He knew this about her, had always known it, but it angered him now. "My God, Lydia, he's investigating Janis's murder."

She rubbed the back of her hand across her mouth and glanced away—out toward the trees, down at her white sandals, anywhere but at him. "I didn't mean it like that," she said softly, contritely. "I loved her, too, you know." She looked at him again. "She was my friend before you ever knew her, Alex."

As though that gave her an edge on sorrow.

"But you could have removed my name from the list. You can't imagine how annoyed Barker is. The cops, then that detective, now more calls for appointments, for more questions. He's been unfit to live with."

What she was really saying was that Barker blamed her for all this because she had been Alejandro's patient, a fact he was sure would cost him votes in the election. And the more obsessive Barker got, the less stable the marriage became. Barker's roving eye wasn't a secret to Lydia.

"I'm afraid my life these days doesn't leave much room for sympathy, Lydia." As Alejandro got up, her eyes followed him, chameleon eyes that seemed to constantly change color, absorbing and reflecting light in some new way. "You'll have to excuse me, but my dinner's getting cold."

She stood quickly, her small, delicate hands smoothing the front of her shorts. "I'm sorry for just dropping by, I know I should have called first." She gave his arm a squeeze. "Don't think badly of me, Alex. I don't mean to be such a self-centered bitch, but this campaign is making me crazy." Then she rolled onto the balls of her feet, brushed her cool mouth against his cheek, and left as silently as she had arrived.

He watched her car until the darkness swallowed it. For moments nothing existed but his anger. Then the all-too-familiar heat rose inside him with the suddenness of a desert wind. He lurched down the steps and ran among the melaleuca trees, his arms clasped against his chest, his hands tucked under his armpits.

He flew past the swimming pool toward the safety of the pines just beyond it. The heat swept through him in waves, each worse than the one before it. It was like pain, this heat, and it blinded him, stupefied him. Branches slapped him in the face. He was in the pines; there were roots everywhere. He stumbled and sank to his knees, clutching himself at the waist, rocking forward so far his forehead brushed the pine needles. A soft moan escaped from him, a hideous sound, and the heat leaped away from him and into the dark.

After a while, he didn't know how long, he toppled to the side. His cheek rested against the pine needles and he drew his legs up against his chest. He could breathe again. The pain was gone; so was the heat. He felt as though he had been scooped out inside, vacuumed clean.

When he felt stronger, he struggled to his knees and sat back on his heels. He patted his pockets for the penlight on his keys, turned it on, and shone it around. The thin beam skipped over pine needles, small rocks, broken branches. Maybe, he thought. Maybe he'd been lucky this time.

Then the beam impaled an anthill the size of a dinner plate. Fire ants. They were among his first lessons when he had come to this country. They weren't particularly large, and their nests appeared wherever they happened to surface from their subterranean network of tunnels.

They were relentless, aggressive ants, and aptly named. Their stings felt like fire and could cause violent allergic reactions that ranged from angry red welts to convulsions. But these ants weren't going to be stinging anyone in the foreseeable future. Dozens of them littered the surface of the mound, little dark corpses that might be mistaken for a handful of sunflower seeds.

As he stared, the queen ant weaved out of the hole, stopped, sank against the dirt, and died.

Alejandro turned off the penlight and pressed his knuckles against his eyes. Dear God, it was happening again. First the glass of the picture window at the airport, now the fire ants. What would be next?

Freak, degenerate, mutant, savage, beast. The words bumped around inside of him as he stumbled to his feet and made his way back toward the house.

7

Shortly after seven Tuesday morning Rita Vail breezed through Quin's front door, a brunette Rita Hayworth, after whom she'd been named.

She was dressed for court in a conservative black suit and a pale pink silk blouse. Her hair was pulled back with a pink scarf, one of those casual touches that Quin could never quite perfect. Her makeup was sparse, mascara and a touch of pink on her mouth, not that she needed even that. In her presence Quin felt like an aging Tallulah Bankhead.

Rita had come bearing gifts, naturally, she usually did: Danishes, two cups of caffè latte, and a bright yellow bucket filled with Legos for Michelle. The Legos promptly ended up scattered across the floor of the kitchen, a colorful barrier of geometric shapes.

"She likes them," Rita said, beaming. She watched Michelle as she fitted the little pieces together.

"You could give her a pie tin, Rita, and she'd like it. Aunt Ree is up there with Barney."

"Who's Barney?"

This, Quin thought, was the sort of question that separated her from her friends who didn't have kids. "A purple dinosaur."

"Ah." As if that explained everything.

Michelle, aware that she was the topic of conversation, plucked her spoon out of the container of coffee yogurt on the floor beside her and offered it to Rita. "C'fee, Ah Ree?"

Rita laughed and quickly took the dripping spoon. "Got my own, sweetie. Now open wide, this bee wants to get in."

Michelle opened her mouth without a whimper.

"You missed your calling," Quin remarked.

"So the Republican attorneys in court are always telling me." Rita swept her napkin across the clumps of yogurt on the floor, then joined Quin at the kitchen table. "Why don't I chuck the bench and become a nanny. What assholes. Oops, sorry. You didn't hear that, Ellie." She put her hands over her ears and Michelle mimicked her and giggled.

Quin said, "She's heard worse."

"Does she understand?"

"About assholes? Probably."

Rita laughed. "About Mac, I mean."

"She saw him shot. She knows what a hospital is. She keeps asking when he's coming home." Quin broke one of the Danishes in half. "I need a favor, Rita."

"Let's hear it."

For ten years the mere mention of Rita's name had sent shudders up the collective spine of the prosecutors in the state attorney's office. Those who had never come up against her in court knew her by reputation: She had won nearly half of the cases she'd defended. The idiots who were deceived by her soft voice and good looks quickly learned better.

Nearly two years ago she'd won a vacancy on the bench in criminal court. Her next stop would probably be the state supreme court or the governor's cabinet or maybe even D.C. At thirty-eight she was already a political presence in the bastions of county and state governments. If there were answers to be found, Rita was the place to start.

"Let me get this straight," Rita said when Quin had finished. "You need three things: information on who or what prompted the investigation on the Chilean; anything I can beg, borrow, or steal on Barker and Lydia Holden; and ditto for Link Research and Development. Is that about it?"

"Until further notice."

She pointed at the circles under her eyes. "See these? Complicated requests make them deeper."

"I thought long nights of great sex did that."

"Sex?" Rita laughed. "What's that? You ought to see what's out there when you're divorced, pushing forty, and sitting on the bench, Quin. Married attorneys with beer bellies and thinning hair, divorced attorneys with attitude problems, single attorneys just out of law school who think they're hot shit. Not to mention the health risks. Hell, I'd rather abstain."

"Find a guy from the Midwest. I've heard men out there are different."

"I'd find him and he'd turn out to be a Republican like my ex."

Who was a conservative fifteen years her senior and the man against whom she measured all that she found repugnant in life.

"Okay, look," Rita went on, all business again. "I already know what prompted the investigation on the healer. Some of his former clients filed complaints with the state attorney's office. They came to Sasha's attention and she asked them to look into it."

Sasha Colt, U.S. Senator, the incumbent whom Holden was running against and a personal friend of Rita's. Quin knew she was a former schoolteacher from Tampa, a grandmother now in her fifties who'd had no prior political experience before she'd run for a seat in the U.S. Senate eight years ago. Her grass-roots campaign had burgeoned from a two-person operation to a kind of pop-culture phenomenon that had ushered her into politics in an overwhelming victory.

She was still well liked by her constituents and the shift in the national political climate made her a natural for reelection. But Florida's voters were an odd, sometimes fickle bunch—retirees, transplants, Hispanics who tended to be conservative. And it was quite possible that Barker Holden, with his megabucks and his conservative platform, had a better shot at triumph than it appeared this early in the campaign.

"Was she looking for dirt on Holden?" Quin asked.

"She isn't into dirty politics. And I'm not saying that just because she's a good friend. I worked on her last campaign and I'm working on this one because she's exactly what we need in the Senate. She had no idea Lydia Holden had been one of Alejandro's patients until Fitz Eastman wormed it out of him not too long after his wife was killed. And once she knew she was real touchy about doing or saying anything that might be misconstrued. Hell, she was even going to back out of this festival I organized in Fort Lauderdale."

"What festival?"

"Jesus, Quin, don't you read the newspaper?"

"I barely have time to brush my teeth. What is it?"

"A big block party with strangers. Food, music, and politics on Las Olas. We'll have eight blocks, with soundstages at either end. It'll kick off with local musicians and end with the featured biggies, Crosby, Stills, and Nash. In between, tri-county voters get to question Holden and Sasha on the issues."

"And Holden went for it?"

"Sure. The beer company that's helping to sponsor it will donate a percentage of what they make to the Children's Last Wish Foundation. The city will match what the beer company pledges. That means lots of press and anywhere from fifty to a hundred thousand people, so of course Holden went for it."

"Sounds like he's right up there on your list of admirable human beings, Rita."

"Don't get me started on that asshole."

"What do you know about Link?"

Rita shrugged. "They have some pretty big government contracts, but that's it. Are we talking about someone in particular?"

"Eden White, the director."

She jotted a few notes as she polished off her Danish.

"You ever met Lydia Holden?" Quin asked.

"A few times. I used to shop in her store on Worth Avenue until the campaign started."

"Another name for your list of admirable human beings."

Rita shrugged. "The only thing I've got against Lydia is who she married. She's really not so bad, a little weird, maybe, but not intolerable."

"Weird how?"

"I don't know. I mean, how weird is Trump? You live in a fifty-room mansion with two hundred million plus in the bank and your perspective on what's real has got to be warped. On top of it, she's married to Holden. Sleeps with the guy. No normal person would have sex with him, Quin."

"C'mon," Quin laughed. "His politics aside, he doesn't look that bad in the pictures I've seen of him."

"I'm not talking about politics and looks. Barker is . . . I don't know, dangerous, I guess that's the word I'm looking for. After screwing him you'd feel soiled or tarnished or something, like you'd committed an unnatural act."

"I'll be sure to pass that on to Lydia when we have lunch."

"Very funny. When're you having lunch?"

"I'm waiting for her to call me back. John gets to tackle Barker."

"Lucky John. Anything else I should check on?"

"Not that I can think of right this second."

"It'll take me a few days to get some answers."

"Whenever you've got time, Rita. I appreciate it."

She frowned, scrutinizing Quin in that way she had. "You seem to be doing okay."

Quin rocked her hand. "I'm doing better than Mac, let me put it that way."

"If you're free this evening, let's go out for a bite to eat. The three of us. We can go to that place up on the intracoastal where Ellie can feed the catfish."

"The Old House. Ellie's favorite spot."

"Fish," Michelle said, clapping her hands.

Rita reached for her purse, downed the rest of her coffee. "Right now I've got to scoot. Hot date with a guy who's in court for his eleventh count of burglary."

Rita gave Quin a quick hug, then hoisted Michelle onto her hip and they danced, cheek to cheek, into the living room. Quin followed in her robe, her slippers, her tangled hair, vaguely depressed that everyone she knew seemed to have a better rapport with her daughter than she did.

The intensive care unit was a small, self-contained world of hums and clicks and burps. Regardless of the time of day she visited, the place was always busy and always seemed to be twilit, as though time had actually paused at the elevator doors.

The head nurse stopped Quin on her way to McCleary's room and said that Dr. Brattleboro wanted to talk to her before she went in to see her husband. She quickly asked, "Has he taken a turn for the worse?" *Such optimism.*

"No, no, nothing like that. I think he just wants to give you an update. Your husband is doing better than any of us expected."

She paged Brattleboro and he appeared less than five minutes later, his manner oddly effusive. "Mrs. McCleary. Nice to see you again. He's coming along just fine. Vital signs holding steady, no fever, and he's now on a liquid diet."

Sucking meals through a straw. Yeah, terrific.

"We'll be moving him out of ICU sometime tomorrow, so he can have other visitors. If he continues like this, we'll release him in two weeks."

"What's the bad news?"

His demeanor instantly sobered. He didn't preface the bad news with happy horseshit, he gave it to her straight, and she appreciated it. "Due to the concussion, your husband appears to be suffering from an expressive aphasia, where normal words are spoken fluently but without semantic meaning. He can probably understand what's said to *him,* he can still think, but he can't express himself either verbally or in writing."

A door blew open inside her head and a storm roared through.

She simply stood there unable to speak, as trapped in herself as McCleary was in himself.

"The prognosis is usually good," Brattleboro continued. "As the injured areas of the brain heal, recovery occurs over a period of weeks or months and—"

"*Months?*"

"Weeks *or* months, Mrs. McCleary. It depends on the patient."

"Is there any way he can communicate? Hand signals or something?"

"Usually the condition affects nonverbal equivalents of words as well. But if I were you, I would try virtually anything. He's going to be extremely frustrated, so prepare yourself for that. I've called in a neurologist who'll be able to answer your questions in much greater depth."

Another doctor to keep track of, Quin thought. How many more would there be before all of this was over? Would it be over? Would the neurologist be able to guarantee that McCleary would recover completely? That in weeks or months or a year from now he would be as good as new? Could Brattleboro guarantee that? Could anyone?

When she passed the cops outside the room and stepped inside, her first thought was that McCleary didn't look much better than he had when he was admitted. Although he was no longer on oxygen, he was still connected to tubes and catheters and IVs, still zapped on morphine.

But his eyes opened when she said his name, opened instantly, as though he'd been waiting for her. She pulled a chair up close to the bed. Brattleboro, she knew, had told McCleary about the aphasia. And judging from the look in his eyes, he'd understood every word. "It's reversible, Mac. And we're going to work on it. We'll devise some way for you to communicate and—"

"Farmers grow rain. Lakes are dry. Roses dance . . ." His face seemed to come undone at the seams; he pressed her hand between both of his own, and her heart broke.

"Look, don't try to talk. The more frustrated you get, the harder it will be. I'll be meeting with the neurologist and we'll know more then. Brattleboro says you'll probably be coming home in a couple of weeks. Just remember this other thing isn't permanent."

Thing: she had already relegated it to a realm of objects, something that could be controlled and directed. And then she quickly changed the subject by reiterating what they knew at this point about the investigation that had led to his shooting. Facts, speculations, suspicions.

But in the telling the details seemed minute, impoverished. Now and then something glimmered in his eyes, recognition or hope, she didn't know which.

They were interrupted by a nurse, who took his temperature, blood pressure, then connected a new bag of antibiotics to his IV. After her came two lab technicians who drew blood, then another nurse who attached something to his chart. McCleary waved his arm at her and snapped, "Fire drills for fools."

The nurse gave Quin a sympathetic look and beat a hasty retreat. When she looked back at McCleary, his head was turned away from her, an arm covering his eyes. She left the hospital with a hole the size of Greenland in the center of her chest.

≈

McCleary watched the slow drip of fluid through the IV, the flickering light from the TV on the far wall, and the cops outside his door as they paced, sat, talked, killed time. He wondered what their joke about this assignment was. He imagined a new breed of jokes to replace the Polack jokes, the cripple jokes, the jokes about blacks and Jews.

McCleary shut his eyes, waiting for the pain. It was there, bright and insipid, his constant companion. But as long as he didn't move abruptly, the morphine kept it within tolerable limits. He wanted to sleep, to sink into the dark seduction of the drug, but he couldn't. His mind moved with the sluggishness of a snail, thoughts looping in on themselves like some vast highway that led nowhere.

He went through the alphabet, counted to five thousand, silently recited his social security number, Quin's social security number, his address, his home and office phone numbers.

He remembered what Quin had been wearing when he'd met her,

the night she'd discovered the corpse of the man she'd been living with. The man's name was Grant Bell. At the time McCleary had been seeing a woman named Robin. He remembered the first time he had made love to Quin, his departure from Miami's homicide department, his affair with Sylvia Callahan; he remembered dying two years ago during emergency surgery. And he remembered his sister's murder and his daughter's birth.

It was all there, the great and the small, the wonders, the triumphs, the betrayals, the guilt, the entire complex history of his life. But when he opened his mouth to whisper yes, he was whole, he was alive, everything broke down, synapses misfired, the system collapsed, and nonsense came out. "Smoking's green."

He turned slowly and reached for the pen and paper Quin had brought him yesterday. *Write hello. Go on, write it. H-E-L-L-O.* He touched the pen to the paper, moved his hand. *Hello* emerged as *sky*.

Your name. Try your name.

Mike came out as *cat*.

Quin: house.

Ellie: paper.

Hospital: phone.

Tark: luck.

He made a hideous sound, then stabbed the paper, puncturing it, tearing it as nonsense streamed from his mouth. His hand rose and fell, rose and fell, again and again, until the paper was strewn like confetti around him and his bed was riddled with small blue holes.

≈

Compared to the rest of South Florida, Alejandro thought, Jupiter Farms was another world.

Trees outnumbered people, only a fraction of the roads were paved, and most of the homes occupied lots that were an acre or larger. Alejandro had wanted to buy a home here, but Janis had thought it was too far from Palm Beach, too rural, too redneck. When he had pointed out that it was good enough for Burt Reynolds, who owned a ranch there, she had simply rolled her eyes as if to say that

Reynolds was hardly in the same league as the Kennedys, the Trumps, the Holdens.

Reynolds is just a good ol' homeboy with some money, Alex.

He passed the Reynolds ranch, which was open to the public and housed a feed store, a pizza parlor, a small petting zoo, a gift shop filled with career memorabilia. Two blocks later he turned west on a dirt road lined on either side by massive banyan trees. Their branches knitted together overhead, creating a tunnel of leaves. Night sounds echoed inside it, the glow of his headlights washed across it.

Eden lived on one of the side roads, at the end of a cul-de-sac. Her house was a rambling split-level on five wooded acres. At one time she had kept horses out back for her kids; now the barn was as empty as her personal life.

She was home, just as he'd expected. She rarely stayed at Link past five and it was already seven. He pulled into the driveway behind her Blazer and started up the wood-chip path. He hadn't seen Eden for months, since her negative remarks about him in the press, and he felt uneasy about coming here. But the priest had raised questions that begged for answers. Were Jim and Bob working for her? Was she behind the experiments? And if so, did she know about Francesca and Miranda?

She answered the door wearing shorts and a T-shirt, her feet bare. Her extraordinary eyes widened with surprise. "Alex."

"Hi, Eden. Do you have a few minutes?"

She hesitated, her body blocking the door as though she expected him to shove his way past her and into the house. "Actually, I was just getting ready to go out."

"This won't take long."

Her lustrous hair was loose and she flicked it off her shoulder, her silver bracelets clicking together, then she stepped outside. In the old days he had been welcome in those cool, cluttered rooms.

"So how've you been, Alex?"

"Not bad," he lied, enjoying her unease, her awkwardness. It was painfully apparent that she didn't know what to make of his visit, that she was, in fact, frantically searching for something to say. "How about you?"

"Pretty good. Busy, real busy." She looked down at the ground, kicked at a fallen leaf. "I want to apologize for not going to Janis's funeral, Alex." She raised her eyes and in the spill from the porch light, her skin seemed luminous. "With, uh, everything that had gone on last fall, I just felt it was better if I stayed away. Now I regret it."

"Don't," he said. "She wouldn't have wanted you there."

She drew back a little, unable to mask her astonishment at his bluntness. Shadows moved in her topaz eyes, shadows cast by the spin of some complex, internal mechanism that was sizing him up, figuring his motives.

"If you've come to place blame, Alex, just spit it out."

"That's not why I'm here. I was going through Janis's papers and realized she never got copies of your records on those experiments we did several years ago." *Twenty-six months of experiments, Eden, but who the hell's counting?* "If I remember correctly, your agreement with her was that we would be notified, in writing, of the results."

Her topaz eyes darkened to an indescribable color and she shook her head slowly, pensively. "I don't remember any such agreement, Alex. But even if I did, the records are long gone. I tossed them out last fall, when Janis refused to let me observe you anymore. Besides, I told her about the confusing ambiguity, the erratic results."

"C'mon, Eden. I know you better than that. You never toss out files, and even if you did, you wouldn't get rid of your personal notes."

She folded her arms at her waist and looked at him as if he'd lost his mind. Her mouth turned upward slightly at the corners. "My notes are my personal property, Alex. What makes you think you have any right to them?"

She kept talking, but he no longer heard her. Blood pounded in his ears; rage surged from some dark, musty place inside of him, rage at her, at Janis, at Lydia, at the men who had taken his daughter and his sister, rage at his wife's faceless, anonymous killer. He didn't realize he had grabbed Eden's wrist until she gasped, "You're hurting me," and twisted her arm, twisted hard, and broke his hold.

Then she was stumbling away from him, shaking her head as if to clear it, blood oozing from her nostrils. She wiped the back of her hand across her nose and her stricken eyes darted from his face to her blood-streaked knuckles to his face again. The sight of the blood bubbling from her nostrils and oozing over her lips burned against his retinas.

"Jesus," she hissed, tilting her head back and pressing her hand against her nose to stem the flow. "Leave m-me alone, just leave me alone." She threw open the door and weaved into the house, slamming the door.

The lock clicked.

The chain clattered.

Alejandro backed away from the door, then walked quickly away from the house to the Porsche and sped out of the cul-de-sac. How long? How long since something like that had happened? Ten years? Twelve? Not since a thief in Santiago had tried to snatch Carmelita's purse. Not since then.

In his memory the thief was still stumbling backward down that Santiago street, his eyes wide with horror and disbelief as he wiped frantically at his bloody nose. Now the beast was awake again, awake, hungry, and raging.

When I was six or seven, I discovered in myself a capacity for deceit.

It began with small things, white lies uttered with a straight face, loose change pilfered from the pile of coins on my father's dresser, shoplifted objects that I wanted. I was never caught; people like me rarely are. It's not that I'm smarter or luckier than people who get caught, just that my darker self and I were comfortable together.

But deceit was a long way from murder. In the weeks after I killed Janis, I suffered. I smelled traces of her blood on my skin even though I washed my hands incessantly and showered five or six times a day. I had insomnia, high blood pressure, a short fuse. I bought some relaxation tapes; they didn't work. I tried acupuncture, herb teas, homeopathic remedies. None of it did a damn thing.

I resorted to thirty milligrams of Librium before I went to bed, fell into a light sleep for a few hours, then woke with a dry mouth and a slight hangover. I doubled the dosage. I wanted to be knocked out, oblivious for at least eight hours. It succeeded. For a while.

On nights when the insomnia was particularly bad, when nothing worked, when my skin was wrinkled from all the showers I'd taken, I obsessed about things—the snails that were consuming my yard, the irritating click in the engine of my car, the stubborn stain in my favorite blouse, a broken nail on my left hand, the migraines that had plagued me intermittently for years and that seemed to be getting worse. I also obsessed about Janis's pillowcase.

I had saved it. I shouldn't have, but I did. It smelled of gunpowder, of blood, of her perfume.

That scent haunted me. Odor and memory, such complex connections. The perfume cost about two hundred an ounce, stuff most people would wear for special occasions. But not Janis. It was just part of her morning routine, no different to her than a tube of mascara or lipstick.

One whiff of that perfume and I could see her, she was right there in front of me: Janis with her exuberant laughter, Janis when she'd had too much to drink, Janis and her distinctive grace even in her worst moments.

The other thing about that pillowcase was the pattern of the blood on it. I knew it was a code of some kind that begged to be broken down, deciphered. I knew it was a sign. But the meaning eluded me.

Sometimes I smoothed the pillowcase flat against the floor and studied the pattern. Other times I taped it to the wall and looked at it from different angles, in different kinds of light, hoping to see the message. Occasionally I was sure the pattern changed even as I stared at it, that the bloodstains elongated or spread or shrank. Once I saw eyes, another time a nose and a mouth, and most recently I saw a snake.

Freud would have had a field day with that one.

The stupid pillowcase and its indecipherable message obsessed me until even the Librium didn't cut it anymore. I got rid of it and decided sex would be the perfect soporific.

Aside from the obvious risk of disease, sex with someone you have only just met is riddled with uncertainty. Too many nuts running around loose out there. And quite frankly I wasn't quite sure how to go about it. Did I cruise? Bar-hop? Hire someone? All of this led to Moreno.

Eduardo Cortez Moreno was his full name, but around me he called himself Eddie Brown because he thought, I guess, that I preferred American men. He was a lawn man, the guy who showed up like clockwork every week with his pollution machine, his deafening grass blower, his electric hedge clippers.

He was part Nicaraguan, solidly built, compact, dark as a raisin, and tall for a Latino. He had a tattoo on his right shoulder, Wonder Woman with her ridiculous boobs, her muscular arms and legs, her silly outfit. Wonder Woman, please, that great outdated icon of male fantasies.

I'm no expert on tattoos, but this one seemed rather large.

Wonder Woman began way up on his right shoulder and extended down onto his upper arm, so her hair seemed to tumble over his skin, an ink-colored waterfall. Because of her height I could never look at Eddie straight on without enduring her scrutiny. Her eyes disturbed me, made me squirm inside, but I didn't understand why until much later. When Eddie flexed his muscles in a certain way, Wonder Woman danced, the rumba, the tango, a slow, intimate waltz.

Eddie liked me, I think, because I talked to him. He would stand there in the sun, an elbow resting on the lawn-mower handle, his eyes hooded and strange but attentive. We talked about grass. Grass, for Christ's sakes. I'd never talked about grass to anyone, the weeds that attacked it, the chiggers that lived in it, the droughts that killed it.

To Eddie I was just this woman who worked in the same neighborhood where he did lawns. So one afternoon as he was packing up his truck, I suggested we go get a beer. He picked the bar, a real basic place where you drink beer from the bottle and eat pickled eggs. We played pool, we danced, we got pretty drunk, and then we went back to his cramped, dirty sloop on the intracoastal and we fucked.

I liked it, liked it in a purely visceral way. He made me feel good. He made me come. There was a clarity about it that appealed to me, no fuss, no games, nothing romantic.

He told me about a certain kind of lizard that attracts its mate by puffing out a colorful flap of skin at its throat. The female plays hard to get at first, approaching the male, backing off, venturing close again. Even though both lizards know the female wants it as badly as the male, her game is the dance of seduction.

"Meaning what?" I asked, wondering if he was saying that I was like the female lizard.

"I hate the dance."

"That's a relief, since I don't know how to dance."

"C'mon, chica, you know how to dance if you need to. You just don't need to with me."

Which was how I came to discover that Eddie Moreno mowed lawns in Walden Lakes, the development where the McClearys lived. Eddie, in other words, was another sign, my triumph or my nemesis, I'm still not sure.

s

~~~~~~~~

It was a day that northerners would kill for in February, Tark thought. The sky that Wednesday morning was a heartbreaking blue, the temperature was in the low seventies, and the Hungry Pelican was jammed.

He stood at the periphery of the crowd at the bar, loud music pounding at the back of his head, and tried to get Estelle's attention. She finally saw him and broke away for a few minutes. "Hey, Gabby. I think I've got something for you. Can you come by the house after I get off tonight?"

"What time?"

"I'll get out of here around midnight."

Someone at the bar hollered for her and she rolled her dark eyes. "Gotta run. See you later."

And just that quickly she was gone, a flash of black hair and dark skin. Tark watched her as she whipped up drinks and opened bottles of beer, watched her as she flirted, laughed, and did what she got paid to do, kept that cash register ringing.

He headed south to Boca Raton for his meeting with Noel Unward, the physicist who had been one of the healer's staunchest supporters. The irony of Boca, he decided, was that a town with such an unflattering name—its literal translation from Spanish was Mouth of the Rat—was considered such a desirable place to live.

Much of the town actually existed outside of the city limits, within housing developments that were like walled cities. Gates, guardhouses, blockades of concrete. It wasn't entirely clear to Tark whether the walls were intended to keep intruders out or the residents in.

Over time the expansion west had crippled Boca's downtown. Small businesses moved or went bankrupt, shopping centers folded, and the area barely limped along. Then a few years ago the construction of Mizner Park had provided the boost the downtown had so badly needed.

It consisted of a single, very wide boulevard that was divided by a landscaped median strip half as wide and lined by shops, restaurants, and businesses on either side. To Tark there was something magical about it, as though it had been lifted from a different South Florida, one in which cars weren't necessary to get around, where you could actually walk, browse, and sit in a sidewalk café.

He and Unward were supposed to meet outside of Liberties' Books & Music. But since Tark was early, he went inside to browse. It was the kind of shop book lovers loved: well stocked, spacious, with a cappuccino bar, tables, chairs, a place that invited you to poke around as long as you wanted.

He browsed at the dumps in the front of the store and settled on the latest Dean Koontz book for McCleary. Then he wandered into the New Age section to find a comprehensive book on alternative medicine. The choices were staggering: acupuncture and aromatherapy and reflexology; visualization, meditation, vitamins, and diet; biofeedback, yoga, homeopathy. The message, he thought, was abundantly clear. Take charge of your life and your health and leave the conventional health-care system to its inevitable demise.

He found a much smaller section that featured books on famous psychic healers like Edgar Cayce, Katherine Kulman, José Arigo, and the controversial psychic surgeons of the Philippines. He picked a biography on Arigo because he was a Brazilian whose humble beginnings were similar to Alejandro's.

His last stop was the Florida section. It seemed to include every book ever published about the state or that featured the state in some way. He ran across an unexpected gem, a tome on Palm Beach's five most prominent families that included about a hundred pages just on the Holden Cereals clan. The material began in 1901 with Grandpa Holden, who had started the business, and ended with Barker Holden, Jr., who had sold it twelve years ago for an estimated sum of two hundred million dollars.

Twenty minutes after entering the store, Tark left nearly fifty bucks poorer. Unward showed up a few minutes later, a beanpole of a man with the lean, weathered face of a sailor. His eyes were the same navy blue as his slacks, his thinning hair the color of dirty sand. His bushy mustache drooped at the ends. Late forties, Tark guessed, a man whose best days in academia were probably behind him. He pumped Tark's arm as though he hoped it would eventually yield water and apologized profusely for being late.

Unward was a fast talker and griped about the traffic, the tourists, how it had taken him twenty minutes to find a parking spot, and would Tark like a beer? They crossed the street to one of the cafés and claimed a table on the sidewalk. He positioned himself like a spy, his back to the café so that he had a clear view of the boulevard. His eyes roamed, darting after cars and pedestrians in a way that suggested he believed he had been followed.

Tark ordered beer and Unward, a double scotch on the rocks. "So you have some questions about Alejandro, Mr. Tark?"

"A few."

"For the sheriff's department."

"I'm taking up where Detective Eastman left off."

Unward stirred his drink, then went at it with a determination that suggested he would be loaded within an hour. "I spent half a morning answering Detective Eastman's questions about Alejandro after Janis was killed. Then after that a fellow named McCleary showed up on campus and I blew an hour with him. How is he, by the way? I heard on the news that he got shot."

"He's still critical."

"That's a shame. Any idea who did it?"

"Not yet."

"He was jogging when it happened, wasn't he?"

"Right. With his wife and daughter."

"Jesus." He rubbed the back of his neck and shook his head. "You just never know, do you."

"It wasn't a random shooting, Mr. Unward. We think it was connected to this case."

This elicited a noncommittal grunt from Unward, whose eyes were roaming again.

"What's your professional opinion of Alejandro's talents?"

Unward's shrug made his shirt pucker at the shoulders. "The guy's for real. Let's just get that clear from the beginning. I told Detective Eastman and Mr. McCleary the same thing. He can do what he claims he can. I've seen it. He removed a lipoma from my arm. A benign tumor." He held his right arm out and indicated a spot on the inside of the upper arm. "It was right about there. No scar, so you'll have to take my word for it."

"Removed it how?"

His eyes swept through the street like a radar. "With a rusted switchblade. About a year ago." From a pocket in his slacks he brought out a pipe, a pouch of tobacco, a lighter, and proceeded to fill the pipe's bowl. "Now picture this, Mr. Tark. We were outside at his ranch, in a patio area behind the house. There must've been fifty people out there waiting to see him. I showed him my arm and he asked for a knife. Someone produced the switchblade. He told me not to watch while he made the incision, so I looked at the student I'd brought with me, who was doing the videotaping.

"Next thing I knew, Alejandro slapped the tumor into my hand. I didn't feel a damn thing—no pain, no discomfort, not even the blade cutting into my skin. He handed me a Band-Aid, wiped his palms on his apron, and moved on to the next patient.

"Since it was done without any attention whatsoever to sterile conditions, I felt I should at least douse it with alcohol. But I didn't. I decided that at the first sign of infection I'd get myself to a hospital. But it healed within two days, less than half the time normally required, and there was never any infection. None, Mr. Tark."

"Do you still have the videotape?"

"No, unfortunately I don't. I mailed it to a colleague, who still has it. I must've watched it a hundred times." The sweet scent of tobacco rose with a puff of smoke. Unward's eyes swept through the street again, where cars were pulling into and out of parking spaces. Then he ordered another double scotch and glanced at Tark, who shook his head. He was still sipping his beer.

"The procedure took about six seconds. Alejandro made two incisions in my arm, like an X, and spread the skin open with his fingers so the tumor was visible. Then he squeezed it like a pimple and it popped out."

"So if he's the real thing, why did you withdraw your support?" Tark asked.

Unward took another puff on his pipe, another hefty gulp of his scotch. "I was doing this on my free time, and between teaching and research, I don't have a whole lot of that. Besides, once the state attorney's office started nosing around and asking questions, I realized anything I said might do Alejandro more harm than good because technically he had practiced medicine on me without a license. That's the main reason I backed off."

"How's it work?"

"How's what work?"

"His ability."

"Ask me something easy."

"You don't have any idea?"

"Sure, I have a few ideas. But that doesn't mean they're valid. You know anything about physics?"

"The apple and Newton, that's about it."

Unward smiled. "That's more than some of my students can remember." He held the lighter to his pipe again. "In 1964 a physicist named John Bell came up with a rather disturbing theory that some scientists consider the most important discovery in the history of science. Basically, it suggests that the mystic's view of the universe is true, Mr. Tark. All things are intimately connected, in the deepest sense of the word, beginning at the quantum level."

He picked up his two plastic swizzle sticks and set them side by side. "These are spinning particles in a two-particle system, okay? We separate them." He pushed them to opposite sides of the table. "Now we slow down or speed up the spin of one of them. According to Bell's Theorem, when you change the spin in one, the spin in the other is affected simultaneously, even if they're widely separated. *Simultaneously*, Mr. Tark, that's the key word here."

"I thought Einstein proved that no signal moves faster than the speed of light."

"See? You know more than you think about physics." He picked up the swizzle sticks, twisted the ends together. "Obviously it takes time for the signal to reach the particle's twin, so the exchange can't be instantaneous because that would be faster than the speed of light. But in spite of what we believe to be an immutable law, this simultaneous exchange occurs."

"Telepathy?"

"Possibly." He pulled the swizzle sticks apart. "In another twenty years Bell's Theorem just might prove to be the scientific basis for telepathy and other phenomena that make scientists squirm. But I think it points to a great deal more than that, Mr. Tark. It suggests an elemental oneness to the universe, an invisible wholeness that unites all things, from rock to insect to man."

"Quite a speech. But certain cultures have known that for centuries, Dr. Unward. It's not exactly a new concept."

"It's new for physics. The controversial part is the implication that what applies to the world of atoms applies uniformly to the world of men. Up until Bell's Theorem the idea of a significant connection between the observed and the observer, between consciousness and the environment, was unthinkable. It implied that the mere act of observing and measuring an experiment, for instance, somehow influenced the parameters, the event, the outcome."

"How does it apply to Alejandro?"

"He has the capacity to connect with that world of atoms." His gaze drifted again, roaming the street, pausing on cars, pedestrians. "To *alter* it."

"Telekinesis?"

"You keep trying to label it." Unward looked annoyed and polished off his second scotch. "The labels may apply, but they aren't the full story. I think we're all born with these abilities to one degree or another and for whatever reason—culture, religion, education—we don't exercise them and they atrophy.

"But Alejandro was born into a culture where these kinds of talents aren't viewed as strange or demonic or what have you, a culture where his talent was allowed to flourish. He's essentially a simple man. A fisherman. He had no preconceived notions about what was possible."

Fine, Tark had no problem with that part. And on an intellectual level, as an idea, an abstract, he didn't find any of this difficult to believe. But when he thought of the abstraction embodied within the skin and bones of a man who was alive now, who lived just up the road, then he had trouble with it.

"But how does he do it?"

Unward shrugged. "Hey, I could sit here all day and cite ideas and theories that would run the gamut from ancient philosophies to the cutting edge of quantum physics, Mr. Tark. But none of it would answer your question. I don't know *how* he does it, I just know that he does.

"When he's healing, his brain waves synchronize with the patient's. They become virtually identical, Mr. Tark. His heart begins to beat to the same rhythm as the patient's; he breathes like the patient breathes. It's as if he fuses with the patient's energy field, what mystics call the etheric field, what New Agers call the aura. He and the patient essentially become *one*."

"Then why can't he heal everyone who comes to him?"

"I don't know. You look at me and what do you see, Mr. Tark?"

"A middle-aged guy playing with swizzle sticks."

Unward emitted a nervous *yuk-yuk* and pointed one of the swizzle sticks at Tark. "I need someone like you in my classes, Tark. You'd liven things up."

"Invite Alejandro."

His mirth vanished and he set the swizzle sticks down. "I did. He told me to check his schedule with Janis. She said forget it, he was booked solid."

"So I see a middle-aged guy playing with swizzle sticks. What would Alejandro see?"

Unward's eyes were glassy from the scotch. "Let's keep it simple. Let's say he sees a stomach ulcer. Most physicians treat an ulcer with diet or a drug that blocks vagus nerve activity. They treat the stomach. But not Alejandro. He treats the whole organism, Mr. Tark. He scans it for all the malfunctions that ultimately express themselves through the stomach. And in doing that he *accelerates* the healing process."

"Give me an example."

"Well, for a stomach ulcer he might prescribe an herb for nerves. He might prescribe something that would reduce acidity in the mouth and the esophagus after a meal. Or he might heal some imbalance in the blood. Like that."

Tark nodded.

"I've lost you?" Unward asked.

"No, I guess I'm just puzzled. If Alejandro can do what you say, if he can actually alter atoms, then it seems to me any researcher would leap at the chance to study him. To learn from him."

"You'd think so, but it comes down to money. Research money. The grants don't come as easily to scientists who investigate the weird and the strange. That's why most of the psychic research in this country has been privately funded and is usually conducted through universities. Okay, so it's not as tough as it was in the early days of testing at Duke University. But it's still not mainstream. I mean, think of it, Mr. Tark. Can you imagine a grant proposal to study Alejandro crossing the desk of some jerk of a bureaucrat in D.C.?"

He started to laugh, then laughed so hard tears streamed down his cheeks. Tark smiled; he'd obviously missed the punchline.

"I'm sorry. Forgive me." Unward swiped at his eyes with the back of one hand and patted the air with the other. His laughter subsided with sharp intakes of air, as though he were swallowing it. "The whole fucking thing just makes me a little crazy sometimes."

"What thing?"

"Thirty years ago a guy named Bell stumbled across something and scientists are still grappling with the fallout. Along comes Alejandro, the living proof in goddamn Technicolor, and suddenly everything gets twisted." Unward again twisted the ends of the swizzle sticks together, clumsy motions, as though his fingers were made of rubber.

"Twisted how?"

"Twisted," Unward said again, his voice soft, brittle with emotion. "You don't understand."

"Help me understand, Dr. Unward."

One of the swizzle sticks snapped. Unward tossed it on the table, wiped the back of his hand across his mouth, and looked at Tark, blinking rapidly as if to clear his vision. Although it wasn't warm, bright beads of sweat stood out on his forehead. His eyes were fixed on something over Tark's shoulder and Tark turned around to see what it was. More people, but otherwise the street looked no different.

"Is something wrong?" Tark asked.

He attempted a smile. A muscle ticked violently under his left eye. "Maybe we should get together again in a few days, Mr. Tark. I don't like talking out here. We're so . . . exposed, you know?"

Exposed: only a man with something to hide would think of it that way.

Unward signaled the waiter for the bill and, until it arrived, fussed with the remaining swizzle stick, now broken by the ravages of his constant fiddling. He went on, his voice quick, urgent, as though he were pressed for time.

"In one experiment I did with Alejandro, he was asked to influence, at a distance, a student who was in another room. He was supposed to influence certain areas of the student's brain, so we measured the blood flow in the student's head with a rheostat. It appeared to change only when Alejandro was trying to do whatever the hell it is he does. We had to end the experiment because the student developed a bad nosebleed and was so dizzy he could barely stand."

"Alejandro caused the student's nose to bleed? Is that what you're saying?"

Unward raised his small blue eyes; he looked utterly wasted.

"That's exactly what I'm saying. If we hadn't stopped the experiment, there's no telling what other tiny capillaries or veins might have burst."

"C'mon." Tark laughed. "You can't be serious."

But he was, of course he was. Men like Unward were burdened by their egocentrism. His cheeks reddened with agitation and spittle flew from his mouth as he said, "Take any technology and I'll show you its dark side. I'll show you the side that makes scientists wish they'd never meddled. Einstein's work ushered us out of an intellectual ice age but it also brought us the atomic bomb. Like that. The good and the bad."

"Did Alejandro know what had happened in the experiment?"

"Good God, no. He wouldn't have continued if he'd known."

"What about ethics?"

"Ethics?" His smile was sad, resigned. "Ethics don't have a hell of a lot to do with it."

"I didn't realize you had tested him, per se. When did this take place?"

"Three years . . ." He stopped, eyes frozen on the street, then looked at Tark again. "Call me in a few days, Mr. Tark. Next week sometime. Maybe I've got a copy of that tape, I'll go through my things and look for it. I'd better shove off." He dropped two tens on the table and vanished into the crowd before Tark had even gotten to his feet.

≈

They arrived late Wednesday afternoon, a pair of giants who lumbered into his space with questions and good intentions. The woman greeted him in a *gringo*'s Spanish and had a name that Alejandro mispronounced, Keewin. She was gracious enough not to correct him. The man had tragic eyes and spoke Spanish like a Peruvian.

They sat in the breakfast room over coffee and pastries Carmelita had made that morning and the man and the woman asked the same questions the other detectives had asked. About his work, about Janis, about the night of her murder. He told them the truth, that

Janis had refused to attend the wedding reception at the Breakers because they had argued about her drinking and she'd been furious with him. He had gone on alone and returned at midnight and found her.

On the couch. Dead. Her skin like ice, already turning blue. He was surprised that he was able to talk about it so calmly. The black, bottomless grief that had crippled him in the first few weeks after her death had been replaced, he realized, by worry over his sister and daughter.

"How did the room look?" Quin asked. "Was anything out of place?"

"No."

Tark said, "According to forensics, she'd been shot through a pillow. Where was it when you found her?"

Alejandro thought for a moment. "On her stomach. I remember because it didn't have a pillowcase on it. That struck me. My wife was very tidy, Mr. Tark, very exacting. Even when she was drunk, things had to be just so. Pillows always had cases, beds were always made."

"Did you find the pillowcase?"

"No. And I don't have the pillow. The police took it."

"That pillowcase is missing," said Carmelita, coming out of the hall with a set of folded sheets in her arms.

"Are those the sheets?" Quin asked.

"*Sí, señora.*"

She showed them the fitted sheet, the top sheet, the lone pillowcase. Quin ran her hand over the fabric. "Silk," she remarked. "It's a beautiful pattern."

And it was, Alejandro thought, a royal-blue background with lustrous black and gold geometric shapes on it. His wife's impeccable taste permeated the rooms in which she had lived.

Carmelita returned the sheets to the laundry room and Quin said, "Mr. Domingo, I think you already know that my husband, Mike McCleary, was investigating your wife's murder for the sheriff's department. He was shot six days ago. There may be a connection between her death and the shooting, so I'd greatly appreciate anything you can tell us."

Alejandro felt a sudden hard pressure against the inside of his skull. "Despite Janis's efforts to gain official acceptance for my work, there was considerable animosity in the community. Perhaps this was someone's way of getting back at me."

"Does Eden White have anything against you?" she asked.

"She thinks I'm a fraud."

"Are you?" Tark asked bluntly.

Alejandro laughed. "I guess that depends on what your concept of a healer is, Mr. Tark."

Carmelita, who was now refilling their mugs with coffee, shot Tark a sharp, disdainful look. "You have obviously never been to a healer, Mr. Tark," she said in Spanish.

His eyes, hard and cynical, creased deeply at the corners when he smiled. "I don't even go to doctors if I can help it." He looked at Alejandro again. "So what is it you do exactly?"

An old anger stirred inside him. Tark, like so many others over the years, was challenging him to a demonstration. *Show me, prove it to me, convince me, and I'll be your ally.* "I'm not a carnival performer, Mr. Tark."

"I'm not asking you to perform. I'm just trying to get some idea of how you work. In the Philippines, healers supposedly perform surgery with nothing more than their hands. In the Amazon, shamans use complex rituals and ancient knowledge of plants. Give me an analogy, Mr. Domingo."

"Arigo," said Carmelita, still hovering. "The analogy is Arigo."

"What's that?" Quin asked.

"Who," Tark replied. "José Arigo was a Brazilian healer."

"Then you know of him," Alejandro said.

"I lived in Iquitos, Peru, for a long time and traveled quite a bit in Brazil. Arigo is something of a legend there."

"Like Edgar Cayce is here."

"I guess. So let's see. Cayce slept when he diagnosed and Arigo claimed that a dead German physician whispered in his ear. How is it for you, Mr. Domingo?"

Tark was still goading him, but Alejandro ignored it. "When I touch someone, my hands seem to become separate from me. They feel detached. They tingle. Sometimes the tingling sensation runs from the tips of my fingers to my shoulders. When I diagnose, I rarely remember what I say. If necessary, the diagnosis is in medical terms. When I'm healing, my palms become very hot. I feel like I'm plugged into the sun. Or into some vast energy source . . ."

"God?" Tark interrupted.

Alejandro shrugged. "Cayce called it God, Katherine Kulman called it the Holy Spirit, Arigo said it was Dr. Fritz. I haven't found any easy answers."

"Can you heal yourself?" Quin asked.

"No, in this way I am also like Arigo. I can't heal myself or any members of my family."

"How did you heal your wife's cancer?" Tark asked quickly.

This man, Alejandro thought, would test him every inch of the way. "She wasn't a blood relative and we weren't married at the time. Maybe the flaw is in me, I don't know. I can't heal everyone who comes to me."

"Why not?" Tark prodded.

"I don't know, but that's how it is. Sometimes I believe the soul has its own agenda, Mr. Tark, and uses an illness to push an individual in a new direction. Other times I think the soul is nothing but a myth and my ability is a whimsy that will vanish tomorrow. Believe me, my life was much simpler as a fisherman."

"Noel Unward believes that when you heal, you're actually altering atoms," Tark said.

Noel and his double-talk, Alejandro thought. "Until I came to this country I'd never even heard of an atom. Then one day Noel sat me down and explained what an atom is. He gave me books to read. He drew diagrams, pictures, showed me slides. So now I know what an atom is. But I still can't touch, see, taste, feel, or hear it. I still can't tell you what, if anything, it has to do with my ability to heal."

Tark persisted. "You must have some idea what's going on."

"Can you tell me precisely what happens when you breathe? When you walk? When your stomach digests food?"

Tark thought about it, then shook his head.

"That's how it is for me when I touch a patient. Something happens, I don't think about how it happens. Perhaps all I do is trigger the person's own immune system. It might be as simple as that."

"But there would still be a question about *how* you do that."

"Oh, c'mon, John," Quin said. "Let it go. He's told you what he knows."

Alejandro held up his hands. "No, it's all right. You're asking the same questions I've asked myself hundreds of times. The only thing I know for certain about healing is that it seems to work best when the patient has gone through a profound shift in awareness. I might be able to trigger a patient's immune system so it can fight off a disease like cancer. But unless the individual makes a leap in consciousness and learns to motivate his or her own healing, the cancer will return."

"Did your wife's cancer ever recur?" asked Quin.

"No. I think when she rejected traditional therapy and flew to Chile, this shift in consciousness had already happened for her and it was just a matter of time before her body reflected that fact. All I did was bolster her immune system."

Alejandro glanced at Tark, expecting him to ask another question, but he didn't and Quin apparently wasn't going to give him the opportunity. She said, "I understand Lydia Holden was one of your patients."

"Yes."

"What were you treating her for?"

He hesitated, then realized that if he didn't tell her, she would just ask Lydia. So he explained. "Fibroid tumors, PMS, scar tissue from an ectopic pregnancy. The thing she wants most is to conceive, but I couldn't help her in that way."

"Why hasn't she come to your defense?"

He shrugged. "Why should she? She paid for my services. She owes me nothing beyond that."

"Paid?" Tark said. "I thought people could make donations if they wanted to but weren't obligated to pay."

Alejandro's irritation was apparent in his voice when he spoke, but he didn't care. He was beginning to dislike this man. "It's a tax formality, Mr. Tark. The people who were able to *donate* did so.

Those who couldn't afford to didn't. And that seems to have gotten me in trouble with the IRS."

Quin gave Tark a dirty look, then asked, "Would any of your patients kill your wife to get back at you?"

"Possibly."

"I doubt it," Carmelita said. "His patients are grateful, not hostile."

"Do you know of anyone who hated her enough to kill her?" Quin asked.

"Not offhand."

"Had she been married before? Is there an ex-husband drifting around?"

"No."

"What about former lovers?" Tark again.

"I don't know."

"Was your wife having an affair with anyone, Mr. Domingo?"

This elicited a sharp retort from Carmelita. "What kind of question is that, *señor?*"

"An honest one."

Alejandro felt a tightening in his chest; he had wondered the same thing himself. "I don't think so. But it's possible, I guess. Right now almost anything seems possible."

"When did Noel Unward test you?" Tark asked.

"Shortly after I came to this country. He was Dr. White's assistant."

Tark looked puzzled. "I didn't realize he worked for White. Or that they knew each other."

"Eden was the first person in this country to test me. Noel was her assistant at the time and has since gone on to his own research and teaching."

"How many times did my husband talk to you?" Quin asked.

"Several."

"Did he talk to your daughter as well?"

"Yes. Twice, I think."

He turned the conversation away from himself by asking her about McCleary, where he was shot, the extent of his injuries, the prognosis. Outside, a mockingbird sang as though its heart were breaking. A pleasant breeze drifted through the open windows. He suddenly wanted nothing more than to sit out on the porch and shut his eyes.

Carmelita sensed it and so did the man and the woman. When they rose to leave a short time later, Tark said they would be in touch. Alejandro didn't doubt it. He sent his best wishes to McCleary for a speedy recovery and, as he watched them walk outside, prayed for a release from his prison of lies.

9

"You're a cynic, Tark."

"Just because I asked him if he's a fraud?"

"For starters, yeah."

"We have a right to know what we're dealing with."

"So ask his former patients."

They were speeding south on I-95, through the evening rush-hour traffic. She was surrounded by cars with out-of-state license plates that were driven by people accustomed to the madness of Manhattan streets or the wide-open spaces of the Midwest. The New Yorkers cut and honked, the Midwesterners daydreamed, and the locals were their usual schizophrenic selves. At least it wasn't raining, Quin was grateful for that. Rain usually sent South Florida drivers into paroxysms of frenzy.

"When I was living in Iquitos," Tark said, "a good friend of mine contracted malaria, went to the local medicine man instead of a doctor, and died. I guess that tainted my opinion of healers."

Quin suspected the friend had been female. Tark didn't seem to have many male friends other than McCleary and R. D. Aikens, the chess whiz they'd met in Miami Beach last summer. She wasn't even sure R. D. counted; he was only sixteen. Although Tark got along with Eastman and the other male investigators in their office, it wasn't the same thing as friendship. But considering the business he had been in, it didn't surprise her. Hit men couldn't afford to have friends.

"Just because one medicine man screws up, you condemn all of them."

She glanced at him, but he was already looking at her, looking in a way that made her distinctly uncomfortable. "Whenever you're pissed, you call me Tark instead of John. Did you realize that?"

"Stop changing the subject. You heard what Fitz said. We don't judge the guy. That's not the point."

"It may be the whole point, Quin. Let's say he *is* for real. Let's say someone like good ol' Dr. White with her inconclusive report has some slick scheme for turning the talent into a viable commodity. But Alejandro refuses. So White or whoever puts the squeeze on him. His wife gets killed. The man investigating the wife's murder gets shot."

"What kind of commodity?"

"That's part of what we need to find out."

"Talk to Zelda again." The honey from Link.

"Waste of time. We've still got some leads to check out."

"I've got a lunch date with Lydia tomorrow. You heard from Barker?"

"Not yet. I'll give him another day before I turn Fitz on him."

And then what? More waiting? More maybes? More ifs and buts? She'd grown to detest those words; they implied a precarious balance, something tottering at the edge of a yawning abyss.

Tark had turned his face toward the window, his attention elsewhere now. She sensed the wheels spinning in his head, charging toward some vague abstraction of a plan that would coalesce, assume shape, and be rearranged a dozen times before he ever uttered a single word of it to her. Assuming, of course, that he planned to share the plan at all.

"Would you do me a favor? If you're cooking up something, let me in on it. If Mac had told me to begin with that he was working with Eastman, this whole thing would be a hell of a lot easier."

He nodded, but there was nothing convincing about it.

The road opened up two miles later, revealing an ambulance, a fire truck, and pavement strewn with glass and chrome. The remains of the cars involved in the accident were blocking one lane. A person was being lifted into the ambulance on a stretcher. Two women were sitting on the shoulder of the road, comforting each other.

A brief lapse in attention, she thought, a moment when your mind is elsewhere, and suddenly your life slides into blackness. She knew the feeling, all right. She and Tark drove on without speaking.

≈

The old joke about Lake Worth was that it was inhabited by the living dead, the retirees who had come here to die then hung on with surprising tenacity. Tark's grandmother had lived here for the last fifteen years of her life, hunched and fragile in her aging bones.

Ida had occupied two rooms in the Lake Worth Hotel, a town landmark on the corner of the main street. At one A.M. the place looked haunted, washed in the glow of sodium vapor lights. But in those days it had been the center of the world for Ida and her clutch of eccentric buddies, most of them widows like herself.

Her closest friend had been Sheila Graham, gossip columnist and mistress of F. Scott Fitzgerald. She'd lived a mile away, in a small condo on the beach, and every Saturday, she, Ida, and some of their cronies had gotten together at a nearby park. Tark had met Sheila the summer he was sixteen, when his parents, foreign diplomats, had returned to the States specifically to convince Ida that she should live with them. For a summer of Saturdays he'd joined them in the park, listening to their stories, enthralled by Sheila's tales of Fitzgerald's final days.

Before the family had left—minus Ida, of course—Sheila had given him an autographed first edition of *Beloved Infidel*, her account of her tumultuous affair with Fitzgerald. He still had the book. Its well-thumbed pages were now yellowing with age, the inscription almost too faded to read. *For John, who listened with such innocent rapture.*

She passed away in the late eighties, nearly a decade after Ida's death. Tark had been living in Iquitos then, an emotional cripple twisted with grief over the deaths of his wife and daughter, a man who hired himself out to the highest bidder. He'd read her obit in the international edition of the *Miami Herald* and wondered how that innocent sixteen-year-old kid he had been had grown up to be such a monster.

Now he cruised the shadowed streets of that faded summer, a man in his early forties who wondered if he would ever be entirely free of his violent past. He passed the park, where the ghosts of Ida and Sheila still walked, and felt an enormous regret for many of the choices he had made, for the lives he had changed, the lives he had ended.

He crossed the bridge over the intracoastal canal and turned off two blocks later. This neighborhood was as old as the town. Small concrete-block homes with carports and jalousie windows slumbered beneath banyan trees that resembled tremendous umbrellas. Spanish moss hung from the branches, swaying in the chilly breeze like dark ectoplasmic ribbons. Yards lay neglected, overrun with weeds and junk. Chain-link fences marked off property boundaries. No home-owners' covenants governed what was permitted, the residents weren't that fussy. Live and let live was the only rule. Which was, of course, why Estelle had settled here.

The house was set back from the road, partially shrouded by trees and dense foliage that kept it cool during the summer and damp in the winter. Her rusted VW Bug was in the carport and the porch light was on, which meant that she was alone and it was okay for him to use his key.

He parked behind the Bug, then walked through the overgrown yard to the back of the house, where the wind bit through his nylon windbreaker. It was at least twenty degrees too cold for him, in the low fifties, and he quickly unlocked the utility-room door and stepped inside.

Laundry was piled on top of the washer and clean clothes were folded neatly in a basket. Curled on top of the clothes was Elvis, the raccoon that had belonged to William Boone, the old man who'd been involved in the case that was responsible for Tark's new life. His reformed life. Elvis lifted his head and yawned as Tark squatted by the basket.

"Too cold out there for you, too, huh, guy." Tark scratched Elvis behind the ears and the coon nuzzled his jacket pocket for a goodie. "Hold on, I didn't forget you." He pulled out a Baggie that contained one of Elvis's favorite treats, a piece of rye bread smeared with crunchy peanut butter. Elvis took it between his front paws and nibbled at it with complete delicacy.

"You spoil him, Gabby," said Estelle, leaning against the door-jamb, arms folded at her waist. She wore a long terry-cloth robe the same deep red as her fluffy slippers and was sipping at a mug of something hot. "The vet said peanut butter could give him a urinary infection."

Tark laughed. "C'mon, raccoons eat garbage. How's peanut butter going to hurt him? I'd change vets if I were you. Where's Fox, anyway?"

Fox was the tabby cat that had also belonged to Boone. "Probably sleeping where it's warm. How about a mug of tonight's special toddy?"

"Depends on what's in it."

"Picky, picky." They moved into the kitchen, where she filled a mug from the kettle on the stove and handed it to him. "I guarantee you'll like it."

Hot plum wine. "This stuff's great. You make it?"

"Yeah, sure, Gabby. I've got a distillery in the back room. A guy at work owed me some money and paid me with the wine. C'mon, let's sit in the living room."

The TV was turned on low and a space heater had toasted the air to just the right temperature. The coffee table was cluttered with the usual travel books and maps, which she studied for months in preparation for one of her many trips.

She paid for her wanderlust from her substantial stash, money she had ripped off when she was the middle person in a drug deal in Broward County five years ago. She had taken off for the Keys, the dealer had turned state's evidence, the buyer was doing ten to fifteen, and Estelle no longer arranged drug deals.

They had met when they were each approaching the end of something—her stint in the Keys, his life as Fernando Gabriel. Her contagious immediacy was exactly what he had needed then and now, a reminder that his point of power lay in the present, not in a past that had trapped him for a decade.

The irony was that as he released the past, the very instinct that had enabled him to track, to find virtually anyone or anything, seemed to have shriveled up and died.

"So how is it going back on nights?" he asked, settling beside her on the couch.

"Fair to middling. About a hundred bucks a night in tips. More if I work double shifts. How's Mac doing?"

"I haven't seen him yet. He just got out of intensive care." He gestured toward the travel books. "Have you decided where you're going?"

"Lots of places look good. I'm sort of leaning toward the Galápagos, but that could change tomorrow." She hooked strands of her short dark hair behind her ears. "You been there?"

"I always meant to but never made it."

"I think Darwin was full of shit, but those tortoises fascinate me."

"You think any authority figure is full of shit."

She grinned. "I guess I do at that."

As she tucked her feet under her, the folds of her robe slipped open, exposing a thigh, the curve of a breast, skin the same smooth brown all over. The robe was her concession to the chill; usually she lounged around the house in the nude. She also sunbathed in the nude, slept in the nude, and probably would have gone to work in the nude if there hadn't been laws against it. Under the robe she wore nothing; it aroused him, it always did, and she knew it.

He leaned toward her, his hands slipping inside the robe, against all that softness. Her small, coy smile swung in place, and she locked her arms around his neck. "Admit it, Gabby, you missed me."

"I never said I didn't." Her mouth tasted like the toddy; the skin at her throat smelled faintly of Ivory soap; her nipple was a rough, hot pebble against his tongue. "You're the one who moved out."

"Your place is too small for you, me, Elvis, and Fox." She sank back against the cushions, fingers working at his fly, the buttons on his shirt. "You were always stepping in the litterbox."

"You were always moving it."

"I was trying to find a spot where it'd be out of the way."

"Domestic details tripped us up." He shucked his clothes and she pulled an afghan over them. "Is that it?"

He nuzzled the space between her breasts and she didn't reply. Her fingers slipped through his hair. She nibbled at his ear like a small, hungry fish. She held his head against her cool skin. He listened to the quickening beat of her heart.

In the years since his wife's death, there had been three women in his life, a Peruvian, a German, and Estelle, who was half American and half Greek. Of the three, she was the most like Tark himself, a nomad, a malcontent, a restless soul in search of something.

They had come together because of their respective pasts, but he didn't know if that was enough to forge a common future. In fact, they rarely mentioned the future. She wasn't interested in the future, except where traveling was concerned. She had led him to believe there were other men in her life, other lovers, and whether it was true or not was beside the point. The mere implication had set the tone of their relationship, made it clear from the beginning that she expected nothing of him, nothing but this languid, timeless present where his hands roamed.

There: the flare of a hip, the softer skin on the inside of her thighs, the incredible warmth between them. The afghan slipped to the floor as his mouth followed his hands, down across a belly as flat as an envelope, lingering at her navel, which dipped, a tiny, round crater. Tark slid his hands under her and her hips lifted as if on a cushion of air. A dry, hot pulse drummed behind his eyes as he touched his tongue to her. And for long moments she was Quin. It was Quin against his mouth, Quin who drew him into the heat of some other sun, Quin who shuddered when she came.

"Gabby, you awake?"

"What I am is freezing." They were in her bedroom, where the windows were all open and the air was so cold he could see his breath. Even the animals had burrowed under the covers at the foot of the bed. "You mind if I shut the windows?"

"I guess I can stand it. This is a down comforter, you know. There's nothing warmer."

"Tell it to Elvis and Fox." He shut the windows and leaped back into bed.

"Happy now?"

"Better."

"Good. Now I've got a bedtime story for you." She fluffed her pillow up against the headboard and reached for what was left of the wine. She took a swig, passed him the bottle. The stuff was now as cold as the air in the room, but that didn't diminish the taste. "The word I hear is that McCleary's routine was pegged down before he was shot."

"Who'd you hear this from?"

"A slime who slobbers when he drinks too much."

"Does he actually know anything?"

She picked up a pack of cigarettes from the nightstand, lit one, opened a drawer, and brought out the half shell that doubled as an ashtray. "He has in the past. That doesn't mean he does now, though. Like I said, he drinks too much. It's worn his brain smooth."

"Who is he?"

"Harry Rimalto. He tends bar at the Breakers. Hears a lot of stuff. Half of what he says is probably bullshit. But the other half . . . well, who knows. I think it's worth looking into. He won't know it came from me. He was pretty drunk when he was at the Pelican the other night."

He watched the glow of her cigarette in the dark. "So who is supposed to have nailed down Mike's routine?"

"He didn't say. But I could tell he's nervous about it now that Mike's been shot. When I mentioned that, he just sort of shrugged like it was no big deal, said McCleary's an ex-cop with some enemies, let people draw their own conclusions. He didn't use those words exactly. Harry's IQ is a couple of points above Elvis's. No, I take that back. Elvis is smarter."

"How well do you know this guy?"

She laughed. "Even I have better taste than that, Gabby, if that's what you're asking."

"So he just drinks at the Pelican sometimes."

She hemmed, she hawed; Tark poked her in the ribs. "You screwed this guy."

"No way."

"Then what?"

"Hell, I guess it doesn't make any difference now. We did some business together a few years back, before I moved to the Keys. A couple of deals. Nothing major, just grass. I can't believe I did business with the asshole. Now we end up in the same goddamn town again. Karma, Gabby, never underestimate it."

"How'd he know Mike's an ex-cop?"

"I don't know, he probably heard it on the news. Maybe you should listen to the news once in a while."

"The news depresses me."

"You? Come on."

"Anything on the Holdens?"

"That's trickier. I know their housekeeper, Madge. She doesn't like him much, but she likes the job. Good money, good benefits, a good reference, she doesn't have to live in, all that. I gave her a call at home after I saw you and Quin on Monday. She stopped by the Pelican. Since you weren't specific about what you wanted to know, I had to play it close. How's it going, anything new, blah blah blah."

"And?"

"She says Lydia Holden's not too crazy about Barker running for the Senate. Seems she likes her life the way it is. A while back she was seeing this healer and Barker wasn't happy about it. He thought it would cost him votes. Anyway, they had a heated argument, and two or three weeks later the state attorney's office decided to poke around to see if the healer was practicing medicine without a license."

"And Lydia no longer consults the healer."

"You got it."

"Now the healer's wife is dead."

"That woman shot up in Jupiter?"

"Right."

"Krieger, the Palm Beach socialite, yeah, I remember now."

"Is Lydia helping with her husband's campaign?"

"Not really. She owns an import-export shop on Worth Avenue. That keeps her busy." She put out her cigarette and sipped again from the bottle of wine. "And in case you're interested, she eats lunch every day at Cheri's on the Avenue."

"What's she look like?"

"Like all these Palm Beach women. Pampered, spoiled, perfumed."

"C'mon, give me more than that."

"Short blond hair, not very tall, I don't know. I only saw her once when I picked Madge up at the house."

"Did you meet Holden, too?"

"Yeah, he was outside when I drove up. He seemed okay—real friendly, almost flirtatious, not stuffy like I'd expected." She stifled a yawn. "And that pretty much sums it up until the next installment, folks. Stay tuned."

They passed the bottle back and forth until the wine was gone, then she lit a joint and they smoked it. "So tell me about this healing, Gabby. This guy for real?"

"Some people seem to think he is."

"You don't?"

"I've yet to see him do anything." As he related the gist of his conversation with Noel Unward, his thoughts wandered through the labyrinthian riddles of the quantum world. It was all mind stuff, that was what Unward had said.

"Nosebleeds?" Estelle exclaimed. "He actually did that?"

"Apparently."

"I saw Sai Baba once, did I ever tell you that?"

The Hindu holy man. "How'd you get close enough to see him?"

"I waited in line for three days. I was maybe six feet away from him when a rose materialized in his hand. A rose, for Christ's sakes. And after the rose he materialized some sort of ash—"

"Holy ash."

"Whatever. But each time he shut his fist without having touched anything, then opened it and there the stuff was. So did he pull it out of his sleeve? Did it fall out of his mouth when I wasn't paying attention?" Her shoulder brushed his as she shrugged. "Beats me. All I know is that his hands were facing the crowd both times when it happened, and I felt, I don't know, like the skies were going to open up and God was going to speak or something."

"In Vegas I saw David Copperfield turn a business card into a rose. He did it for the woman who was sitting next to me. I smelled the rose. Touched it. Damn thing was real. So what's that make him?"

"C'mon, he's a magician, Sai Baba is a holy man."

"Maybe David Copperfield is a holy man masquerading as a magician and Sai Baba is a magician masquerading as a holy man." Stoned logic: they both laughed. "There's no market in India for magicians, but there is for holy men; here the reverse is true. That's the difference."

"So what're you saying?"

"Shit, I don't know."

"Yeah." She laughed. "That's what I thought. I'm going to make us some sandwiches. Be back in a jiffy."

Sandwiches, Christ. He might as well stay awake to watch the sun rise. Tark shut his eyes for a moment and bolted awake suddenly with sunlight on his face and the hands of the clock at seven. His heart was pounding. He'd been dreaming, the old dream about the explosion that had killed his wife and daughter.

He could still see it, the stained-glass window in his father-in-law's restaurant in Little Havana, the glass flying inward. But in the dream he never heard the explosion, just his wife's scream and then a deep, horrifying silence. His father-in-law, Alfie, had died six months ago in the same restaurant, in another explosion, one more death, the final death, the punctuation mark at the end of Fernando Gabriel's life.

For months after he'd met Estelle, he hadn't dreamed about the explosion until the version where Quin had been his wife, bleeding on the glass-strewn floor. Now the dream came every few weeks, a reminder, a warning that he wasn't as free of the past as he had hoped.

He slipped quietly out of bed so he wouldn't wake Estelle, who would probably sleep until noon, and went into the bathroom to shower. She poked her head in before he was finished. "Room for two?"

He tossed her the soap and she joined him. This time she wasn't Quin.

≈

Quin had arrived and left and so had McCleary's neurologist and his internist. And that was the point, wasn't it?

Everyone had split and he was still there, connected to an IV, trapped in a bed where he couldn't see the window, the sunlight, not even the goddamn sky. He was being held hostage in a body that couldn't piss on its own, that hurt when he moved, a body whose brain failed to translate his thoughts into their verbal equivalents. The short-circuit was in the Broca's area of the brain, his neurologist had said, as though any fool knew where that was.

He'd been moved out of ICU earlier in the week, moved with his clothes and a dozen plants and bouquets of flowers from well-wishers. Now he was in a private room on the seventh floor. The nurse had neglected to open the blinds and when McCleary had attempted to ask her to do so, nonsense had rushed out of his mouth.

He groped for the button to raise the head of his bed. As it came up, he heard voices outside his room and a moment later Eastman strode in. He was with a tall, husky man with curly gray hair, a gray mustache, strange silver eyes. McCleary recognized him from one of the photographs that had been in the shoebox.

"Mike, this is Jim Granger from the U.S. marshal's office," said Eastman. His voice was a shade too loud, as though he thought aphasia meant hard of hearing.

Granger, wearing a charcoal-colored suit and polished shoes that squeaked, brought two chairs over to the bed. He smiled at McCleary, who didn't smile back.

"As you know, the feds have had Alejandro under surveillance for the last several months. He'd like to ask you a few yes-or-no questions. Just nod or shake your head, okay?"

McCleary didn't give any indication that he'd understood what Eastman had said. "The cow jumped over the moon."

Granger frowned; it thrust a pair of identical creases down either side of his nose. "I thought you said he understands what's said to him."

"I'm just passing on what the neurologist told me."

Got that, Granger? "Radio springs eternal," McCleary said.

Granger looked irritated. "If you understand, Mr. McCleary, nod your head."

"Hawks pee, grass turns blue."

"Let's try something else." Granger leaned close to McCleary's face, close enough for him to smell the lemon candy on the man's breath. A thin cigar poked up from his jacket pocket. "When you understand, tap the railing on your bed."

"Blue corn for breakfast."

Granger sat back. "Must be too soon."

"It's only been a week since he was shot." Eastman rubbed his chin. "They've still got him on heavy painkillers."

Like I'm not here, McCleary thought. "Gulls shit on the table."

"I'll drop by in a couple of days." Granger pressed his knobby hands against his thighs and pushed himself to his feet.

"Call me first and I'll meet you here. No one gets in without approval." Eastman smiled as he said it, but the message was clear: the rule of entry included feds. Even though Granger didn't look too pleased about it, he was smart enough not to argue the point. "Sure thing. Talk to you soon, Fitz."

Granger left and Eastman spoke to the cops outside the room, then came back in and shut the door. "We've got to work out some way of communicating, Mike. If you understand what I'm saying, nod your head."

McCleary nodded once; Eastman laughed and slapped his thigh. "White boy, you are one sly fucker."

Ask me questions, Fitz. "Find the rocks."

"We'll find the rocks, all right." He sat down again. "Thumbs up for yes, thumbs down for no, right palm up if you don't know, left palm up if it's a maybe. Got it?"

His thumb shot up.

"I take it you don't like Granger."

Thumbs up.

"Good, we agree on that. I think Granger knows more than he's saying and I'll make it clear he doesn't get in here unless I'm present. That suit you?"

Thumbs up again.

"Okay, down to business."

McCleary shook his head. "Lizards eat ants." He wanted Eastman to ask him if he'd seen Granger before. But Eastman didn't understand.

"What?"

McCleary pointed at the door.

"Granger?"

He nodded.

"You've seen him before?"

Thumbs up.

"Where? No, never mind." He rubbed his jaw, thought a moment. "Look, let me just ask questions, then we'll come back to Granger. Okay, this Blue Pearl who sent you the note. You talked to this person?"

Thumbs up. McCleary held his fist to his ear, indicating they had spoken by phone.

"A man?"

Another thumbs up.

"Did you meet with him the night before you were shot?"

Thumbs down.

"Did you get something from him?"

Thumbs up.

"What?"

"Watch the thorns, walk the dog . . ."

"Yeah, sorry. This takes some getting used to."

You ought to try it where I am.

"We'll stick to yes-and-no questions."

Ask me about the key, Fitz, the goddamn key.

"Okay, this Blue Pearl fellow gave you something, not a note, but evidence of some kind that relates to Janis Krieger's murder."

Yes. He nodded.

"You stashed it somewhere. The key Quin found in your den fits the place you hid it."

Yes, yes, c'mon, McCleary thought, nodding.

"Does it have something to do with Alejandro Domingo?"

Thumbs up.

"Where is it? No, wrong question. Is it at the house?"

Thumbs down.

"At the office?"

Thumbs down. *Give me a phone book and I'll show you.* He touched the phone and was glancing around for a book when Eastman went on.

"You called someone? Is that what you're saying, Mike? Someone you called has the information?"

McCleary shook his head, held up his hands. *Wait.* He yanked open the drawer of the nightstand, found one of the paperbacks Quin had brought him, set it beside him on the mattress. Then he slapped his hand against it.

"Book," said Eastman.

Thumbs up. McCleary dropped his hand to the phone.

"Phone book."

Yes, yes. He nodded.

"The person is in the phone book!" Eastman exclaimed. "Is that it?"

No, that isn't it, McCleary thought, but it was close enough. Thumbs up.

Eastman searched the nightstand, didn't find a phone book, and told the cops outside the door to get one pronto. They did, but it was only the white pages. McCleary shook his head and looked around for something yellow. But there wasn't a spot of yellow in the room, of course not, this was a hospital, for Christ's sakes, not a day-care center.

"Okay, let's leave that alone for now." Eastman paced.

McCleary grabbed the pen from Eastman's shirt pocket, slapped the paperback book down on the table, and flipped it open. He tried to write *yellow.* He tried to write anything. But his hand began to tremble, then shake. He flung the pen; it struck the wall and rolled across the floor. Eastman stared at it. McCleary stared at it.

"Fuck it," Eastman said. "Let me find a dictionary." He hurried out into the hall and returned several minutes later with a pocket dictionary. "See how you do with this."

Key. McCleary flipped to the *K*s, saw the word on the page, but when he tried to point to it the same thing happened again. His hand shook violently.

"Forget it." Eastman took the dictionary from him, set it down. "We stick with hand signals. You have any idea about who shot you?"

The moment had passed. McCleary sank back against the pillows and held his thumb up.

"Did you see the car?"

He nodded.

"Can you describe it if I ask you the right questions?"

Given time, yes. But there were other, more important questions that Eastman should ask. Thumbs down.

"Quin thinks there were two people in the car."

Left palm up for maybe.

"Someone who knew your routine."

Definitely.

"Who'd had you under surveillance."

Probably. But they had no hand signal for that. He turned his left palm up again for maybe.

"Do you know what Alejandro's hiding?"

Thumbs down.

"Does this information Blue Pearl gave you connect Link Research to the case?"

Left palm up for maybe.

"Through Eden White?"

Who else? He nodded.

Eastman resumed his pacing, moving between the bed and the window. "You have a problem with Quin on this case?"

Look at me, Fitz. "Cats weep."

Eastman glanced up. "Oh, sorry."

He repeated the question and McCleary hesitated. He had plenty of problems with Quin investigating this case, not that it would make any difference. So he shook his head.

Eastman seemed to understand. "I couldn't keep her away from it, Mike. But you have my word that if there are any incidents, no matter how small, she'll be off the case."

Sure. McCleary laughed. "Birds in heaven."

"No shit, man. But I'll do my best to keep her off this thing if it gets ugly. Does anyone beside Quin and the neurologist know you can respond to yes-or-no questions?"

Visitors like Rita and Quin's sister might suspect, but only Quin and his doctors knew for sure. Thumbs down.

"Good. Let's keep it that way. I don't have any problem with Tark's knowing, but just the four of us. When you're released, I'd like to transfer you to a safe house in the Keys. You game?"

Let me think about it. Left palm up for maybe.

"Fair enough. Give it some thought. Okay, back to Granger. You've seen him before. Does that mean you've met him?"

McCleary shook his head.

"Had he followed you or something?"

Possible, but he didn't know for sure; he shrugged.

"Was something about him included in whatever Blue Pearl gave you?"

Thumbs up.

Eastman grinned. "It's a start. We'll talk again. You need anything?"

A weapon. "Good day for sun."

Eastman squeezed his arm. "Hang in there, buddy."

As though he had a choice.

10

~~~~~~

Quin spent most of Thursday morning searching the public records. They were housed in the courthouse downtown, in a tremendous room that was nonetheless cramped and claustrophobic and smelled of sweat and dirty feet.

The windows were sealed, the AC rarely worked well enough to provide comfort in either summer or winter, and the people who worked at the front desk redefined the Peter Principle. The lines that morning were long; the waiting was endless. Once she got a carrel, she laid claim to it with a briefcase that contained a notebook and a bag of munchies so that she could come and go without losing her spot.

Her search began with Eden White. Eight years ago she had gotten divorced from her husband of three years, under that great catchall "irreconcilable differences." Shortly afterward she had paid close to two hundred grand for her home in Jupiter. No children had been born to her in Palm Beach County. She had never sued anyone or been sued or been arrested or charged with any crime in the county.

Several months before the divorce, she had sold eight acres of land out near Lake Okeechobee for thirty grand and change. A pittance, even for the sticks, but the sale probably had been a way to keep the property out of the divorce settlement. The intriguing point was that Holden had bought it. Had he just happened to be in the market for eight acres? Or had he and Eden White known each other well enough to strike a deal?

Aside from the land he'd bought from White, Holden owned a dozen pieces of real estate in the county, most of it beachfront. His mansion, which he had inherited from his old man, cost him a pretty sum in taxes—roughly three hundred grand a year. The property he'd bought from White was zoned agricultural—sugarcane—so the taxes were a fraction of what he would have paid had he owned eight acres on the beach. Any beach between here and Dade.

He'd been born in Palm Beach and, in between exotic jaunts, had been raised there. But he apparently hadn't married Lydia or anyone else in this county. He had never been divorced, sued, charged with a crime, or arrested and no child had been born to him in this county.

Link R & D was owned by a private company called Cantrell, Inc., of Durham, North Carolina. The same outfit also owned Link's two other subsidiaries, one in Camden, South Carolina, the other in Virginia Beach. Five years ago a Christine Redman of Winston-Salem had sued Link for malfeasance. Since the charges had been dropped before the case ever made it to court, Quin couldn't uncover any details.

She didn't find much on Noel Unward. He and his wife had bought their home in Boca Raton six years ago for $95,900, about right for a college professor and researcher. No suits, no kids born there, no arrests, nothing unusual.

She was curious about the Holden mansion, who had built it and when, and a search of the real estate records turned up an interesting bit of information. Holden's grandfather had bought the property in 1918 for twenty-five grand, a fortune in those days. The seller had been Janis Krieger's grandfather.

The connections among Palm Beach's old-money families, Quin thought, was a kind of nepotism perpetuated down through the generations. She wondered if there were any other links between the two families and looked through the index for the local newspaper. Although nothing had been indexed before 1965, there were a number of references to both families and several that appeared on the same date. Society puff pieces, probably, but she decided to take a look.

She chose an article from a Sunday in June 1969. It was on microfilm and the machine, a temperamental antiquity, gave her fits. It creaked, it skipped frames, it chewed up one section of the film and snapped it in another place. She had to tape it back together, then thread it through the machine again. But it was worth it.

The article covered a graduation bash at the Breakers for Barker Holden, then twenty-two and Janis Krieger, seventeen. They were photographed together in the ballroom, a striking couple, self-assured and confident that the world would always be at their feet.

But the longer Quin looked at the image, the more apparent it became that the shutter had snapped at a transitional moment. Janis's eyes were just slipping away from Barker, their fingertips were almost touching. They looked as if they'd just gotten away with something.

Yeah, and so what?

They were a couple of Palm Beach brats tossed together because their families were friends. It didn't mean they were particularly fond of each other and it sure as hell didn't mean they'd been lovers. Even if they had been, the photo had been taken nearly twenty-five years ago.

Before she left the building, she bought a *Miami Herald* from the newsstand and a Cuban coffee and a roll from the espresso bar. Then she walked into the newer section of the courthouse to do what she rarely had a chance to do at home: catch up on the news.

This area was part of the city's refurbishment project, an attempt to lure more businesses into downtown West Palm. The center of it was a courtyard with tables and chairs, benches, a fountain, and lush tropical foliage. Covered by a tremendous glass dome, it was bathed in perpetual sunlight.

At a table near the fountain she scanned the front section. South

Florida news, it seemed, was rarely upbeat and had become even less so since Hurricane Alfred had slammed into the coast six months ago. A new tent city had been set up for hurricane victims whose homes still hadn't been rebuilt. The storm had cost insurance companies nearly three billion in claims and two major companies had announced that they would be pulling out of Florida altogether.

There were the usual pieces on crime, the drug busts, the shootings, and the newest Miami road game, which the media had labeled Crimes Against Tourists. In the most popular version a gang of thugs targeted a rental car on the interstate and rammed it from behind. When the driver pulled over, the thugs robbed the occupants and, in several instances, had also killed them.

Who needs it, Quin thought, and shut the paper. As she looked up, she spotted Rita striding toward her in a conservative navy-blue suit, briefcase in one hand, an espresso in the other. "We're really on the same wavelength this morning." She set her briefcase on the floor, claimed the other chair. "I was just going upstairs to call you. What're you doing here?"

"A little research."

"I stopped by to see Mac yesterday. I think he looks pretty good, all things considered."

"I guess so." Quin wasn't able to muster Rita's optimism. The reality was that McCleary still couldn't make himself understood. "At least he's out of ICU."

"Well, I've got a tidbit that should cheer you up. On Eden White. I don't know if it's significant, but she was something of a wunderkind in her day. She graduated from Harvard med school at twenty-four, joined the Peace Corps, and went to Thailand."

"Do you remember what year she graduated?"

"Late sixties, I think. Why?"

"Holden was at Harvard around the same time, in the business school."

"Along with six or eight thousand other hopefuls."

"Yeah, but he bought some property from Eden about eight years ago. I think they've known each other a long time."

"Maybe. Anyway, White apparently stuck around the Orient for a while after her stint with the Peace Corps ended. When she finally came back to the States, she landed a juicy research post at Walter Reed. She must've liked the work. Other than a sabbatical, she was there until Link nabbed her a decade or so ago."

"Now she's designing space toilets for NASA. Big deal."

"NASA's small potatoes, Quin. Link's biggest client is something called Blue Pearl. Ever heard of it?"

Only as a signature on the note that had been left on the windshield of McCleary's car. "No."

"Me, either."

"Where'd you get this information, Rita?"

"I called in a favor."

"From whom?"

"A woman who works at Link. Her brother got busted a year or so ago and I got him probation."

"What's her name?"

"Zelda."

The sweet young thing who had flirted with Tark. "Yeah, we met her. What's she say about Blue Pearl?"

"She doesn't have any idea who they are or what their business is with Link. She dug the name out of their computer's financial bowels."

"Have her dig a little deeper."

"She's afraid White might get wise and she doesn't want to lose her job. But I'll see what I can do."

"Thanks, I appreciate it." Quin told her about the connection between Janis's family and Holden's.

"Hey, this is Palm Beach, Quin. All these Republicans know each other. Their granddaddies probably all played polo together." Rita just shrugged; she had bigger things on her mind. "Listen, Sasha's going to be in town this weekend and I'd like the three of us to get together."

"Sure."

"Great. I'll give you a call when I know more about her schedule." She tapped her watch. "Right now, I've got to run. An honest-to-God date, can you believe it? And the best thing about this guy is that he's not an attorney." She was gone before Quin had the chance to ask if it was anyone she knew.

≈

The Breakers Hotel & Club loomed at the edge of the Atlantic, an extravagant monument to the good life, Palm Beach style. It sprawled across one hundred and forty acres of primo real estate, a pink palace with more than five hundred rooms, two eighteen-hole golf courses, an oceanfront pool, and half a mile of private beach. It also had more snobs per square inch, Tark thought, than Buckingham Palace.

They tootled to the front door in expensive cars, zipped across the golf courses in electric carts, drank champagne in eight-hundred-dollar-a-day suites, sunbathed in designer string bikinis. Even the employees had a touch of snobbery about them, a certain arrogance he found mildly irritating. Harry Rimalto was no exception.

He was the head honcho at the pool bar, a muscular man with thick black hair. The top three buttons of his short-sleeved shirt were unfastened, revealing a gold St. Christopher's medal tangled in the hairs on his chest.

He moved around the busy bar with the ease of a pro, wiping down the counter with one hand, fixing a margarita with the other. Harry seemed to know just about everyone but minded his p's and q's; he was friendly but not too familiar, didn't drink on the job, thanked customers for their substantial tips, and didn't stare at the women in the string bikinis.

He wasn't quite the slobbering slime Estelle had led Tark to believe he was. But then again he wasn't drunk and this wasn't the Hungry Pelican.

Tark ordered an espresso and just sat for a while, sipping it and observing Harry. When he'd decided how to handle him, he plucked one of the fancy cocktail napkins from a small straw basket and printed on it: *You've got 24 hours to make The Man a happy camper, Harry, so let's talk about it.* He folded it in half, slipped a box of Marlboros from his shirt pocket, and put it on top of the napkin.

When he saw Harry on his way over, Tark pressed down on the lid of the box, activating the tape recorder inside. It was one of the more useful gadgets he owned, identical in every way to a pack of

Marlboros. If you flipped open the lid, you saw cigarettes inside. But they were cut off just below the filters to accommodate the recorder.

"Would you like a refill on that espresso, sir?"

"Yeah, thanks. In a cup to go." He slipped the folded napkin out from under the Marlboros and slid it across the bar. "Guy left this for you."

"Thanks." Harry took it, whipped his damp cloth across the counter surface, then headed toward the espresso machine. He stopped midway there and glanced back at Tark, who simply shrugged.

Harry stuffed the napkin in his shirt pocket and waited on three customers before he drew the cup of espresso. It was filled to the brim when he set it down in front of Tark with exquisite care. "Who left that?"

"I did."

He swirled the damp cloth across the bar again and, without raising his eyes said, "You tell that motherfucker I did what he paid me to do."

"He thinks otherwise. He says you didn't finish the job."

Harry's eyes darted to Tark's face. In them he saw a fear peculiar to laboratory rats who have encountered an unexpected twist in the maze. "That's bullshit," he hissed.

"Hey, Harry. I'm just delivering a message, okay? You got twenty-four hours to repay the money." Tark slapped a five on the bar, pocketed the Marlboros, picked up his espresso, and walked off.

He took his time crossing the space between the pool bar and the hotel. Sure enough, Harry didn't disappoint him. He fell into step beside Tark, four inches shorter and at least thirty pounds of muscle heavier. "Okay, man, what the fuck he want?"

Tark heard sweat in Harry's voice. "His money."

"Money's spent."

"That's not my problem, Harry."

"Besides the money. What's he want besides the money?"

Tark laughed, stopped, and looked at Harry as he downed the last of the espresso. "C'mon, Harry. You got your chance and The Man says you blew it."

"Look, I already told you, I did exactly what he paid me to do.

'Get a handle on the dude's routine,' he says, so I did that. Did it on my days off, four days total, and then I gave him the information and he paid me. How he used it was up to him."

"Hey, Harry. I sympathize, I really do. Guys like you, hell, it's a waste, you got your whole life ahead of you. I don't want to bust your skull open, Harry, believe me. But I got my work and you got yours. You know how it is." Tark started walking again and Harry did, too.

"That cocksucker's pushing his luck."

"Probably." He'd bought the bullshit, actually believed Tark had been hired to waste him. But then why shouldn't he? Good ol' Harry Rimalto was a man with a tarnished conscience and Tark had been in the business of killing long enough to sound like the real thing. "But that's how the asshole is."

Harry laughed, a weird, nervous laugh, pathetic in its way. "Shit, you don't like Eddie either."

Eddie, a name. "You don't have to like the man who pays the bills, Harry."

They were inside the hotel now. Tark dropped the cup in an upright ashtray and moved down the hall toward the restroom signs.

"Look, man, I can give him back two-fifty of what he paid me. Tell him that. That'd make us even."

"Like I said, Harry, I'm just the message boy. But I'll pass on what you said." He pushed open the door of the men's room; Harry was right behind him. No one stood at the urinals; the stalls were empty.

"The fucker isn't—"

Tark spun and kneed Harry in the groin. His eyes bulged in his pleasant face, a broken sound fell from his mouth, and he sank to his knees, moaning. Tark grabbed his hair, jerked his head upright, jammed a .38 under his jaw. "Let's get it straight between us right from the start, Harry. I don't like you any better than I like Eddie. He never tells me what's going on, you know what I mean?"

"Yeah," he gasped. "S-sure, man, I know what you mean."

"So maybe we can work something out."

"N-no problem."

"You give me some information on Eddie that I can use and I'll forget about that bullet. Sound fair, Harry?"

"What do you want to know?"

"For starters, what he paid you."

"Six hundred for nailing down McCleary's routine. He ... he couldn't do it, he had some other shit to take care of."

"You wouldn't lie to me, would you, Harry?" Tark yanked hard on his hair.

"F-fuck, take it easy. I'm not lying, I swear."

"And all you had to do was watch McCleary?"

"Yeah, find out his routine, that's it."

"Harry, Harry." Tark jerked on his hair again. "You've got to do better than that if I'm going to forget the bullet with your name on it. Where's Eddie live? The bastard's never even invited me to lunch."

"On ... on a sailboat. He anchors in a cove on the intracoastal. In Lantana. Where the Old House Restaurant is, that place where you can feed the catfish. Know where I mean?"

Yeah, he knew.

"If he's on board the *Rusted Nail* you'll see his truck in the park."

"What kind of truck?"

"It says Brown Lawn Service on the side. Brown." He laughed, a choked sound. "His name's Moreno and the shit translates it, figures he'll get more Anglo customers that way."

Tark released his hair, slipped the .38 inside his shoulder holster, and zipped his windbreaker again. "I think you and I may have a deal, Harry. I'll be in touch."

He left Harry on his knees and hurried out, smiling to himself as he turned off the recorder.

≈

"The car is still back there," Carmelita said, eyeing the side mirror. "You see it? In the right lane?"

Alejandro glanced in the rearview mirror at a maroon Lexus four or five car-lengths behind them. He had noticed it when he and Carmelita had stopped to get gas shortly after leaving the ranch. It had remained some distance behind them, always too far back for Alejandro to see the driver or the license plate. *"Maricónes,"* he muttered. "What's the point? Where would I go?"

"To heal," Carmelita said. "They've forbidden you to work on people. They want it all stored up for their lab, Alejandro. Think about it. Just think about it."

"For all they know, I'm going to the grocery store." He exited the interstate and so did the Lexus. He turned into a convenience store parking lot and the other car did the same. He stopped and the Lexus stopped at a gas pump, but no one got out.

"They don't even give a shit if we know," he said.

"Maybe they want to race."

"Yeah, maybe they do."

They glanced at each other and laughed. As soon as they were on the interstate again, the Lexus several car-lengths back, he opened the Porsche up as wide as it would go. It shot forward, sixty grand worth of car that his wife had kept tuned and oiled and running like a top. The speedometer swung past seventy, eighty, ninety, and there wasn't so much as a shimmer in the steering wheel. He couldn't even hear the wind.

Trees lost their shapes and melted green across the windshield. Traffic blurred into a thin ribbon of gray. The road in front of him was wide open, the vast blueness of the sky beckoned; the speed seduced him. Carmelita emitted a soft, startled gasp and he slowed, checking the rearview mirror, then glanced at her. Her hands were covering her eyes.

"No sign of them," he said, and leaped across a lane of traffic to make the next exit. Her hands dropped away from her eyes. "You okay?"

She turned to him, her face flushed, and grinned. "Now," she said, "I think I am ready for Space Mountain."

He laughed and turned into the parking lot outside of the emergency room. As he nosed the Porsche into a space, Carmelita scooped a plastic bag off the floor in front of her and opened it. "Clerical collar," she said, handing it to him.

He snapped it on.

"Crucifix."

He slipped the chain over his head.

"Wire-frame glasses."

He slipped them on.

"Bible."

He set it on his lap, combed his fingers back through his hair, and said, "Well?"

She frowned, scrutinizing him, then straightened the collar and grinned. "Go hear confessions, Padre."

"Give me an hour."

She checked her watch as she got out and came around to the driver's side. "I'll go to the mall and be back by two." She slipped behind the wheel, put on her sunglasses, and drove off.

From a pay phone just outside the emergency room, he called the main number for the hospital.

"West Palm General. How may I direct your call?"

"Mike McCleary, please. He's a patient."

"Just a moment, sir." Then: "That's room seven-twelve. I'll connect you."

As soon as it started to ring, he hung up and went inside. The waiting room was crowded; a line of people waited at the front desk. The overworked volunteer didn't bother asking who he needed to see in the ER; she simply pressed a button that opened the electric doors and he hurried in.

He passed doctors, nurses, technicians, orderlies, patients. No one stopped him, no one questioned his right to be there. If you looked like you belonged, you were treated as though you did.

He pushed through the double doors that led to the hospital, quickly located the stairs, and climbed the seven flights to McCleary's floor. He emerged at the end of a hall, a safe distance from the nursing station. It was visiting hours and most of the rooms he passed had at least one other person in them besides the patient.

He quickly realized that 712 was on the opposite hall. Rather than cross in front of the nursing station, he turned down the next connecting corridor and stopped. Two men in suits were outside of McCleary's room. Cops, he thought. One of them was reading a book, the other was talking to an orderly and jotted something on a clipboard before he allowed the man to enter the room.

Alejandro ducked back into the corridor and wrote a note in Spanish on the inside of the Bible's front cover. *In case I can't get past the barricade, call me at home. We need to talk and I would like to keep it private.* He signed it *Ancud*, the name of his village, then walked down the hall to 712; the door was now shut.

"Can I help you with something, Father?" asked the cop who had stopped the orderly.

"This is a private room, I hope."

"Right."

"Good, good. I just have one left." He held out the Bible. "Our parish has donated Bibles for the rooms that were lacking them. It's used, but I hope the patient won't mind."

"No problem, Father. We'll see that he gets it."

"Thanks very much."

He headed for the elevator but the doors opened before he reached it and Detective Eastman stepped out. Alejandro did a quick about-face and left by the stairs. He was pretty sure Eastman hadn't seen him, but in the event that he hadn't arrived alone, Alejandro decided to cut back through the emergency room, which was at the far side of the building. It would be safer to exit there than through the main lobby.

As soon as he entered the ER, it was obvious that something had happened: a natural disaster, an explosion, a gang war. Gurneys lined the halls, all of them occupied by people who were bleeding, groaning, dying. The rule of triage no longer applied; everyone needed help fast. Doctors barked orders, the PA system crackled, the examining rooms were filled, and the spillover patients were being treated where they lay.

Their collective pain washed through him with paralyzing intensity. He struggled to breathe, to move, to shut himself off. But he couldn't; he was wide open, beyond resistance.

He had no sensation of movement but suddenly found himself inside an examining room, where a young black woman hovered, weeping, over a man on his side on a gurney. He was groaning, covered in blood, and she kept sobbing, "Don't move, Ricardo, you're not 'sposed to move, they don't know where the bullet is, sweet Jesus, what's taking them so long? I'm goin to find a nurse, a . . ." Then she saw Alejandro and rushed over to him, asking him to stay, please stay, while she went to find someone.

The room shrank to the size of a pea and inside it were the man and his agony, the only things that existed. Alejandro's hands were burning when he touched the man, spoke to him, calmed him, dulled his pain. Information raced through his fingertips about the gunshot wound to the man's left shoulder, about the bullet lodged a quarter of an inch from the cervical just below his hairline. Beyond that, he was aware of nothing until the young woman ran back into the room with a nurse and two orderlies.

The world swam into focus again. He was clutching a bloody bullet and his Swiss Army knife, which was open, the blade damp and red. He snapped it shut, shoved it into his pocket, and hastened out of the room and into the hall. There was so much commotion that no one paid any attention to him. No one saw him pause briefly at a cart outside one of the rooms and drop the bullet into a metal bowl.

This woman was a specialist, she was supposed to know about migraines. But all she did was ask me a bunch of questions.

"How did you feel before your last migraine came on?"

"Anxious."

"About what?"

I couldn't tell her the truth. "I don't know, just anxious."

"What had you eaten prior to the migraine?"

"I don't remember."

"Are you under any stress?"

C'mon. "Some, yes."

"Have you been treated for migraines before?"

Yes, I had. The migraines had started some years ago, when I began to think that every time I turned off an electric light my father would die. I then felt compelled to touch the light switch again and take back the thought. But I didn't want her to know that, I was afraid she would refer me to a shrink and I didn't need a shrink. I'd already been labeled, it was just medical jargon. I mean, if I say obsessive-compulsive neurosis, what does that really tell you about me? Not a damn thing. So I lied and told her I'd never been treated for migraines.

"Is your sex life adequate?" she asked.

I nearly choked on that one. My sex life? It'd been fantastic since I met Eddie. I really wanted to tell her about that, about Eddie, but of course I couldn't. That was the worst part, see, that I had no one I could talk to, not about him, not about Janis, not about the seemingly random patterns that kept invading my life, begging to be decoded. That's when I started making these tapes.

I needed to hear the sound of my own voice, needed to hear myself say these things out loud. I needed to climb out of my head, can you understand that? Believe me, I know why people go mad in solitary confinement. When I first saw Papillon, the worst part wasn't Steve McQueen eating roaches to survive; it was the way he crawled around that miserable cell for five years talking to himself.

These tapes are like that, me talking to myself. But when I play them back, I find an odd comfort in them, as though I am listening to some other woman tell this story. As though this woman and I are sitting over coffee somewhere, chatting like old friends, confiding in each other.

A tricky thing, trust, even between women.

I trusted Janis, but I hated her.

I never trusted Barker, but I loved him.

That's how it is between men and women, turned around, unbalanced, all mixed up.

The woman doctor, this specialist, prescribed a new medication for migraines. I got the prescription filled, but I never took the pills. I was sick of pills. And that night when I felt a migraine coming on, I didn't lie down. I didn't succumb to it. I got in my car and drove to the Parrot, this great little beach bar in Fort Lauderdale.

I drank beer until it drove the pain out of my head. I played pool.

I danced with this biker from Seattle who had tattoos all over his arms, not just the busty broads like Wonder Woman but weird images, cobras, snake charmers, the tusk of an elephant.

While we danced to some slow, mellow ballad, our bodies pressed together like strips of tape, I said, "I killed this woman."

And he didn't even draw back and look at me or anything. He just muttered, "Uh-huh," and ran his hand over my ass.

"Did you hear what I said?"

"Sure. You killed a woman." He looked at me then, his beard untrimmed, his eyes bloodshot, his breath ripe with the stink of smoke and booze. "So go on. I'm waiting for the rest of the story."

"I shot her."

"With what?"

"A .38."

"Where?"

"In the chest, point-blank."

He shook his head and pressed his cheek against mine. "A .357 in the face woulda been better."

He was perfectly serious, the sanctity of life didn't exist for him. And suddenly the pain slammed into my head again. I felt so sick I broke away from him and rushed to the restroom and threw up. Next thing I knew I was in bed. I didn't remember driving home. I didn't remember anything. There was just this big fat blank space in my head.

That was when I got out the tape recorder and started talking.

11

Quin stewed in a line of noon traffic that snaked behind her for probably two miles, waiting for the raised bridge. She could see the string of boats waiting to make a languid passage down the intracoastal, cabin cruisers and yachts, sloops and ketches and tall fishing vessels. The toys of Palm Beach's elite were headed seaward early for the weekend, to places like Bimini and the Caymans, Nassau and the Keys.

The bridges in this county had become a constant source of irritation to her. They were antiquated structures, metal jaws that took half a lifetime to clatter open for the ever-burgeoning number of pleasure vessels that plied the intracoastal waters. During the tourist season the bridges opened every half hour. Unless she timed her crossing just right she could expect to be delayed fifteen or twenty minutes. And that was only if the bridge didn't get stuck.

Please, don't get stuck. She had a lunch date with Lydia Holden at one, a date made through their respective secretaries late yesterday afternoon, and she wanted to stop by the office first.

Her head ached from hunger and she went through her purse for a snack, a stick of gum, anything. She finally resorted to a small box of Cheerios that she kept in the glove compartment for Michelle. She consumed them by the handfuls, dry Cheerios. They were the ultimate insult to an appetite that longed for fettuccine smothered in clam sauce, fresh whole-wheat bread with honey butter on it, a crisp salad with honey and mustard dressing. Plebeian taste, she thought, but better than Cheerios.

She emptied the box and, disgusted, tossed it to the floor. Did Holden Cereals have anything comparable to Cheerios, that great favorite of the toddler set? What about Crunchy Flakes, one of their best-sellers? Or Dino Delights? Or Mango Munchies? Too sweet, too salty, too exotic, no no no.

But with twenty-two varieties of hot and cold cereals, who cared?

She went through the glove compartment again, hoping she'd overlooked something. But the car was emptier than Mother Hubbard's cupboard.

This deprivation, as silly and small as it was, suddenly symbolized everything that had gone awry in her life in the eight days since McCleary had been shot. It was as if her physical hunger were merely a reflection of some deeper, emotional hunger. But a hunger for what? For the order of her life before the shooting? Who the hell was she kidding?

Her life hadn't been ordered since she'd stopped teaching fifteen years ago. Order had nothing to do with it. She hungered for release from her resentment and anger toward McCleary for having thrust her into this case, for not having confided in her, for getting shot. Even that.

She was fed up with the risks he took, his appetite for a specific kind of chaos. If he was looking for thrills, why didn't he scale cliffs? Climb mountains? Hunt for Bigfoot? At least then the risk would be only to himself, not to her and Michelle as well.

But more to the point, she was tired of the inequities in the marriage, of the spats and disagreements that arose in the course of a single day simply because they worked together. When something went wrong at the firm, it invariably carried over into their personal lives. The reverse was true as well. An argument at breakfast didn't end when they left the house; it shadowed them, it insinuated itself when they passed each other in the hall, it became a presence.

Then there was the rest of it, she thought, child care, household chores, the unequal division of labor, his affair with Callahan, their subsequent separation, issues she had never fully come to terms with. Maybe that was at the heart of the whole thing, that before the marriage or her life could move forward, she needed to resolve those issues.

Horns blared and her head snapped up. The bridge had descended, traffic was on the move again, cars were pulling out from behind her. She quickly cranked up the engine and joined the parade traversing the canal.

St. James & McCleary was ideally located just two blocks off Ocean Drive and four blocks north of Worth Avenue, the Rodeo Drive of Palm Beach. On one side was a jewelry store, on the other stood a bakery, and directly across the street was a small city park.

They had the bottom floor of a two-story building, about three thousand square feet of space that cost them a small fortune to lease. But their business had doubled in the nearly three years they'd been there, which had necessitated an expansion in their staff. There were now three other detectives besides themselves, two secretaries, and one part-timer, R. D. Aikens, the kid they had met last summer in Miami Beach.

Quin ducked into the bakery first for a cup of coffee and a pastry, then entered through the rear door of their building. The secretaries were alone, as they often were, and were eager to know how McCleary was. She said his condition was still guarded, which, considering the aphasia, wasn't exactly a lie, and left it at that. She beat a hasty retreat to her office and shut the door, grateful for the solitude.

She'd been into the office twice since the shooting, but you'd never know it by the stack of mail, phone messages, and files. Fortunately, the secretaries and Tark had handled the items that had required immediate attention. He had attached hastily scribbled notes to some of the files explaining what he had done. She hadn't seen him since they'd visited Alejandro's ranch earlier that week, and although they'd spoken once on the phone, she realized she'd missed him. Missed the personal contact, missed his presence.

A dangerous musing, that. Tark certainly qualified as one of the unresolved issues in her life.

Quin spent an hour on the phone with friends and professional acquaintances who had called about McCleary. It took her another hour to look through his active files for one on Janis Krieger. She couldn't find it, neither of the secretaries had it, and there was no entry for it on the computer. Either McCleary had never started a file or he had hidden it somewhere.

She exited the word-processing program and at the c prompt accessed GEnie, the electronic network to which he subscribed. He had no new letters waiting for him in E-mail, but she requested all the letters he'd sent and received in the last six weeks. She downloaded them and printed them out.

McCleary was active on the boards; even loners hungered occasionally for human contact. And in all fairness to the technological wonder of cyberspace, the boards were the ideal way for people of like mind to connect, to network. McCleary's contacts lived all over the country and most were in law enforcement or the gumshoe business, but they ran the gamut from writers to general weirdos with an ax to grind.

Half of McCleary's twenty-two letters were from a guy named Randy Tract, an ex-cop turned free-lance writer in Seattle, with whom McCleary had obviously been communicating for quite a while.

Tract, who had been shot ten years ago while answering a robbery call, was a fellow flatliner. His near-death experience, like McCleary's, had raised many questions for him and led him into researching and writing about different kinds of mind stuff, as he called it.

He evidently had numerous contacts in the field and this had prompted McCleary's inquiry about Alejandro Domingo. Their last exchanges, dated the week before McCleary was shot, were particularly interesting.

TO: M.McCleary2
FROM: R. Tract
SUB: Alejandro Domingo
     My sources at three research facilities have never heard of this guy. But I can tell you a thing or two about Eden White. She was very prominent in parapsychological research ten or twelve years ago. Her passion, if I'm remembering correctly, was healing. White tested a psychic now in your neck of the woods, Christine Redman.
     Five years ago a skeptics' group went after her just as she was garnering quite a reputation as a clairvoyant. They maligned her in print; she sued. The whole thing was tied up in the courts for nearly two years, and when she lost, she went bankrupt.
     Around this same time she also sued Link R & D for malfeasance but dropped the suit. She lives at 513 South Dixie, Apt. 6, in Boca Raton. She can probably tell you a thing or two about the spirit of scientific investigation. Keep me posted. Randy

TO: R. Tract
FROM: M.McCleary2
SUB: Christine Redman
     She's got a new name now, Randy. New name, new life, and she refused to talk to me about any of it. When I mentioned Eden White, she slammed the door in my face. Tell me more about White and where she tested Christine. Mike.

     Twice in two days she had run across Christine Redman's name; that definitely qualified as a lead.
     Tract's last response, the day before McCleary had been shot,

was that he would get back to him as soon as he had some answers. Quin accessed the E-mail again and sent Tract a note explaining who she was and what had happened to McCleary. She asked Tract to get in touch with her through her handle, Q. McCleary, which would appear on her computer at home.

Armed with a little more information than she'd had when she'd left the courthouse yesterday, she walked the four blocks to Chéri's, a French restaurant on Worth Avenue. The menu posted in the window confirmed what she'd already suspected, that the prices were out of her budget.

"Shrimp pasta for twenty-three fifty? Who're they kidding?"

Tark. His reflection now took shape in the window, a very tall man in khaki chinos and a blue shirt peering over her shoulder at the posted menu. Tark, who had approached on feet of silk. "Neat trick," she said to his reflection. "You'll have to teach me how to sneak up like that." She turned. "What're you doing here?"

"I hear Lydia Holden is a daily patron. I thought she might like some company."

"Then join us."

His brows lifted. "You didn't tell me she'd called back."

"Our respective secretaries set it up."

Inside, the maître d' showed them to a booth at the window. Tall fans of palms in huge clay pots provided privacy from the other diners, and since they were early, they had the booth to themselves.

"How're we going to spot her through all these palms?" Tark grumbled.

Quin, mimicking the maître d's accent, said, "I'm sure, dah-ling, that she'z told everyone she iz meeting someone."

"Look for a pretty blonde."

"You know what she looks like? I thought this was the woman who has an aversion to cameras."

"Where'd you read that?" he asked.

"Some slick Palm Beach rag. Who's your source?"

"Estelle."

"Estelle knows her?"

"She knows Holden's housekeeper, Madge."

Interesting. But before she could pursue the subject, Tark men-

tioned he'd visited McCleary, then she gave him an update on everything, including what her courthouse visit had yielded. She gave him
more than he needed and Tark listened as he always did, with a rapt,
disturbing attention, his hazel eyes fixed on her.

His eyes bothered her, they had since they'd met that night in the
courtyard in Miami Beach. It was as if his entire history resided in
those colorful swirls, in the blackness of his pupils, layers upon layers,
complex and inscrutable. If she could peel the layers away, it would
all be there: his childhood in Miami and abroad, his early marriage,
his years as owner of a flight chartering service, the deaths of his wife
and daughter, the blacker years in Iquitos. John Tark and Fernando
Gabriel, the light and the dark, the man, the enigma.

And I'm married, she thought. "What leads did you check out?"

"One that could yield some answers." He told her about Harry
Rimalto and a lawn man named Moreno. "Does your development
have a lawn service?"

"Just for the common areas. Otherwise the homeowners take care
of their own lawns. Most of the people on our block use a neighbor
who has a lawn service. I don't know about the rest of the development. Walden Lakes has got four hundred homes in it, John."

"You recall seeing a truck with Brown Lawn Service written on
the side?"

"No, but even if I had, I probably wouldn't remember."

A busboy came over with a basket of warm rolls and pats of
butter. Quin helped herself to a roll and passed the basket to Tark.
"At one time Mike had access to the computer at the sheriff's department. Do you know if he still does? I'd like to run these names."

"That was an arrangement he had with Fitz." One of many. "I
don't know if it's still in effect or not. Why don't you just let Fitz run
them?" Quin asked.

"I'd rather we keep things to ourselves until we know more."

"You must have something illegal in mind."

"Let's just say Fitz wouldn't go for it."

"Uh-huh. Definitely illegal."

He pretended not to hear that. "I drove down to Lantana yesterday, where Moreno lives. His sailboat's anchored in a cove about
three hundred yards offshore with half a dozen or so other boats. I'm

going to keep an eye on him for the next few days and try to get a handle on his schedule."

"You know what B and E carries in Florida, Tark?"

"I take it that means I get no help from you."

"You really think this Moreno fellow works for whoever is responsible for the shooting?"

"It sounded that way, but until I get on the boat and have a look around, I can't say for sure."

"Then count me in for whenever. You hear anything more from Noel Unward?"

"Nope, he hasn't returned any of my calls. But Holden's secretary finally called. I got my appointment. At the house. What's on your schedule for the rest of the day?"

"Another trip to the library, paperwork at the office." And then she would tend to her daughter, her husband, her animals, her life. If she was lucky, she would fall into bed by eleven and Michelle wouldn't wake up three hours later, wanting a banana or juice or company.

The maître d' materialized like a ghost, accompanied by a shapely woman in white designer jeans and a pink silk shirt with Indian symbols on it. White, in the middle of the winter. Never mind that it was a Florida winter. In Palm Beach white was forbidden before May.

The blouse looked as if it hailed from someplace like JC Penney or Macy's and the sandals had probably been woven by an Ecuadorian woman who had been paid fifty cents a shoe. JC Penney, for Christ's sakes, and her husband's net worth was several hundred million, not to mention what she pulled in from that fancy import shop of hers. And yet Lydia pulled it off with style.

Yes, she was pretty. But a lot of women in South Florida were pretty. The difference was that Lydia Holden knew she was a looker. She knew the effect her face had on people. She was used to the envy it no doubt engendered in women and the craving it triggered in men. And she played it to her best advantage: that soft voice, the directness of her gaze, a subtle coyness with Tark.

Tark, naturally, picked up on it and poured on the charm. He asked what she recommended on the menu and they chatted briefly in French, a language Quin hadn't known Tark spoke.

"You speak the language like a true Frenchman, Mr. Tark. Where did you learn it?"

"French Guiana."

"Fascinating. Did you live there?"

"For a few years when I was growing up."

"Were your parents missionaries?"

Missionaries. Now wasn't *that* a snob's question. Why not ask if they were peasants? But Tark just laughed. "They were diplomats."

Lydia's soft blue eyes lit up. "So were my folks. In Thailand. My dad worked for the U.S. embassy in Bangkok. I still think the best book and film about life in diplomatic circles is *The Comedians*."

They evidently shared a passion for the book and for its author. Lydia spoke quite eloquently about Graham Greene's accurate depiction of Haiti under Papa Doc and Tark talked about what Haiti was like now. They switched back and forth between English and French with equal ease, which only deepened Quin's irritation. She had never been to Haiti, had no desire to go there, she didn't speak French, and on top of it she was starved and their order hadn't been taken yet.

At the first lapse in conversation, she leaped in with a question. "Is Thailand where you met your husband?"

"Yes. We had mutual friends at the embassy." Then she turned her attention to Tark again. "Where else besides French Guiana was your father stationed?"

"Venezuela, Argentina, Brazil. Every two years for ten or eleven years we packed up and moved on. Are your parents still in Thailand?"

"No, shortly after Barker and I were married, my dad retired. He and Mom now live in the Canary Islands."

The waiter appeared with a bottle of red wine and a communal platter of escargot smothered in butter. "I hope you don't mind, but this is what I usually start off with every day," Lydia said.

Snails, Christ. Snails and anchovies were the only two foods Quin couldn't stand.

The waiter went through his routine with the wine, and Lydia tasted it and nodded, then the waiter poured a glass for each of them. Lydia ordered in French. The waiter replied in French and glanced at Quin. "Madame?"

A burger, make it rare. "I don't know yet. Go ahead and order, John."

Which he did, in French. The waiter nodded his approval of Tark's order, then said a few words in French and glanced at Quin again.

"Try the scampi," Lydia said. "It's divine."

"Fine, the scampi." At $23.50 a shot.

Quin settled into a moody silence, nibbling at a hot roll as Tark and Lydia jabbered away in French and devoured the snails. By the time their meals arrived, the two of them were on a first-name basis and laughing like old friends. They included Quin in their newfound familiarity simply because she was there, taking up space. She finally butted in with another question.

"How well did you know Janis?"

Her smile faded like a tan. "I already went over all this with your husband, Quin, and frankly, I find the subject enormously depressing. Janis was a good friend and I miss her terribly. But like I told your husband, I don't have a clue about who might have killed her or why."

"How did you meet her?" Tark asked.

"Through Barker. Their families went back a ways. She had a boutique in those days that was a few doors down from my store, so we used to have lunch together, shop, whatever, and got to be friends rather quickly. After her mother died, she had to sell the boutique to pay bills.

"Then she was diagnosed with the cancer and didn't want to go through chemo and the rest of it. She'd heard about a healer in Chile and decided she was going to get help from him. I lent her the money and she left. When she returned eighteen months or so later, she was married to Alejandro and her cancer was in remission."

"And that's when you became one of Alejandro's patients?" Quin asked.

"Yes, not too long after that."

"You obviously believed Janis had been cured."

"You bet I do. I saw the before and after MRIs. And Alex certainly helped me out with a few health problems. This business with the state attorney's investigation is a waste of time and tax money. He's helping people, that's the important thing."

"*Was* helping," Tark said.

"That's exactly my point, John. They drove him out of business."

"Why didn't you come to his defense?" Quin asked.

"It would have done him more harm than good. Besides, it's not the kind of publicity that would help Barker's campaign. Anything that smacks of faith healing or whatever is a political risk. Look at where Pat Robertson ended up."

"Alejandro isn't a faith healer," Tark said.

"That's true. He's never once said that his talent comes from God. He's never called himself a reverend. He doesn't have a church. But he does claim to heal people, John, and in the minds of the voting public, that can get mixed up very easily with the religious right. Barker's platform is that of a moderate conservative, not a fanatic. How'd you like the scampi, Quin?"

Always trying to distract, to change the subject. "It was good." Before Lydia could seize another tangent, Quin asked, "Do you know Eden White?"

"Sure. She and a number of other researchers have observed Alex. Janis wanted her seal of approval for Alex because she's well regarded in the research field. But she ended up blaming Eden for the negative press he got last fall and refused to let her near him after that."

As the table was cleared, Lydia recommended the chocolate mousse for dessert. Tark passed; Quin ordered just coffee and quickly returned to the topic. "Janis cut her off from her research, in other words."

"Yes, I guess you could say that."

Whether that was a sufficient motive for murder, Quin thought, depended on how significant the research had been to Eden White.

"Look," Lydia said, sliding her fingers back through her blond curls. "I'm sure you've heard that Janis could be a bitch on wheels. And I'm not going to tell you otherwise. If you did something that she construed as an attack on Alex, then she slammed the door in your face, it was that simple. She held grudges. She never forgot a slight. But I guess you could say that about all of us to one extent or another."

When Lydia's dessert arrived, she dipped her spoon ever so delicately into her chocolate mousse, little finger curled. Did they teach that in prep school? At Vassar? At the embassy in Thailand? Was it a sign that you were, as the Latins sometimes put it, from a good family?

Dessert seemed to signal the end of the business discussion for Lydia and she turned her attention back to Tark. Quin, unable to abide another round of their twittering, excused herself and went in search of the restroom.

When she returned to the table, Tark was alone, checking over the bill. "Where's your buddy?" Quin asked, slipping into Lydia's side of the booth.

He tilted his head toward a table of eight on the other side of the room. "Making the rounds." He pulled $85 from his wallet and set the money down with the bill. "She's invited us to stop by her shop when we leave."

"Lunch with the woman is enough for me. I'm going to see if I can run a few names on Mac's computer."

He looked amused. "That bad, huh?"

"C'mon." Quin made a face, then unzipped her purse and got out her wallet. She handed Tark a pair of twenties for her share, dropped the wallet back into her purse, and eyed Lydia's designer bag. It was a rich brown leather with a flap on the front that was unsnapped. Before she could change her mind, Quin pulled it over next to her and stuck her hand inside.

"Tell me when Lydia heads this way again, John."

"Are you doing what I think you are?"

"Never pass up an opportunity to go through a woman's purse." A McCleary axiom, one of many.

Out came Lydia's wallet, bulging with credit cards, a checkbook, photos. Quin immediately went to the checkbook. The balance was twelve grand and change—*for a goddamn checking account*—but she'd written only five checks in the last two months. Two were to Madge LePorin, Estelle's friend, the housekeeper, and the other three were for cash. Rather large sums of cash, too, three to five thousand a clip. Hell, this was probably her household account.

She was carrying about eight hundred in bills and had two dozen credit cards. There were half a dozen photos of her and Holden—at a party, on a yacht, getting into a private plane, in front of an Oriental temple, on a ski slope somewhere.

Quin dug around in a zippered compartment and found two business cards for local bookstores and two condoms. These weren't just run-of-the-mill Trojans, either. They were the kind that were sold out of machines in restrooms in bars, truck stops, greasy spoons.

Tark said, "Here she comes."

"Okay, okay." She slipped the wallet back inside the bag, pushed the purse over to where it had been, the flap still unsnapped, and folded her hands on the table.

"Well?" he asked.

"French ticklers."

"What?" He laughed.

"Two of them. For the quickies on the campaign trail, I guess."

They were still snickering when Lydia sat down again.

≈

Tonight Bob handed him a thermos of milk that he was supposed to drink on the way to the windowless room. Milk, the very thing they had told him not to drink the times before.

Jim was waiting in the backseat with a new tape from Miranda, shorter this time but chatty, as though she were on vacation and enjoying herself immensely. Alejandro wondered what lies they had told her and why there had never been a tape from his sister. He realized he didn't want to think about that too closely.

"Any questions, Alex?" Jim asked as he turned off the recorder.

"Next time I'd like to hear my sister's voice."

"I'll think about it." He gestured toward the thermos as the Lincoln started down the driveway. "Drink up."

"I'm not in the mood for milk," he said, and tipped the thermos to the side, pouring the stuff over the floor of the car. Then he dropped the thermos and sat back, waiting for Jim to react.

C'mon, give me an excuse to squeeze the inside of your head like a goddamn orange, Jim.

Jim picked up the thermos and set it in the front seat with Bob. He lit one of his thin, fetid cheroots and said, "All right, Alex. Next time there'll be a tape from your sister. Anything else bugging you?"

As though Jim were the therapist and he the patient. "Stop having me followed."

"I'm afraid I can't do that, Alex. And if you pull any more stunts like you did yesterday, that's it for the tapes." He slipped a kerchief out of his pocket. "Now put this on."

The beast reared up inside him and he felt an overpowering urge to turn it loose on this bastard, to let it squeeze the soft, pulsating mush of his brain until it burst. He would do to Jim what he had done to the glass at the airport, to the fire ants, to Eden, only he would do it worse.

And Miranda will die.

With that thought the beast shrank away and Alejandro took the kerchief and tied it over his eyes.

When they removed his blindfold a long time later, he was in a small, cool room dimly lit in blue. There was a bed, a nightstand, the usual machines to track his vital signs, his brain waves, the dampness of his skin.

"We're going to monitor your sleep, *amigo*," Bob said. "The machines will tell us when you're dreaming, and as soon as the REM cycle is over, we'll wake you up. Just say the first thing that pops into your head. Any questions?"

A million of them, but none that he would ask. He shook his head.

"Okay then. Use the restroom, brush your teeth, whatever. You'll find everything you need right in there." He pointed at the door on the far side of the room.

"And I suppose there're hidden cameras to record how long I piss."

"C'mon." Bob flashed one of his irritating grins; the blue light glinted off his glasses. "We're not that bad, Alex."

"Yeah, you're worse."

The bathroom was as cold and sterile as the bedroom. Although it appeared to be private, he knew that it wasn't. So he took his time to get even with them and realized it gave him enormous pleasure to keep them waiting. After a leisurely shower he slipped on the bathrobe that had been folded on a chair and walked out with his clothes draped over his arm.

Bob entered a moment later with a glass of milk. "One more for the road, *amigo*. Then we'll get down to business."

Alejandro drank it down, milk but with a chalky aftertaste. Probably drugged.

"Go ahead and stretch out." Bob pulled back the covers on the bed. "Get comfortable. I've got to hook you up to this hardware. Oh, you're supposed to wear the earphones, too, just like you've done before. Snooze music, *amigo*. But this time you go to sleep listening to it and you'll hear either me or Jim telling you to wake up at the end of the dream cycle."

"Fine."

He lay back on the bed while Bob started hooking him up. He wondered if this room was in the same house they had brought him to all the other times. The air here smelled the same as it did in the other place, sterile and cold. The floor was tiled, the walls were newly painted, there were no windows, just like before. The one-way glass was absent, but cameras were mounted in the corners farthest from the bed.

When Bob was finished, wires trailed from Alejandro's scalp, wrists, chest, and cuffs around his index fingers. "Comfortable, *amigo*?"

"Don't be ridiculous."

Bob poked at his glasses. "It's not as restrictive as it seems. You can squirm around all you want. Try the earphones. They feel okay?"

"Yeah."

Bob signaled the camera and moments later music flowed through the earphones, a strange, haunting melody, flutes and drums that seemed to echo through some vast canyon. It was interrupted by Jim's voice, asking how the volume was.

"All right." The music resumed.

Bob dimmed the lamp and left the room. For a while Alejandro remained on his back, his head elevated on several pillows. It seemed he could feel every place on his body where an electrode was stuck to his skin. The spots itched and burned and chafed when he moved. He finally turned on his side and began to feel the effect of whatever he had drunk.

Just before he slipped over the edge of sleep, he thought he heard something else inside the music, threaded through it. He strained to hear it again, but there was only the haunting melody of the flutes.

≈

In the control room they watched the computer screens where Alejandro's brain waves and vital signs were being tracked. "He's about to enter REM," Eden said, glancing at Holden.

He adjusted a knob that caused the camera in the bedroom to zoom in on the Chilean's face. "Is the subliminal still running, Jim?"

"Yeah," said Granger. "It's on a continuous loop. As soon as the dream ends, Bob will wake him up. We'll know then if it took."

"And what the hell are you going to do if it doesn't work?" Eden asked.

Holden disliked the tone of her voice. "Then we'll do it again tomorrow night."

"You can't keep pushing him, Barker."

"And why's that, Eden? Because he's going to come undone? Because he'll crack up? I don't think so. He's not the type."

"You don't have any idea what type he is," she spat, and pushed away from the computer. She picked up her bag and slung it over her shoulder. "I'm going home."

"Home?" Jim Granger exclaimed. "You can't leave in the middle of this."

"Watch me." She slammed the door on her way out.

Bob Clarion rolled his eyes. "She's been real touchy lately."

"She's a pain in the ass," Granger said. "Want me to go after her, Barker?"

"No, I will." He caught up with her outside, just as she was getting into her car, and grabbed hold of the door before she could shut it. "Hold on a second, Eden."

"Christ." She flicked her braid off her shoulder and sat back against the seat. "Look, I'm tired. You didn't bother asking my opinion before you and Jim put this whole thing into motion, so I really don't see any point in my being here."

"I need you inside."

"You don't get it, do you, Barker. You don't have the slightest idea what makes Alex tick. You can't kill his wife, snatch his sister and kid, strip him of everything that's familiar, and then force him to do tricks. It's going to backfire."

"I didn't kill Janis."

"Oh, right. Pardon me. Jim and Bob did it and you were just fucking her. Janis, me, Lydia—who else do you fuck, Barker?"

Holden grabbed her by the chin and felt an almost irresistible urge to snap her goddamn neck. "Let's get something straight, Eden. You've been compensated from day one for your involvement. Now if you'd like to call things even as of right now, that's fine with me. I'll save roughly four million a year."

She wrenched her head free, slammed the door, and sped away.

≈

"Rise and shine, *amigo*."

Bob's voice. Alejandro's eyes fluttered open, then shut again. He tugged the covers over his shoulders. Go away, he thought. Go away.

"What comes to mind, Alex?"

He'd been dreaming of the sea off the coast of Chiloé, of the old days when he had fished those cold Pacific waters. He could feel the weight of the net in his hands; the taste of salt coated his tongue. In the dream he had seen the *pincoya*, the mermaid, facing the sea, a sign that the day's catch would be a good one. The mermaid never lied.

"Alex?" Bob's voice persisted.

"Sea. Fishing," he replied sleepily.

"Anything else?"

"The *pincoya*."

"Very good, Alex. Go back to sleep."

12

~~~~~~

Freedom, McCleary thought, was no machines, no tubes, no catheters, no IVs. It was wearing your own pajamas, eating solid food, drinking *real* coffee instead of Nescafé. It was everything he had taken for granted until he'd been shot.

By early next week the stitches would be out, and by the end of next week he would be released. Those things were guaranteed. But no one was willing to venture a guess, much less guarantee, when he would be able to speak normally again. Not his neurologist, who was supposed to be the expert. Not the nurses, who would probably be delighted to see him depart with his police guards, and not his speech therapist, who sailed in as he finished his last spot of breakfast coffee.

Sally was early, just as she'd been for the last two mornings. She was in her late twenties, had short, curly red hair that bounced when she moved and a face as fresh and open as Huck Finn's. She was an unbridled optimist, one of those people who referred to a cloudy day as partly sunny and for whom a glass was half full, never half empty. She meant well but she got on his nerves.

"Morning, Mike. My God, it's gorgeous out there, a real Florida February day. Midsixties, supposed to climb up into the seventies by this afternoon. I don't miss Pennsylvania at all. Talked to my mom last night and she said they were expecting ten inches of snow. Ten inches, can you believe it? I'd die in ten inches of snow."

From the nightstand she picked up the tidy pile of magazines and books that Quin had brought him from home and put them on the chair. Then she set down a notebook computer, flipped open the lid, and booted up.

"This is a pretty nifty program one of my professors designed. Go ahead, sit down here." She patted the bed, shoved the nightstand over in front of him, and stood on the other side, her green eyes bright with enthusiasm. "Our first two days together gave me some idea about the extent of your aphasia. Now we're going to focus on therapy."

Then get on with it, he thought, and nodded to show he was listening.

"Did you know, Mike, that if you destroy eighty percent or more of the visual cortex in a rat's brain, it's still able to respond correctly to visual patterns? So where's the function actually *located*?" She leaned forward, smiling at her secret. "Everywhere, that's where. The parts contain the whole, Mike, like a hologram. That's the beauty of the brain. So we're going to remind your brain that its language function doesn't reside only in the part that's damaged."

She wasn't quite the flake he'd thought.

She sat beside him on the bed, played the keyboard. A row of simplistic pictures appeared on the left, numbered one through ten. To the right was a column of verbs, *A* through *J*. "You match the verbs to the picture by typing in the correct letter. See this first one? A girl batting a ball. Now you look down this column for the right verb. *B*. For *bat*. As you type, you say the word." She typed in *B*, said, "Bat. Like that. You try the next one."

A picture of a kid crying. He hit *C* for *cry*, said the word in his head, but when he spoke it out loud it came out wrong. "Farm."

"Next one," she replied, undaunted.

And so it went for the next two hours, different sets of pictures and words: nouns, verbs, adjectives. He missed all fifty.

After this there were columns of letters that he was supposed to match to words that began with those letters. A for ant, B for boy, and so on. He was to say the letter first, then the word, stuff a three-year-old could master. But when *A* rolled off his tongue it became *wick*. His *B* came out as *van*. This continued through the alphabet until he reached *N*.

"En," Sally said. "This one's fairly easy. Just take a deep breath and as you exhale the sound starts at the back of your tongue and ends with the tongue touching the roof of the mouth. Try it."

He held the sound in his mind as he took a breath, then exhaled. "Enyeh."

"Hey, that's close, Mike." She beamed. "Just get rid of the 'yeh' at the end. Try it again."

"Enyeh, enyeh, enyeh." *Hear it, Sally? Do you hear it? That's Ñ, the Spanish N, the N with the squiggle over it.* His brain thought in English but his tongue insisted on speaking Spanish. "Enyeh, enyeh."

"Good, that's good. But shorten it." She touched her thumb and index finger together. "En. Short and to the point."

She didn't get it. And when he tried to communicate his excitement, the nonsense streamed out again, larger and uglier than before, a mockery. She patted his arm.

"Look, you've done just fine. You start out making progress in baby steps, then you proceed to giant steps."

She might as well have been talking about the case, he thought.

"We've been at it two hours. Let's give it a rest until tomorrow. We'll keep this up every day until your release, then arrange a schedule for two or three days a week."

Not if he went to a safe house.

She exited the program, snapped down the lid on the laptop. "When you get a chance, watch TV with the sound on, okay? Saturate your brain with good ol' American drivel." She patted him on the arm again as though he were a cute pet and left.

Palace, say the Spanish word for palace. Palacio, *say it, say it.* "Weeds grow in the field." *Try it again.* "Dogs frolic."

Maybe the Ñ was a fluke.

He got up and went over to the window. The view wasn't great if you looked straight down, just the parking lot, the usual landscaping. But when he raised his eyes, the blue of the unobstructed sky made his heart ache. Nowhere else on earth did a winter sky look like this, the blue almost luminous. He wanted to feel the February air on his face. He wanted to hold his daughter, to fall asleep next to his wife, to roam through his house, to see his dog, his cats. Never had the prosaic seemed so ideal and so unattainable.

His neurologist referred to aphasia as an "idiosyncratic syndrome"; to McCleary that meant medical science didn't know a hell of a lot about it. In practical terms, though, it might explain why he could punch a key on a computer for a particular word but not point to it in a dictionary. Until something changed, he was incapable of making the connection between the key and a locker at the gym for Quin.

Every day when she stopped by the hospital she gave him the Report, as she called the update on the investigation, and asked him questions to which he could reply through hand signals, yes, no, maybe, I don't know.

It was excruciatingly slow, frustrating beyond belief, and he wondered what the hell he would do if he had to spend the rest of his life like this. He felt as if he'd fallen through the looking glass and come to in an upside-down world through which Alice's white rabbit hurried, muttering that he was late.

He watched cars entering and leaving the lot and spotted Quin's Explorer as it turned in. Behind her was Tark in his silver Grand Cherokee. They found parking spaces and met on the sidewalk. They started walking; she laughed at something he said. They looked remarkably compatible, which disturbed him. No, *disturbed* wasn't the right word. He was jealous, jealous that she and Tark were working the case together, that Tark could walk without stabs of pain, that he could drive, talk. And the emotion was raw, undiluted, powerful.

Forget the safe house. He needed to reclaim his life.

He had suspected for some time that Tark's attraction to Quin had begun with the case on Miami Beach, where she'd been posing as Liz Purcell, a divorcée. He sensed the chemistry was mutual, but neither of them had acknowledged it, much less acted on it. He wasn't sure how he would react if they did.

In a strictly pragmatic sense it might balance the books for his affair with Sylvia Callahan. Even though Quin claimed she understood why the affair had happened, he knew she'd never entirely forgiven him for the indiscretion. But balancing the books wasn't going to change what had happened with Callahan. And, bottom line, he didn't need the complication. McCleary liked Tark, respected him. He had brought in an impressive amount of business in the six months he'd worked for them. But the discomfort that would result in their professional situation would be nothing compared to the stress it would put on the marriage.

A scene from *The Big Chill* came to mind, when Glenn Close's husband and her best friend had bedded down with her full knowledge and blessing. So the friend could conceive. He would be hard-pressed to muster Close's generosity.

He was still standing at the window when the cops waved Quin and Tark into the room. She was wearing a black skirt flecked with turquoise and white, a turquoise blouse, black flats, and pale stockings that set off her slim, muscular legs. Her hair, with which she battled six months out of the year when the weather was humid, seemed uncommonly tame, falling nearly to her shoulders in waves.

As she hugged him hello, the fragrance of her perfume enveloped him, triggered a flurry of intimate memories that stirred his slumbering libido. He wanted to touch her, but Tark's presence inhibited and irritated him.

It was tough to remain irritated, though. Tark was genuinely delighted with McCleary's improvement and talked about the investigation as though he were actively involved in it. He didn't act like a man who hoped to seduce the wife of a friend. He didn't behave any differently, in fact, than usual. Neither did Quin.

She had brought him an early Valentine's Day gift, a coffee-table book on impressionism with a cat card that said "I Love You" inside. She kissed him when she gave it to him, kissed him in front of Tark, who made a crack about no smooching allowed.

Yeah, you wish, McCleary thought, irritated with him again.

They adjourned to chairs that Tark and Quin pulled into a tight circle. Tark began the Report, Quin finished it, and it was thorough. Some of it he'd already heard from Eastman, some of it was new.

Quin's attempt to talk to Christine Redman had failed, but she intended to try again today. Noel Unward hadn't returned any of Tark's calls; he was meeting with Barker Holden today. No more news from Rita. The make they had run on Moreno had turned up an arrest and conviction seventeen years ago for manslaughter. He had been clean ever since. Tark had his sailboat under surveillance.

In short, nine days after his shooting, they had hit an all-too-familiar plateau, the Between, that was what they'd called it when he'd been in homicide. It was the limbo where some investigations got stuck and died. But if he could communicate to Quin or Tark about the key, about what it fit, the material he'd stashed would boot the investigation right out of the Between and into the land of the living again.

"Bring the towel," he said, rapping his knuckles against the windowsill. "Fly the kite, get the bike, drive the car . . ." He stopped when he saw the glance Tark and Quin exchanged. "Fuck the duck," he snapped, and paced over to the closet where his clothes were hanging.

He found his key case, dropped it on the table, glanced at Quin, then at Tark. He was watching McCleary closely and was the first to move forward, to say something.

"Keys, your keys. You want to leave? Is that what you're saying?"

McCleary shook his head, then shut the door to the room so they wouldn't be overheard. He removed one of the keys from the case, put it on the table, pointed at Quin. In the den. He thought the words in Spanish, but they came out in English in the usual way. "Orchids walk."

"A key, a key," Tark repeated. "Okay, a house key?"

McCleary shook his head.

"The key I found in the den," Quin said, hurrying over. "That's what you're saying, right?"

He nodded, smiled. Yes, yes, keep going. Ask the right questions and you win the big stuffed dog.

Tark moved restlessly back and forth across the room. "Does it fit a mailbox?"

Thumbs down. McCleary looked at Quin and she said, "A safety deposit box? No, I asked you that before."

"A padlock?" Tark asked.

Close, close. But McCleary had no hand signal for that. "Free the frogs, fence the dogs." Christ, he had to do better than that. He walked over to the closet again, shut the door, banged his fists against it. He felt a sharp discomfort in his chest and stopped.

"A closet? The key fits a closet?" Quin asked.

Keep going, give me something else. He pulled the door open again, grabbed his jeans from the hanger, folded them, set them on the closet floor, shut the door. He drew his hand across his forehead as though he were wiping sweat from his brow. He rubbed his calves, kneading away imaginary knots in the muscles. They still looked perplexed.

Mike McCleary, mime. He went over to one of the straight-back chairs, straddled it, pumped his legs, and hoped he looked as if he were on a bicycle. He grew short of breath and had to stop.

"Your bike, right. And you keep your bike in the garage," Tark said, excited. "So the key fits something in the garage."

"Or maybe in the attic," Quin added. "The door to the attic is in the garage."

McCleary sank to the edge of the bed, shaking his head, sucking at the air, too winded to say anything. Even if he could speak, what difference would it make? *The cow jumps over the moon, the bear shits in his spoon.* Yes siree, and here he sat with a deflated lung and a brain that had turned to mush.

Tark said, "Let's leave it alone for a while." He pulled over a chair and Quin sat down on a corner of the bed. McCleary continued to wheeze. "Did you talk to Christine Redman at any length, Mike?" asked Tark.

Thumbs up.

Then Quin: "Did you get anything out of her?"

He supposed that depended on your definition of *anything.* Christine Redman had listened to what he said, listened without interrupting, and then had told him to get the fuck off her doorstep and not bother her again. But her singular terror would have been apparent to a blind man. He had no way of explaining this, so he simply turned his thumb down.

"Well, your GEnie pal from Seattle left me a note in E-mail. He said Eden White tested Christine Redman at Duke six years ago, when she was a visiting researcher. At the time she called Christine her most promising subject. But a year later when the skeptics massacred her, White sure didn't come out in her defense."

"I still think Moreno is our best bet," Tark said.

"Christine Redman may come through yet," Quin said.

Tark shrugged. "If she does, make sure you find out why Eden White concluded she was a phony."

"Bring it up with Lydia Holden when you see her today," Quin remarked with a smile.

"If I'm lucky she won't be there today," Tark replied.

It was an innocuous exchange, innocent, and yet to McCleary it hinted at a private joke, something between just the two of them, news passed back and forth over drinks or an intimate little dinner. McCleary suddenly wished they would both leave. He craved his solitude, such as it was.

Tark must have sensed it because he left a few minutes later. McCleary moved higher on the bed, which was raised to a sitting position, and shut his eyes. Yes, it was easier like this, his wife blocked out, Tark gone.

But on the inner screen of his eyes he could see them, Quin and Tark, alone somewhere, at the house, in a car, the place didn't matter as much as the fact that they were alone together. One reached for the other. They embraced, they kissed, they held each other. The image skipped ahead, to a couch, a bed, maybe even a floor. Again the place wasn't as important as what they were doing: Quin undressing Tark, Tark undressing Quin, the flash of skin, the breath of passion, all that chemistry.

The more he dwelled on it, the more specific the images became, a home movie unrolling in his head. Where would it happen? Tark's place? A motel?

Would it happen in *his* bed?

Would *his* daughter be home?

Jesus, he had to get out of here.

"Mac?" Her voice was soft, and when he opened his eyes, her face was very close to his. He touched the back of her head and drew her face toward him. His mouth brushed hers; she pulled back, ran her fingers through his beard, said that she loved and needed him, things he desperately wanted to hear.

But she didn't kiss him back. She picked up her briefcase, set it on the table, snapped it open. She brought out his .38 and set it on the bed. "I'll sleep better if you have this. I never thought I'd say it about a gun, but what the hell." McCleary slipped the gun under his pillow, with the box of shells she put beside it. Next she brought out a manila envelope that contained his sketchpad and a half-dozen number-two pencils, all newly sharpened. "I figured you might want this. Actually, it was Ellie's idea. When we were getting ready to go over to my sister's this morning, she came out of the den with the sketchpad."

He picked up one of the pencils, flipped open the sketchpad. Draw a treadmill, he thought. A locker. A key. But when he tried to sketch, it was obvious that his brain interpreted these objects as the equivalent of language. The key resembled a dachshund with serious proportion problems; the locker vaguely suggested a car. He tore the sheet off the pad, crumpled it, shook his head.

"Look, it's okay," she said. "We'll figure it out." Then: "I think you should go to the safe house when you're released, Mac."

Leave it to his wife to worry about the future before it had arrived. He was at least a week to ten days away from release. Plenty of time to make a decision about a safe house. He shook his head. She moved away from him and stopped at the foot of the bed.

"I realize no more attempts have been made on your life. But it'd be difficult for anyone to do that here. Once you're out, it might be a different story. I won't have Ellie jeopardized."

Just what the hell did she think *she* was doing by working this case? "Bobcats streak through the trees, squirrels hide nuts . . ." Screw it. He couldn't defend himself, so why even try?

Exasperated, she went on. "She's the most vulnerable. You could at least do it to protect her. And you could've told me about the case. I know, I know, Fitz asked you not to, but look where the hell it's gotten us."

Go on, get it off your chest, Quin. And while she was at it, she might as well dredge up everything else that had gone wrong in their marriage. She would never have a chance quite like this one again, a captive audience incapable of presenting a defense.

But to his surprise she stopped there. "Just think about it. That's all I'm asking." She let out a short, ugly laugh. "Asking, can you believe it? I shouldn't even *have* to ask, not when it's Ellie." With that; she turned, her shoes clicking against the polished floors. The door opened, shut. He listened until he couldn't hear her footsteps.

Another week in here, with cops at the door and his wife out there with Tark: he didn't think he could stand it. He was at the window when he saw her emerge from the hospital. McCleary watched until the Explorer was just a wink of silver in the February light.

≈

At one time Boca Raton had been touted as the city where one in every forty-third person was a millionaire. The figure was probably one in a hundred now, Quin thought, but it seemed that nearly everyone lived like a millionaire.

The yuppies in Boca favored Beamers, sent their toddlers to pre-schools that cost as much as other people's mortgages, and hired illegal aliens to keep their mansions clean. There was only one de-pressed area in the entire town, a mile stretch along Dixie Highway that was inhabited by poor blacks. But even it looked pretty good for a slum. And wasn't that what Boca, like Palm Beach, was all about? Looking good, living well, succeeding. The American dream in a nutshell.

The dream, though, had bypassed the building where Christine Redman lived. It was at least twenty years old, a mere infant in a city like Paris but ancient for Boca. It shrieked for a face-lift. The grounds needed weeding. The wooden fence that ran along one side of the property listed permanently to the left. The cars in the lot were, for the most part, tired old warriors whose wounds hadn't healed.

The parking lot was small and most of the spaces were reserved for residents. The slot for apartment six was occupied by a rusting Honda with a loose tailpipe; the lady was home. And probably still asleep. The last time Quin had tried to talk to Christine Redman, she'd answered the door in her robe. According to a neighbor Quin had talked to, Christine worked the swing shift at the Boca Hospital as an LPN and kept "late hours."

Quin nosed into a vacant visitor's spot. Before she got out, she slipped a cassette recorder into her purse. This wouldn't be admissible in court, but she and Tark had agreed to tape-record their interviews as a precaution from now on. The tapes would be transcribed, then put in the firm's safety deposit box. Rita Vail had asked for a copy of Tark's conversation with Noel Unward, which Quin would deliver when she met her and Sasha Colt for lunch tomorrow.

Christine's place was a corner apartment on the ground floor. Quin rang the doorbell and stepped to one side so that she wouldn't be visible through the peephole. When Christine asked who it was, Quin didn't answer.

"You goddamn kids get away from my door," Christine barked. The inside chain clattered and she stepped out, a short, stocky woman in a neon-blue robe whose sable eyes and hair were several shades darker than her skin. Her forehead puckered when she saw Quin. "You again? Jesus, girl, get your ass outta my sight."

She started to shut the door, but Quin wedged her foot between it and the jamb. "Tell me why Eden White decided you weren't the prize she'd claimed you were, Ms. Redman. That's all I need to know."

"Name's Henderson, not Redman. Now move your foot, bitch."

"Please." Quin grabbed the edge of the door and shoved it open. "Help me out. I think Eden White may be responsible for the murder of Janis Krieger and for the shooting of my husband, Mike McCleary."

She rolled her eyes and jammed her hands into the pockets of her blue silk robe. "Lady, I don't know how to make it any clearer than I already have. My name's Loretta Henderson, not Christine Redman. I never heard of no Eden White. I never heard of Janis Krieger. And if McCleary's the fellow who tried to push his way through my door a few weeks ago, then you got ten seconds to march your skinny white ass right out the door. Ten seconds or I call the cops."

"I'm working for the cops."

"I don't give a shit who you're working for. You got eight seconds."

"Six years ago you were tested at Duke University by Eden White. You were her star clairvoyant. A year later, just as you were starting to gain national prominence, a skeptics' group went after you and things went down the tubes. You sued Link for malfeasance, then dropped the suit. I need to know what really happened."

Something changed in her expression, small, subtle details that wouldn't have amounted to much if they'd occurred separately. But the cumulative effect was strange, unsettling. It made Quin feel like the ugly American who had offended her host in a foreign country. She suddenly felt compelled to apologize for her rudeness and make herself scarce.

"C'mon, c'mon," Christine said sharply, impatiently. "Get your ass in here so I can close the door." Her plump, dimpled hands made quick, sweeping motions until Quin was inside. Then she shut the door, walked past Quin, murmuring, "Be back in a minute," and went into the kitchen.

Quin peered down the long hallway into a living room where the walls were bare and the furnishings were worn and faded, used stuff picked up at garage sales. A clunker of a TV, a nicked stereo, a few plants, a low shelf crowded with books. A life that is quickly disassembled, she thought.

"I want you to listen good, girl, because I'm only going to say this once."

Christine stood in the kitchen doorway with a silenced weapon aimed at Quin's chest. She gripped it like a cop. The safety was off. It seemed to take twenty years for Quin's eyes to move from the 9mm to Christine's face. Blood roared in her ears. "I'm listening."

"You come back here again and I blow you into next year. We understand each other?"

"Loud and clear."

"Good. Now I got something to show you." She reached around the side of the doorway for something on the counter, then her hand returned clutching a bulging photo album, a cheap thing found in discount bins at K mart. "Look in there." She held it out, Quin took it. Christine didn't lower the gun. "Go on, look at it."

Inside were numerous press clippings with headings like "Clairvoyant Predicted California Quake" and "Local Psychic Aids Police." Some were from weekly newspapers, some were from the heavy hitters, and others were from magazines both large and small. There were photos of a slender, attractive black woman with dreadlocks who bore only a faint resemblance to the present Christine Redman.

Quin scanned a few of the clippings. She kept turning the pages. And Christine Redman waited.

When the clippings ended, there were photographs, family snapshots of Christine with a man and a boy of seven or eight. The last page was an obituary from a Winston-Salem newspaper:

> Samuel Redman, 8, died yesterday of injuries sustained in a car accident. He is survived by his mother, Christine, 33, and his father, Ronnie, 36, of Durham.

Quin shut the album. "I'm sorry, I didn't mean to—"

"Forget the sympathy shit. When my boy died, so did Christine Redman and all her grief. But maybe she didn't die like she should've. Maybe she kept in touch with a few too many people and that's how your man McCleary found her. Maybe he told the police." She snatched the photo album from Quin's hand. "Or maybe you're going to tell them you talked to Christine, huh?" She stepped close to Quin and pressed the end of the silencer to the tip of Quin's nose. "What about it? You a snitch?"

A muscle kicked under Quin's left eye. Sweat popped out on her skin. She heard the soft, even tick of a clock somewhere nearby. *If a gun's in your face, you do what you have to do to stay alive. You lie, you cry, you beg, you weep, you tell the guy with the gun whatever he wants to hear.* Another McCleary axiom. But this wasn't some stupid doped-up punk who wanted her wallet. This was a woman who had suffered something unspeakable and needed the truth as badly as she did.

"Your name appeared on a computer network. It was given to my husband by an ex-cop named Randy Tract."

She obviously recognized the name. Her liquid eyes narrowed, her nostrils flared, and the pressure of the muzzle against Quin's nose seemed to ease a fraction. "Go on."

"All I know about him is that he's an ex-cop who died but didn't die and the experience changed his life. He lives in Seattle. When my husband was investigating Janis Krieger's death, he apparently asked Tract if he knew anything about Janis's husband, Alejandro Domingo, a local healer.

"Tract checked with several research centers. No one had ever heard of the healer. But Tract thought it might be significant that Dr. White had tested both you and Alejandro. So he gave my husband your name and address. I don't know how Tract got the information."

"I didn't bury Christine as well as I should've, that's how. When did Eden test this guy?"

"Within the last five years."

"That bitch still messing around at Duke during the summers?"

"Not that I know of."

As Quin explained about Link Research & Development, the pressure against her nose slowly eased. Christine finally stepped back, her gun aimed at the floor, but her eyes never left Quin's face. She felt that if she moved too quickly—a sneeze, a sudden itch, it would take that little—she might not live long enough to scream for help. She might not live long enough to even feel pain.

When Quin was finished, Christine Redman tucked the gun in the pocket of her robe, where it bulged like some ludicrous appendage. "Best advice you'll ever get is to turn around and walk out that door, then start running as fast as them long legs will take you. You fuck with these people you end up like me, okay? That clear enough for you?"

She strode to the door, opened it, and walked just as quickly away from the door, past Quin, and into the living room. She stopped at the stereo, set the needle on a scratched rendition of gospel music. The open door beckoned, but Quin wasn't about to leave things like this.

"It's my turn now, Ms. Redman." Quin went over to the stereo and turned down the volume. "My husband was shot while he, my daughter, and I were running in our neighborhood. He was shot by someone in a moving car. He has a punctured lung and talks like a mental patient on bad drugs. My daughter is nearly two. I have a life. It may not always be the best life, but it's *my* life and no one's going to force me to surrender it and become what they want me to become.

"If you want to keep running, if it makes you feel better, then fine. Do it. But if you want to get even for the death of your boy and the years you've lost, then call me. Quin St. James. I'm in the book."

She resisted the urge to slam the door on the way out. Once she was inside the Explorer, she started to shake. She wrapped her arms around herself and pressed her forehead to the steering wheel. She could still feel the pressure of the gun against her nose.

13

～～～～

In a town like Palm Beach, where most things existed larger than life, the evidence of enormous wealth had become almost commonplace for Tark. Even so, as he stood at the wrought-iron gate outside the Holden estate Saturday morning, he had to admit the place was impressive.

It occupied five acres on Ocean Drive, the millionaires row of Palm Beach, and looked as though it had come straight out of *Gone With the Wind*. White pillars, a dramatic front porch, floor-to-ceiling windows. The grounds were magnificent: slopes of green broken up by roses, gardenias, and impatiens, palms and acacias and mango trees. Off to the right was a pond encircled by weeping willows.

Up near the house a gardener in coveralls and a wide straw hat knelt by a berm of flowers, his back to the gate. To the left of the house was a four-car garage, the doors closed. Two cars were parked outside, a BMW and a Mercedes. Behind the house, shrouded by trees and foliage, was the ocean.

Tark rang the bell under the intercom speaker. It crackled and a female voice said, "Yes? May I help you?"

"John Tark to see Mr. Holden."

"Just a minute, please."

He wondered what it would be like to wake up every morning in a place like this, in a life like this. It was, according to what he'd read in the book he'd bought at Liberties', all that Barker Holden had ever known.

He'd been born with the proverbial silver spoon in his mouth, an only child groomed from birth to follow in his father's footsteps. He had inherited Holden Cereals when he was twenty-four and fresh out of Harvard Business School. He then spent the next decade doing what all good businessmen do and he had done it better than most of his competitors. By the time he had sold out, boxes of Holden Crunchy Flakes and Dino Delights graced at least half the breakfast tables in America.

Holden, who was then thirty-six, single, and enormously wealthy, had left the country for two years. There were numerous speculations in the book about where he had gone and what he had done. One rumor was that he'd joined an ashram in Thailand, another placed him with power brokers in Europe and Japan. Whatever the truth, he had returned with a wife, Lydia Holden, who was eight years younger. It was the first marriage for both.

In the twelve years since Holden had sold the cereal company, he had dabbled in politics but always in the background. He was a name behind the scenes, part of the power structure that backed a particular candidate, a man who seemed to know everyone who was someone. He had never run for political office until now.

A shot at the U.S. Senate seemed like a mighty long leap from this quiet estate on Ocean Drive. But stranger things had happened in American politics, Tark thought. Especially when your net worth was in the neighborhood of several hundred million.

"You can come on through," said the voice on the intercom. "The gates will open automatically."

"Thanks." Tark returned to the Cherokee. The book on Palm

Beach's prominent families, which he had been reading at stoplights and on surveillance, was on the dashboard. He stashed it under his seat and started the engine.

The gates yawned open soundlessly and he drove on through. A pair of golden retrievers loped out of the trees, barking, and charged alongside the Cherokee. A collie joined them before Tark reached the house, and all the commotion caused the gardener in the straw hat to glance around, to stand.

Lydia Holden. Her feet were bare, her coveralls were stained; she held a small hoe in one hand.

The dogs bounded over, panting and barking, as he got out of the Cherokee. They were beautiful, pampered animals that made a lot of noise but were otherwise harmless. "Sit!" Lydia snapped, and they did. She nudged her straw hat back farther on her head as she came over, a polite smile fixed on her very pretty face. "Hi, John."

"I didn't recognize you."

She laughed and hooked her thumbs at the sides of the coveralls. "My most effective disguise. C'mon, I'll take you in to see Barker." She dropped the hoe on the ground, brushed her hands against her coveralls, and whistled for the dogs. They followed at a discreet distance, tails wagging. She gestured toward them and smiled again. He liked her smile. It was crooked, imperfect, and added humanity to her face. "They're supposed to be watchdogs."

"Maybe they know I have an appointment."

"Yes, maybe they do at that."

As they headed toward the house, Tark drank in the landscaping, the arrangement of colors, the intimate touches no hired hand could pull off. "The grounds are beautiful."

"Thanks, but I can't take credit for it. I just putter." She was nearly a foot shorter than he and had to crane her neck to look up at him. "It's only fair to warn you that Barker isn't in the best of moods today. He just got home an hour ago from a campaign thing up in Tallahassee and he's leaving again this evening and is really annoyed about this appointment. I guess he thought I was supposed to answer all your questions at lunch yesterday."

Too bad, Barker, old boy. "He's the one who grew up with Janis."

"That's what I told him." Another smile. She removed her hat and fanned herself with it as they climbed the porch steps.

He realized he hadn't given much thought to what the interior of the Holden home might look like. But even if he had, it probably wouldn't have prepared him for the reality. The place was a palace. The open-beam ceilings were fifteen feet high, the floors were polished black tile, the halls were as wide as his entire apartment. The tremendous rooms were filled with sunlight and plants and small trees in huge hand-painted ceramic pots. The air possessed the stillness of an empty cathedral.

The rooms he glimpsed all had different motifs: Spanish, Southwest, Oriental. It wasn't just the furniture that followed the individual patterns, but the rugs, the art on the walls, every detail right down to the figurines. Lydia noted his interest and paused here and there to explain the origin of a piece of art or a story connected to a particular vase. She was in no apparent hurry and neither was he.

As they stood before a wall mural in the Oriental room, a young woman in a black and white uniform paused in the doorway. "Where will you be having your coffee, Mrs. Holden?"

"In Mr. Holden's office, Madge. Mr. Tark and I will be joining him shortly."

Madge, Estelle's buddy.

"Yes, ma'am." She smiled at Tark, obviously recognizing his name, and hurried off. He wondered what Estelle had told her, how she talked about him to her women friends.

"I have a certain fondness for this particular room," Lydia said when they were alone again. She walked over to an Oriental throw rug, curled her bare toes against it. "Barker and I bought this rug at a bazaar in Thailand. And that vase . . ." She pointed at a four-foot-tall black porcelain vase standing against the wall in front of them. "We shipped it back from Hong Kong."

She looked up, that crooked smile in place again. She seemed to be waiting for him to say something. When he didn't, she gestured toward a delicate black ceramic lamp with a tissue-thin shade that stood on an end table. A green dragon was painted on the side, its mouth open, spewing bright orange flames. "The day Barker and I were married, the owner of the hotel in Bangkok where we stayed gave us that lamp."

These intimate peeks at her personal history seemed to require some sort of response from him. "It sounds like you miss the Orient."

She shrugged. "I guess I just have a certain nostalgia for the diplomatic life. It's very . . . I don't know, clear-cut or something. You know what I mean?"

He nodded. The fact that she was a brat of the diplomatic corps, like himself, had brought her into sharper focus for Tark. He had grown up with people like Lydia Holden, Americans whose childhoods overseas had made their frames of reference strikingly different from their contemporaries. He was a prime example.

They walked out into the hall again. His shoes squeaked against the tile. He wondered how many people it took to clean this place. "How many rooms are there?"

"Sixty."

Fifty shy of Trump's estate, but the Holdens had twice the land Trump did. The homes had been built around the same time, Trump's place by the Post Cereal family and this palace by Holden's grandfather. "You ever get lost?"

She laughed. "Not anymore. But I did when we first moved in. I'd be on my way to the kitchen and end up in the solarium."

"It's interesting that Janis's grandfather sold the property to Barker's grandfather."

If she was surprised that he knew, she didn't let on. "That's how it was in Palm Beach in those days."

They passed a game room, a family room, a dining room that seated fifty. There wasn't a speck of dust in sight, not a stick of furniture out of place. "Will you keep the house if Barker wins the election?"

"Definitely."

Nothing equivocal about that, Tark thought.

"I'll probably spend most of my time here." She glanced at him; a dark brooding had entered her eyes. "I detest politics. This is Barker's game, not mine. And it's not *if* he wins, it's *when*. That's how he looks at everything he covets."

He wondered if it was just a personal observation about her husband or a veiled warning.

They turned down another hall and climbed a few steps to a landing where several pairs of shoes were lined up. "Shoes off, John. Oriental habits die hard." Then she opened an oak door with a plaque on the front that read BARKER'S WORLD. And it was certainly that, a world so different from the rest of the house that it belonged in another galaxy.

Everything was white. The thick rug, the walls, the office furniture, even the computer, the phones, the fax, the doorknobs. To Tark's left a pair of white Persian cats snoozed at opposite ends of a white couch. He felt as if he'd walked into a movie director's version of the afterlife.

The campaign posters that covered one of the walls weren't white, though, and neither was the barefoot woman behind the desk. She was Oriental, thin and chic, possessed of that odd serenity that seemed almost genetic with Oriental women. Her shiny black hair was stylishly cut to just below her ears and moved as she moved, following the motions of her body as she came out from behind the desk.

As soon as she greeted Lydia, Tark recognized her voice as that of the woman who had called and made this appointment. She offered her hand to Tark. "Jenny Ming, Mr. Tark. Nice to meet you." Her hand was cool and soft, but her grip was like a man's. "Barker's still on the phone. It's been nuts around here."

"Jenny is Barker's personal assistant," Lydia explained.

"We talked the other day," Tark said.

"I apologize for taking so long to get back to you," Jenny said. "But we were in and out of town with the campaign." She gestured toward the sliding glass doors. "Let's go out onto the porch. Madge left us some coffee. You joining us, Lydia?"

"Sure."

It was clear that Lydia Holden's authority ended at the threshold of Barker's world. In his absence Jenny called the shots. Lydia didn't seem to resent it; the two women actually appeared to get along well. They chattered back and forth about the trip to Tallahassee, the status of the campaign, future public appearances.

Lydia poured coffee into blue china cups and passed the matching platter of finger-size pastries. Jenny filled china bowls with fresh fruit and handed one to Tark, along with a shiny silver spoon and a linen napkin. Tark was beginning to feel like a kid at a tea party.

The blue of the ocean glimmered through the profusion of trees below and a pleasant breeze carried the scent of salt and sun. Tark watched a gardener moving along a length of hibiscus hedges with a power trimmer; the ground behind him was littered with peach-colored flowers. Another man was washing the downstairs windows along the side of the house, and Madge was sweeping leaves off the wooden decking that surrounded a piano-shaped pool.

Ordered lives, he thought. A cook to prepare meals that were served right on time; floors mopped and polished by an army of hired hands; grounds tended by one or two lawn services; a maid to wash, iron, and polish the lovely silverware; a housekeeper at your beck and call throughout the day.

"So, Mr. Tark," Jenny said. "You mentioned over the phone that you were unclear about a few points in Barker's previous statements to Detective Eastman and Mr. McCleary."

"Yes, that's right."

"Is there anything I can clear up for you?"

It annoyed him that Holden had her and his wife running interference for him. "I don't think so."

Her mouth twitched with irritation. "Would you like a copy of his campaign schedule in the event you need to speak to him again?"

"That'd be great, thanks."

"I'll have it ready for you when you leave. Let me go see if Barker is off the phone." With that, she pushed up from the chair and went back inside.

"Is she Thai?" Holden asked.

"Her parents were from Hong Kong, but she was born here. She's incredibly efficient. Barker was lucky to find her. She came into my shop one day several years ago, that's how we met her."

The sliding glass door opened again and Holden stepped out in casual clothes that were obviously tailored and no doubt expensive. He didn't look much different in the flesh than he did on his campaign posters: six feet tall, lean, sandy hair with the right touch of gray, not particularly good-looking but with a face you could trust. Rich brown eyes, the color of teak, quick to smile. But the posters failed to capture the power of his bearing, a magnetism that commanded your full attention.

He shook Tark's hand and didn't waste time on amenities. "I had hoped Lydia would be able to answer whatever questions you and Mrs. McCleary have. Since that apparently isn't the case, I've asked her to join us so we won't have to repeat this."

Fuck you, too, pal. "This is a murder investigation, Mr. Holden. You may have to repeat this scenario a dozen times whether you like it or not."

Holden looked appropriately apologetic. "You're right, of course. I'm sorry. I've been so wrapped up in the campaign that I tend to forget what's going on elsewhere." He glanced at his watch as he sat down; Tark wondered how much time he'd been allotted.

"When was the last time you saw Janis?"

"Two days before she was killed. We ran into each other at the courthouse. But I'm sure Detective Eastman already told you that, so why ask it?"

"Some people have short memories."

"Well, I'm not one of them." He smiled and flicked at something on his dark slacks; Lydia seemed fully absorbed in straightening the brim of her straw gardening hat. "I'll be quite frank, Mr. Tark. Janis and I hadn't been on good terms since the negative press about Alejandro started appearing last fall. She accused me of initiating the investigation by the state attorney's office, which simply isn't true."

"So you didn't have any problem with your wife seeking Alejandro's help with her health problems?"

"Not personally. But politically I had problems with it. And that's a hell of a thing, Mr. Tark, because I'd known Janis for years and I'm fond of Alejandro and I thought he might succeed with Lydia where doctors had failed."

Throughout this little speech Lydia didn't say anything. Now she glanced up. "I wasn't seeing Alex anymore when the state attorney's office started their investigation."

"Because of the campaign?" Tark asked.

"Because there was nothing more he could do. But Janis misconstrued everything. She accused us of turning against Alex, of betraying him. . . ." She made an impatient gesture with her hand. "All that."

"Eden White said pretty much the same thing," Tark remarked.

"It was probably warranted with Eden," said Lydia. "She claims she was grossly misquoted in those newspaper articles about Alex. But if that's true, then why didn't she call the papers and demand a correction or something?"

"Maybe she did and was told to forget it," said Holden.

"Sure," she replied. "And maybe this and maybe that."

"How well do you know Eden?" Tark's question was directed to Lydia, but Holden answered.

"Eden and I met at Harvard years ago and have mutual friends now, but that's about it."

So Quin's supposition had been right. Tark started to mention the land Holden had bought from White but thought better of it. "Did you ever run into her at Alejandro's?" he asked Lydia.

She no longer seemed quite as eager to talk about Eden White. "A few times."

"What's your impression of her?"

"A little aloof, but nice enough."

"What time did you and your wife arrive at the reception the night Janis was killed?"

"We went there straight from the wedding. It must've been, what, Lydia? Eight? Eight-thirty?"

"Thereabouts. I guess we left around one."

"Did you see Alejandro that evening?"

"Sure. We sat at the same table for dinner," Holden replied.

"And he and I danced several times during the evening," Lydia added. "He seemed in good spirits despite Janis's absence."

Holden glanced at his watch. "Is there anything else, Mr. Tark?"

"One other thing. Exactly how long did you know Janis?"

"Most of my life. Our parents were friends, we got thrown together a lot as kids. But once we both went away to school, we didn't see all that much of each other. We were never particularly close."

A few minutes later they walked back through Jenny Ming's office to the hall. Holden said the things Tark had expected, that he hoped

their chat had helped, don't hesitate to call, and so on. But it was
Lydia who accompanied Tark downstairs, into the immense silence
that suffused the rooms on the ground floor.

"Barker hates to admit it, but he and Janis were a lot alike. He
fights to win; so did she. He's opinionated; so was she. He's stubborn;
so was she. Alejandro and I used to joke that they should've married
each other. You married, John?"

"Divorced." It was easier to lie than to say he was widowed,
which usually prompted the inevitable "Oh, I'm sorry" or, worse,
"How did she die?"

"Sometimes I think of marriage as a country. Well, not just marriage, but any romantic partnership. In the beginning it's a strange
and wondrous country that keeps you on the edge of your seat. Then
as you learn your way around, you encounter its hidden places, its
secrets, its dark passages, its dangers. So you find a spot within the
country that's safe, ordinary, habitual, and that's where you live out
much of your life."

It wasn't how marriage had been for him. But if this was actually
how she perceived her relationship with her husband, then he supposed her safe spot, her harbor, was money and lifestyle. "Don't ever
become a travel agent," he said with a laugh.

That crooked smile swung into place again and she opened the
door for him. The light against her face rendered her features in
exquisite detail: the soft, pouting mouth, the porcelain skin, the
vibrant blue eyes. An enigma, this Lydia Holden. "Nice talking to
you, John."

"Thanks again."

When he got into the Cherokee, an envelope was sticking out of
the glove compartment. Madge, he thought.

He removed it but didn't open it until he was parked in the lot
of a shopping center in West Palm Beach. Two color snapshots were
inside. One was faded, tattered at the corners, and depicted two
young men and a woman, all of them laughing, arms around one
another's shoulders.

The second photo was of the same three people seated on the
deck of a boat, but they were at least twenty-five years older. There
was nothing written on the snapshots to indicate where or when

they'd been taken or who they were. But Tark recognized two of them—Barker Holden and Eden White.

He dug a magnifying glass out of the glove compartment and studied the people in the older picture. They all looked to be in their midtwenties, a cocky, arrogant trio in bell-bottom jeans and cable-knit sweaters. The background suggested a college campus.

Buddies at Harvard in the sixties. Holden in business school, Eden White in med school.

And the other guy? Which school at Harvard had he attended? Political science? Law? But more to the point, who the hell was he and what did this connection mean?

≈

Alejandro stopped in the doorway of his wife's room and looked around slowly. He'd been in here only twice since her death, to gather up his belongings and move them to a downstairs bedroom. Otherwise the room was exactly as it had been the night she died, preserved like an artifact in a museum.

Strips of sunlight fell across the king-size brass bed and spilled onto the cedar chest at the foot of it. Janis's vanity and chest of drawers, also made of cedar, stood against the far wall, on either side of another window. Makeup, bottles of perfume, and Janis's mysterious lotions and creams were neatly arranged on the vanity. On the chest of drawers was a small gallery of photographs, moments snapped from happier times, frozen in brilliant color.

All of the photos occupied oval brass frames that stood on three brass feet. In the center was their wedding picture, the largest in the collection, taken in the garden behind his brother's home in Ancud. Janis wore a soft yellow dress with white stockings and matching yellow flats. Sunlight streaked her short pale hair with gold. She was laughing at something he'd just said and looked like a bride is supposed to look. Happy, serene, utterly radiant.

Alejandro picked up the photo and stroked her face with his thumb. Sorrow filled him, but it wasn't the debilitating grief he'd felt in the weeks right after her death.

In his mind's eye she was many women: the pale, thin *gringa* waiting on his patio one spring morning with dozens of other patients; the young American staying at the Ancud Hotel who the townspeople called *La Rubia*, the blonde; the feisty woman who disputed a hotel bill when they were in Santiago; a mother who sang her daughter to sleep at night. She was a passionate lover, an acute businesswoman, a spendthrift, a drunk, a shrew. He no longer knew who the real Janis had been.

He set down the photo and opened the top drawer of the dresser. It contained underclothes, nightgowns, everything neatly folded and arranged in individual piles. For Janis, everything had had a place, a niche. It was as true of the way she had arranged her clothes as it was of the way she'd arranged her life.

Alejandro dug through silks, rayons, cottons. He didn't know what he was looking for. Evidence of a secret? Something that would tell him what had gone wrong in their marriage? The dresser yielded nothing. Neither did her vanity nor her closet with its many shelves, its boxes of shoes.

The bathroom was next. It was a tremendous room with a shower, a tub, double sinks, his and hers. The windows overlooked the swimming pool and the forest of melaleucas beyond it. French doors at the foot of the tub opened onto a small balcony with a Jacuzzi. Janis had sometimes sunbathed there in the nude.

In the beginning he had balked at the extravagances, the space, the luxuries. After all, he had grown up in three damp, crowded rooms with cement floors, a fireplace for heating, and an outhouse. But his seduction hadn't taken long, just a few weeks, so in that way he was as guilty of excess as his wife.

Alejandro searched the linen closet, the medicine cabinet, then opened the doors under the sink. Supplies, more supplies than two people could use in a year: twelve bottles of Redken shampoo; nine bottles of Tylenol; two dozen bottles of a coral-colored nail polish; eighteen bars of Dove soap; six tweezers; three hair dryers and four curling irons; six bottles of children's Tylenol; and ten bottles of hydrogen peroxide.

He also found an array of contraceptives: two diaphragms and four tubes of the goo that went with them, a dozen contraceptive sponges, and a box of condoms. He knew she hadn't wanted more children, but this seemed excessive. Hell, it all seemed excessive. It was as if his wife had been buying against a future when these items no longer existed.

Naturally, everything was neatly arranged, with brands crowded together in numerous plastic trays. Alejandro removed each tray, checked to make sure it contained only what it appeared to, and set it aside. He worked his way to the back of the deep, spacious cabinet and found a wooden cigar box.

The writing on the lid had long since faded, the edges were starting to crumble, and it was held together with a fat rubber band. He carried it into the bedroom, sat on the edge of the mattress, snapped off the rubber band, and flipped open the lid.

The box held an odd assortment of memorabilia: Janis's college ID card from Smith; a black-and-white snapshot of her parents, circa 1951; a sorority pin; mementos from her life long before he'd known her. On the bottom was a blue velvet drawstring bag, which Alejandro jerked open and turned upside down, dumping the contents onto the bed.

Pieces of paper fluttered out. Notes. Printed, unsigned notes. *Meet me in the field at noon*, said one. *I have to touch you*, said another. *Did you make love to him after you left me? Did you?* demanded a third. Then a longer note:

> *Meet me somewhere, Janis. Anywhere. We need to talk. I go to sleep thinking of you, wake up thinking of you, I dream of you, I hate my life without you in it.*

Alejandro knuckled his eyes. What field? When? And why? But he knew why. In the year before she had died, he'd worked from eight in the morning until nine or ten at night, six days a week, attending to other people's needs, other people's pains. His free time had gone to his daughter, not to his wife. It wasn't that he had loved Janis less, only that Miranda had seemed to need him more.

Besides, he'd been operating under the apparently mistaken assumption that he and Janis had been working together toward something. She had coordinated nearly every aspect of his waking life, from scheduling his patients to balancing the books to the press coverage he received. He'd believed they were partners.

And yet there were signs, of course there were: sudden eruptions of temper, her increasingly frequent absences, her spending, her drinking, the nights they turned away from each other in bed. But he had dismissed these details as temporary, as pieces of the vast and puzzling mystery of marriage.

There were no envelopes with the letters, so he couldn't tell when the notes had been mailed. Maybe Janis's lover had been one of the many observers who had drifted through here in the past two years, journalists, scientists, people like Eden White and Noel Unward.

Meet me in the field at noon.

The house was surrounded by fields.

Was that what had happened? Had she and her lover crept away from the crowds and fucked in the fields? He could imagine it, could almost see it in his mind, his wife and this man stealing away for thirty or forty minutes.

Alejandro read the remaining four notes. Two referred to a motel he'd never heard of where Janis and her lover had met when he and Miranda had gone to the zoo. He remembered that Sunday, remembered it clearly, Janis begging off, saying she didn't feel well. Carmelita hadn't been working that day, Francesca had been in Miami, there had been no witnesses to his wife's deception. The third note held a desperate tone, the voice of a man suffering acute withdrawal, and the last was an ultimatum: *Don't make me do something we'll both regret, Janis.*

What kind of something? Tell the oblivious husband? Make threatening calls? Kill her? For this she had died? For some dirty little affair conducted in fields, beach motels, and dark culverts on dead-end streets?

He leaped up and hurled the cigar box, great, silent sobs shuddering through him, waves of heat sweeping from him into the room. The cigar box struck the far wall and splintered into a dozen pieces. The perfume bottles on the dresser suddenly burst on their own, one two three four, soft, rapid explosions like faulty firecrackers. Bits of glass flew out in every direction, the odor of perfume suffused the air. When Carmelita rushed in seconds later, streams of perfume were running over the sides of the dresser, the floor was bright with shards of glass.

For seconds he and Carmelita just stared at each other, neither of them moving or uttering a sound. The steady *drip drip drip* of perfume punctuated the silence. He felt as if his insides had been scooped out, emptied, and any second now the weakened walls of his body would simply crumble. Then his knees buckled and he sat down hard at the foot of the bed, ashamed and humiliated by the depth of his anger and despair. But more than that, he was terrified of the heat that had rushed out of him.

"*Dios mío*," Carmelita whispered, waddling over to him. "What happened?"

He shook his head, at a loss for what to say. He pushed to his feet, crossed the room, and began picking up the pieces of the cigar box. Carmelita stooped to help, her face eaten up with concern, her unasked questions crowding the air.

"You would tell me if this had something to do with Miranda and Francesca, wouldn't you?"

"Yes. It doesn't." He paused, and when he spoke again, the words nearly choked him. "Janis was seeing someone."

But even that wasn't the whole truth.

"It does not surprise me."

"You suspected?"

"Nothing so strong." She removed her apron and used it to sop up the perfume. "It's the kind of woman she was, Alejandro. There was a terrible darkness in her, a spiritual corruption. Even Miranda sensed it sometimes."

Her voice had taken on a thick, languid quality, as though she were a voice in a dream. "I think in the beginning, in Chile, when you were working on her and she was starting to improve, you were her saint, her guardian angel, her Christ. She married the healer, not the man."

Alejandro said nothing.

"It's happened before," she went on. "Remember the village women in the early days? You were their miracle."

She sounded like the priest. "I was nothing of the sort, Carmelita.

It was easier for them to come to me than to take the ferry into Puerto Montt."

"No, you're wrong. Remember when the bishop from Santiago came to see you? That was no accident, Alejandro. The village women's belief in you was so strong they contacted him about you. When they didn't hear from him, they raised enough money among themselves for a round-trip train fare to Santiago.

"Their emissary made the trip and had an audience with him. That's how he ended up in Ancud. After that, word spread and patients began to come from all over Chile, from Argentina and Uruguay, even from Brazil. You were the next Arigo. Those women felt proud, like they had discovered you. But they never knew you as a man, Alejandro, because they felt you were a Christ. I think Janis felt a little like that, too."

The room was suddenly too warm, too closed, too cloying. He moved to the open window, where the warm air smelled green, vast. The water of the swimming pool below was a perfect blue, like the sky, like paint, like the sea where he had fished. But this was not his world. It had never been his world. He wasn't a Christ, a saint, or a miracle. He was an immigrant, a transplant, a stranger to these shores, an outsider. And that, he thought, would never change.

"Carmelita, remember that time when we were in Santiago visiting friends and that thief on the street snatched your purse?"

"Sure." She had fetched a broom from the hall closet and was sweeping up the glass.

"Tell me what you remember about it."

"You went after him. When I reached you, you had my purse and the man was on the ground, clutching himself and groaning. Then he lifted his head and . . ." She stopped and they looked at each other. *She knows*, he thought. *She knows the truth and denies that she knows.*

"And what?" he prodded.

She shrugged, swept the glass into a dustpan. "What's the point of talking about it?" she said crossly, impatiently. "It was a long time ago."

"The man died, Carmelita. He bled to death in seconds."

"He was ill, he—"

"No. I killed him."

The words hung in the air, weighted and ugly. Carmelita stood there with the broom in one hand and the dustpan in the other, her eyes dark, inscrutable.

"It was an accident," he went on. "One moment we were struggling for the purse and he was hitting me and the next moment he . . . he was bleeding." Alejandro leaned back against the windowsill, rubbing his hands over his jeans, not looking at her now. "It's like a beast inside of me. I don't know what wakes it up, I don't know what releases it, I don't know how to control it. It seems to be tied in to certain emotions—anger, despair, grief—but not with any consistency. When I read the notes her lover had written her, I . . . it leaped away from me."

He looked at her. Her gaze roamed around the room, comprehension like a wound in her dark eyes. "The box didn't hit the perfume bottles," she said.

"No."

When she finally spoke, her voice was very soft. "Duality exists in all things, Alejandro."

"But only recently has this . . . this thing come awake again. For years, since that night in Santiago, it never surfaced."

"Because all of your energy was focused on healing. You haven't worked, really, since Janis's death. All that . . ." She paused, her hands moving through the air as if to seize the right word. ". . . that power builds up, Alejandro. It seeks release in whatever way it can."

He glanced out the window again, where Neruda was stalking something at the edge of the pool. He wasn't sure he agreed with Carmelita. He'd felt good when he'd left the hospital yesterday, he'd felt elated, euphoric. But had he felt depleted? Used up because he had worked on someone? He didn't know, but he was willing to try anything.

"When you go into town, Carmelita, would you call Padre Cardenas?"

"Yes, of course." She brightened. "What should I tell him?"

"That I will do as he asks, but without the bishop there. And it won't be at the church. I'll go to the migrant camp. He knows the situation with Miranda and Francesca, but you might remind him."

"Anything else?"

"No cameras, no recorders, no reporters, only one other priest from the church besides him."

She dropped the pillow on the bed. "We need a few things from the market, Alejandro. I'll be back in a while."

"Drive carefully."

"Como siempre." She walked out, humming to herself.

It was two Sunday morning when I pulled into the park and stopped next to Eddie's truck. I couldn't see his boat from shore because it was anchored in a cove. I had no way of knowing whether he was even on board. And if he was, maybe he had company. So I waited for a sign.

It arrived in the form of an owl. I heard it before I saw it, that soft, mournful hoot coming from the trees, then a fluttering of wings and there it was, a large dark shadow against the moonlight. It settled on the branch of a nearby tree, close enough so I could see it.

If it flew toward me in the next five minutes, it meant Eddie was on board. If it landed nearer to his truck than to my car, it meant he was with someone. If it just flew away, then I should do the same. Simple. But five minutes is a long time when you're waiting and other thoughts crowded into my head. About Janis, about Barker, about

Eddie. I felt a sudden, urgent need to wash my hands. All that water out there, I just couldn't stand it.

I removed the small bar of soap I kept in the glove compartment, stripped off my T-shirt and shorts. My nylon tank suit was black and so was the waterproof pouch I buckled around my waist. Perfect for nighttime swimming.

I stuck my car keys in the pouch with the other stuff, then I slipped over the seawall into the cool, moonlit canal. I treaded water for a few minutes, while I washed my hands. I really worked up a lather, spreading the suds up my arms, all the way to my shoulders, then over my throat and the back of my neck. The last spots I got to were between my fingers and under my nails, where the worst stuff gets stuck.

It nauseated me, thinking of the things I had touched in a single day: fruit in a produce bin that hundreds of other fingers had squeezed; utensils and glasses that Christ knows how many other people had handled; paper, vegetation, wood, other people's hands. It wasn't just the germs and microbes and viruses that appalled me, but my certainty that some peculiar essence was also transmitted in this way. And if you had no defenses against this essence, it entered you, attached itself to your soul like a barnacle. Perhaps, ultimately, it possessed you, I didn't know. I didn't want to know. But I wasn't taking any chances.

When I finished washing up, I tossed the soap over my shoulder and dived underwater, washing the suds off. There is something undeniably sensuous about swimming at night, especially when your skin is squeaky-clean.

The tank suit was like not wearing anything at all. I could feel the chill of the water, its stroke against my skin, the way it held me. I could feel it like a weight between my legs.

Eddie's sloop wasn't far, a quarter of a mile if that. It hugged the curve of a shallow cove, a cove shallow enough for me to stand in. But I didn't stand. Couldn't. The bottom was a black, oozing muck, filthy muck but strangely soft.

I dreamed about that dirty softness sometimes, the same dream, images replaying themselves like memory. The dream always ended when I fell facedown into the muck and couldn't lift my head out of it. Couldn't breathe.

I swam faster toward the sloop, splashing now, my strokes harder. Then I felt the smooth wood of the ladder around my fingers and hauled myself up, breathing hard, noisily, blinking water from my lashes.

No lights on board. Not a sound. I was already chilled and rubbed my hands over my arms as I made my way toward the cabin door. It was open; Eddie said he usually keeps it open during the winter when the bugs are scarce.

I moved carefully down the steps to the cabin and stopped just inside the door. My eyes were already accustomed to the dark. I could make out the counter in the galley, the sink faucet, the fridge. I unbuckled the bag at my waist, dropped it on the counter, and stripped off my suit. I left it where it fell, molted skin at the threshold of my secret life, and made my way toward the bunk, my hands out in front of me like a blind woman's.

He was awake, he had probably heard the splash of the water, and moved over to make room for me on the narrow bunk. "Epa, chica," *he murmured.* "I knew you would come tonight."

"I didn't."

He pulled the damp sheet over us, a cocoon, and then his hands were everywhere, large, callused hands that scratched across my skin like sandpaper. Small, hot fires erupted on my body and he extinguished them with his mouth. His tongue swirled over my nipples, licking away the salt. It was warm and slightly rough, like a cat's, and as precise as a cat's. It darted, lingered, and inscribed what felt like letters against my belly, a little alphabet, a code that his thick, relentless fingers unlocked when they climbed inside me.

This man who knew nothing about G spots, who had probably never heard of The Joy of Sex *or Masters and Johnson, broke me down piece by piece until I was as wet and slippery as an eel. His body was wedged between my thighs, his hands were sliding under me, I could smell the earth in his sweat, the sea, the sun that had beat down against him today, the grass that he had cut, the bushes he had pruned. I could smell the dirt under his nails.*

He raised my hips, murmuring something in Spanish, and that was when I noticed her, the Wonder Woman tattoo. She quivered in the moonlight, danced, came alive. Her hair cascaded over her shoul-

ders like thick, shiny vines. Her arms unfolded from her body like wings. And at precisely the moment when he pushed into me, she lifted from his shoulder and flew off into the dark, her wings beating the air.

I knew then that she had been the owl that had watched me in the park, that hadn't moved because she didn't want me here. She was jealous of me; Eddie was hers.

"Tell me about the tattoo," I said later.

"Not much to tell."

"So tell me anyway."

Eddie was sitting back against the pillows, smoking. It was very dark in the cabin, the sky had clouded over, covering the moon. The end of his cigarette glowed in the dark, a bright, singular red eye. "Got drunk one night down in Miami with some Cuban dudes I knew and woke up with the wonder lady on my shoulder." The glowing red eye moved as he touched the tattoo. "Hated her at first. I felt like killing the asshole that did it. I'd asked for Madonna, a small Madonna, not something this big.

"But after a while, I don't know, there she was, looking back at me in the mirror when I shaved and I, like, started talking to her and shit. I figured we were stuck with each other. Now I'd feel like I was missing a hand or a leg or something if she wasn't there. Stupid, huh."

He sat forward and flicked the cigarette through the porthole. We both watched the red glow arc through the darkness until it struck the water.

"She have a name?" I asked.

"She's Wonder Woman, she doesn't need a name."

"That's what you call her when you talk to her?"

"Well, no, when I talk to her she's Gloria."

Gloria. He was into celebrities, Eddie was, but I could think of only two Glorias and I was pretty sure it wasn't Steinem. "You named her after Gloria Estefan?"

I felt him smile in the dark, pleased that I'd guessed. "You got it, chica.*"*

I went into the galley for my bag. I had an old spread draped around my shoulders because it was cool and damp inside the cabin. It didn't cover me completely and I could feel Eddie's eyes watching me. Eddie's and Wonder Woman's.

As I sat on the bunk again, he slipped his hands inside the spread and brought them up under my breasts. "I like these," he said, and I laughed and he grinned and closed his mouth over a nipple, nibbling at it.

My fingers slipped through the dark, springy hair on his chest, my eyes wanted to close, I wanted to lean into the wall behind me and float away. But it would be light soon. "I can't, Eddie. I've got to get going."

He lifted his head, his hands still against me. "You ever come like this? Just the tits?"

If I said no, he would insist on showing me and the sun would rise before I got out of here. If I said yes, he would want to show me he could do it better. Either way, it would take time. "I can't, Eddie, really." I moved away from him and unzipped the bag. "I still owe you some money." I counted out ten one hundred dollar bills.

He looked down at the money, then up at me, and lit another cigarette. "That dude I staked out."

"What about him?"

"What was his name again?"

"McCleary."

"Yeah, right. McCleary."

Another silence, then he said: "Read in the newspaper he got shot."

My throat tightened. "That's what I hear."

I knew he was waiting for me to say something, to explain. But no matter what I said the fact remained that I had paid Eddie two grand to find out McCleary's routine.

"So what was your business with him, chica? *What was I staking him out for?"*

"Like I told you, Eddie, his company owed me a refund for some work they'd done for me. The wife wouldn't talk to me about it, the check had been cashed, you know what I'm saying? I figured if I could talk to him alone, we could reach some sort of agreement."

"You never said whether you reached an agreement."

"Yes, we did."

I could feel him mulling this over. He flicked his second cigarette out the porthole and I leaned toward him, into the deep, thick odors of his skin. "C'mon, Eddie. It's me, okay?"

One of his large, powerful hands came up under my jaw, neither gentle nor rough, just firm, forcing me to look at him. "A while back, seventeen years ago, I was in a bar down in Texas. A dude came at me with a broken bottle, he was loaded, it was either him or me. I killed him. I couldn't afford no lawyer, they assigned me a dick of a public defender. He said to cop a plea, I told him no fuckin way, it was self-defense. So I sat in a piss hole of a jail for eight months, waiting for my trial.

"The white boy I killed wasn't trash, you know what I'm saying? But he'd been in trouble before, he was a general pain in the ass to everyone in town. So even though they nailed me for manslaughter, the judge only sentenced me to two and a half years, with credit for time I'd already served. With gain time I was out in thirteen months. But it was long enough. Kid of twenty grows up real fast in a piss hole like that.

"When I was sprung, I beat it from Texas fast. Never went back, never been in trouble since. And I want to keep it that way. So if you had something to do with this dude getting shot, I need to know about it. I'll just pack up this old boat and sail on outta here and leave you to your business."

"I told you what happened."

I ran my hand down his arm and after a moment felt the muscles loosening. But on his shoulder the tattoo quivered and Wonder Woman's pale blue eyes glared at me and I knew that she knew I was lying and that she was going to make sure that Eddie knew it, too.

14

Quin stood in the warm light waving at her sister's van as it pulled out of the driveway Sunday morning. Michelle, wedged in the back seat between her cousins, blew her a kiss. Quin pretended the kiss smacked her in the forehead and rocked back on her heels as if it had bowled her over. Michelle laughed, everyone waved, Hank honked, then the van turned out of the development.

Gone, just that fast.

She remained where she was, her head filling with only the worst scenarios: an accident on the interstate, Michelle lost at Ocean World, Michelle slipping at the edge of the dolphin tank and sinking like a penny. Guilt, she thought, this was guilt speaking. Once again Michelle had been adopted for the day, whisked off to some grand adventure with her cousins.

These were the times she would remember when she was older

and looking back. Disney World with Ricky and Rebecca, Ocean World, Sea World, all those Florida worlds. She would remember that her parents had equipped her with the basics, how to wash her hands and brush her teeth, but that it was her aunt and uncle who had coached her in the nuances of living.

Thoroughly depressed now, Quin walked back into the house. What might her life have been like if she and McCleary had met just out of college, before either of them had much of a personal history? Would the mutual chemistry that had drawn them together in their thirties have existed if they'd met in their twenties? The romantic in her wanted to think so, but the rest of her knew better.

They had met, she thought, at exactly the right juncture in their lives. If certain events had happened differently, thus speeding up or delaying that crossroad, they would not be married. They might know each other, they might even feel a kind of pressure in each other's presence, the phantom of that other life, those other selves. But they would not be married.

Maybe that could be said of most unions, that it was timing, not destiny or karma or whose moon fell in which house. Timing, pure and simple, just where you happened to be at a particular point in your route to wherever.

See, my dad got shot, Michelle would say to her therapist. *And my mom freaked out and that's when things started to go bad.*

Had she freaked? Was she freaking now? Freaking as she hugged her plump black cat and walked her dog and dressed for a brunch she really wasn't up to?

I'm coping, she thought, and believed it until she was on the road, eyes brimming with tears.

The Fish Shack was a funky little restaurant on the beach just north of Boca. It was about as a laid-back as you could get outside of the Keys: simple wooden tables, a floor covered with sawdust, no printed menu. It was Rita's choice for Sunday brunch.

Quin was early, naturally, she was always early, a trait that had begun to irritate her nearly as much as McCleary's chronic lateness. She waited at a table on the long deck that overlooked the beach, a perfect spot that would be unbearable when summer rolled around.

The hard-core sunbathers were already soaking up the rays, their beach chairs and coolers marking the areas they had claimed for the day. Quin watched a young couple strolling hand in hand along the water's edge, talking, laughing, pausing now and then to pick through shells. She envied their absolute absorption in each other and wondered if she and McCleary had lost that or simply misplaced it.

Sometimes she believed the marriage had been doomed since the beginning. Murder had brought them into each other's lives and had dogged them ever since. It had often blurred the fine line between their professional and personal lives and made her yearn for another profession.

Something safe like dentistry, for instance.

I knew you shouldn't have pulled Mr. Smith's wisdom teeth, Mac.

She broke open a warm roll from the basket the waiter had set on the table, nibbled at it, and watched the young couple charge into the surf. Waves broke over them. They went under, surfaced farther out, and embraced. Had McCleary felt like that with Callahan? Would she feel that way with Tark?

Did she want that to happen with Tark?

She didn't know. And not knowing disturbed her more than anything she had ever imagined about what had gone on between McCleary and Callahan.

Quin glanced away from the young lovers and saw Rita threading her way between the tables. She was dressed for a casual Sunday: jeans, a T-shirt, sandals. Slightly behind her was a slender woman who was about five and a half feet tall, with copper hair streaked with gray. Senator Colt. She looked as inconspicuous as a Cleveland housewife on vacation: sunglasses, black Levis, a black and white cotton blouse, and sandals.

Was there a certain etiquette to be observed when you met a senator? Was Ms. Colt, like the president, supposed to be addressed by her title? Should she stand? Bow? What?

But Rita set the mood when she introduced them by their first names, making it clear that formality had no place here. Sasha smiled warmly and shook Quin's hand. "It's a real pleasure to meet you. Rita has talked an awful lot about you and your husband. How's he doing?"

"Better, thanks."

Rita plucked a roll from the basket and passed it to Sasha. "I thought this would be the ideal place for the three of us to get together. None of the press people I know hang out here and neither do the local political heavies. Besides, Sasha and I are playing tourist this weekend."

"Actually, we're both playing hooky," Sasha said with a laugh, tilting her sunglasses back into her short copper hair. She was a rather ordinary-looking woman except for her eyes, which were large, expressive, the color of sunlit aluminum. "Twice a month or so we get together to work on the campaign."

"Work, ha. This isn't work," Rita said. "What we do, Quin, is go to the beach and brainstorm."

"Or we go fishing," Sasha said, buttering a roll. The only jewelry she wore was a simple gold wedding band. Her nails were short, painted with clear polish. "Well, actually, I fish and Rita watches."

Rita wrinkled her nose. "I can't stand to touch bait. It's so . . . so slimy."

"Lures aren't slimy, Rita."

"Yeah yeah yeah. But if I caught something, I'd have to cut the line. No way am I going to work a hook out of a squirming fish. Jesus, just the thought makes me queasy."

Sasha rolled her eyes and Quin laughed. They sounded like sisters who squabbled out of habit but who had long since accepted each other's differences.

"Never try to change Rita's mind when it's made up," Quin remarked.

Sasha nodded. "Don't I know it."

She slipped her sunglasses back on when the waiter came over to take their orders for drinks and to recite the day's specials. Once he'd left, Rita leaned toward Sasha. "Take my word for it. You don't need the shades, okay? No one who gives a damn comes here." Then to

Quin: "She was in Miami yesterday at the new tent city they've set up for hurricane victims. Six months and some of those people still don't have places to live. The press wouldn't leave her alone."

"It's not the press," Sasha said. "I just never know for sure when one of Barker's boys might be around and I'd rather he not have any inkling about this meeting."

"Then we should've met at your daughter's condo," Rita said. "Barker couldn't possibly know about it."

"He might. But it's too pretty a day to stay indoors."

Rita sighed with mock exasperation and shook her head. "You see what I have to put up with, Quin?"

"It sounds like a draw to me." She was still puzzling over the remark concerning "Barker's boys." "Oh, before I forget. Let me give this to you." She took a cassette tape from her purse and handed it to Rita. "This is a copy of John's conversation with Noel Unward." She hadn't made a copy yet of the tape she'd recorded at Christine Redman's.

"Fantastic. Thanks." Rita dropped the tape in her own purse. "We'll listen to it this afternoon. I've kept Sasha informed about all this, Quin."

And since one good turn deserves another, Quin said, "Then you won't mind telling me what's going on." She looked at Sasha. "Noel Unward seemed to think Alejandro is the real thing. Personally, I don't care one way or the other, but there's obviously more to this or you wouldn't be here."

"I think there's a great deal more to it," Sasha replied. "My office had gotten a number of complaints about Alejandro. Disgruntled customers, mostly, people who had gone to him in the hopes that he would make them well, had been pressured by Janis to donate to the organization, then felt ripped off when their medical problems didn't improve. I asked the state attorney's office to investigate.

"When they discovered that Lydia Holden was one of his clients, I became a little wary about the whole thing. I didn't want this to be construed as my launching a smear campaign against Barker. A psychic healer would put Lydia in the same category as Nancy Reagan after people found out about her astrologer. You see what I mean?"

Quin said, "Personally, I thought the astrologer bit humanized her."

"So did I," Sasha replied. "But, believe me, we're in the minority." She paused as the waiter brought their coffee, then sat forward, talking more softly. "Anyway, I just kept the information to myself. Then Janis was killed, Alejandro went into seclusion, and the state attorney's office suspended their investigation. Up to that point it was all pretty run-of-the-mill.

"A few weeks ago I discovered that Barker Holden has had me followed for the last six months, probably in the hopes of uncovering a few skeletons he can bring out right before the election. I don't like Barker. I know how that sounds since he's my opponent, but even if he weren't my opponent I still wouldn't like him. And it pissed me off that he'd had me followed."

"How do you know he's responsible?"

"Oh, I had a little chat with one of his hired hands in Georgetown who wasn't very discreet. Unfortunately, the guy knew only as much as he needed to know, which wasn't a hell of a lot. So I started doing a little digging of my own into Barker's background and found some interesting bits of information.

"After Barker sold his rights to Holden Cereals, he left the country for two years. It's pretty common knowledge that he was in the Orient, where he met his wife. But that was toward the end of the trip. Most of his first eighteen months were spent traveling back and forth behind the Iron Curtain." She shook her head. "It sounds so archaic now. The Iron Curtain, the Berlin Wall, the Cold War."

"He was just traveling?" Quin asked.

"No, not quite," said Rita, picking up the story. "Thanks to a few friends in high places, he was making the rounds of Soviet universities and research labs where the investigation of psychotronics was very serious business. That's what the Soviets called the investigation of psychic phenomena. Back then they poured enormous amounts of money into it in the hopes of finding a way to adapt psychic skills to warfare, spying, whatever."

"In other words, they were searching for a practical application of psychic ability," Sasha added. "Imagine having a trained group of good citizens who are able to spy by doing nothing more than shutting their eyes and focusing on the latitude and longitude coordinates they're given. That's just one example."

"Military uses?" Quin asked. "That's what the Soviets were after?"

"That seemed to be the government's primary thrust," Sasha replied. "But they were also experimenting with dowsers who could be trained to locate oil and minerals; with clairvoyants who might be trained to police the populace; with telepaths; with all the stuff we Westerners tend to call fiction. But this was a respected field of study in the Soviet Union.

"Anyway, Barker's primary interest seemed to be telekinesis, the ability to influence matter. That's what Alejandro, as you probably know, supposedly does when he heals."

"How'd you find out all this?"

"From a former Czech diplomat who met Barker while he was over there and who now lives in this country. He was Barker's escort through eight research centers. I had a friend in the State Department check Barker's passport records; they coincided roughly with the approximate dates the Czech had given me. Given all this, the real question is what the hell was Barker after?"

"I hope you have an answer."

"It's not that simple yet, but I have a theory or two." Sasha combed her fingers through her short copper hair, sat forward, back, forward again. She had obviously given this a great deal of thought and it seemed important to her to get it right. "I thought Barker had probably reached a crossroad in his life. He was burned-out on the perpetuation of his cereal empire and was looking for answers. He'd probably had an interest in this area and decided to indulge himself.

"But after a check of his passport records, I think he was interested long before he sold the company. There were three dozen trips to areas known for their healers—the Philippines, Brazil, Haiti. So in a sense he'd had his on-site education and the stint in the Soviet Union was the logical next step, to see if it was possible to apply these talents in a practical way."

"Why not investigate in this country?" Quin asked. "There're healers here."

"I think he probably did, then decided to expand his search."

The waiter brought their meals, and when they were alone again, Rita picked up the story. "Then along comes Alejandro, who's practically in Barker's backyard and who happens to be married to a Palm Beach girl—"

"Whom Holden had known for a long time," Quin interrupted. "Their families were chummy. Janis's ol' grandpappy sold Holden's ol' grandpappy the property their mansion sits on."

"In light of her murder, that *is* intriguing," Sasha remarked.

"And hardly surprising," said Rita. "I put nothing past Barker. His wife becomes Alejandro's patient, Barker gets to know him, they make sizable donations to the Domingo coffers. Then when the shit hits the fan with the state attorney's office, the Holdens are gone like the fucking wind and Barker gets all worried that Lydia's association with Alejandro is going to cost him votes. I don't buy it."

"He's rich, he apparently has some eccentric interests, so what? Nothing you've told me indicates that he's broken any laws," Quin said.

"That's what I said to myself," Sasha remarked. "But my curiosity was piqued, so I dug a little deeper. You probably already know that shortly after Janis's death, Alejandro sent his daughter and sister back to Chile. Their names appear on the flight roster, but according to my diplomatic sources in Santiago, Francesca and Miranda Domingo aren't in Chile. The family believes they're still here."

"Maybe your sources are wrong," Quin said.

"That's unlikely. My guess is that they never made it to the plane because they were abducted."

"And Barker Holden is responsible?"

The question wasn't addressed to one or the other, but Sasha answered. "We think it's a possibility. We also think it's possible that he believed your husband had figured out a little too much."

"But this guy's trying to win an election, not hang himself."

"Which makes it just that much more puzzling."

Rita spoke up. "Remember the source I mentioned at Link Research?"

"Zelda. Sure."

"Well, she went back to the company computer to see what else she could find out about Blue Pearl. Turns out it's an experiment that's been attracting three to four million a year in grants for Link during the last five years."

"For fifteen to twenty million it must be one hell of an experiment. What's entailed?"

"I don't know," Sasha replied.

"Are these government grants?"

"Not that I've been able to track down. It's probably private funding. Barker's funding, but I can't prove it. I think Alejandro is pivotal to it, but I can't prove that, either, and Alejandro isn't talking. Even worse, if Barker is behind it, I don't know what his motives are."

Disappearances, secret agendas, possible conspiracies. Quin's head began to ache. *You fuck with these people you end up like me,* Christine Redman had said. Which people? Eden White, who had tested her and Alejandro? Barker Holden, who might be financing an experiment at Link? Or some other faction?

But it seemed equally possible that Sasha Colt had her own agenda despite what Rita had said. After all, Barker Holden wanted her spot in the Senate and maybe she did intend to pull out Lydia Holden's dirty laundry. Maybe she knew more than she'd told Rita. And that was the problem, really, too many unanswered questions, too many maybes and what ifs.

She suspected where the conversation would be headed from here and wasn't sure how she would play it until Sasha spoke. "Even if Rita or I confronted Alejandro, it's unlikely he would confide in either of us since I was responsible for the investigation by the state attorney's office and Rita is working on my campaign. We need your help."

Yes siree, Quin thought. We all need help.

"I realize you're working for Fitz Eastman on this, Quin, and I'm not asking you to violate that confidence. But perhaps we can work together and find the answers twice as fast. I have resources that Eastman doesn't. I'll talk to him about it, but I wanted to speak to you first."

Fair enough. But until Quin knew more, she intended to keep the bulk of what she knew to herself.

≈

Moreno's sailboat, the *Rusted Nail*, was snuggled back in a cove sheltered by mangroves. This was the first time Tark had watched the sloop from the water: thirty-five feet of fiberglass, the cabin portholes clearly visible from here. He didn't know enough about boats to even venture a guess at what Moreno had paid for it, but he suspected it hadn't come cheaply.

Since it was Sunday and tourist season to boot, there was a lot of waterway traffic. No one paid any attention to him and Estelle; they were just a couple fishing from a Zodiac raft directly across from the cove. The raft was hers and she was seated at the front, a can of beer tilted to her mouth, a pole propped between her knees, a denim baseball cap tugged low over her forehead.

"Lots of action on board today," she said, tossing the empty can into the cooler.

"Popular guy, this Eddie Moreno."

Music blared from a boombox on deck, where a dozen or more people were having a fine ol' time and more were arriving by the minute. Men and women in pedal boats, in Zodiacs, in cigarette boats that emitted thick clouds of gray smoke.

"I think it's time we joined the party," she said, her head turned toward the cove. "We have enough brew here for an army, that'll make us popular, and who's going to know?"

Tark laughed and reached into the cooler. "Catch." He tossed her a beer, her arm flew up, and she caught the can without even looking. "It'll be a zoo."

"Shit, I work in a zoo." She reeled in her line. "Hit it, Gabby. I'm ready to party."

They followed another Zodiac into the cove and tied up on the starboard side. Hands helped them on board, each of them with a six-pack, and Estelle immediately started working the crowd. She didn't just do it well, he thought, she did it like a seasoned politician.

Every man on board either watched her or hit on her or both. There were certainly women who were better-looking, but she possessed a flamboyance that had an odd effect on men. That black hair, that laugh, that irreverence, the tight shorts, the brown legs, the bikini top, that hot Greek blood. It was like a scent that she radiated. She looked exotic. She looked forbidden.

Tark drank from his can and wandered toward the bow of the sloop, where he had seen Moreno. The party animals on board were Anglos and Latinos but otherwise weren't a particularly diverse lot. The men had longish hair and beer bellies. The women were usually younger than the men, in some cases much younger. They were the sort of women who rode on the backs of motorcycles not because they enjoyed it but because their men were wedded to their machinery.

"Hey, man, good to see you," one guy said over the blast from the boombox, slapping Tark on the back. "Didn't know you were in town."

Tark smiled and nodded, knowing he had never seen the man before in his life. He poked his head into the cabin, where two women were parking beers in a tub of ice. They were chattering away and didn't notice him, which gave Tark a chance to glance quickly around.

Moreno presumably kept business records of some sort, a list of customers, an account of who had paid him, who owed him. But Tark didn't see file cabinets or anything else where such records might be kept.

"You looking for someone?" asked one of the women.

"For Eddie."

"At the front."

"Thanks."

Moreno was at the bow of the boat, playing a raucous game of poker with three other men. He was taller than many Latins, five ten or so, and he was large—not fat, just large and solid. His skin was naturally dark and took well to the sun. His black hair was thick, short in front, long enough at the back to pull into a ponytail. He was good-looking in a raw, coarse way, husky and macho, and Tark didn't think he was Cuban. Ecuadorian, Mexican, Nicaraguan, maybe even Peruvian. Indian blood.

The lime-green tank top he wore with his swimming trunks showed off his musculature and the Wonder Woman tattoo that covered most of his right shoulder. Tight, springy black hairs covered his chest, arms, shoulders and sprouted from the backs of his hands and thick fingers.

Behind him was a huge trash bin that was filling rapidly with beer cans; in front of him was a pile of bills—ones, fives, tens, twenties. Moreno had obviously been winning big.

"I raise ten," he said, slapping a bill in the center.

"I'm outta here," replied the guy across from him. He dropped five low cards, grabbed a beer from the cooler next to him, and walked off.

"Chickenshit," Moreno said, laughing, and looked up. "C'mon, let's get someone else in here. We'll deal again."

Tark sat in the spot the other man had vacated. "Count me in. What's the ante?"

"Five," Moreno replied. "Ten's the limit on bets."

Tark pulled a five out of his wallet and dropped the bill in the center.

The guy to Tark's right shook his head. "I'm gone. I'll play at Rico's Thursday night when the ante's a buck."

"Anyone else?" Moreno shouted.

"Sure, I'll play." Estelle stepped forward and took the empty seat. From the pouch buckled at her waist she pulled out a fifty and asked for change. "Who's dealing?"

Moreno stared at her, his eyes fixed on a point between her breasts and her mouth. "I don't play poker with ladies."

Estelle laughed. "I'm not a lady. Let's raise the ante to ten with a twenty-buck limit on bets." Her eyes darted to Moreno. "You gonna give me some change or not?"

Moreno handed her five tens and dropped a twenty on the table. "I raise your ante and fifty's the limit on bets."

"Twenty it is." She made up the difference and looked at Tark. "What about you, Gabriel?"

"In." He dropped an additional ten and a five and hoped the first game didn't bust them.

"Me, too," said the man to Tark's left.

Estelle gathered up the cards, shuffled them like a Vegas dealer, put the deck in front of Moreno. "Ladies deal first, right? Seven-card stud."

Tark hit a full house on his first hand and won four hundred bucks. Moreno won three hundred on the next hand. Estelle took in seven hundred in the next two games, and in the fifth she and Moreno traded fifty-dollar raises until Tark and the other man dropped out on the fourth card.

When she raised the bet on her seventh card, Moreno called her. Tark guessed there was close to two grand in the pile.

"You don't want to raise me?" she asked.

"Shee-it. Just drop your fucking cards."

She flicked them out one by one: a ten, a jack, a queen, a king, an ace, all in diamonds.

Moreno slammed his cards face down. When he raised his eyes, they were glazed with booze, anger, humiliation. Estelle just opened her hands and shrugged as if to say, *Better luck next time, guy,* then reached to scoop up the bills. But one of Moreno's large, hairy hands slapped the center of the pile.

"Five-card stud. You and me. Double or nothing."

"No thanks." She pushed his hand away, started stuffing the bills in her bag, stood.

"No fucking way, bitch." He swayed on his feet as he grabbed her wrist. "We play again."

She was the wrong woman to bully. Moreno was too drunk to sense it, but the guy next to him wasn't. "Cut the crap, Eddie. She won fair."

Estelle, still smiling, said, "I think you'd better let go of my hand, asshole."

"Or what?" Moreno laughed. "Just what the fuck you going to do?"

"Jerk." Her left leg jackknifed and suddenly Moreno was flat on his back, gasping for air. "You're a piss-poor loser, Eddie. I hate poor losers." With that, Estelle walked off through the crowd.

Tark, barely able to contain his laughter, picked up the rest of the money and shoved it in the pockets of his shorts. He heard someone saying, "Breathe deep, Eddie, that's right, man, just take it easy. You ain't dyin, for shit's sakes."

Not yet, anyway, Tark thought.

When he climbed over the side of the sloop, Estelle was already in the Zodiac, its puny outboard idling. She winked at him and he grinned and dropped inside.

"Hey," he said, as they chugged out of the cove. "When're you going to teach me that trick?"

"Whenever you're ready to teach me some of yours."

He laughed and they headed back across the water.

≈

Several minutes before three that Sunday afternoon, McCleary walked down to the sun room on the seventh floor. The cops who stood guard outside his room were accustomed by now to his numerous treks through the halls and didn't accompany him.

As always, he was winded when he reached the sun room and mildly depressed that he was unable to complete the walk in less time than it had once taken him to run two miles. Sharp, bright stabs of pain in his back and chest forced him to sit down.

From a pocket in his robe he removed the note Alejandro had scribbled in the Bible and read it through again. McCleary had run across it by accident only this morning, when he'd been going through the nightstand drawer looking for a pen. The cop Alejandro had given it to apparently had left it in the room when McCleary wasn't around, and one of the nurses had probably put it in the drawer. He had called Alejandro's house early this morning and, with Alejandro asking the questions and McCleary grunting in code, they had agreed to meet at the elevators at three.

The Chilean stepped off the elevator several minutes after three, saw McCleary in the sun room, and came right over. He shook McCleary's hand and spoke in Spanish. "I feel I am partially responsible for this."

McCleary shook his head and motioned toward a nearby chair, inviting Alejandro to sit down. Give me answers, he thought. But Alejandro glanced around, then said, "Is there anywhere else we can go where we won't be interrupted for a few minutes?"

McCleary thought a moment, then nodded, and they headed up the hall to a vacant room. "When I didn't hear from you, I figured

you hadn't gotten the Bible or hadn't seen the note in the front,"
Alejandro said as he shut the door. "I was reluctant to try to see you
again, for fear it would be a risk to you. It may still be a risk. But I
feel I owe you this much." He pulled a chair over to the window.
"Sit down, my friend, and let's see if I can help you."

Once McCleary was seated, Alejandro stood behind him. He
rubbed his hands together hard and fast, then moved them inches
above McCleary's head and shoulders. His breathing pattern
changed. A fierce heat radiated from his palms. He didn't say anything, but from time to time he touched McCleary—on the crown of
the head, the temples, the back of the neck, the throat. Then he
moved his hands down through the air over McCleary's chest and
back and around his arms.

The first thing McCleary felt was a lessening of the pain in the
deeper, still traumatized muscles in his chest. He found he could
breathe more easily, think more clearly. A sense of well-being came
over him and spread through him like liquid. He shut his eyes, surrendering himself to it.

He had spoken to enough of Alejandro's patients to know that
the experience wasn't the same for everybody. There appeared to be
no fixed pattern, nothing predictable. Some people had reported that
they hadn't felt anything. McCleary definitely felt something, but he
couldn't have said exactly what it was. An infusion of energy, deep
relaxation, both, neither, something else altogether.

They were interrupted by a nurse, who asked them in a rather
chilly voice to please use the sun room. McCleary still couldn't speak
in a way that made sense, but something inside of him felt altered
somehow. It was like trying to describe some subtle shift or nuance
in emotion.

As they left the room, McCleary spotted one of cops striding up
the hall. Alejandro saw him, too. "I'd rather not be seen here. But
once you're out of the hospital, we'll work together again." Then he
grasped McCleary's hand in both of his and hurried toward the stairs.

I cruised past the row of condos on Delray Beach where Eddie would begin work in fifteen minutes or so. It was 5:30 Monday; he liked to start his days early and finish early.

I parked parallel to the canal on the other side of the street, where the trees were low and full. The monstrous building directly across from me was ten stories of concrete shaped like a quarter moon, with the inner curve facing the Atlantic. The cheapest condo went for more than a quarter of a million, a cramped box that offered nothing but a side view of the ocean.

It sat high on a man-made mound trimmed in flowers that Eddie would weed. He would trim the carpet of grass to a crew cut. For a self-employed lawn guy like Eddie, these condo contracts were probably his mainstay, steady and lucrative.

He showed up right on time. His truck clattered to a stop along-

side the road, dispersing the tendrils of fog that snaked over the asphalt. A heavier fog rolled in from the ocean, drifting like steam or smoke from between the buildings and across the road. It would burn off as soon as the sun rose and the air warmed up. But I liked the mood it created, the fog behind him as he got out of the truck, a dark, mysterious stranger who had blown into town with trouble in mind.

He held a cup in one hand, coffee probably, and manual hedge trimmers in the other. He wouldn't mount his noisy mower until later in the morning, when most of the residents were sure to be awake or gone.

Despite the brisk air, Eddie wore just a tank top and jeans. I was too far away to see Wonder Woman but realized she was the reason I was here. I needed to peer into her face, find out what she had told Eddie, get a better sense of her game.

He stood outside his truck for a few minutes, finishing his coffee, enjoying the solitude. But he doesn't miss much; if there's something out of place in his environment he notices it. Even though I was parked under a row of pines two doors down and across the road, he noticed my car rather quickly.

He crumpled his coffee cup, tossed it into the back of his truck with his equipment, and lit a cigarette. Then he started toward me. I unlocked the doors and he climbed in the passenger side. The air immediately filled with the smell of him: grass, earth, wind, all of it mingling with the scent of the smoke, an aphrodisiac.

His dark, smoldering eyes took in all of me, then he cracked the window and flicked out his cigarette. "Kinda warm for a leather jacket," he said.

It was fifty-six degrees outside. "Sort of brisk for a tank top."

"If you're so cold, why don't you wear something that covers your legs?"

"I don't feel like it, that's why."

I couldn't wrench my gaze from the tattoo. Wonder Woman— Gloria, I reminded myself, that was her name—looked different somehow; she had changed since I'd seen him last. Maybe it was her eyes, which seemed larger, brighter, more mocking. Or the arrogant tilt of her head. Or just the brazen way she stared at me. I suddenly understood just how dangerous she was.

"*Wonder lady must like fresh air, huh.*"

He smiled and rubbed his callused palms over his jeans. "*Yeah, I guess. So what's going on, chica?*"

I began unbuttoning my jacket and moved closer to him. "*I felt bad about the way we left things the other night.*"

"*What things?*"

Like he had no idea what I was talking about. "*That I couldn't stay.*"

He shrugged. "*You do what you gotta do.*" A line he'd probably heard in a movie. "*And tonight's no good. I got a poker game. Got to make up the money I lost yesterday. If I hadn't been drinkin, I could've beat this bitch.*"

A poker game, a tub of beer, loud music, women in string bikinis: I could see it, see the details of Eddie's weekend life, and a kind of shock rippled through me. I knew he had such a life, of course, but I had never thought of it closely. Eddie with friends, Eddie with poker buddies, Eddie drinking too much and boasting about the gringa who came to him in the dead of night.

Wonder Woman winked at me. I could barely speak around the lump of fear in my throat. "*How much did you lose?*"

"*Too much. She walked with all of it. She and this tall dude she came with. You shoulda seen this guy, tall and tough, hardly said a word. I thought he and the bitch were friends of someone on board, but it turns out no one knew them.*"

Tall and tough: that nagged at me. No reason it should have, but it did.

Eddie suddenly started to laugh and closed his hands over the lapels of my coat, which was completely unbuttoned now. He flipped it open. I wasn't wearing anything under it. "*You're crazy,*" he said, staring at me. "*People get arrested for shit like this.*"

I had lost interest in seducing him now; I wanted to think about the tall guy. But when I tried to pull the coat shut, Eddie's hands were already inside of it; his mouth was at my throat, his cheek scratched across my collarbone, my breasts, he was angling my body back against the seat.

I knew if I pushed him away as I had the other night, that would be it, he would cut me off. I would lose whatever hold I had over

*him, and at the poker game tonight or next week the boast about the
gringa might include a name.*

It was too late to say no.

*His tongue was in my mouth, the taste of smoke and grass choked
me, and Wonder Woman was right there in my face, laughing silently.
The upper part of her body peeled away from his shoulder and she
flopped forward at the waist like a paper cutout, giggling hysterically.*

*I pressed my hand over her, she squirmed against my palm as if
trying to burrow into my flesh, and I sank my nails into her. Eddie
didn't understand, didn't know the tattoo was a living thing, a jealous
woman who intended to claim me, possess me, find her way into the
world of the living through me. He thought I was trying to hold him
off because I wasn't ready.*

*"C'mon, c'mon, c'mon," he said hoarsely, impatiently, trying to
position himself between my legs.*

*He gripped my hips, trapping me against the seat, and I lost my
hold on the tattoo. But I could still see her, only her feet anchored
now against his upper arm, her own arms lifted as though she were
about to take flight. Then he hunched over me and she vanished from
view and I felt a dark, wild panic.*

*I grabbed his hair, trying to make him straighten up so that I
could see her, I was afraid she was somehow going to free herself
from him and make her way into me. But Eddie wouldn't budge. His
mouth was fastened to me, his tongue was burrowing inside of me,
and I knew then, I knew, what her plan was.*

*I screamed, a low, muffled scream, and lurched forward with a
strength that shocked me more than it did Eddie. He fell sideways
into the dashboard. I scrambled back behind the steering wheel,
fumbling with the buttons on the coat, my gasps like hiccups.*

*Shower, I thought. Fast. A hot, stinging shower, steel wool, Lysol,
bleach, whatever it took to get rid of her phantom touch on my skin.*

*I didn't think she'd gotten inside me, but I couldn't be sure. She
might be wiggling into my skin at this very second, buttoning herself
into my bones, breathing through my lungs, trying me on for size.*

*Eddie was shouting at me in Spanish, words spewing from his
mouth, his face contorted with rage. Then he threw open the door
and leaped out and slammed it so hard the windows rattled.*

I screamed at him, screamed that he didn't understand, but he pretended he didn't hear me. He sprinted across the road and through the fog, toward the now pale sky. I started the car and screeched away from the curb. I thought of possession, of zombies, of hauntings. I thought of Navajo skinwalkers that worm their way inside you and invade your dreams, claiming you bit by painful bit until you die. I felt her crawling around under my skin and I sobbed, I prayed for a sign.

It came later, after I had showered, scrubbed, and gobbled a handful of vitamins and antibiotics. It came, the sign, while I was brooding over Janis's pillowcase, trying to divine the meaning in the random arrangement of bloodstains. The man who had been on Eddie's boat playing poker, the tall, tough guy, was Tark.

Somehow Tark had found out about Eddie. And if he knew, so did Quin.

The only way that could have happened was if Eddie had told someone he'd been hired to stake out McCleary's house. That was the moment when everything changed.

15

When the phone rang at seven Monday morning, Quin had just stepped out of the shower. She grabbed a towel and ducked into the den to take the call, certain it was Eastman with information on the photos Tark had turned over to him.

"Mrs. McCleary, please." A slightly accented male voice.

"Speaking."

"If you're interested in the truth about Alejandro Domingo, he will be at the Campo Alegre migrant camp tomorrow night at seven-thirty. It's four miles west of Belle Glade. The gate will be open."

Before she could reply, the man hung up. Campo Alegre: Happy Fields. It sounded like a mental institution, not a migrant camp. She phoned Eastman and told him about the call. "I think it's worth checking out the migrant camp, Fitz."

"Yeah, I agree. Take John with you. I'd go with you myself, but I've got a briefing I can't miss."

"A briefing on this case?"

"Indirectly. I'm catching some shit about what it's costing the department to keep Mike under surveillance. I'm hoping I can hold the captain off until Mike's sprung at the end of the week. But if I can't, he's probably going to remove the cops and tell me to send Mike to a safe house."

"I don't think he'll go."

"You need to talk him into it, Quin."

"What makes you think he listens to me?"

"He'd better listen to someone."

"I'll do my best, but don't hold your breath, Fitz. Oh, before I forget. You have anything yet on those pictures John gave you? Of Holden, White, and the other guy?"

Caution crept into Eastman's voice. "I'm working on it. We'll talk about it when I see you. One of you call me when you get back from Belle Glade tomorrow night."

Her last call was to her sister, asking if she could keep Michelle for a while tomorrow night. Again. She hated to ask, felt guilty about it, but short of taking Michelle with her or finding a sitter on such short notice, she didn't have much choice. Ellen was as gracious about it as usual and asked if Michelle could go with them to the Keys that weekend for three or four days. "We thought you and Mac might like some time alone when he's released."

Disney World six months ago, the Keys this weekend, and where six months from now? Europe? Australia? The Far East? "I'll let you know, Ellen. I appreciate the offer."

Appreciated it even though her daughter would grow up believing Ellen and Hank and their kids were her family, that their house was her home.

The shop on Worth Avenue was called Lydia's Place, a rather homey name that made Quin think of old-fashioned ice cream parlors. The dark blue awning over the picture window shaded a pair of round metal tables and matching chairs. One of them was occupied by an aging matron, decked out in silk and gold, and her white poodle. The woman was sipping coffee from a delicate china cup, the poodle was lapping the stuff from the saucer.

Inside, the place was tremendous, much larger than it looked from the street. The shiny wooden floor was broken up by Persian carpets that seemed to float like colorful islands against the sea of wood. Vases made from every conceivable material and in a variety of shapes stood in the soft, muted light, watchful and grand. There were animals of copper, brass, jade, and silver; chess sets carved of lapis lazuli; china figurines. The merchandise hailed from Chile to Curaçao, from Thailand to Trinidad, and all of it was lovely. But you would have to live in a palace or a mausoleum to own it and forget about having kids. An exuberant toddler could demolish this place in seconds flat.

Five well-dressed young women were waiting on customers, a sixth was ringing up a sale and eyeing Quin as though she might be a potential shoplifter. She stepped just inside the doorway of a second, smaller room.

Mirrored walls and a mirrored ceiling reflected what was surely a fortune in exotic imports. Gold snakes with ruby and sapphire eyes, an emerald frog the size of her hand, a doll's house carved from jade, lamps with shades studded in pearls: those were the items that immediately leaped out at her. Everything was locked away under glass, only one of each item and none of it with a visible price tag.

"May I help you with something?" asked a cultured, familiar voice behind her.

Quin turned and the crooked smile on Lydia Holden's face strained to remain in place. She was shorter than Quin and had to look up at her. "Quin, nice to see you."

As if it had been weeks since the lunch at Chéri's. "Hi. John was right about your shop, Lydia. It's beautiful. Do you do all the buying yourself?"

"I used to do a lot of it, but since Barker's campaign got under way, I've only taken one trip." She slipped her hands into the pockets of her silk skirt and her eyes moved slowly around the room, pausing here, there, as if this were the first time she had really looked at everything. "Two of my employees do the bulk of the buying now."

"Are you going to keep it if Barker wins the election?"

Lydia seemed genuinely puzzled by the question. "Why wouldn't I?"

"I figured you'd move to D.C."

As soon as Quin said it, she realized how pedestrian it sounded and how limited her own vision was. People like the Holdens owned multiple homes staffed year-round by employees and they traveled among them on their chartered jets and their yachts and in their chauffeured limos. They had a fleet of accountants, attorneys, and money managers. They dined with presidents, with heads of state. They flew to Zurich for breakfast.

They were, in the truest sense of the word, the power elite in this country, the royalty, and many of them probably believed they were above the law because much of the time they were. After all, if Ted Kennedy wasn't who he was, he might have done time for Chappaquiddick. If Nixon had been anyone other than the president, he would have done time for Watergate. Whatever justice there was in the judicial system occurred at much lower economic levels.

It wasn't as if any of this was really new to her, but she had never perceived it in quite this way, with a member of the elite standing in front of her.

"I detest D.C.," Lydia was saying. "And Georgetown is right out of *The Stepford Wives*. Everyone's the same. You have a bunch of clones running around loose."

That description might also fit Palm Beach.

"So were you looking for anything in particular?"

Quin laughed. "Sure." She couldn't tell if Lydia was being snide, sarcastic, or whether she actually believed Quin would find something in here that fell within her price range. With luck, she might be able to afford a paper clip. "That emerald frog would do nicely."

"Good choice. Colombian emeralds are among the finest in the world." She walked over to the case that held the frog, took a small device from her pocket, and punched in a three-digit code. The door of the case popped open and she reached inside for the frog.

The figure was a quarter of the size of her palm, an exquisite sculpture, a breathtaking green. "The clearer the emerald and the deeper the green, the better the quality."

"Then this must be at the top of the line."

"They don't get any greener than this."

Quin suddenly knew that Lydia was referring to her, not to the color of the frog, and there weren't many things that pissed her off more than being dismissed as a flake. "How much?" she asked.

Lydia pretended to think about it, enjoying the game. "I'd let it go for two fifteen."

As in $215,000. "Sold." Quin reached into her purse. "You take personal checks?"

She believed it, Quin could see it in her face. A trust fund, a recent inheritance, no telling where she thought the money came from. Then Quin laughed, and after a moment so did Lydia, but with a certain restraint.

"You almost had me fooled," she said, still smiling.

"Was Janis having an affair with Barker, Lydia?"

The ha-ha-aren't-you-a-riot routine flew straight out the window. Lydia looked as though she had swallowed a bowling ball. To her credit, it didn't take her long to recover and move on. She drew herself up to her full five foot four or five and snapped, "You've got a lot of nerve asking me a question like that. Just who the hell do you think you are?"

"Hey, it was just a question."

"Get out of my store."

She walked off and Quin stared at her receding back, at her firm, slender hips, at the indignant swing of her arms. Fuck you, she thought, and went after her. Quin grabbed her upper arm and spun her around. Lydia was so surprised she just stood there with her mouth open.

"Let me put it this way. Janis either screwed your husband or she didn't, and if this were a routine case I wouldn't give a damn one way or another. But my life has been kicked in the ass because someone killed Janis. So when I find out who did it, Lydia, and I definitely *will* find out, that person is going to wish I'd never been born."

Quin released her arm and left, anger slamming around inside her. She crossed the street to the Esplanade, a Spanish-style shopping arcade, and ducked into an espresso shop that faced Lydia's Place.

She bought a double cappuccino and a pastry and sat at a window table, watching the shop for more than an hour.

Lydia didn't leave, but her husband dropped by. He arrived alone, on foot, and several moments after he'd gone inside, a dark Lincoln pulled into the alley between Lydia's store and the shop next door. The driver got out and slapped a police bubble on the roof of the Lincoln. Quin recognized him as the mystery man in the photo of Holden and his two college buddies. His hair was thick and gray, he wore a dark gray suit.

He went next door to the ice cream shop and settled at one of the sidewalk tables, licking his cone like a teenager. Another man joined him, a guy with sandy hair and a beard who was wearing wire-rim sunglasses, chinos, and a guayabera shirt. They spoke briefly, then the second man darted across the street and headed in her direction.

Quin had a sudden premonition that Lydia had known all along where she was and had called Holden about it. Or maybe she'd called Holden to accuse him of screwing Alejandro's wife. Either way, the guy in the wire-rims was the end result and she wasn't in the mood for a chat.

She grabbed her purse and ducked out of the espresso shop, into the stream of shoppers. But she wasn't fast enough. The guy in the wire-rims spotted her and started after her. Quin hurried through the crowd, bumping into women with bulging shopping bags and men with golf-course tans. She ran up the stairs to the second floor of shops and the man was right behind her.

A purse shop, a shoe shop, a maternity shop—she flew past them all and into B. Dalton. It was quiet inside. Hardbacks were stacked from the floor to the ceiling on shelves that divided the place into an intricate maze and she threaded through them, darting up and down aisles. She finally stopped in the children's section.

She sat in a munchkin-size chair next to a cute little girl who was maybe four years old and opened one of the books scattered across the munchkin-size table. *The Three Little Pigs*, pop-up style. Her back faced the door. She dug a scarf out of her purse and tied it over her hair. She stripped off her jacket and wadded it up in her lap. Then she rested her arm along the back of the little girl's chair.

"Will you read me that story?" the little girl asked.

"You bet," Quin said, and read it without hearing a word.

She sensed the man's presence when he entered the store. She felt him moving through the aisles, pausing here, there, browsing through books that he picked randomly from the shelves. She knew the instant his roaming eyes zeroed in on her and leaned toward the girl and whispered, "You'd better go find your mommy."

The girl said okay and wandered off. Quin gathered up the children's books with one hand and slipped the other into her purse. Where her 9mm was. She flicked off the safety and kept the gun hidden under her jacket.

"I hate to repeat myself, Mrs. McCleary," the man said, turning one of the pint-size chairs and straddling it. He was smiling pleasantly, a rather ordinary-looking man who kept poking at his wire-rims, nudging them farther up the bridge of his nose. He was close enough for her to see the gray threaded in his beard. "So I'm only going to say this once. Mr. Holden is a senatorial candidate who has cooperated fully with the police on a homicide investigation. If you or your employees continue to harass him or his wife, he will be forced to seek a restraining order against you. Do I make myself clear, Mrs. McCleary?"

"Who're you, the family butler?"

He reached into the pocket of his chinos, pulled out his wallet, flipped it open. The badge read BOB CLARION, U.S. MARSHAL. "Have a nice day, Mrs. McCleary." And he got up, still smiling, and walked away.

≈

McCleary was surprised when Quin breezed into his room at two that afternoon. He was sitting in the chair near the window, his speech therapist's notebook computer on his lap.

"You can write?" she exclaimed.

"Catch the wings." He turned the computer so that she could see the screen, the baby words, the little tests he continued to fail.

Her disappointment was palpable. "Well, it'll happen." She set her briefcase on the bed, snapped it open. As she moved things around inside, searching for something, she told him about her visit with Lydia Holden. "She bothers me, Mac. I mean, suppose Barker *was* having an affair with Janis and she knew about it and gave him an ultimatum to break it off or she'd divorce him. Barker couldn't afford a big divorce scandal in the middle of his campaign, so he agreed to break it off with Janis.

"Then Janis gets killed. Lydia thinks Barker did it, right? So she can't tell anyone that he and Janis were involved with each other because there's the motive."

McCleary rapped his knuckles against the armrest to get her attention. With his thumb and index finger he made an *L*. Once again, Quin understood what he was trying to say.

"Yeah, that occurred to me, too. That Lydia found out about their affair and killed Janis herself. Supposedly they were all at the Breakers that night. But there were four hundred people at that wedding reception and she could have slipped away for a while without being missed. So could Barker, for that matter. So could anyone."

She removed a stack of construction paper from the briefcase, set it to one side, and brought out a small corkboard. The details of the investigation were scribbled on index cards arranged according to what they knew and what they only suspected. As she talked, she began to move the cards around.

"Even though I think it's entirely possible that Lydia killed Janis, I have a few problems with it. They were friends and had been for a long time."

So what? McCleary thought, and shook his head.

"I know, I know," Quin said. "Maybe the friendship didn't mean squat. But if she killed Janis, then the chances are pretty good that she also shot you. We agree on that, right? That we're looking for one person here?"

Probably, but he wasn't certain; he shrugged.

"Okay, for the moment we'll assume one person. And, frankly, I just can't see Lydia cruising outside our development and taking a shot at you. If she hired this Moreno fellow to do it, then it's a little more believable. Moreno turns around and hires Harry Rimalto to keep an eye on you, to nail down your routine.

"But then I run into a problem again, Mac. If Lydia *did* hire Moreno to shoot you, then maybe she also hired him to kill Janis, and that means she can't afford to let Moreno live. But he's still walking around. John and Estelle crashed a poker game on his boat yesterday. Moreno was drunk and obnoxious, but John says he's no killer."

And he ought to know, McCleary thought.

"Then there's Eden White," Quin went on. "Janis messed up her research by not allowing her to observe Alejandro. If he was pivotal to something her company's trying to develop, that would qualify as a motive."

Eden, the Holdens, Moreno, jealousy, subterfuge, bitter passions, take your pick, he thought. "Dingbats." He started to rearrange the index cards in an attempt to communicate that the key fit a locker at the gym. The cards didn't contain all the words he needed, but even if they had, it wouldn't have made much difference. Somewhere between his brain and his hand, the message broke down.

Quin finally said, "We'll come up with something better, Mac. Don't worry about it."

As she returned the cards to their original positions, he realized that she looked different from his memory of her, although he couldn't say exactly what the difference was. It was as if the days he'd spent here had interfered with his mental picture of Quin, altered it somehow. Or perhaps her appearance had actually changed, molecules and cells rearranging themselves daily as he waited, his life in suspended animation.

He reached for her hand and ran his thumb over the knobby hills of knuckles, the perfect juncture of joints, the rounded half moons of her painted nails. The topography was as familiar to him as his own skin. And yet.

"What?" she asked, and he raised his eyes, searching her face for some hint of what he was trying to communicate. Then she suddenly slipped her arms around him. "Things have got to change, Mac." Her voice was quiet, her mouth close to his ear. "I can't keep living like this. I don't want to keep living like this."

He buried his face in her hair. He didn't recognize the scent of the shampoo she had used this morning, a vanilla scent, rich and sweet. It, like the changes in her appearance, hinted at some invisible shift in their lives. But as his hands moved over her back, against the fabric of her shirt, he found the familiar steps of her spine, the indentation of her waist, the ridges of her ribs. Her body hadn't changed; it was precisely as he remembered it, tight and compact and soft in the right places.

She drew back, looking at him, and suddenly laughed. "Uh-huh. You're definitely on the mend."

He unfastened two of the lower buttons on her shirt and slipped his hands inside. She wasn't wearing a bra and her skin was just as cool as he remembered, except for the heat of her nipple, a point of sunlight against his palm. She giggled like a teenager and said he was nuts, someone would come in, and stepped back. Her hip hit the edge of the table and the corkboard slipped to the floor, knocking loose the tacks that held some of the cards in place.

"Shit," she muttered.

They knelt at the same moment and began picking them up. Without looking at him she said, "You've got to go to a safe house when you're released, Mac. If you don't, I'm going to send Ellie to the Keys with my sister."

"Lighten up," he spat, and didn't realize what he'd said until her head snapped up.

"You spoke."

"Blackbirds singing." Gone, Christ, just that fast it was gone. He didn't know what shocked him more, that he had actually said something that made sense or that she had issued an ultimatum about Michelle as though she alone had the right to make decisions about their daughter's life. He literally saw red. He went to the door, opened it all the way, stabbed a thumb at the hall. *Hit the road, Quin. Pound sand.* "In the dead of night."

She glared at him, then tossed the remaining cards into her purse, slammed the corkboard shut, dropped it into her briefcase, and marched past him, her face bright with rage.

≈

Quin drove to assuage her anger, to tame it. She had no destination in mind but wasn't surprised when she ended up in front of the Breakers. And since she was there, she set her odometer, noted the time, and drove as far as the dirt road that led to Alejandro's ranch.

She stopped alongside the fence that bordered his property to the south and lowered the window. The air had warmed since this morning and smelled of the surrounding fields, of clover and wilderness. She checked the odometer and the time.

With less traffic and maintaining a speed of at least sixty, Janis's killer probably would have made it to the ranch in half an hour. An hour round-trip. How long had the killer spent in the house? Five minutes? Ten? Long enough, she thought, to remove the case from the pillow and wipe away fingerprints. At the most then, Lydia or Holden had been absent from the reception for an hour and a half.

But how had the killer known that Janis hadn't gone to the reception? That she was in the house alone? Had the killer watched the house first? The reception had started right after the wedding, eight or so, and Holden had said that he and Lydia had gotten there between eight and eight-thirty. If that was true, then one of them had driven to Janis's sometime after that, killed her, and then returned to the reception.

Quin drove on to Alejandro's, swung through the gate, and parked next to his dead wife's Porsche. No one answered the door. There were no cars parked in front of the garage apartment where Carmelita lived. Quin walked around to the side of the house where the pool was and saw Alejandro swimming underwater.

She waited through ten laps in which he didn't come up for air, ten laps from end to end, a distance of twenty-five or thirty yards per lap. She grew short of breath just watching him and finally crouched at the edge of the pool and shouted his name. His head broke the surface, he sucked at the air, blinked against the light. "Mrs. McCleary."

"Sorry to just barge in like this, Señor Domingo. Do you have a few minutes?"

"Sure."

But as he got out and grabbed his towel from a chair, she noticed that he seemed uneasy. His eyes swept through the yard and the road beyond it, then paused briefly on the driveway. "I didn't realize Carmelita wasn't back yet. She's out running errands."

They sat at a table with an umbrella poking up from the middle of it. She was tempted to ask him what he would be doing at the migrant camp tomorrow night, but the answer was obvious. He would be healing. She decided to hold that one in abeyance for a while.

"What can I do for you, Mrs. McCleary?"

"Quin, okay? The Mrs. makes me feel old."

He laughed and rubbed his wet hair with the towel. "And I'm Alex."

"Look, I know John Tark has already asked you about this and I'm not sure how to put it without offending you."

"I don't offend very easily anymore. Just say it."

"I think it's likely that your wife was having an affair with someone and that may be why she was killed."

He looked down at the towel in his lap and smoothed his hand over it. A beautiful hand, she thought, large and yet delicately sculpted. Long fingers, short, neatly clipped nails. These hands might have been those of a pianist or an artist, hands that produced something she could see or touch or hear.

"I found some notes," he said softly. "From her lover. I don't know who he was."

"How about Barker Holden?"

"Barker's actually the first one I thought of. They'd known each other for years and I always suspected they may have been lovers at some point."

"Did you ever mention it?"

"Only once. She just made a face and said Barker had never been her type. A smart thing to say, I guess, if she'd been sleeping with him at the time. My wife was a clever woman. I've only recently begun to realize just how clever."

"The night of the wedding reception. Do you remember when you first saw Barker and Lydia?"

He thought about it, then shook his head. "He was with a group of us having drinks out at the pool. But I don't remember if it was the first time I'd seen him that night. Lydia and I danced a few times. She said Barker had two left feet. That's all I remember about Lydia that night."

"I had lunch with Senator Colt the other day. She says Barker hired someone to follow her, to dig up dirt on her that he could use against her."

Alejandro shrugged. "I know very little about how Barker conducts his political business. But I do know that he considers me a political liability. And if he and Janis were lovers, then she was probably a liability as well."

"How do you think Lydia would have reacted if she'd known he was having an affair?"

"I don't know." He draped the towel around his shoulders and tilted his head back, gazing into the underbelly of the blue sky. "Lydia is completely unpredictable in everything."

"Did you know that Eden White and Barker knew each other at Harvard?"

"I didn't know, but it doesn't surprise me. All these people seem to have histories with one another."

"There's a third person, too. Bob Clarion. He's a U.S. marshal." She told him what had happened earlier that day when she was watching Lydia's shop. "Anyway, this Bob Clarion fellow told me if I continued to harass the Holdens, they would get a restraining order against me."

"What'd he look like?"

Quin described him, but Alejandro just shook his head. "I don't think I've seen him."

"Senator Colt brought up something else, Alejandro. She said your sister and daughter aren't in Chile. She checked with her diplomatic sources."

"But that's absurd!" he exclaimed. "I speak to them once a week. They take the ferry to Puerto Montt and call from the phone office. Her sources are wrong."

Quin detected nothing insincere in his voice or his expression. "She says her sources can't be wrong."

"They are." He was watching a plump black cat stalking something at the edge of the pool at the deep end.

"Yours?" she asked.

"My daughter's. Neruda. He used to divide his nights between Miranda's bed and a spot near my wife's head. With both of them gone, he's been out of sorts."

Cats, a commonality. "One of my cats looks exactly like him. Was he inside the night your wife was killed?"

"When I opened the door, he was licking her face and mewing pitifully. For several days afterward he refused to eat. He went into mourning."

They sat silently for a few moments, watching Neruda until he darted off into the trees. "I was counting the laps you swam underwater. I got up to ten and started getting worried. How many can you do?"

"It depends on how fast I swim. At rest, I can hold my breath for about four minutes."

"You sit on nails, too? Like those Eastern yogis?"

"No nails." He laughed.

"Does your physical condition affect your ability to heal?"

"It seems to. I have more energy. And energy is what I work with when I heal. When I'm feeling good, I have more control over my autonomic nervous system, which allows me to work for longer periods of time without tiring."

"Give me an example."

"To one degree or another I can exert control over my blood pressure, pulse, the rise and fall of my blood sugar."

"So you have a biofeedback machine built into you."

"I guess it's similar. You're very inquisitive."

"This stuff fascinates me."

"Healing?"

"Healing, telepathy, precognition, all of it."

"May I have your hand?" he asked.

She stretched out her arm and he took her hand, his long fingers closing around it. His hand was as warm as beach sand, the skin slightly callused. His thumb slipped over her knuckles a couple of times, then he rubbed his hands together vigorously for a moment and took her hand again. It was uncomfortably warm now. His breathing sought a new rhythm, settled into it; she realized it matched the rhythm of her own.

"Incipient arthritis in the right clavicle would benefit from an increase in the body's intake of vitamin C and low-impact exercise that doesn't strain the surrounding muscles.

"Chronic iritis in the right eye occurs when there is something in the environment you don't want to see. Dairy products during a flare-up aggravate the condition, which would benefit from increased vitamin C, less sugar, and less red meat in the diet.

"The strain on the left patella is due to high-impact exercise on a hard surface. Occasional menstrual discomfort would be alleviated by ginseng tea and calcium supplements.

"There's considerable anger in the body. It is released primarily through the musculature, expressing itself as strains, sprains, pulled muscles."

He paused and she waited, stupefied by what he'd just said. After a moment he took his hand away. "I don't sense anything else."

No wonder the AMA hadn't endorsed him, Quin thought. A guy like this would make physicians obsolete. "Was that like a body scan?"

"In a sense."

"You see inside a person through touch?"

"I don't *see* with my eyes. I perceive information."

She couldn't fathom the deep, crushing loneliness his talent probably inflicted on him, especially in this country. "Do you think you could heal aphasia?"

"I don't know. I've had limited success with things that afflict the brain. I worked on your husband for a while yesterday afternoon and hope to do so again when he's out of the hospital."

It was news to Quin. "He spoke his first coherent sentence since the shooting when I saw him a while ago."

"Good, perhaps it helped then."

"I got a call early this morning from someone who said you would be at the migrant camp tomorrow night."

It obviously caught him by surprise, but before he could reply, the cordless phone on the table began to ring. He answered it, listened, said, "Hold on a second," and looked at Quin. "It's my brother in Chile. I'd better take this."

"I've taken up enough of your time, Alex," she said, and thanked him.

"We'll be in touch."

Yes, indeed, she thought, we sure will.

16

~~~~~

Alejandro walked up the beach toward the Holden estate. Several joggers and swimmers were already out, people who probably lived in the slumbering mansions that lined the beach. His presence was noted, but no one challenged his right to be here, on a Tuesday morning at half past seven.

The beaches in Florida were public land and as long as you didn't cut across someone's property to get there, you weren't trespassing. It meant you could sit on the beach in front of any one of the mansions and the owner couldn't do a damn thing about it. So in the parts of Palm Beach where homes had been built on the ocean instead of across the street from it, the city hadn't provided public access. It meant Alejandro had to park the Porsche half a mile north, where there were no homes on the ocean side of the road, and walk in. But at least this way his arrival would be a surprise and he wouldn't be turned away at the gate.

From the back the mansion looked forbidding, rising beyond the ten-foot-high seawall like a castle of concrete, wood, and glass. The gate wasn't locked, which meant Holden had already been out for his morning jog. Alejandro pushed it open and climbed the half-dozen steep steps to the outdoor pool and the wide deck beyond it.

Lydia was doing laps in the pool, her strokes swift and graceful. She saw him when she turned her head for air. "Alex."

He merely nodded and walked on toward the porch, where two people were having breakfast. He heard her say his name again, but he didn't stop, and after a moment she fell into step beside him, a towel wrapped around her shoulders. "You can't just barge in like this, Alex."

"You knew, didn't you, Lydia."

She touched his arm. "C'mon, Alex, slow down a minute. What is it I'm supposed to have known?"

He didn't reply. He saw Holden, rising from the breakfast table while the other person turned around. Eden, it was Eden, her face tight with astonishment, her eyes darting toward Holden as if she expected an explanation from him.

"Isn't this cozy," Alejandro said dryly. "Old friends plotting the campaign over breakfast. Or is that just your excuse to see him, Eden?"

Flustered, Eden pushed up from her chair. "You're way out of line, Alex. You—"

Holden interrupted her. "What the hell's going on, Alex?"

Alejandro suddenly understood just how much of an edge he had. By barging in he had violated an unspoken code of behavior and etiquette and Holden wasn't quite sure how to deal with it. He reached into the pocket of his shorts and pulled out an envelope. "I thought I'd just drop by, Barker. It's been a while, hasn't it. I've seen Lydia and Eden recently, but not you. We haven't seen each other since the funeral. I can understand why, though."

He held up the copies he'd made of the love notes. "I found these in Janis's things. You'll like them, Lydia." He looked at her, standing there like a statue, water beaded on her face and shoulders. "And, Eden, given your relationship with Barker, I'm sure you'll get a kick out of them, too. This one's my favorite note. 'Meet me somewhere,

Janis. Anywhere. We need to talk. I go to sleep thinking of you, wake up thinking of you. I dream of you, I hate my life without you in it.' Would you like to hear more?"

He glanced up and took enormous pleasure at the sight of a muscle ticking wildly under Holden's left eye. Lydia's face had drained of color; her gaze was riveted on him. " 'Meet me in the field at noon,' " Alejandro said without looking at the notes. "Does that sound familiar, Barker? Or how about this one. 'Did you make love to him after you left me? Did you?' "

Holden snatched the notes from his hand, his eyes cold blue with rage. "Get out of here, Alex."

"Just for your information, Barker, I have the original notes. I think the police will be quite interested in them."

"Don't threaten me," Holden said softly, taking a step toward him, his fist clenched, but Eden grabbed his arm, holding him back. "No, don't, Barker."

Her eyes were fixed on Alejandro as she said it, a topaz sea darkened with fear. *She knows,* he thought. *She knows exactly why her nose bled the other day.* And how much else did she know or had she guessed? This was the woman, after all, who had scrutinized his talent, analyzed it, broken it down like components in a radio. He was suddenly certain that she had designed the experiments that Jim and Bob carried out. If so, then she had to know about Miranda and Francesca.

He turned without another word and slammed the gate on his way out. It banged against its metal posts, clattering, as he made his way back up the beach.

≈

Seventy miles stretched between West Palm Beach and Belle Glade. It wasn't much, Tark thought, in a state where it took about sixteen hours to drive from the Keys to the Georgia border. But at night the journey across this flat, surreal plain of sugarcane seemed to move back in time a year for every mile traveled.

The bright clarity of the stars swept across the velvet blackness, a celestial highway. The ever-thickening odor of the land itself, the hidden waters, the fields of sugarcane and other crops suffused the air inside the Cherokee. It reminded him of the incomparable lush smell of the jungle around Iquitos and he found himself reminiscing about Peru, something he rarely did.

Quin listened with rapt attention as he talked about the deep green mystery of the jungle where everything existed larger than life: plants as huge as condominiums, bugs as big as a man's fist, fish that walked on land, water lilies the size of a car, vines thicker than tree trunks. And through it all flowed the river itself, almost four thousand miles long and so powerful that the water at its mouth could supply New York City with enough water for a year.

He described the noise and bustle of Iquitos and the fierce struggle of its people to eke out a living in a country doomed by its warring factions: the Shining Path, the drug lords, the corrupt government, the peasants and the *ribereños*, the tribes and terrorists and tourists.

She worked off her running shoes and drew her denim-clad legs up against her. "Life here must be pretty boring in comparison."

"Life here is a relief." Tark glanced at her, moonlight spilling down her nose, the tall, dark stalks passing beyond her.

"I wish you wouldn't do that," she said.

He nearly replied, "Do what?" But he knew what she was referring to and said, "Sorry. It's a habit I can't seem to break."

She was silent for a moment. "I don't think we're talking about the same thing."

"Sure we are. We're talking about this." His hand moved in the air between them. "About whatever it is that's been going on between you and me ever since Liz Purcell slipped in that courtyard in Miami Beach last summer."

"I'm not looking for an affair, Tark."

"I know." The Cherokee bounced over potholes. Lightning flashed in the distance; a storm was moving over the Everglades. "But suppose you were single, Quin?"

"I'm not."

"If you were."

"But I'm not."

Drop it, he thought, and realized he couldn't. "Look, all I'm trying to say is that when I'm with you, everything feels right. When I'm not, something is missing, there're holes in my life." It was more complicated than that, but at least he had said it, said it after six months of wanting to say it and never being able to muster the courage. She was quiet for so long he was sure he had offended her. "I'm sorry, I shouldn't have—"

"I've thought about it," she said quietly. "About you and me. I've thought about it a lot." She paused and Tark waited. "But I'm not twenty-five anymore. Any decision I make affects Mac and Ellie, too. It affects the way we make our living. It's different for you."

Was it? Was it really so different? He didn't think so.

They rode for a long time without speaking, the air between them weighted and awkward. He finally broke the silence. "When I was in the chartering business, there was a woman who flew for one of the other companies. The chemistry between us was mutual and the situation was similar. I was married, with a daughter, and she was single."

"What happened?"

"Nothing."

"Do you regret it?"

"Sometimes."

She turned her face toward the window, watching the moonlit fields. "When we were living in Miami, Mac had an affair with a woman he'd been involved with before we'd met. She was killed during the investigation that had brought them back together, but I used to drive myself nuts wondering how things would have turned out if she had lived. The weird part is that I liked her, I understand why it happened."

The things you discovered about people when you weren't looking seemed to come more easily than the information you searched for, Tark thought. "Does it bother you now?"

"Sure."

"When you and Mac were separated, was there anyone else?"

"For him or for me?"

"For you."

"Not really."

The ambiguity of the response irritated him. "Meaning what?

That you just dated? That you didn't sleep with anyone and wanted to? Or that you slept with someone and it didn't amount to anything?"

"Christ, John. You're worse than I am. I didn't sleep with anyone when we were separated because I didn't feel like it, okay? Mac claims he didn't even date anyone during those seven months, but how the hell do I know if that's true?"

"Because he said it's true."

"Yeah, right." Her feet dropped to the floor again and she stretched out her legs and ran her hands over her jeans. "It isn't so much that he slept with Callahan but that he wasn't honest about what was going on with them. Distrust grew out of that.

"And maybe that's the whole thing, you know? People who have successful affairs are able to compartmentalize their lives so neatly they don't feel guilty. And if they don't feel guilty, their other sexual relationships don't get messed up. But I'm lousy at compartmentalizing, I don't keep secrets very well, and I don't want to sneak around. A relationship predicated on lies doesn't appeal to me in the least."

Then get separated again, he thought. Get divorced. *Give me a chance.* But instead he blurted out: "Are you happy?"

"Are you?" she shot back.

"Happier than I was in Iquitos."

She didn't say anything. He slowed as they approached the outskirts of Belle Glade, a Florida cow town, a punctuation point at the southern tip of Lake Okeechobee. During the 1926 hurricane the lake had overflowed and dumped tons of black silt that had made the soil the richest in the state. Sugarcane loved the stuff and with the cane came the migrants, following the seasonal harvest, sugarcane here, citrus in Vero Beach and Orlando, peaches in Georgia. The town also had the dubious distinction of having the highest incidence of AIDS per capita in the nation.

He headed west through town on a bumpy two-lane road, walls of tall, leafy stalks rising on either side of them. In the now intermittent moonlight the stalks seemed luminous, strange, possessed of an elementary consciousness that took note of their passage.

The fields on the right gave way to pastures, open meadows, and the eerie glow of the migrant camp. The place was hardly impressive.

It was an enclave of dirt roads, trailers, bleached concrete buildings, and prefab structures that would collapse in a high wind. A dimly lit slum in the middle of nowhere, enclosed by a wire-mesh fence: that's what this was.

Tark drove through the open gate and followed a line of battered pickups and old cars moving slowly toward a cluster of trees at the far end of the camp. They passed campesinos on foot, men in jeans and jackets, women in skirts and shawls, children bounding alongside. Dim lights burned in the windows of the impoverished homes, music from a boombox somewhere drifted through the cool, breezy dark.

The camp vaguely reminded him of Leticia, Colombia, a dusty border town at the edge of the Amazon River. Walk south in Leticia and you stepped into Brazil; head across the river and you landed in Peru. But in Leticia a promise of violence rippled through the air, never too far beneath the surface of things. Here in the migrant camp all he sensed was resigned despair.

Tark pulled out of the line of vehicles and turned down one of the dark, deserted side streets. He parked in front of a *tienda* that had been closed up for the night. "You carrying?" he asked Quin.

"Uh-uh. You?"

"Nope."

"That might be our first mistake of the night."

They got out, Tark left the doors unlocked. There were no sidewalks and the recent rain had left puddles of water in the rutted road. Off to the left an emaciated dog foraged in garbage from an overturned trash can. Stray cats lurked through the shadows. Shards of glass glinted in the moonlight. The alleys between the dilapidated buildings were littered with beer bottles, rotting cardboard boxes, rusted cans, wrappers. The stink of urine hung in the air.

"Third world," Quin said.

"Third worlds are worse."

As they rounded the corner to the main road, the brisk breeze swelled with different odors, different sounds. Fried foods and thick, steaming soups, music and a crack of distant thunder. Tark buttoned up his worn leather jacket, dug his hands into the pockets, and wished he were a foot shorter. Few of the people around them were taller than five and a half feet; he and Quin were Gullivers in comparison.

"Tark?"

"Yeah?"

"Thanks."

"For what?"

"For clearing the air."

"Is that what I did?"

"Isn't it?"

"I don't know. Maybe it was easier the other way."

"Guessing, you mean."

"I don't know what the hell I mean, Quin."

"Swell. And all this time I thought you were the one with the answers."

They started to cross the road, but she suddenly did an about-face. "That guy in front of the Laundromat is the one who followed me yesterday. Bob Clarion, fed."

Tark glanced across the road. A bearded guy in jeans and a pullover stood next to a Volvo, as conspicuous as they were. Light glinted off the lenses of his glasses as he stuck a cigarette between his lips, then bowed his head to light it. He followed the rest of the crowd.

"Let's stay behind him."

Tark lost sight of the man several times as the crowd closed around him, swallowed him, and emptied into an oasis of green, a playground encircled by ficus trees. Strings of Christmas lights were still threaded through the branches and winked like stars in the dark. People sat around in the grass, on towels or blankets or in beach chairs, like spectators at an outdoor concert. Their kids climbed over the jungle gym, their laughs and exuberant shrieks a barricade against the misery in which they lived.

A van was parked at the far edge of the playground and two priests stood next to it. One of them kept glancing at his watch and finally approached the crowd. In Spanish he apologized for the delay and said he was sure Señor Domingo would be along shortly.

"Our fellow *gringos* don't look too happy about waiting," Quin said, nodding toward the other side of the crowd. The bearded guy stood there with his arms crossed like a sumo wrestler. Two hundred feet to his right was a man with a basketball cap pulled down low over his eyes. He was puffing on a thin cigar and blew three perfect smoke rings in quick succession. For seconds, that was all, just seconds, his eyes looked on Tark's, seized them. Tark recognized him.

"Holden's Harvard pal," he said.

"I know. I saw him yesterday, too. Look, I'll meet you back at the Cherokee in fifteen minutes," she said, raising the hood of her jacket. "Keep an eye on those two."

Before he could ask where she was going, she had slipped away through the crowd.

≈

Quin threaded her way between the parked cars that now lined both sides of the main road through the camp. People from Belle Glade, she guessed. Word had gotten around. Except for several teenagers and a couple of women carrying baskets of laundry, the road was devoid of people.

The Volvo was wedged between a pair of pickups and was quite visible in the wash of light from the Laundromat. Through the open door she saw three women loading or unloading washers and dryers. Safe enough, she decided, and walked over to the Volvo as though she owned it.

The driver's door was locked and a quick glance through the window confirmed that the other doors were as well. No lights glowed on the dash; the car apparently wasn't equipped with an alarm. She dug her pocketknife from the canvas bag buckled at her waist, chose a long, narrow blade, inserted it into the lock. She jiggled it, snapped it to the right, the left, the right again.

Nothing happened.

The window was cracked open along the top. She worked the flat of the blade into the space and moved it up and down, trying to widen it, to push the window down enough so that she could hook her fingers over the glass. It wouldn't budge. A hanger, she thought. A hanger might do the trick.

She put the knife into her jacket pocket and hastened into the Laundromat. Quin smiled at the woman closest to her and in her embarrassing Spanish asked if she could have a hanger, that she had locked her keys in her car.

"*Sí, sí, claro. Necesita ayuda?*" Did she need help?

You bet, she thought. But not for this. She thanked the woman and returned to the car, twisting the hanger until it broke in a corner. She checked the road, then pushed the hooked end of the hanger through the crack and fished for the lock stem. On the third try it popped up; she slipped quickly into the Volvo and shut the door.

The Laundromat provided enough light to see fairly well and there was a lot to see. A police radio, a cellular phone, a computer keyboard under the dash that was connected to a small terminal built into the dashboard, six books on the passenger seat. Quin glanced at the titles and flipped through one on José Arigo and another on parapsychology. The texts of both were heavily highlighted in yellow. One missing book might not be noticed, she thought, and set the parapsychology book on the dash to take with her.

The lock on the glove compartment surrendered easily to her knife. Inside were assorted maps, a box of raisins, and three clips for an automatic, eleven rounds each. Nothing was hidden under the front seat; the backseat was empty.

She glanced up to check the road. Headlights were moving toward her, a car searching for a place to park. She slipped low in the seat, waiting for it to pass. It slowed instead and she hunkered down even lower, her head now well below the windshield and windows.

Then the headlights moved on and she inched upward and watched it through the rear window. A sedan, nothing special about it. But she had a bad feeling, a get-out-here gut feeling, and slipped from the Volvo clutching the book in one hand, the hanger in the other. She ducked into the Laundromat, tossed the hanger in the trash, and claimed a bench off to the side. She opened the book on her lap and hoped she would be mistaken for a customer waiting for her laundry to finish.

The car made a second pass. And a third. And on the fourth pass it vanished into a space between the Laundromat and the prefab next to it. She heard a car door slam. The fifteen minutes she'd given herself had come and gone, but she didn't move. She stared at the mirrored wall across from her, waiting to see the driver.

A tall figure in jeans and a navy-blue windbreaker with a raised hood stopped next to the Volvo and looked up and down the street, his back to Quin. She lowered her eyes to the book; the words melted together. She glanced up again.

Now the man turned sideways, toward the playground, and Quin recognized the profile, the regal nose, the high forehead. Not a man: it was Eden White.

Here.

Waiting for the bearded fellow.

But it was the man in the baseball cap who appeared a few moments later, the mystery man in the photograph, the third member of the Harvard trio. He and Eden stood outside the car, arguing. Quin couldn't hear what they were saying, but Eden's gestures made it clear that she was the one with the gripes. The mystery man opened the door of the Volvo for her and she got in. He walked around to the driver's side and slid behind the steering wheel but didn't start the car.

Only their heads were visible, but it was enough; she could tell their argument continued. Ten minutes later Eden exited the Volvo and marched off. Definitely not a happy camper and the man didn't seem to know what to do about it.

He got out, stood by the open driver's door, called to her. *Hey, Eden, hold on.*

But she didn't stop, didn't miss a beat; she headed straight for her car. The man was still standing by the Volvo when Eden backed out into the road and sped toward the gate.

He stared after her, weighing his options, and finally walked off in the direction he'd come from, apparently to wait for Alejandro. But Quin suspected the Chilean was going to be a no-show and that it might be her fault. She shouldn't have mentioned the migrant camp when they'd talked yesterday.

She slapped the book shut, sprang to her feet, and dashed out into the dark. When she hit the other side of the road, she cut through an alley, ran down an unlit side street, charged up another road, and suddenly realized she was lost. She couldn't remember where Tark had parked the Cherokee.

Campo Alegre wasn't just a makeshift slum in the middle of nowhere. It was a little Marrakesh, a labyrinth where dusty blocks twisted back in on themselves and where every corner looked like the one before it. She ran toward a deserted intersection, stopped again, ran, and suddenly saw the Cherokee, a long vehicle on a shadowed, silent street. The passenger door swung open and she leaped inside.

"A book?" Tark exclaimed. "It took you all this time to steal a goddamn book?"

"I got lost."

"Lost?"

Like he didn't know the meaning of the word. "Yeah, you know, which way is north, which way is east. Lost."

"Quin, this place isn't big enough to get lost in."

"Just get us the hell out of here, Tark."

The inside light was still on and she recognized the look on his face. She had glimpsed it in McCleary's expressions when she had done something he couldn't fathom, something he ultimately relegated to a gender quirk, the result of PMS or female rage.

"C'mon, drive, will you?"

And he did.

Twenty miles beyond Belle Glade, rain hammered the roof of the Cherokee, streamed over the windshield too fast for the wipers to clear it, and rendered visibility to zero.

It had been raining like this the night she'd met him and she felt superstitious now about him and rain, as though his nature were linked somehow to the kind of tempest that had ushered him into her life. She was relieved when he pulled into a dimly lit truck stop and suggested they go inside until the rain let up.

They dashed for the front door and entered the diner half soaked. Country-western music twanged from a jukebox; the air smelled of fried food. Business was slow and they had their choice of spots.

They settled in a booth at the back, on opposite sides of the table. While they waited for their coffee, Quin pulled the parapsychology book out of her jacket and flipped it open.

"He really marked up the text," she said, glancing at some of the highlighted passages on J. B. Rhine's early research at Duke University.

"Maybe he's a serious student of the occult."

"Right, a fed who conjures and plays with a Ouija board."

Tark laughed. "Flip to the index."

There were two, a subject index and a name index. Tark moved to her side of the table, tore out the subject index, and looked through it while she went through the names. She didn't find an entry for Alejandro but ran across other names she recognized. Arigo, Cayce, Uri Geller, Peter Hurkos, even good ol' Nostradamus.

Geller and a woman named Nina Kulagina had check marks next to their names. Quin turned to the section on Kulagina, whom she'd never heard of, and she and Tark read through it.

Kulagina was supposedly able to move small objects that weighed no more than five grams simply by concentrating or by holding her hands inches above them. Like Alejandro, she couldn't always command her talent. Sometimes nothing happened; other times it took as long as three or four hours of intense concentration before she was able to move even the smallest items. She was tested extensively by the Soviet government and they were impressed enough to consider her a national resource.

"This woman sounds like the type Holden might have wanted to see in action when he made his tour of Russian psychotronics labs," Tark said.

"Why do you think that?"

"Noel Unward said that Alejandro's talent is basically telekinetic, the ability to influence matter. That's supposedly what this Kulagina woman does. Same thing, different focus. Senator Colt told you that Holden had visited all these countries known for their healers, right? Then he went to Russia, where psychic research at the time was focused on practical application."

"So?"

"Skip ahead. One of Holden's Harvard pals has tested Alejandro, the other may be a fed who has him under surveillance. Holden's wife has been a patient and the woman who may have been his lover was married to the guy. That strains the parameters of coincidence, Quin, particularly when you look at Holden. Business whiz, multi-millionaire, political wannabe. It's not healers he's interested in. It's telekinesis. How it works, why it works, and if he can use it to further his own agenda."

"Use it how? For what?"

"I don't know. That's the missing piece."

"You've met the guy. Would he nab a kid to further his agenda?"

"I think he'd do whatever he felt he had to do. Murder his lover, nab a kid, fund research to the tune of four or five million a year."

"At Link? C'mon. The only connection we have between Link and Holden is Eden White."

"But I think we're getting closer." He checked the page number in the subject index that he'd been looking at earlier, then found the section he wanted. "Take a look at this." It was entitled "Energy" and the first paragraph read:

> The energy emitted when a healer works is sometimes visible to the naked eye. It may appear to crackle from the healer's fingertips, like a bluish electricity, or may look like a luminous blue globe of light. Among certain Eastern religions, this globe is called the Blue Pearl.

≈

The storm had passed and trees sparkled beneath the glow of the streetlights in the McClearys' development. It was only eleven, Tark thought, but the road was deserted, windows were dark, the neighborhood was sealed up like a coffin.

"You want to call Fitz or should I?" she asked.

"I'm going by his place when I leave here." He stopped in the driveway and glanced at Michelle. They had picked her up at her aunt's house and she was curled under a quilted blanket in the backseat. "I don't think rock music at full blast would wake her," he remarked.

"No, but a monster under her bed at three A.M. will."

"You need some help with her?"

"I don't think so, thanks."

She exited the car quickly, as if she were afraid he might resume their earlier conversation, and opened the rear door to get Michelle. Tark watched as she hurried down the walk and vanished around the side of the house. He heard the gate clatter shut, heard Flats barking. A light came on in the front window.

He stared at it, at the window, imagining her as she tucked Michelle into bed, fed the cats, let Flats outside, fixed herself a snack. He wasn't sure how long he sat there, but he suddenly felt like a voyeur, doomed to a life on the outside looking in.

Get out of here, he thought, and reached to turn the key in the ignition. It was then that he saw the book on the floor in front of the passenger seat. He scooped it up before he could change his mind and got out to return it.

When he came through the gate, she was standing in the yard in a long terry-cloth robe, watching something beyond the fence, down near the lake. She glanced around. "Hey, I thought you'd left."

"You forgot this."

"Oh, thanks. Thanks very much." She took it in one hand and shook the bag of dry dog food she held in the other. "I was going to try to entice Flats back into the house. He took off the second I let him out and leaped the goddamn fence."

"I'll do it."

She looked at him then, the pale light of the moon touching her forehead and cheeks, her eyes bright with questions. Before she could speak, Tark put his hands on her shoulders and kissed her. For a beat or two she didn't move, didn't react. Then she dropped the things she was holding and her arms went around him, her mouth opened against his.

Impressions flew at him almost too quickly to process: the taste of mint, the erotic softness of her tongue, the stab of a hip, the texture of her hair against his cheek. His hands, hungry for sensation, seemed to move with a volition of their own across her back, up through her hair, down over her arms, then slipped inside the robe.

There: the ridges of her ribs; here, the smooth swell of a breast; and there, the drumming of her heart. He felt an abrupt, violent shift within himself, as if the tectonic plates of his emotions, sealed since the death of his wife and daughter more than a decade ago, were suddenly torn open, flooding him with excess. It shocked him.

Tark wrenched back at the same moment she did, breaking the embrace. Starlight rushed into the vacuum between them. Quin stepped back again, her fingers fussing with the tie of her robe. She shook her head once, just once, as though answering some question she had posed silently to herself.

"I'm not ready for this." She raised her eyes. "All the way back here tonight I was thinking about this. One night, I thought, just one night with you. But it wouldn't be once, it'd be a full-blown affair."

She stooped to retrieve the fallen book, ignoring the dog food that had scattered across the grass. She stood there, giving him a chance to reply, but he didn't know what to say. His hands burned from her skin, the taste of mint lingered on his tongue, he was still hard.

"I'll see you tomorrow, Quin."

He sped out of the development a few minutes later and didn't look back.

17

～～～

Eastman's Caddy was parked in its usual spot behind his building and the lights in his second-floor apartment were still on. Apparently he had just gotten home; he answered the door still wearing his shoulder holster.

"John. I was about to call you. C'mon in. How'd it go?"

"Alejandro was a no-show and Blue Pearl is energy, Fitz."

"Huh?"

Tark explained as they walked into the spacious kitchen. It, like the rest of the rooms, was decorated with Eastman's photographs. The ones in here were mostly in black and white and, at first glance, appeared to be rather simple. Portraits of children, scenes of urban decay, shots of his native Liberty City in flames during the riots in 1980.

But whenever Tark was here, he saw details in the photos that he'd missed before. They were as layered and complex as Eastman himself and it was a relief to be in these rooms, out of the car, off the road, with some distance between himself and Quin.

"Are you saying that someone at Link sent Mike the note?" Eastman asked.

"It's possible." Tark sat down at the kitchen table. "But who?"

"Not Eden White, I can tell you that much." Eastman opened a kitchen drawer, took out an envelope, and brought it over to the table. He dropped it in front of Tark, then joined him at the table. "Your pictures. I didn't want to say anything until I had what I needed."

Tark removed them from the envelope, pointed at the mystery man. "He was there tonight. At the migrant camp. He met briefly with Eden White."

"Jim Granger, U.S. marshal. In 1968 he was at Harvard on a full scholarship, pursuing a degree in criminology. He and Holden were fraternity brothers and Eden White belonged to their sister sorority.

"Granger graduated in 1969, first in his class, John, so we're not talking about a dumb shit. He went to Nam with the Special Forces, won himself a Purple Heart, came back and joined the FBI. Eden joined the Peace Corps, then went to Nam with the Red Cross. When she came back to the States, she landed a spot on a research team at Walter Reed. Cancer research. Holden went home to take over his old man's empire."

"How long was Eden at Walter Reed?"

"About eight years. But then she took a leave of absence and started publishing papers on psychic research she'd been conducting at a private facility in the Ozarks called Beacon. So I called the place. It's amazing what you can find out when you're a rich old fart who might be tapped for a donation. Lady I spoke to was real helpful.

"According to her, the facility was nearly running on empty until 1982, when it was bought by Cantrell, Inc., the name Quin turned up in the public records. They changed the name to Link Research and Development and sold out to a group of investors in the late eighties."

"Quin said the place was still owned by this Cantrell outfit."

"The public records obviously haven't been updated. The woman I talked to insisted that Cantrell had sold out."

"How long was Granger in the FBI?"

"Seven years. Then he spent four years with the NSA and finally arrived at the U.S. marshal's office. He's been investigated twice by internal affairs for complaints lodged during arrests, but otherwise his record is clean. He's been in the West Palm Beach office now for three years.

"According to my source in the U.S. marshal's office, Granger has a lot of autonomy, comes and goes pretty much as he pleases, and likes these tax investigations the IRS throws his way. The one on Alejandro Domingo and Janis Krieger supposedly started last spring, when the IRS got an anonymous tip on Alejandro's 'medical practice.' "

"Any idea who the tip came from?"

Eastman shrugged, sat back, rubbed his hands over his face. "Maybe a customer who felt like he'd been ripped off."

"Or maybe by someone who wanted to put the squeeze on Janis, like one of the Holdens. Lydia might've done it to get even with Janis for screwing Holden."

"She might've killed her for the same reason."

"Or hired someone to do it."

A light of recognition flickered through Eastman's bloodshot eyes. "Like a guy named Eddie Moreno?"

Tark couldn't contain his surprise. "How did you—"

"Mike's computer. C'mon, man," Eastman said with a laugh. "Modems work two ways, you know. When I gave Mike the access code to the computer at the department, we agreed that I'd be able to access his records whenever I wanted. The stuff you downloaded on Moreno was all there. Date, time, the works. I didn't say anything because I wasn't sure if it related to this investigation or not. You should've mentioned it."

"Correct me if I'm wrong, but I seem to remember your saying that if we did something that wasn't above board, you didn't want to know about it."

Eastman sat forward, his voice softer. "Two weeks ago I was dumb as dogshit. I actually believed it was possible to bring down someone like Holden without breaking any laws. But it just ain't going to happen that way.

"The captain had a few surprises at tonight's briefing. The budget's tight, he says. We can't afford you and Quin and we can't afford the twenty-four-hour guard outside Mike's room. You two are off the payroll as of tonight."

"Then we work for free. But what about Mike?"

"The captain says he'll keep the guards outside his room until he goes to a safe house Friday."

"You believe him?"

"I think he'll do what he can, but he's catching heat from the top. He assures me the safe house is okay. It's cheaper and he can justify the expense because Mike has already been a target. So that's where he's going Friday, even if I have to haul his ass there myself."

"You may have to do exactly that."

"The captain figures that if we cooperate with the feds, with Granger, the investigation becomes their expense. I told him to go piss in the wind. And you know what he says to me? Cooperate or collect unemployment. Hell, I'm supporting three kids and two ex-wives. So the rules have changed, John."

"We need a list of Moreno's customers, the people whose lawns he services."

"Then get it. Do whatever you have to do to build a case against Holden that will stick. The prosecution is going to need all the evidence it can get. I don't want this fucker to get off, John."

"I'm not all that convinced that Holden's responsible for Janis's murder or for shooting Mike."

"I'm not, either. But my gut says he's at the center of all this. It wouldn't surprise me if Holden hired a guy like Moreno to do his shit work."

"Once we have a list of Moreno's customers, we can check it against the association's master list of homeowners. If there's even one in Walden Lakes, it'll be enough to bring him in for questioning."

"When can you do it?"

Tark thought for a moment. He remembered one of Moreno's poker buddies mentioning a game at Rico's on Thursday night. "Thursday."

"What's wrong with tomorrow?"

"Moreno's a homebody. Once he knocks off work, he tends to stick around the boat. But Thursday night he's got a poker game."

"Then Thursday it is. Before I forget, I swung by Christine Redman's apartment after class today. Figured we'd have a friendly chat or I'd bring her ass in. But Quin's visit must've spooked her. She's moved out. A neighbor saw her loading up a U-Haul early yesterday morning and the hospital where she'd been working said she resigned Sunday. She didn't leave a forwarding address with personnel, but she's supposed to pick up her last check in a couple of weeks."

"We need answers before then. I'll drop in on Unward tomorrow."

"Good." Eastman stifled a yawn and finally shrugged off his shoulder holster. "And make it clear that he either talks to you or he talks to me at the station."

"I'll pass on the message." Tark rapped his knuckles against the table and pushed to his feet. "And now I'll let you hit the sack."

Eastman walked him to the door. "I'll fill in Quin and Mike at the hospital tomorrow morning. We're going to nail these shits, John."

Tark nodded, but he wasn't able to muster optimism about much of anything just then. As he left Eastman's, he dreaded the thought of returning to an empty apartment, to the silence that would drive him into the dark, brooding spaces of the past. So he headed south to spend the night with Estelle, who would ask no questions.

≈

At six Wednesday morning Quin opened the door to let the animals out and saw the corner of an envelope protruding from under the mat. It was soggy from all the rain and had probably been there when she'd gotten home last night. Thanks to Flats's escape and Tark throwing her for a loop, she hadn't seen it.

Her name was typed on the front and the letters had smeared. Although the paper inside was damp, the note was legible.

Don't say I never did nothing for you,
girl. Meet me at the Lantana Airport

at 10 tomorrow morning in front of
the flight service building.

C.

If Christine had left the note last night, then "ten tomorrow" meant in about four hours. Otherwise, it meant ten Thursday morning. Either way, she intended to be there.

She and Michelle left the house at half-past seven in McCleary's red Miata. The trunk was loaded with presents for her daughter's birthday, which they would celebrate at Ellen's this evening. There were cupcakes and party favors on the floor in front of Michelle for a party at school today. And her hospital visit, she thought, would have to wait until later today.

It was just as well. She didn't want to see McCleary until she'd thought about last night, about what she had felt out there in the yard, heat rising in her blood as though she were some hormonal adolescent.

The Miata hadn't been driven in two weeks and the engine stuttered and coughed several times. The interior smelled faintly of McCleary, the familiar, indescribable scent of his skin and hair. She imagined what it would be like to lead a double life, to drive this car, for instance, after spending a few stolen hours with Tark. She didn't think she had it in her, the furtive meetings and frantic sex, the lies and duplicities, the dark intensity of a soap opera. And yet it held the visceral appeal of the forbidden.

Was that what had brought Holden and Janis together? Not love, not sex, not even passion, just this business of forbidden fruit? This reenactment of the fall from paradise? And was it precisely that which had killed her?

Every investigation seemed to possess a particular mood, a motif that ran through it like the refrain of a song. This theme, she realized, bore uncanny parallels to issues she was wrestling with in her own life: deception, infidelity, betrayal. It was the internal made manifest, the universe's little joke on her. *Pay attention, Quin,* it seemed to say. *You've asked the right questions, now go find the answers.*

Yeah, and between the asking and the seeking her life had turned to shit.

. . .

Lantana Airport was strictly a general aviation facility. Charter out-fits, a flight school, a glider company. Quin was forty minutes early and parked in one of the visitors' spots at the front. She bought coffee and a pack of peanut butter crackers from a machine in the breezeway. The coffee tasted old and sour and the crackers were stale, but she consumed both. A gnawing anxiety had left a hole in her stomach a foot wide and she needed to fill it with something.

She called the hospital from a pay phone. She wanted to let McCleary know that she would be by later today. But Eastman answered. "Fitz, it's Quin. I thought you'd be at class by now."

"Where the hell've you been?" he snapped. "I've been here since seven-thirty waiting for you."

"I didn't say I'd be there at seven-thirty," she replied testily, suddenly irritated with his rules and expectations. "Since when do I have to report to you about what time I visit Mac?"

He quickly apologized. "I just figured you would be here and I wanted to update you and Mike on those photos."

"So update me." She felt ungenerous toward him despite the apology. "I'm listening."

He gave her an abbreviated version about the background on the Harvard connection, the sheriff's department's financial woes, the strategy he and Tark had discussed the night before. He topped it off with the news that Christine Redman had apparently split.

"Well, she hasn't gone far," Quin said. "I'm meeting her at ten."

"Convince her to—"

"Be a witness for the prosecution. Yeah, I know, Fitz."

Eastman's laugh was that of the man she'd known before all of this had started. "Okay, I'm a control freak. I admit it. Should I put Mike on?"

"Just tell him I'll be by later this afternoon."

She hung up and walked back to the Miata. There was a note on the seat that read: *The silver and red Cessna 150 in the tie-down area. Hop to it, girl.*

Quin laughed, crumpled the note, and stuck it in the pocket of her leather jacket. She locked the doors and moved quickly through the breezeway and out onto the airfield. A silver and red high-wing Cessna was taxiing out of the tie-down area. Quin ran toward it waving her arms, her sunglasses thumping up and down on the bridge of her nose. The plane stopped and a door popped open. The propeller continued to spin, stirring up dust devils.

Christine was behind the wheel. She was wearing a bulky pullover sweater, jeans, a wool scarf, and sunglasses. She looked like a barnstormer, an adventurer, like Snoopy the Red Baron on drugs. "C'mon, c'mon," she shouted crossly over the din of the engine. "I don't got all day."

Quin climbed in, buckled up, and the plane resumed its taxiing. "You really know how to fly this thing?"

"You'd better hope so, girl." Then, with a quick glance at Quin, she added: "You're not going to puke in here, are you?"

"You'd better hope not."

Christine laughed and the Cessna swung out onto the runway. When she had clearance from the tower, she pushed the throttle in and worked the rudder pedals with her feet, keeping the plane straight and steady down the yellow line until she reached lift-off speed.

Then the hunk of tin rose into the air, listing slightly to the left, and the coffee Quin had drunk sloshed around inside her. She shut her eyes, appalled that she had actually gotten into the plane, that nothing but a thin tube of metal and a spinning propeller stood between her and annihilation.

"This your first time in a small plane?" Christine called over the noise.

Quin opened her eyes and stared into the vast blue of the sky. "No. But it's not my favorite way to travel."

"I had you figured different."

"I could say the same for you."

Quin's fingers tightened over the edge of her seat and she dared a look below. The view literally stole her breath. Houses and cars no larger than Tinkertoys, trees like paper cutouts against a concrete landscape, and directly beneath them a pale ribbon of beach. Off to her right the Atlantic loomed like a bluish-green continent, an unknown world.

"Sort of snaps things right into place, you know what I mean?"

Christine said. "Everything to its proper size. That's why I fly. I needed some perspective after my old man and boy were killed, and I always wanted to fly. He had a small life-insurance policy, my old man did, that's what paid for the lessons."

"Your husband died, too?" Quin asked.

"Yeah. A few months after my boy. He was on the wrong end of a drug deal."

She cut back on the throttle, fiddled with the dials, then settled in like a tourist enjoying the view. "The job in Boca paid me a pretty penny and I saved like a miser. This plane cost me less than five grand, can you believe that? Bought it in an estate sale when one of my patients died. Guy's family just wanted to unload it. Been flying about three years now. Figure there's no place safer to talk, that's why I used to bring Noel up here. Until he got sick right there where you're sitting."

Noel Unward. "How do you know him?"

"He was Eden White's assistant for a while when they were testing me at Link."

"I thought Eden tested you at Duke."

"That's where it started. But she was just there for a summer, and when the summer ended, she wanted more tests. They paid me a thousand bucks a weekend, plus airfare and expenses. Me and my old man, he was still alive then, we needed the money. He wasn't working then."

"All this because you tested so well at Duke?"

"That counted, sure. But it wouldn't have meant shit if I hadn't gotten the endorsement. See, that summer at Duke, Eden asked me if I'd read for some friends of hers. I got the idea it was real important to her, that she needed these people's support to go on with our testing, so I said sure, no problem. I felt like I owed her, you hear what I'm saying? She was paying me a hundred bucks a day. Me, who'd been doing readings at psychic fairs for fifteen a shot." She turned a dial on the radio and a weather report crackled through the speakers.

"Who were these friends of hers?" Quin asked.

"I'm getting to that. They flew into town one evening, a couple of white folks, educated, polite. And since they were friends of Eden's,

I opened up nice and wide for them. Read them backwards and forwards and sideways and didn't much like what I saw."

She tipped her sunglasses back onto the top of her head and glanced at Quin. "And just so there's no mistake about it, girl, I've read for cons, dopers, hookers, wife beaters, even read for a guy who ended up on death row. I know bad when I see it, okay? And I got to tell you these two had hearts like black ice, but it was all prettied up with money."

"Barker and Lydia Holden."

"You got it. But I didn't know who they were then. I never ate Crunchy Flakes in my life."

"What did you pick up on them?"

"Bunch of things. Like the marriage wasn't doing too good. He was dippin his wick where it didn't belong and it was messing things up between them."

"Did she know about it?"

"Sure, I think she did. It mighta been buried pretty deep, but at some level you always know when the one you love isn't lovin you back the way you should be loved."

Quin had the impression that the remark was intended for her. "What else did you pick up?"

"That he was aiming to get into politics and go all the way to the top. The White House, you hear what I'm saying? But he knew there were steps he had to take, he saw it like a game, this move here, that move there.

"I'm making it sound like he was easy to read for, but he wasn't. She was, but not Barker, no way. The inside of his head was, I don't know, like honeycombs in a beehive. Some rooms I couldn't get into, he'd sealed them off, he'd *learned* to do that, okay? Studied how to do it. But I kept picking up the word 'colt' and thought he owned horses or had investments in horses or something. It wasn't till I moved down here that I realized 'colt' was Senator Colt."

"Did you pick up any other names besides Colt?"

"Probably, but I don't remember 'em now. This was five years ago and that part of me has gone to rust. And don't forget, I didn't know Colt was a name until just recently."

"Why did it take Barker until now to run for Colt's Senate seat?"

"This is a man who likes everything lined up nice and tidy, girl. He wanted to be sure he was gonna win. Also, the Mrs. was against it. She had this idea of a regular life, kids, a family, a place in the country. Like I said, she was easier to read, and since I did them separate, I spent more time with her. There was lots of anger in her, sexual anger. I told her she'd better get rid of it because it was beginning to mess her up inside."

"The Chilean healer treated her for female problems."

"Doesn't surprise me none." She glanced out the window as the plane banked inland, then reached for a map tucked inside a flap on the door and unfolded it in her lap.

"Where're we going?" Quin asked.

"Sightseeing."

"Tell me more about the Holdens."

"You got a one-track mind, all right."

"I can't afford not to."

"Things gone to hell pretty fast since your man got himself shot, huh?"

"Yeah, you might say that."

Her gaze lingered on Quin for a moment and she felt distinctly uneasy. Then Christine resumed her story. "Lydia asked a lot of questions, too. Was she going to have kids, where would she be living in five years, shit like that. I saw a pregnancy that she wouldn't carry to term, success with her store. Just about everything else was wide open."

"What do you mean by 'wide open'?"

"Possibilities, choices. Way I see it, we come into the world with certain lessons to learn, things the soul needs to experience or resolve before it can move on to a higher level, you know what I'm saying? We're born with talents that help us on that path. But whether we use them or not is up to us. Nothing's written in stone, girl. Nothing. We make up our future as we go along.

"I could see Lydia was going to have to make some big decisions around the time her husband got into politics. And I told her that what she decided would carve out the path she'd probably follow the rest of her life." She pointed below. "Over there, two o'clock. Recognize it?"

"Link."

"Right. Eden's world, that's how I used to think of it." Christine continued her story about the Holdens. "Lydia and Barker musta been impressed with their readings, because the next day they came over to the lab to watch the testing. Simple stuff that Eden already knew I did well. ESP cards, holding objects or photographs and giving my impressions, shit I'd done with cops on cases.

"Then Barker wanted to try an experiment he'd come up with. Far-viewing, remote-viewing, they got different names for it. Basically what happened was that Lydia drove to a spot she picked out while she was driving, then tried to send me impressions of the place. I musta done okay because after that Eden wanted to do more of it.

"She said she was going to teach me how to shift my focus, how to transmit instead of receive, like I'm a fucking radio, right? But I got to admit it was fun. One day I changed the spin of a compass, another day I messed up a computer, like that. Sometimes it took hours, but it made me feel powerful."

The plane banked again. Lake Okeechobee loomed in the distance, a huge ink stain against the flatness, its circumference dotted by towns and crops. Christine circled a field, spoke softly into the mike, then began to descend.

"We're landing here?" Quin exclaimed.

"Sure thing. Mighty fine spot for breakfast. No power lines, no buildings, no people."

Breakfast. In the middle of nowhere. The plane touched down in weeds and high grass and stopped just short of a wooded area. A dirt road angled into the Australian pines, but otherwise there was no sign of human habitation.

Christine unloaded the baggage compartment, the excess flesh at her jowls quivering with the exertion. They carried an ice chest, bags of groceries, and several gallons of water into the trees. A small wooden house was hidden under the sagging branches of the pines; Christine's battered Honda was parked in front.

"So this is where you split to," Quin said.

"Friend of mine up in Durham owns the land—power comes from a generator, nearest phone's about fifteen miles south, got a septic tank I pump out once a year."

"What about water?"

"I tapped into the sprinkler system that waters some fields out yonder. Won't find this place on no map, girl."

"Sort of drastic, isn't it?"

"Listen, I lost my life once. That's not gonna happen again. My place got trashed about a week after your husband came to see me and a few days after your first visit. Last time I saw you I was already getting ready to leave."

"Any idea who did it?"

"Eden, I reckon. Or one of Holden's men. Dunno for sure. But Noel figured it was time for me to move on." She pushed the rickety door open with her foot and they put everything on the counter in the tiny kitchen. "And he took a sabbatical, left town two days ago."

No wonder he hadn't returned Tark's calls, Quin thought, glancing around. Besides the kitchen, there was one large room with a foldout couch, the old stereo Quin had seen at Christine's apartment, a scuffed bookcase, a table and two chairs, a newer model TV than the one in her apartment, and a VCR. Christine threw a switch on the wall and the generator powered up.

"Noel left a tape for that Tark fellow. It's over there on top of the VCR. Pop it in. I'll get us something to eat."

The tape was labeled "Alex: 1989–1991." Quin turned on the TV and VCR and put it in. "Is this Noel's tape?" she asked.

"Yeah. He copied it from Eden's tape file when he left Link. She'd shit if she knew it."

Quin walked over to the bookcase. There weren't many books, maybe three dozen, and they ranged from horror to classics, Stephen King to Mark Twain. A framed black-and-white photo stood on top of the bookcase, a younger, slimmer Christine with her husband and son. The boy looked to be about three.

"Those two are the reason you're here," Christine said, coming into the room. "I owe them this much." She set a paper plate of pastries and slices of cheese on the table. "Coffee'll be done in a minute. Make yourself comfortable." She picked up the remote control, fast-forwarded the tape, stopped it. "You can turn this tape over to the cops, but you'd be hurting someone who's already been hurt enough."

She didn't know who Christine was referring to and at the moment was more concerned about Noel Unward. "If Noel knows something, why didn't he just go to the cops himself? It would've been a lot simpler."

She shrugged. "He's got too much to lose. Don't forget, he was there when these experiments were going on. That makes him just as unethical as Eden. No denying that. But he's changed since then. He saved my ass, he was trying to steer your old man in the right direction, and he—"

"He's Blue Pearl?"

Christine rubbed her fleshy hand across her mouth. "Yeah. He talked to your old man and left some stuff in his car for him the night before he was shot. I think Holden's people suspect something like that."

"Jesus." Quin felt sick at the thought that so much of what had happened could have been avoided.

"He never got it?"

"He stashed it somewhere but can't tell me where because of this aphasia he's got. And so far I haven't been able to find it. Where was his car that night?"

"Noel never said. He figured the less I knew, the safer I would be." She smiled, a sad, resigned smile that dimpled her plump cheeks. "We sure fucked up on that count. I think when Noel talked to Tark, he realized something had gone wrong and that's why he left this tape."

"And took off."

"Yeah, that, too. By now he's someplace in Mexico." She went into the kitchen again, returned with coffee, then sat down, aimed the remote control, and hit PLAY. "Okay, here we got Alejandro isolated in one room, hooked up to Eden's goddamn machines. In the next room is a student volunteer. Alejandro is supposed to influence the student's brain, right? He can do it any way he wants, send a mental image, trigger an emotion, increase the flow of blood into the brain, it doesn't matter."

"Noel told Tark about this one. The student gets a nosebleed."

"Uh-huh." And there was the student, stumbling from his chair like a drunk, blood streaming from his nose. "But there were twenty volunteers, not one, Noel didn't tell Tark that part. And eighteen of them ended up like this guy. You can watch the whole tape at home, but I just want to show you one more thing.

"This section you're going to see now happened toward the end of the time when Eden was testing Alejandro. Noel wasn't there that night, you won't see him on the tape. He found out later and that's when he resigned."

She fast-forwarded the tape. The sequence began as before, with a volunteer in a soundproofed isolation booth. But the volunteer this time looked like a homeless drunk, not a student. He was hooked up to machines and squirmed like a kid on a car trip. His eyes darted around, paused on the camera, moved on. "Hey, nothing's happening," he called once. "These wires are drivin me nuts. Hey, you hear me?"

Then Eden White's voice: "Sit back and take deep breaths, Howard."

A few moments passed. Howard rubbed at his temple, winced. "Listen, I don't feel so hot," he said. "My head's hurtin something fierce. Hey, you hear me?"

Eden replied, "I'll be in there in a sec—"

Howard suddenly started shrieking and leaped to his feet, hands gripping the sides of his head, blood rushing from his nose. Wires and electrodes tore away from his body and he stumbled blindly, knocking over machines, his shrieks high, sharp, panicked. Drops of blood bloomed in the corners of his eyes, oozed from his ears. In the background Eden White was shouting, "Cut off that goddamn camera, cut it off!"

Then Howard pitched forward, the door to the room flew open, and Eden and several other people rushed in, crowding around the body on the floor. "He's dead, Jesus, he's de—" The tape went black.

For long moments the only sound in the room was the buzz of the television. Christine finally got up and punched the rewind button. "It was an accident," she said. "That's why she had the camera turned off."

"Let me get this straight," Quin began, but Christine interrupted.

"What's there to get straight? Alejandro blew apart the inside of the guy's head. He didn't know it, it wasn't like he meant to do it, but it happened. A cerebral blowout, okay? That's how powerful this guy is. And he didn't even know it."

And who would believe it? Quin thought dimly. Who?

"So Eden had a corpse on her hands, but fortunately for her it was some guy who wasn't going to be missed. They'd stopped using student volunteers by then, they were recruiting people from the streets, five or six of them by the time ol' Howard got in there. Drunks, hookers, nobodies, okay? Howard's probably in a pauper's grave. Or buried on Holden's property." She started to laugh; it sounded like she was choking. "Hate them fuckers, hate them all, girl."

The information Rita's contact at Link had dug out of their computer suddenly made sense. The Blue Pearl experiment wasn't about healing, it was about killing. And it was being funded to the tune of four to five million a year. "You keep referring to Holden, Christine, but so far we don't have anything concrete that ties him into this."

Her eyes widened. "You don't know who owned Link?"

"Some outfit called Cantrell, Inc. So what?"

"Cantrell is Lydia Holden's maiden name."

"Where do you go from here, girl?"

"I don't know."

They were sitting inside the Cessna, which was in the tie-down area at Lantana Airport. The doors were thrown open and a cool breeze blew through the plane. Quin could hear the noise of traffic on Lantana Road, the din of a twin-engine plane as it sped down the runway, the sounds of the ordinary world.

"I'm not talking to no cops, just forget that."

"This guy isn't just a cop," Quin said. "He's a friend. Fitz Eastman. Born and raised in Liberty City and not a fan of Barker Holden's. He wants to nail Holden, Christine, but he can't do it without evidence."

She tilted her sunglasses back onto the top of her head and clicked her tongue against her teeth. "You didn't hear a goddamn thing I said. What good would it do if I told this Fitz dude all this? Only thing I know about Howard is his first name. And Eden didn't kill him. She probably got rid of the body, but she didn't kill him. Alejandro did."

"Just talk to him, that's all I'm asking." Quin jotted down Eastman's home and office numbers on the back of one of her business cards. "Keep this. Think about it."

"You won't hear no promises from me, girl. Promises are against my religion."

"Yeah? And what religion is that?"

"The cover-my-ass religion."

Quin laughed and swung her legs out of the door. "Thank Noel for the tape. And thanks for talking to me."

"Wait. You were asking about names, did I remember any names besides a Colt. I remember another one. It's something to do with the mix-up about 'colt' in Holden's reading." Her eyes narrowed and she gazed at a point just over Quin's shoulder, as if struggling to read a billboard in the past. "A lawyer, I know she was a lawyer. Marie, Risa, something like that. No, Rita. Yeah, that was it. You know a Rita?"

Impressive, Quin thought. "She's working on Senator Colt's campaign."

"She wasn't working on no campaign five years ago. She was one of Holden's ladies."

Not so impressive, she thought, and started to laugh, she couldn't help it. "The Rita I know wouldn't go near Holden, much less screw him."

"She a lawyer?"

"A judge."

"Was she a lawyer five years ago?"

"Well, yes, but . . ."

"Ask her. Just ask her about Holden. You ask her about Holden and I'll seriously consider talking to this Fitz dude. This lady's got something to tell you, believe me."

"All right, all right. I'll ask and you consider."

Christine smiled. "You're okay for a white girl, Quin."

It was the only time Christine Redman had called her by name. "And you're okay for a black girl, *Loretta*. If you ever want a job using your psychic talents, let me know."

"Shit, I'm retired from that. The seein part of me is all burned out, that's why I can't give you nothing but clues about the past. Now go on, outta my plane. And don't go thinking you can give your buddy Eastman directions to my place, girl. Haven't met a human being yet who can find their way back."

With that, she reached over and slammed the door and turned the Cessna back toward the runway and the cool blue sky.

I didn't swim to the boat this time. I didn't take the raft, either. I waited in my car in the park, waited for Eddie's contraption to roll in, his pickup and that U-Haul attached to the back that held his lawn equipment.

I felt uneasy, I don't mind admitting that. I was nervous about what he would say when he saw me waiting there, nervous that he might not say anything at all, that he might pretend he didn't even see me. And I was nervous about the other part, about why I was here.

Waiting.

I'm not very good at it.

In my old dreams about Barker I'm always waiting for him, waiting for him to turn around, for him to notice me, for him to do, to act, something, anything. But he sits there like a Buddha among

*his subjects, a man who definitely marches to a different drummer.
Not so unlike Eddie, really. It's just a matter of degree, this difference
between them. One born to everything, the other born to nothing.
Privileged versus disadvantaged, isn't that the oldest story in the
book?*

*There were people in the park today and that worried me, too.
Mothers with kids, men and women entering and leaving the library
on the east side. It meant I would have to stick around at least until
dusk, when the park cleared out.*

*Eddie rolled in right on time, just after four. He had a six-pack
tucked under his arm and despite the cool weather was wearing a
tank top as usual. I couldn't see his tattoo from where I was, Wonder
Woman in all her red and blue glory. But I sensed her and was sure
she sensed me, too. Eddie was our conduit and through him, through
his mouth, his saliva, she had deposited something of herself inside
me. It was small and hard, like a seed, but it radiated a heat that I
could feel even now, as I waited for him.*

*The heat grew in intensity and I wondered if it was a kind of
signal that alerted her to my presence, that connected us directly,
bypassing Eddie. I was suddenly certain that if I shifted my focus
ever so slightly I would feel her quiver against Eddie's flesh, rousing
herself from the deep slumber she sank into when he worked. I would
feel her eyes blinking, her tongue wetting her lips, her arms stretching
over her head. I might even hear her whispering to Eddie, telling him
to turn his head as he was doing now.*

*He saw me as I walked toward him and I smiled hesitantly,
making it clear that I knew I might not be welcome. He didn't smile
back. He didn't lift his hand in greeting. He just watched me the way
construction men watch women on the streets, his eyes peeling away
my clothes. It made me feel like a cliché and I hated him for it.*

*Then I saw her, tattoo Gloria mounted against his right shoulder
like a Boy Scout badge, a war medal, a seal of approval. She was
grinning at me, her lips pulled away from her Pepsodent teeth, her
hair dark and shiny in the afternoon light. And for moments the heat
of whatever she had left in me grew so fierce and brutal, it blistered
my insides. The fetid stink of scorched tissue, of organs and bones,
surged upward, nearly choking me. I coughed, my eyes watered, I*

couldn't see, I could barely breathe. I stumbled and Eddie grabbed my arm.

"Cuidado, chica."

And just that fast the heat receded, clean air rushed into my lungs, and I could smell the grass on his skin, the wind, the sun. I looked into his dark face, but my attention was focused on her. At first she seemed to twitch like a muscle, then she began to vibrate as if she were struggling to free herself from the prison of his skin and leap on to me, into me, to fit herself into my bones.

"I owe you an apology for the other day, Eddie."

"You're one crazy gringa." He maintained his grasp on my elbow as we walked toward the dock, where his skiff was tied up. "And that's okay. I got no problem with locas. But don't show up where I work, me entiendes?"

"Fair enough."

We got into the skiff; he started the outboard and we putted across the still water and into the cove. He killed the engine and tied the rope to the ladder. I started to get up, but he said, "No, wait," and I sat back down again.

"I don't fuck with you when you're at work, I talk to you with respect, the way the lawn man's supposed to do. I don't even look you in the eye when you're at work. You should do the same for me."

"I hear you, Eddie."

The skiff was so small our knees were touching. He leaned forward and brushed the hair from my cheek, a proprietary gesture that annoyed me, then put his hands on either side of my face, forcing me to look at him. "Yeah, yeah, you hear, but do you listen, chica?"

"What the hell do you think I'm doing now?"

Those smoldering dark eyes seemed to bore through me, as if he were looking for something inside me, the seed, maybe, the thing his tattoo woman had planted in me. His cheek rubbed mine, pressed against mine, and he licked the edge of my ear, his tongue tracing its fetal shape from earlobe to hairline, then dipping inside, swirling against cartilage and skin. The sensation was exquisite, electric, strangely tender. It aroused me and he knew it.

He kissed me, something he rarely did. One of his hands dropped from my face to my thigh and slipped under my skirt. My knees snapped shut, a prim, nice-girl reflex, a vestige of all that childhood conditioning.

He laughed, a low, hoarse laugh, and pushed my knees open with his hand, then drew back and looked at me, our faces so close our noses were almost touching. "Right here, chica. *I'm going to make you come right here." His fingers climbed along the inside of my thigh; his other hand stroked the back of my neck. "In my boat. In my cove. I'm choosing the place, not you."*

I was aware of sunlight against my head, shadows crossing my back, the distant sound of a boat, the lap of water against the sides of his sloop, the smell of his skin. My skirt rustled and beneath it his hand moved like a small, burrowing animal.

Barker and I had done this in places far more public. The first time it happened on a beach while other people were playing volleyball, swimming, sunning themselves. We were sitting in the sand, playing cards. We looked quite normal, really, the sun beating hard against the sand around us, the smell of Coppertone mixed up with the aroma of salt and sand, gulls pinwheeling through the blue overhead. Normal, except that we were groping at each other under a towel.

Afterward, we both acted guilty, ashamed; proper people like us didn't do things like that in public. But I seized my pleasures now, seized them without regrets and in spite of the occasional nice-girl reflex. Eddie, of course, never had the inhibitions to start with.

When we were on board, Eddie opened a couple of beers and we went into the cabin and finished what we'd started. This time it wasn't so good because I could see Gloria clearly and I could feel the thing she'd left in me, feel it heating up again, growing, swelling.

I suddenly understood that the seed, this hard thing inside me, was the essence I had always feared, the substance that could attach itself to your soul. And that's what Wonder Woman was after, my soul, and she would suck at me until she had it, until I was dead and she was alive. That was her ultimate purpose. Life.

She couldn't very well suck away Eddie's energy because she needed his skin to exist. In return, she kept him company and told him other people's secrets. Their symbiosis had worked just fine for years, despite his relationships with other women. So Gloria had bided her time, waiting for a woman in the right circumstances. Someone like me. Now I was to be her vehicle. Through me she would make her transmigration to flesh and bone and I would be reduced to some dry, shriveled husk.

She left me no choice.

While Eddie dozed on the bunk, an arm thrown over his eyes, I got a knife from the galley, one he used to clean fish. The blade was thin, sharp, sturdy—the only qualities that matter in a knife.

I stood for a moment at the side of the bed, watching him sleep as the cool breeze dried the sweat on his face, and felt a piercing regret. I liked him, after all, which I couldn't say for Janis, and he intoxicated me sexually. But even if he'd consented to have the tattoo removed, there would still be a problem. He was the only thing that connected me in any way to McCleary.

I touched the blade to his throat, pressed down, and whipped my wrist to the left. It felt like a knife cutting through melon.

His eyes flew open, wide and panicked, and I suddenly wanted to press my hands over the wound, stop the flow of blood, save him. But it was too late by then, too late for Eddie, too late for me.

He somehow managed to bolt forward and I wrenched back and back again and again until my spine was up against the far wall. Blood bubbled from the gash. His hands clawed impotently at the air, as if to tear a hole in it that would allow him to breathe. The noises he made were hideous—gasps, gurgles, hisses like a snake.

Sweet Christ, I didn't mean for him to suffer, he was supposed to die quickly, like Janis. So when he tried to get to his feet, when his arms reached out to me for help, something broke inside me. My knees crumpled. I slapped my hands over my mouth to stifle my cries and the knife clattered to the floor. Then he was on his feet, he was actually standing there, swaying back and forth like a tree in a high wind, his hands mashed against his throat, his eyes bulging in their sockets.

And she moved, that was when the tattoo woman moved, throwing out her arms as if to grab on to something so that she could pull herself off of Eddie's shoulder. But he pitched forward and slammed against the floor. His head landed a few inches from my feet.

I sat there on my heels, weeping into my hands, my eyes squeezed shut. The thing inside me burned and burned.

After a time, seconds, minutes, I don't know how long, his scent reached me, grass and wind and sun. Then the stink of death swallowed it and I stumbled to my feet and into the galley and vomited into the tiny sink.

I felt better then, not great, but okay enough to think, to function. I washed my hands first, washed them hard, vigorously, then I put on the rubber gloves Eddie wore when he cleaned fish. My hands shook. I found Ajax, Lysol, and scrubbed down everything I had touched and probably things I had never touched. I overdid it, scrubbing the boat from top to bottom, then I went over to Eddie and crouched beside him.

The knife was under him and I needed to roll him off of it. And I needed to see the tattoo before I would know for sure that the hard thing inside me had died with her, with him. I wedged my hands beneath his shoulders and pushed. He flopped onto his back, a beached whale, and Wonder Woman gazed up at me, no more malefic than a pimple.

A trick, I thought. It was just a trick. She made my head ache, my eyes water; I couldn't think about her just then. I moved away from her, from him, and went back to clean the cabin, scrub scrub scrub.

Afterward, I washed Eddie's body with a dishcloth and warm, soapy water. I even used a fingernail file to clean under his nails. There was no blood on him when I finished, no trace of my body fluids, nothing to connect me with this place, with him.

Except for his business records. Those would come last.

I'd been naked all this time and his blood was on me. I showered until the hot water ran out. I looked down at one point and saw Eddie's blood, swirling pink down the drain, and for a few seconds nausea gripped me again.

When I was clean, I wiped out the shower with a wad of paper towels, attentive to details like the drain. The shower was one of those prefab things; it was easy to clean. But I took my time, I wanted to be sure. I finally shoved the towels into my purse to take with me and went back into the cabin to search for Eddie's business records.

It took me a while to find them. Eddie wasn't a file-cabinet sort of man, he didn't own a computer or a typewriter or an adding machine. I was forced to look in unusual places and laughed, actually laughed, when I opened a recipe box on top of the fridge and there they were.

One customer to an index card. The entries were neat, with annotations about what each customer required—lawn, hedges, fertilizing, weeding, whatever—and payments received. I put the box in my purse.

My state of mind had improved when I returned to his body. In a situation like this, something happens to your sense of time, everything accelerates. I had accepted his death, accepted that I had killed him. I pulled the sheet off the bunk and covered him with it, drew it up over his feet to his waist. I shut his eyes. I kissed him on the mouth and whispered his name around the lump in my throat. Then I took care of the tattoo, bye-bye Gloria, you're no Wonder Woman now.

I boarded the skiff when it was dark and chugged back to the dock. Stars struggled through a bank of clouds to the east. I tasted rain in the air. Some mechanism clicked madly away in the back of my mind, checking to make sure I had done this or that, but I was fairly confident I hadn't missed anything.

Tark wouldn't find me now and neither would Quin. I was safe, wasn't I? Safe.

18

~~~~~~~

Michelle's birthday party was under way by dusk. Rita arrived around eight, breezed in with gifts for Michelle and quick hugs and kisses for everyone else, and of course she brought food. Lasagna for the adults, candy and party favors that were stuffed into a piñata for the kids.

She was a local celebrity in this household, Quin thought. While they sat on the porch watching the kids smack the piñata, Quin's brother-in-law plied Rita with questions. He asked about cases she had tried, about cases on which she had sat in judgment, and he asked about Senator Colt, her favorite topic. She was a facile, eloquent speaker when she felt passionate about something. She even managed to tone down her cynical comments about Republicans.

She was the first to clap when the piñata finally gave way and surrendered its goodies, Gummy Bears and M&Ms raining out of the papier-mâché bull with a gaping hole in his belly. But when the adults—Ellen, Hank, and some of their neighbors—poured out of the screen door to help the kids pick candy out of the grass, Rita remained behind. So Quin did, too.

"I bet your brother-in-law voted for Reagan and Bush, didn't he," she said.

Quin laughed. "Gee, what gave him away?"

Rita sipped from her glass of wine. "He actually had me guessing until just a few minutes ago. He argues both sides equally well."

"And what about you, Rita? You keep people guessing?"

"Yeah, sure," she said with a laugh. "I'm about as subtle as a semi with overheated brakes on a Colorado slope." She glanced at Quin, a frown thrusting her dark eyes closer together. "PMS, right?"

"What?"

"PMS would explain the tone of your voice, Quin. Did I offend your brother-in-law or something? Is that why you're pissed off at me?"

"I'm not pissed off."

"Then what's eating you?"

Quin had wondered how to say it tactfully, but she had never been very good at tact, so she blurted, "Have you screwed Holden, Rita?"

She burst out laughing. "You can't be serious." She made a face and when Quin didn't laugh, she stared at her as if Quin had lost her mind. "My God, you *are* serious."

"Yeah, I guess I am."

"*C'mon.* We're talking about Barker, not Mel Gibson, for Christ's sakes."

Quin shrugged. "I needed to ask."

"Why don't you ask me if I've screwed Mike, Quin? That would make as much sense."

"Okay, okay, I'm sorry."

"I need a refill," Rita murmured, and got up and went inside the house.

She circulated after that, avoiding Quin and charming everyone she talked to. During supper she sat next to Michelle at the long picnic table set up outside and fed her. Quin felt uneasy watching them, her daughter and wonderful Aunt Ree who could do no wrong.

Around nine when Rita was ready to leave, Quin walked outside with her. The sky was clouding over and a brisk breeze skipped through the palm trees in the front yard, rattling the branches like castanets.

Quin apologized for what she had said earlier. "I'm beginning to feel that if I don't get out of this business pretty soon, I'll start suspecting my parents of dark deeds."

Rita lit a cigarette, an infrequent indulgence, and leaned back against her BMW. "I did screw him," she said. "I'd rather not remember it, but you deserve an explanation, Quin."

"Let's walk."

They strolled north through the neighborhood, along a bike path that passed large, expensive homes, swimming pools, landscaped yards. A trimmed perfection, like a movie set.

"When I was going through my divorce," Rita said, "I went to some of these Palm Beach bashes just to get out of the house, to circulate. I kept running into the Holdens. Barker and I would trade barbs and go on our separate ways.

"Then there was this costume party on a yacht, an all-night deal that ended up in Nassau for breakfast the next morning. I started dancing with this court jester. He didn't say anything, he just mimed, right? I'd had a lot to drink. We went out on deck and continued to dance, talking to each other by miming. This guy made me laugh, Quin, and Christ knows I needed some laughter then."

She dropped her cigarette to the ground, stepped on it, then picked it up and pocketed it. The seminal conscientious citizen, Quin thought. "Holden was a court jester? That has possibilities."

"I didn't recognize him. He was wearing a mask and he didn't talk. On top of it I was feeling no pain. One thing led to another, we went down to his cabin, and by the time he took his mask off, it was beside the point."

"That's it? End of story?"

"I wish." She jammed her hands into the pockets of her jacket and kicked at a rock on the bike path. "A few months later I get a call out of the blue, right? He asks me to dinner. I was curious about what he was up to. I knew there had to be an angle to it. So I said sure.

"We flew to the Caymans, Quin. For dinner. Private jet, limo, the works. I hate to admit it, but I had fun. I was home by one and he shook my hand at the door and said, 'Friends, Rita?' He never even tried to touch me."

"Where was Lydia?"

"Out of town. He didn't make any bones about it. He said they had an agreement. She had her life, he had his, but they also had a life together."

"An open marriage."

"Open, hell, there's nothing open about it. They just don't ask each other questions."

They cut through a low hedge to a playground and sat in the swings. "Did you ever find out what his angle was?"

"Not for months. It was this cat-and-mouse game we played. He'd call me up on the spur of the moment and we'd fly off someplace for lunch or dinner. As long as we didn't talk politics, it was fine. Then we started sleeping together and that went on for seventeen or eighteen months."

"I thought you detested the guy, Rita."

"I do. But I didn't then. There was something, I don't know, thrilling about it, I guess that's the word I'm looking for. The private jet, the yacht, the way he spent money, the things he talked about. Books, theater, history, traveling . . ." She shook her head and pushed her feet against the ground until the swing began to move. "Christ, I'd never known anyone like him."

Quin wondered how Holden could possibly keep his life straight. "How often did you see him?"

"Twice a month at the most, usually less. But it got so that I was waiting for his calls. Serious waiting, okay? Canceling dates to wait for the goddamn phone to ring. And I used to go to restaurants that I knew he frequented, to parties where I knew he would be. I was obsessive, Quin, and completely hooked. It's not that I was ever in love with him, but I was hooked. He knew it, too, and that's when he asked me to be his campaign manager for the Senate race."

She paused and leaned back, her face turned skyward as the swing moved.

"That was his angle all along?"

"Of course it was. He'd done his research. He knew I'd worked on Sasha's last campaign and that I'd be working on this one, too. Maybe he figured if I was on his side it would undermine her campaign and win him votes he might not get otherwise. Or maybe it was just the challenge of stealing me from his opponent, I don't know. But he knew he couldn't get me just by asking, so he went about it this other way."

"What'd you do when he asked?"

"Told him to go fuck himself. We were sitting in this run-down old fish shack of a restaurant in the Virgin Islands somewhere. I didn't make a scene or anything, I just said my piece, got up, and left. I bought a seat on the next flight back to the States. And that was it. We haven't said two words to each other since, except when I was arranging this festival on Las Olas. I think the only reason he consented to it was to rub salt in the wounds."

"Does Sasha know?"

"Sure. I told her before this campaign started."

"I wish one of you had mentioned it when we had lunch, Rita."

"It didn't seem like the right time or place."

"What was Sasha's reaction when you told her?"

"She said I have lousy taste in men." Rita shrugged. "Look, I know I should have told you this before and I'm sorry I didn't. But Holden isn't one of the prouder moments of my life."

Quin could think of several men she'd known when she was single who weren't among her prouder moments, either. She certainly sympathized in that respect. "Did you know he had an affair with Janis Krieger?"

"It doesn't surprise me. I was just the twice-a-month lady and I figured there was some other fool in between. Hell, he was probably poking Eden White, too."

"Yeah, that's occurred to me," Quin replied, thinking of the Harvard photo, Eden and Holden and their buddy Jim Granger.

"But what's Holden's angle with Alejandro? That's the real question, Quin."

She told Rita about her conversation with Christine Redman, about the tape. "And I'd appreciate it if you kept that to yourself until Fitz decides how to handle this, Rita. I think if we give Holden enough rope, he's going to end up hanging himself."

"This guy Howard actually died? You're sure of it?"

"As sure as I can be without having been there."

"And Alejandro supposedly did it with just this . . . this energy, just by concentrating."

"That's my understanding."

"It sounds like science fiction to me."

"I agree. It's possible the guy had weak blood vessels in his brain and one just happened to pop. But keep it to yourself until Fitz decides what he's going to do."

"Or until Barker hangs himself."

"Right."

"The fall of the Holden empire. Man, I'd buy front-row seats for that one."

They walked back toward the house to the distant roll of thunder, the subject of Holden now settled between them.

≈

The clock chimed twelve times. The sound echoed through the dark silence of the house, a reminder, a mockery, a resonance of his solitude. Alejandro sat in a rocker at the window, the Levolors open so he could see the driveway and the road beyond it.

Be ready by one, Bob had said when he called. Bob, a U.S. marshal who had told Quin to stop harassing Holden or else. He had recognized her description. How much clearer did it have to get? "*Hang in there, amigo,*" Bob had said before he'd hung up. "*We're almost there.*"

Almost where? At the end of Holden's twisted rainbow? And then what? Would they release his daughter and his sister, put the three of them on a plane, and send them back to Chile? Yeah, sure.

He rose quickly from the rocker and sprinted upstairs to toss some clothes into a bag. He wasn't going to be here when Jim and

Bob arrived. He needed help and he needed proof to get that help. One way or another, Eden was going to turn over her files and her notes and tell him where his sister and his daughter were.

He wasn't sure how Bob and Jim would react when they discovered he wasn't home. But he was fairly certain they wouldn't do anything drastic at this point, not this close to whatever they had planned for him. To cover himself, though, he scribbled a note and taped it to the front door.

He sped out of the driveway at 12:20 and turned into Jupiter Farms half an hour later. He parked a block from Eden's, under some trees in a vacant lot, well off the road so his car wasn't visible. It was probably an unnecessary precaution, no one was out and there wasn't another car in sight. But now that he'd decided to do this, he didn't intend to be seen.

Her car was in the driveway, the windows of the house were dark. He walked around to the back, where the screened porch was, and hoped that Eden was still a creature of habit. He dug around in the potted plants on either side of the door, golden pathos ivy with tremendous leaves. Sure enough, the spare key was exactly where it had been nearly three years ago when he'd been welcome here. He unlocked the utility room door and stepped inside.

Silence, vast and deep.

The glow of the night-light in the kitchen was sufficiently bright for him to make his way down the hall and into her den. He shut the door, pleased that it didn't squeak, and turned on his penlight. The file cabinet was to the left of the desk, four drawers, none of them labeled and all of them locked.

He used a fingernail file to jimmy the lock on the top drawer, which was jammed with hanging files arranged by topic. They had probably been alphabetized at one time, but no more. Eden was a clutter bug, the polar opposite of his wife in that regard. He glanced through a file on cancer and another on AIDS. Articles from medical journals, magazines, newspapers—that was it.

In the next drawer the files were considerably more interesting. There was one on José Arigo that dated back to Eden's early years in medical school, when she had been part of the first American medical team to investigate the Brazilian healer. He found a file on a clairvoyant named Christine Redman, one of Eden's test subjects at Duke, who he remembered her mentioning during the early months of their association. He set those two files aside to take with him.

The files in the third drawer contained articles on every conceivable aspect of psychic phenomena, from telepathy to precognition to telekinesis. He went through the one on telekinesis, saw that she had scribbled notes in the margins, and decided to take it with him as well.

The fourth drawer contained only office supplies. Disappointed, he moved to the laptop computer on her desk, a new model that weighed five or six pounds. He booted it up and glanced through the directory listings in the word-processing program. His name didn't appear, but he hadn't really expected it to. If her notes on him were in there, the directory would be coded or hidden.

Alejandro accessed the word-processing program and went into the files one at a time. The fourth, entitled Beacon, requested a password, and so did the eighth, which was called Blue Pearl. He backed them up, pocketed the disks, then started in on the desk drawers.

He was so engrossed in what he was doing he didn't hear the door when it opened. The light suddenly blazed and Eden said, "There's a gun at your back, fucker."

He raised his arms, said, "Hello, Eden," and turned around.

She aimed a silenced weapon at his chest. Her face had hardened like stone, freezing her features in an angry mask, but he saw surprise in her eyes. "You're a goddamn fool, Alex. I'd be doing all of us a favor by shooting you."

"But then you'd have to get rid of my body and answer to Barker. What's he have on you, Eden? What is it he knows about you that makes all this worthwhile?"

"Sit in the chair, Alex." She gestured with the gun. "Go on, do it!"

When he was seated, she stepped into the room, the hem of her silk robe rustling against her ankles. "I told Barker this wasn't going to work, but it was too late by then. He and Jim had already put things in motion and—"

"Where's Miranda?"

"I don't know. I didn't have anything to do with that part of it.

And since Barker created this problem, he can just damn well deal
with it."

She reached for the phone and glanced away from him momen-
tarily to punch out the numbers. Do it, he thought, and hurled himself
out of the chair. She fired, but she wasn't fast enough. He had dived
for the floor; he was rolling as she was turning, then his feet slammed
into her legs and she stumbled back, arms pinwheeling, the gun aimed
at the ceiling when it fired again. He tackled her.

Eden struck the floor like a giant and they struggled for the gun,
rolling across the floor until they hit the wall. The gun went off, the
bullet flew wild, and she sank her teeth into his wrist and hung on
like a starving wolf. Just when he didn't think he could clutch her
any longer, ugly, rasping noises erupted from her throat. Her hands
flew to her head and the gun clattered to the floor.

Alejandro grabbed it and scrambled away from her, his wrist
bleeding where she'd bitten it, his temples pounding, his body on fire.
She writhed on the floor, clawed at her head. Blood streamed from
her nose and ears and oozed from the inside corners of her eyes. The
face of the thief in Santiago flashed like neon in his head and he
dropped the gun and lurched forward to help her, to undo what he
had done. She died before he touched her, her eyes wide and blank,
blood pooling on the floor around her.

"*Dios mío.*" He blinked hard, rubbed his hand across his mouth,
looked away from her, at her, away from her again, at her again. His
knees cracked as he crouched beside her and felt her neck for a pulse
he knew he wouldn't find. Her skin was still warm; his face was
reflected in her dilated pupils.

Get out think fast what did you touch in here?

Everything, he had touched everything, the doorknobs and the
handles on the file cabinets and the computer and the gun and the
. . . Oh, Christ, what now? What was he supposed to do now? His
hands dropped to his thighs, his gaze dropped to Eden's face. Her
lips were turning blue.

Alejandro pushed to his feet, shrugged off his windbreaker, and
used it to wipe off everything he could remember touching. Then he
zipped the gun into a pocket of his windbreaker, jammed his arms
through the sleeves, jerked the zipper up to his throat.

He looked down at her. Vacant eyes. The tip of her braid lay in a pool of blood.

Her phone rang and his head snapped up at the sound of it, loud and abrasive, a demand. The answering machine clicked on; her voice drifted into the room. He stepped around her, scooped up the files on the desk, slapped down the lid on the laptop. He yanked the plug out of the outlet, wound the cord up, tucked it into its space at the back. Then he grabbed a box of disks from the bottom desk drawer and shut it with his foot.

Beep.

A gravelly voice said, "Eden, give me a call."

It took him a moment, but he realized the voice was Jim's, Jim of the gray hair and the gray eyes and the high blood pressure. Jim, who sounded as though he had a cold.

He didn't have to be a college graduate to figure out what he wanted to talk to her about. Right about now Jim was stewing in the windowless room and his blood pressure was shooting for the moon. And sooner or later, Alejandro thought, they would come here, Jim and Holden, Jim and Bob, Jim and someone.

Alejandro stepped over her body and remembered to wipe the doorknobs as he fled.

≈

Holden read the note out loud. " 'Had to take Carmelita to Miami, didn't have a number I could call. Leave a message on the machine and I'll call in and pick it up.' " He crumpled up the note and glanced at Bob Clarion. "Did you go into the house?"

"Yes, sir. One of the windows was open. I went through his closet, but I couldn't tell if anything was gone. There were no messages on his answering machine; the cat wasn't in the house. I found two phone numbers on the refrigerator: a number in Puerto Montt, probably for one of his brothers, and Mike McCleary's home number."

"Uh-huh." Holden rose from the couch in the room without windows and watched Jim Granger pacing back and forth in front of one of the video cameras. "Did Eden call you back, Jim?"

"No."

"Did you leave your name?"

"No."

"Did you disguise your voice somehow?"

"Yeah." Granger stopped pacing. "So what do you want to do?"

"We wait for his call. And in the meantime we pressure McCleary."

"We can't get anywhere near McCleary," Clarion said.

Holden, smiling, walked over to Clarion. "Oh, I think you can if you really want to, Bob. I think you and Jimbo are just about the best in the business when it comes to doing the impossible." Then he grabbed Clarion's head in a neck lock and forced his mouth open and shoved the wadded note down his throat. Clarion started to gag; his hands jerked up and his fingers clenched over Holden's forearm. "Lesson one, Bob," he said softly, his mouth close to Clarion's ear. "I've got a shitload of money invested in our buddy Alex and I hate to lose. You understand what I'm saying, Bob?"

He dug the wad of paper out of Clarion's mouth and stepped back as the other man coughed, gasped for breath, coughed again.

"I think Bob's got the picture, don't you, Jim?"

Granger just shook his head. "Yeah, Barker, I think you made your fucking point."

"Good, Jimbo. Delighted to hear it. Call me at noon with a progress report."

He slammed the door on his way out.

19

Thursday evening McCleary stood at the window, watching Quin and Michelle as they crossed the parking lot seven floors below. His daughter's little legs were moving very quickly to keep up with Quin, who had shortened and slowed her own stride considerably.

Quin was carrying a shopping bag filled with gifts Michelle had opened here at the hospital. Her second birthday party in two days. The remains of her Aladdin cake, courtesy of a local bakery, were on the table behind him. His trash can was stuffed with wrappers and ribbons. A faint candle scent curled through the air. It had all happened a day late, but considering the general state of things, it was miraculous it had happened at all.

Birthday number two, come and gone.

He turned away from the window and his foot came down on a Lego. McCleary laughed and had to crouch to pick it up; he was still too stiff to lean over. His stitches had come out this afternoon, he had seen his daughter for the first time since he'd been shot, and his bag was packed for the safe house tomorrow.

But he wouldn't be going.

He had realized it when Quin had updated him on the case and Eastman had admitted he didn't know what to do about the videotape Christine Redman had given Quin. To act or not to act, if this, if that, the endless weighing of options: that was what Eastman was up against. The larger picture.

McCleary's own world was considerably smaller at the moment: a green Lego in his hand, a packed bag in the closet, and no safe house in his future. That was it.

His decision had been facilitated by the departure of his guards, who had been yanked at noon today, victims of the department's fiscal woes. Eastman was furious, Quin was worried, McCleary was relieved.

He had thought things through and knew the broad strokes now, where he would go and how he would get there. Only the finer details eluded him, getting to the gym before it closed tonight, where he would spend the night, where he would view the videotape in the shoebox.

McCleary sat at the edge of the bed, got up, sat down again, and polished off a piece of Michelle's birthday cake. *My daughter, my wife.* My, he thought, as in ownership, possession, as in what was yours. The very notion was fallacious.

In all his years in this business, both as a cop and a gumshoe, he had been shot, he had been knifed, he had been framed for murder, he had killed in self-defense. He had had amnesia, been afflicted with aphasia, and he had died. His life to this point had galloped along like a bad John Wayne movie.

But he had never lost a wife to another man. He had never had a daughter refer to this other man as Uncle John. He had never felt quite as he did now, as if the very fabric of his life were tearing exactly where he had believed it was strongest. In the final count, he thought, you owned nothing, you possessed nothing. The past was gone and the future hadn't arrived yet. You had yourself and you had Now.

So he waited for visiting hours to end, for the moment when the seventh floor would settle into quiet for the night. He waited because at the moment there was nothing else he could do.

McCleary was stretched out in bed, watching TV and waiting for visiting hours to end, when Jim Granger and another man strolled into his room and shut the door behind them. He immediately slipped his hands under the pillow, where he kept the .38 at night, and pushed it under his legs.

"Evening, Mr. McCleary," Granger said cheerfully. "How're you getting on?"

"Donkeys climb the moon."

Granger's companion laughed. He was taller and younger than Granger, with broad shoulders, chestnut hair, a beard, and glasses. "That's how he talks all the time?"

"That's it." Granger stopped on the right side of the bed, his companion on the left. "This is Bob, Mr. McCleary. He's never met an aphasic before. He didn't believe me when I told him how you talked. Quite frankly, I don't believe it, either." Granger leaned into McCleary's face; his breath smelled of smoke and lemon candy. "I think it's a bluff. Your speech therapist, in fact, says your comprehension is fine, it's just responses you have problems with."

McCleary offered the embarrassed smile of a man who doesn't speak the same language and reached for the buzzer. Bob grabbed it and flung it away from the bed. "I don't think so, *amigo*. We don't want any company right this second, do we, Jim?"

"I'm afraid you don't understand what's at stake, Mr. McCleary. And maybe Bob needs to explain it to you."

Bob grinned and leaned into McCleary's face just as Granger had. *Monkey see, monkey do.* "Watch my lips, *amigo*. Noel Unward gave you something and we'd like it back. Simple, huh? If you fuck with us, we'll fuck with your wife and kid. That clear enough? We understand each other now?"

"Red tide at your feet."

"A real comedian." He pressed his hand against McCleary's shoulder, holding him against the pillow. "We'd go to Noel, but he's left town. Left the country, in fact. So we're coming to you, Mr. Mac. You have twenty-four hours to turn it over or your wife and kid pay the price."

"Acid rain on the plains," McCleary said, and snapped his legs upward, wrenching nearly every stiff muscle in his body, and slammed his feet against Bob's chest. He flew back, arms pinwheeling, and crashed into the wall.

Granger went for his gun, but McCleary already had the .38 trained on him. "Turn down the sky," he snapped, and Granger stepped back, his hands in front of him like a shield.

"Just take it easy. We're leaving."

"Crazy fuck," Bob muttered as he got up, rubbing his hand over his mouth.

McCleary swung his legs over the side of the bed and moved forward as the two men moved back. They beat it into the hall and were halfway to the elevators when he glanced out. He quickly shut the door and stood against it, his heart pounding. He experienced a slippage at the back of his mind, a pause like the space between breaths, and suddenly knew that one of those men had shot him and that neither of them had killed Janis Krieger.

Either Granger or his buddy or both of them had been in the car that morning, he thought, and someone else had killed Janis.

McCleary retrieved his canvas bag from the closet, went into the bathroom, and locked the door. He removed clean clothes from the bag, then shucked his robe and pajamas and began to dress. He glanced in the mirror as he was buttoning his shirt, something he had avoided doing, and stared at the scar on his chest. It cut him neatly in half, an ugly red zipper that extended from his breastbone to his waist. He turned slightly and saw its counterpart on his back, smaller but just as unsightly.

The face in the mirror was his but not his. He looked older, thinner, grayer, like a man who would be sitting on a park bench in fifteen years.

He turned away from the mirror and finished dressing. Then he pulled the pajama bottoms over his jeans, shrugged on the robe again, and made sure it was closed at the top to cover the collar of his shirt. He tucked his wallet inside his shaving kit and wrapped his running shoes, socks, gun, and extra ammo inside his towel. On his way to the door he returned the canvas bag to the closet.

It was busy in the hall. Visitors were starting to leave, nurses were dispensing medications, several doctors were making their rounds. A nurse glanced at McCleary, probably noted the fact that the patient in 712 was on his way to the whirlpools, then continued on to wherever she was going.

The whirlpool rooms were closer to the stairs than his own room. At the most he would be exposed for the sixty seconds or so it would take him to reach the stairs. Once he was inside a whirlpool room, he threw the lock and turned on the water, which would be audible to anyone passing in the hall. He removed the robe and pajama bottoms, put on his socks and shoes, then bundled the discarded clothes and pushed them into the trash can.

Next, he shaved off his beard and mustache. He found the black shoe polish he carried in the kit and rubbed it in his hair. The stuff smelled like hell but covered most of his gray. The final touch was a pair of reading glasses. The disguise wouldn't fool Quin, he thought, but it would do the trick as far as the staff on duty.

He zipped the shaving kit inside his windbreaker, put the gun in one pocket and the extra ammo in another, and cracked open the door. Clear.

I'm gone.

He passed a nurse on his way to the stairs, but she merely smiled, probably mistaking him for a lingering visitor. When he was in the stairwell he stopped twice to catch his breath. His daily jaunts through the hospital halls hadn't prepared him for seven flights of stairs and a walk across town. He worried about how long he would have before his absence was discovered. Twenty minutes? Thirty? An hour?

One of the nurses would enter his room an hour from now to offer him a sleeping pill and another would stop by at midnight to take his blood pressure. If the first thought he was in the bathroom or in a whirlpool, then he might have as long as three hours.

But whether it was twenty minutes or three hours, sooner or later someone would realize he had left. Security would be notified. Eastman would be called. Since he was already under pressure to cooperate with the feds, he would probably notify Granger shortly afterward. Granger, of course, would know why McCleary had split and would probably issue an APB. So by one or two tomorrow morning, he thought, the shit would hit the fan.

McCleary stepped out into the lobby. It was virtually empty. The old codger at the information desk glanced up as McCleary passed but just nodded and returned to the book he was reading.

Outside, the chilly February air washed over him, fresh air that invigorated him, filled him, his first fresh air since he'd been shot. He crossed the street, and once he was beyond the hospital lights, his pace quickened. He couldn't hold it very long, he got winded too fast. But he made fairly good time as he ducked up and down side roads, through poorly lit neighborhoods, making his way toward the downtown bus station.

From there he planned to take the Island Hopper, a bus that left for Palm Beach every half hour. It would drop him within three blocks of the office. The firm's van was parked in the alley behind their building. He still didn't know where he would go for the night, but he would definitely be at the gym when it opened tomorrow morning.

≈

After dusk the park was closed to cars, except for those belonging to people whose boats were anchored in the canal. Tark left his Cherokee in a spot at the curb and went in on foot at nine on the nose. He didn't expect to see Moreno's truck in its usual spot under the lone streetlamp and hoped it meant that he had gotten a ride to the poker game. Otherwise this little venture was over before it even began.

The sloop wasn't visible from the park, but if Moreno's skiff was tied up at the dock, then he probably wasn't on board. Tark ducked under the trees, passed the playground, and stopped at the seawall. A Zodiac raft and three wooden skiffs were tied at the dock. Moreno's was the smallest of the three, with barely enough room for two people.

Tark dropped to the dock. The skiff wasn't secured in any way against theft, but who would want the thing? It looked to be on the verge of sinking and flakes of rust covered the fifteen-horsepower outboard. He untied it, pushed away from the dock, and started the engine.

He navigated out into the canal, where he could see the sloop, a dark shape against the greater darkness of the mangroves behind it. No lights on board, no music floating from the deck. *Nada.*

Tark steered the skiff toward it. As he entered the cove, he slipped a flashlight out of his knapsack. He pulled alongside the sloop and throttled way back. "*Epa*, Moreno," he called softly, just in case he was asleep in the cabin. "Hey, man, you home?"

Nothing stirred on board. Tark steered the skiff to the back, killed the engine, tied the rope to the ladder, and climbed on board. He turned on the flashlight and kept the beam aimed at the deck as he moved toward the cabin door. It was shut but not locked and creaked when he nudged it open with his foot.

The smell of Lysol hit him first, a hospital stink that had stalled inside the closed-up cabin like a weather front. It was so excessive that it made his eyes water and burn as he stepped down into the galley. He shone his flashlight across the tidy counter, the pint-size appliances, the portholes on either side. Tark opened them to let some fresh air in, then shone the light around the rest of the cabin, wondering where a man like Moreno would keep his business records.

The beam impaled a dark mound on the floor at the other end of the cabin, next to the bunk. A bag of laundry. But as he neared it he realized it was a sheet, toes poking out at the bottom of it.

Toes.

Tark crouched at the head and flipped the sheet back with the end of the flashlight. It was Moreno, all right, his corpse starting to bloat, his throat slashed from ear to ear, a gaping, bloodless grin.

Bloodless.

His eyes were shut and his nose was pushed to one side, the bridge of it broken, a piece of bone or cartilage poking up against the skin, like a stick inside a tent. His lips were blue, his skin was completely cold and reeked of Lysol. He'd been washed down with the stuff and the Lysol masked the other odor, of death, of decay. Tark guessed he had been dead at least twelve hours, probably longer. If this had been August, the deterioration would have been much worse.

He noticed white flecks of something that had gotten caught in the exposed flesh in the slit at his throat. Cocaine? He opened his pocketknife and used the tip of it to coax out one of the flecks. He examined it under the flashlight, then passed his fingers over the blade and rubbed the fleck between his thumb and forefinger. It felt gritty, like beach sand.

She slit his throat, then stuck around to scrub the blood away with Lysol, to shut his eyes, to cover him with a sheet.

She?

He lifted one of Moreno's hands. It was as clean as the rest of him, with marks under the nails that indicated she had used something sharp to clean them, a nail file or a toothpick.

Tark stepped over the body and went to the porthole closest to him. He pressed his face to the screen, breathing deeply, then pressed the crook of his elbow over his nose and mouth. He went into the head, where the air was suffused with the Lysol stink. He had never seen a shower or a sink so clean. They looked utterly new, straight out of the factory. Around the drain and along the edges of the shower he found more white flecks. Ajax, Comet, some sort of cleanser.

Cleanser, for Christ's sakes, like the Lysol hadn't been enough.

She hadn't just washed Moreno, he thought, she had scrubbed the entire cabin from floor to ceiling. He walked back to the bunk, pulled the quilt away from it. The sheet was gone and the mattress was still damp where she had tried to scrub out the bloodstains.

He returned to the foot of the body and yanked the sheet away. White flecks were caught in Moreno's pubic hair, the hair on his upper thighs, and even in his navel.

But worse than any of that was the mutilation to his right shoulder, where the Wonder Woman tattoo had been. It hadn't been cut away, it had been scooped out like a giant, pesky weed in a garden. The flesh was torn and ragged and the wound was so deep, Tark could see bone at the bottom.

Bits of cleanser adhered to the sides of the wound like uneaten cereal in a bowl. Stabs pierced the skin around it, one to his throat, another that had slammed into his collarbone, a third at the edge of his shoulder that had torn away a chunk of tissue.

Tark suspected these had been inflicted after Moreno's death, when the blood was already cold and thick and had seeped out slowly, like pus, as Moreno lay there in the stink of Lysol, his body scrubbed squeaky clean.

He felt, suddenly, that he was peering into the killer's head, into the swirling miasma of a madness that had broken loose when she had gone after the tattoo. A paralyzing fear seized him, something he hadn't felt in years. It was as if she stood right behind him, her knife poised, her madness poisoning the very air that he breathed. His head snapped around, but of course no one was there. He was quite alone, just he and Eddie Moreno, a corpse not so different from those he had disposed of in his life as Fernando Gabriel.

Men with a price on their head, men he had killed.

A wave of revulsion swept through him, revulsion for who he had been, for what he had done. He pressed his fists against his eyes and thought of Sheila Graham, Sheila of his sixteenth summer, inscribing her message in that trembling hand with an old fountain pen.

For John, who listened with such innocent rapture.

As though his innocence might be captured on that page. He mourned for that long-lost summer, for the kid he had been, for whatever innocence he had once possessed. And he mourned for the instinct that had abandoned him and that might have vindicated him.

He sat there for what seemed a long time, staring at Moreno, whose only mistake had been screwing the wrong woman. Then he fled from the body, the sailboat, the evidence of a madness he understood. And he didn't stop moving until he found a public phone and punched out Eastman's number.

≈

The beauty of Palm Beach, McCleary thought, was that it was deserted at this hour, its residents tucked away in their beds, their sweet oblivion. The shops along Worth Avenue were sealed up for the night. No limos idled at the curbs.

He cut through the park across the street from the office, aware of how deeply his body ached now, of how insidious his exhaustion was. Trees swayed and rustled in the wind, leaves fluttered to the ground, the scent of an impending thunderstorm cloaked the air. Several cars turned off Ocean Drive and McCleary stopped short of the curb until they had passed. Then he slipped across the street, the ghost of Christmas past.

The office windows were dark; no cars were parked out in front. He cut between their building and the pastry shop next door and emerged in the alley. He was relieved to see the minivan parked exactly where it was supposed to be, a lone wolf. He unlocked the van, left his shaving kit on the seat, then let himself into the building.

The night-light in the hall cast enough illumination for him to make it into the staff room without turning on an overhead light. He found a flashlight in one of the drawers and helped himself to a couple of sandwiches and a bottle of cranberry juice in the refrigerator. He put the stuff into a paper bag, took a blanket and a pillow from the storage closet, and set everything near the rear door.

His next stop was his office. From the floor safe he removed eight hundred bucks in cash, an automatic pistol, and four clips. He grabbed the backpack in the closet, which contained a change of clothes, a knife, hammer, other essentials.

He wanted to leave Quin or Tark some sign that he had been here. He couldn't write a note, not with a pen, not on the computer, so he needed something else. He eyed the Ma Bell yellow pages, remembering what had happened when Eastman had handed him a dictionary. Maybe, he thought, and picked it up.

McCleary flipped it open to the Gs. *Gym*, touch the word *gym*. His hand didn't tremble as he brought it to the page, as his finger stabbed the word, and he laughed out loud. Alejandro or just the passage of time? It didn't matter. He began tearing out sections in the yellow pages, circled certain words, then divided the pages between Quin's desk and Tark's, thus making sure one of them would realize he had borrowed the van. With luck, they might figure out what he had in mind and that he'd left the hospital for reasons other than his reluctance to be sealed up in a safe house. Maybe one of them would even connect his departure to Granger.

As for Granger, McCleary didn't believe he would make good on his threat now; after all, a threat wasn't a threat if the guy you threatened wasn't around to know it.

Ten minutes later he crossed the bridge to West Palm Beach and headed for the interstate entrance. None of his options appealed to him. To rent a campsite at one of the state parks along the beach would require talking. He knew safe places in Miami, but it was too far and he would have to battle rush-hour traffic to get back in the morning by the time the gym opened.

Although Alejandro's ranch was large enough to get lost on, McCleary suspected Granger's men might be watching the place. Might be watching his own house by tomorrow, too, in the hopes that he would swing by.

He decided the best spot was long-term parking at the Palm Beach airport. A machine would spit out a ticket as he drove in, someone in a toll booth would take his money and the ticket when he left. The area was patrolled by airport security at night, but he wouldn't be seen as long as he laid low.

He wasn't crazy about remaining in the city tonight. But his hour of grace was nearly up and he definitely wanted to be somewhere before Granger sounded the alarm.

The airport it would be, he thought, and turned onto the northbound ramp on I-95.

≈

The Holiday Inn on Fort Lauderdale Beach was overpriced, but it had two things Alejandro required: a covered garage, where he had parked the Porsche, and room service.

He hadn't left the room since he'd checked in at three that morning. When he'd gotten hungry, he'd ordered from room service, and when he'd felt tired, he'd slept. He'd spent most of his time, though, studying Eden's article files and the directories in her laptop that weren't encrypted. He still hadn't been able to get into Beacon or Blue Pearl, but he had a clearer picture of the intellectual passion that had driven Eden. She'd been searching for a principle that would unify all aspects of psychic phenomena and, thanks to her observations of Arigo, had used telekinesis and psychic healing as her focus.

He tuned the TV to a local channel for the late-night news, then sat at the side of the bed and called his home number to pick up his messages. There were three. The most recent was from Detective Eastman, his voice tight and urgent, asking Alejandro to call ASAP. The next message was from Quin, who said McCleary was definitely getting out tomorrow and she would call again to arrange a time when they could all meet. The last message was from Jim.

"I hope to hear from you by noon tomorrow, Alex. Call my cellular number."

In other words, at one minute after noon tomorrow, all bets were off and Miranda and Francesca would be killed. He pressed a two-digit code that erased the messages, then hung up and sat back against the pillows, staring at the TV. There was a piece on the music festival tomorrow night on Las Olas Boulevard in Fort Lauderdale, which was expected to draw upwards of fifty thousand people.

"Florida's senatorial candidates will take advantage of the large crowds with a short appearance before Crosby, Stills, and Nash come on at eleven." The camera cut to a close-up of Barker Holden and Senator Colt shaking hands at the opening of a new park in Broward County this morning. Just the sight of Holden nauseated Alejandro and he turned the channel to a West Palm Beach station.

He watched the news to the end, but there was nothing on it about Eden. Either the cops hadn't released the news to the press or her body hadn't been found yet. He turned off the TV and picked up the receiver to call Eastman, then realized he didn't know what to say.

The truth, he thought, he would tell him the truth. Eden White had designed certain experiments for Holden, which two federal agents had carried out. These same federal agents had abducted his daughter and sister to force him to comply with these experiments. And then what? That he had killed Eden in self-defense? That he'd accidentally blown apart the inside of her head? Sure. Even if Eastman believed a fraction of it, he would want to know what Holden's motive was, and Alejandro didn't have an answer to that.

We're almost there, amigo, Bob had said, and Jim had given him a deadline of noon tomorrow. Friday, February 19. Why then?

Make the compass spin, Alex. Heal the gull, Alex. What were you dreaming, Alex? Focus and release, focus and release, focus and release. And suddenly he was sure they knew about the beast, that they had known all along. What he had believed to be his most private and desperate secret wasn't secret at all. Somewhere along the line Eden's relentless probing had discovered it, and that was at the bottom of everything Holden had done.

Holden. Senator Colt. The festival tomorrow night. And at least fifty thousand people. *We're almost there, amigo.*

And how would they make him do it? By showing him tapes of the holocaust? Was that what it had all been about in the lab? A conditioning process? *Put on the headphones, Alex. Listen to the music. What were you dreaming? Focus and release. Kill her, Alex, and you can have your family back.*

Its heat woke me that night, the heat of the seed, of the small, hard thing tattoo Gloria had left inside me.

It burned like a small, furious sun in the center of my body, too hot to touch with my hands. I ran into the kitchen, grabbed some ice, wrapped it in a dishtowel, and pressed it against my solar plexus. I thought I could hear the soft, terrible hiss of steam rising from my skin.

When the ice started to melt, the cold rivulets of water ran down the insides of my thighs and made me think of Barker. He once painted my body with ice cubes, leaving long, slick, chilly trails that his tongue followed, licking up the water. I'm sure he did that to Janis, sure that he did with her everything he had with me. Barker and his bag of erotic tricks.

I followed Barker and Janis, did I ever mention that? Followed them one Sunday to a crumbling motel on the beach. While he waited in the car, Janis went into the lobby to rent the room. You should have seen her, dolled up in a scarf and sunglasses and torn jeans like she was some hotshot celebrity traveling incognita. I watched them hurry into the room as if they couldn't wait to get their hands on each other.

It wasn't the only time I followed them, but it was a turning point. She became the embodiment of everything I hated him for, the symbol of my own humiliation. I guess that's when I first thought about killing her. That makes it murder one. Premeditated.

I thought about that sometimes, the meaning of the word in the legal sense, death row and the chair. There is one woman on the row in the entire state, housed in solitary confinement at the women's prison. She killed a cop and now spends most of her time working on her appeal, a jailhouse lawyer. I would probably do the same with nothing but the death chamber in my future.

It's a grim room, the death chamber, stark and small, twelve by fifteen, with the huge oak chair, Sparky, bolted to the floor. There are two telephones behind it, an institutional phone and the hot line to the governor's office.

Sparky is powered by a diesel generator that produces up to 3,000 volts, or 40,000 watts, enough juice to raise the body temperature to 150 degrees. At that temperature your skin literally fries.

The chair faces a glass partition and behind it are twenty-two seats that, during the execution, are occupied by at least twelve official witnesses who are chosen by the prison superintendent. Ringside seats.

Shortly before the execution, the inmate is removed from his cell on the bottom floor of the death house. Six cells stand there, and rumor has it that the closest one is only thirteen steps from the chair. Alfred Hitchcock would appreciate that.

The prisoner is moved from the cell to another room, where his head and right leg are shaved for the electrodes. His head is soaked in salty water, which ensures good contact. When the inmate sits in the chair, a rubber hood is pulled over his head, echoes of old western hangings.

Once the prisoner is buckled into Sparky, the executioner takes his position at the switch. You never know who he is, what he looks like, where he comes from. He wears a hood whenever he's in the death house and he's referred to only as John Doe. He's hired from a pool of applicants for the job. His sole function is to flip the switch when the superintendent gives him the nod. A one-time gig.

The executioner used to make a hundred and fifty bucks for an execution. I'm not sure what it is now. Since money and security obviously aren't incentives for the job, I'm led to believe these executioners are a sadistic lot who revel in the two seconds they get to play God.

Less than four minutes after you've entered the death chamber, it's over. You're history.

Yeah, I thought about that a lot.

I removed the towel from my solar plexus and touched the area with my fingertips. It was nearly numb, red from the cold, and the burning was gone. I moved my fingers over the skin, pressing down, feeling for the seed. I found it, a small, hard kernel like a swollen ovary, and quickly took my fingers away.

Still inside me, and still alive despite what I had done to the tattoo and to Eddie.

I opened the freezer and reached way in the back, under the packages of frozen goods. It was just where I'd left it, a little bundle of tin foil. I peeled the foil open and stared at her, at Wonder Woman in her torn, frozen blues and reds.

She didn't look quite so smug now. Her once lustrous hair screamed for a professional cut and blow dry and a serious tinting. Her mascara had smeared under her eyes, leaving dark circles like bruises. Her lipstick begged for a touch-up. She wasn't moving.

But I was afraid she might only be in a state of stasis, waiting like a caterpillar in its cocoon for some genetic trigger. I was sure now that the seed inside me was keeping her alive. Through it she continued to feed on me, sucking at my soul. I couldn't dig the seed out of myself, but I could make sure she rotted and that she didn't escape until that had happened.

I dropped her on the cutting board, put on rubber kitchen gloves, took a meat skewer from the drawer. I pressed the end of the skewer against tattoo Gloria's navel and twisted it right through her.

The seed in me burned brightly, as if in sympathy, and it seemed her expression changed. A fleeting astonishment, a grimace of agony. I jerked the skewer out, then inserted a fat toothpick in the hole and pretended she was Barker. A little kitchen voodoo.

I didn't put her back into the freezer. Once the bitch thawed out, she would start to rot. I put fresh foil around her, the end of the toothpick poking through it. Next, I cut Janis's pillowcase in quarters and wrapped a piece around the tattoo.

It was lovely in an odd way, the bloodstained fabric molding itself to the chunk of frozen flesh, the stains stretching and curving until they resembled letters. And there it was, the message that had eluded me for so many months, visible only now, with the cloth fitted around the tattoo.

Trophy. As in what a serial killer sometimes takes from his victims.

I started to laugh, I couldn't help it; the very idea was absurd. Me, as a serial killer, a Ted Bundy, a Hillside Strangler, a maniac on the run. The universe loves a good joke.

I sealed the whole thing with masking tape. It required quite a bit of tape because the pillowcase was so much larger than the tattoo and the tape didn't stick well to the fabric. But the end result was a small, compact package that fit into a pretty aluminum box that had once been filled with rose petals.

I stuck it in my purse, where I could keep my eye on her. Now I would hear her if she moved, if she whispered, if she cried out. I delighted in my power over her, the very power she had attempted to gain over me through the hard, pellet thing she had left inside me.

I stuffed the unused portion of the pillowcase into a zippered compartment in my purse to get rid of in the morning. I tried to go back to sleep, but when I closed my eyes, I saw Eddie's face as he was dying and I started to cry. Serial killers don't cry.

I understand why you may find that incomprehensible; people who kill aren't supposed to feel anything. But it's not that way at all, at least it wasn't for me. Emotions were at the heart of everything I did.

20

~~~~~~

Tark sat in Eastman's Caddy watching the cops swarm through the park like hungry ants. A forensics crew had boarded the sloop half an hour ago and Moreno's body was on its way to the coroner's office.

Gawkers had gathered outside the barricade the police had set up at the entrance to the park. More gawkers stood on the bridge and still others watched from the boats anchored near Moreno's. Two of Eastman's men were going from boat to boat asking people what, if anything, they had seen or heard.

"How's your report going to read about me being on the boat?" Tark asked Eastman, who was jotting down notes on a clipboard.

"You'd gone there to ask him about some of his lawn-service customers. You found the body; you left and called me. You didn't run across his records, did you?"

"No. I think she took them."

He tossed the clipboard onto the dash and looked at Tark. "She?"

"A woman killed him, Fitz."

"What makes you so sure?"

"She'd washed his dick, for Christ's sakes."

"That doesn't mean it was a woman."

"Hey, this is just my theory, okay? Moreno and a woman were in the sack, he fell asleep afterward, and that's when she slit his throat."

"Then she rolled him onto the floor."

"Could be. Or he might've lived long enough to get to his feet and then collapsed and broke his nose in the fall. But she definitely killed him in bed. There were bloodstains on the mattress that she couldn't get out. You saw them, Fitz. You saw everything in there that I did."

"His nose could've been broken from a blow with a weapon. Or when she rolled him out of bed."

"C'mon, you've seen enough broken noses to know that wasn't from a weapon."

"I'm not a doctor, John, and you aren't either."

Tark didn't have to be a doctor to know the difference. As Gabriel he'd broken his share of bones, but Eastman didn't know about any of that. "She's actually told us quite a bit about herself. The way she shut his eyes, for instance. She might have a superstition about the dead or she might have cared about Moreno."

"And I suppose she dug that tattoo out of his shoulder because she cared so much for him, huh?"

"She'd lost it by then."

"Lost it," Eastman repeated, as though he didn't know what it meant. "I got news for you, John. Crazies don't remember to clean up the victim and the scene."

Tark realized that Eastman intended to argue every point. "She cleaned up before she took the tattoo. I think that happened last and it's when she went nuts. Until then she knew exactly what had to be done to get rid of anything that would connect her to him. She even cleaned under his goddamn nails, Fitz. A cop would do that. Or a doctor, someone who knows something about forensics."

"Like Eden White. That's what you're saying, isn't it?"

"She's the only doc in the group."

"Doesn't prove shit. Someone who watches the tube would know to do this stuff, John."

"But your ordinary Doe wouldn't have the presence of mind to carry it out. A doctor would. And we've got the beginnings of an M.O. here, too. Both Janis and Moreno were asleep when they were killed. But Moreno woke up."

"And she used a different type of weapon."

"Only because she couldn't fire a gun on board. It might have been heard."

"I still think it's possible that Holden did this," said Eastman. "Maybe he undressed Moreno after he slit his throat and did all this other stuff to make it look like a woman."

Maybe. But Tark knew that Eastman wanted to nail Holden so badly, he would concoct endless variations on the evidence. Nothing he said would change that.

The radio crackled, but Eastman ignored it. "I need more than what-ifs to get a warrant, John."

"Bring Eden in for questioning."

"It may tip off Holden."

"If he's got anything on the ball, Fitz, he already knows we're on to him and he knows we don't have squat that would hold up in court. So what if his wife used to own Link? And so what if he was having an affair with Alejandro's wife? None of that means he killed her and none of it connects him to Howard the drunk who had a cerebral blowout in Eden's lab."

"But Eden was there. If she had reported the death, you would've heard about it. That means she probably got rid of the body. So she's already got a strike against her."

Thunder rumbled through the darkness. A flash of lightning ripped a hole in the sky, and it began to rain. Most of the cops in the park, who had been combing the brush for leads, loped to their cruisers to wait it out.

"Shit," Eastman muttered. "There go whatever leads she left."

"I don't think she left any." Rain danced against the Caddy's roof and streamed over the windshield. Eastman turned on the wipers;

they smeared wide half moons of dirt against the glass. The radio crackled again, and this time Tark heard the dispatcher asking Eastman to come in please.

"You're being paged, Fitz."

"They can wait. It's probably just the captain with another bug up his ass." He turned off the wipers. "What about Alejandro's sister and kid, John? Suppose Senator Colt's right and they never made it to Chile? Suppose Holden is responsible for nabbing them? If I bring in Eden or anyone else for questioning, Holden may get spooked, call off whatever he's up to, and he'd have to kill them. I don't think I can live with that."

"Assuming you're right, they may be dead already."

Eastman didn't reply. He had said his piece, take it or leave it.

"Look, just tell me what you want to do," Tark said.

"I don't know. Alejandro's scared about something and he isn't going to tell us what it is. Quin's tried. If he didn't confide in her, he isn't going to confide in us. Neither is his housekeeper. Did you track down those priests who were at the migrant camp the other night?"

Tark nodded. "I talked to the head honcho at the camp yesterday. He says the priests are from San Ignacio Church in Belle Glade and the one named Carlos Cardenas has worked with Alejandro before. He hasn't returned my calls."

"Fuck the phone. Go out there. See what he knows. If Alejandro won't cooperate, we'll put pressure on the priest."

Tark didn't put much hope on a man who kept secrets for a living. All those confessions, he thought. All those sins. But they had exhausted their other leads. "Can you get anyone to tail Eden and the Holdens?"

"I'll try. I've got a bitch of a day tomorrow. Besides getting Mike to a safe house and teaching a class, I'm going to be sticking real close to the festival on Las Olas tomorrow night."

"Broward County's out of your jurisdiction."

"I've got some friends with the sheriff's department."

"Is Granger going to be there?"

"I'm sure he'll be around."

"Does Quin think Christine will talk to you?"

"She thinks there's a good chance."

The car phone rang and Eastman just shook his head. "Christ, they can't leave me alone for five minutes." He punched the button for the speaker phone and snapped, "Yeah, what is it?"

A young male voice, the dispatcher, said, "Uh, sorry to bother you out there, Detective Eastman. I know you're busy. But I just got a call from the hospital. There's a problem with Mr. McCleary."

Eastman squeezed the bridge of his nose. "What kind of problem?"

"He, uh, seems to be missing. The nurse who called said it looks like he left the hospital."

"Left? Walked out?"

"That's what she led me to believe, sir."

"Christ."

"I, uh, don't know the details, sir. She just asked me to contact you."

"Did it go out over the radio?"

"No, I couldn't raise you on the radio."

"How long ago did she call?"

"Thirty minutes or so. I, uh, had orders to call Agent Granger if anything came up about Mr. McCleary."

"So he knows?"

"Yes, sir."

"Great, that's just great."

"He should be at the hospital now."

"I'm on my way." Eastman punched the button, disconnecting them. His hands dropped to his legs, balled into fists. "I knew I should've gotten Mike out of there today when the captain pulled the guards outside his room."

"Maybe he just walked, Fitz. I can't see Granger or Holden or any of them nabbing him at this point. Killing him, maybe, but not removing him from the hospital to do it."

"I don't think Mike could walk more than half a mile. He'd need a car to get anywhere. It's twelve miles to his house."

Tark opened his door. "I'll follow you in my car."

As soon as Tark stepped off the elevator, he saw Granger. He was talking to one of the nurses, his back to them. Beyond him, just leaving McCleary's room with an orderly, was the other man he and Quin had seen out at the migrant camp, Bob Clarion, who had told her to stay clear of the Holdens.

He was carrying a canvas bag that Tark knew was McCleary's. For some reason the sight of it, of this jerk of a fed gripping McCleary's bag as though he owned it, infuriated Tark. He told Eastman he'd be right back and walked quickly down the hall.

"Hey, guy, that bag doesn't belong to you."

The orderly had just walked off and Clarion glanced around. His cocky smile made it clear that he recognized Tark from the other night. "Excuse me?"

"The bag. You have a warrant for it?"

Clarion laughed. "I don't need a warrant, pal."

"Think again, pal." Tark yanked the bag away from him. "I'll make sure Mike's wife gets this."

The words were barely out of Tark's mouth when Clarion spun and kicked out with his left leg, a maneuver as quick and powerful as a gunshot. His foot struck the canvas bag, lifting it into the air, and then impacted with the small of Tark's back, knocking the air from his lungs. He stumbled forward and fell to his knees, gasping for breath, his kidneys on fire. The bag slammed to the floor less than a foot away.

He grabbed it just as Clarion was coming up behind him and swung it out and up. The fed fell back, blood streaming from his nose, crashed into a wall, and sank to the floor, groaning, "My nose, Jesus, my nose."

Tark walked over to him, barely aware of the voices behind him, of the people stepping out of their rooms. He clutched the front of Clarion's shirt and jerked him away from the wall. "Force Alex to heal it, asshole."

"That's enough, Mr. Tark," demanded Granger. "Just back the hell off."

Tark straightened up, turned, and stared down at Granger. His chest was puffed out like an angry rooster's, his silver eyes were narrowed to slits in his face, his hand was poised for an easy dive into his jacket for his gun.

"You'd best teach your boys not to steal, Granger." Tark walked around him and an orderly who flanked him.

"You okay, Bob?" Granger asked his buddy on the floor.

"Yeah. Yeah, I think so. Just a nosebleed."

"Muzzle your dog, Fitz," Granger snapped.

Tark didn't stop to hear the rest of it. The three elevators were all on the first floor; it would take them half a century to get here. Stairs, he thought, and headed for the exit sign, paralleling the hall where Eastman and the others were.

He reached a hallway that connected his and the other and realized it led directly to McCleary's room, where Granger and Eastman now were. *You just slipped on out and hit the stairs, didn't you, Mike.*

Tark pushed open the door to the stairwell and trotted down seven flights to the lobby. He came out behind the information desk. An elderly fellow was seated behind it but otherwise the lobby was deserted. He exited through the side door to the employees' parking lot.

Okay, Mike, talk to me. Was someone waiting for you here? Or did you just start walking?

Tark strode to the mouth of the entrance. He looked up and down the street, a physicians' row of buildings that looked identical, each one housing a specialist of one kind or another. Their combined education probably totaled well over two centuries and their combined income might even pay off the national debt.

Beyond the row were neighborhoods that had been built when Beaver Cleaver and Donna Reed vied for the top slot in sitcoms. And past them lay downtown West Palm, Palm Beach, and the ocean.

Where to, Mike? The house for his car? Tark doubted it. Twelve miles on one functioning lung would have taken him too long, and McCleary, he thought, had been in a hurry. Tark was certain he had headed for whatever the silver key fit.

He sprinted back to the visitors' lot, where his Cherokee was parked, and drove east toward downtown. McCleary hadn't taken a cab; it would have required that he talk to communicate where he was going. A train was out for the same reason. That left the bus station.

And just like that the rusted gears of an instinct he thought had deserted him began to move and he had it. The Island Hopper. You didn't have to speak to anyone to take the Island Hopper. You simply bought a token from a machine and handed it to the bus driver when you got on. The bus had taken McCleary to Palm Beach, where he had walked a few blocks to the office and borrowed the firm's van.

The Cherokee's tires bounced over the cobblestones in the alley behind their office building. A stray cat froze in the glare of his headlights, a chunk of garbage in its mouth, its eyes a luminous red. The cat was the only sign of life Tark saw.

He parked in the space the van usually occupied. It was possible one of the employees had checked it out for the night, but Tark didn't think so. And as soon as he stepped through the rear door, he knew McCleary had been here. It was as if he had left a spoor in the air, like an animal, that Tark could smell.

In McCleary's office nothing appeared to be disturbed. Except for the phone book and the yellow pages on his desk, it was excruciatingly tidy, just as he'd left it. But his canvas bag, his emergency bag, was missing from the closet and the emergency cash in the safe was gone.

Tark went into his own office for the first time in two days. He glanced quickly through the phone messages, the papers in a wire basket, the stack of faxes. Nothing. Then he raised his eyes to the corkboard. Among the papers and notes tacked to it were several sheets from the yellow pages.

Tark scanned them, puzzled as to how McCleary was now able to make these kinds of connections when he had been incapable of it only a few days ago. Either he'd been faking it or the effects of the aphasia were beginning to wear off.

Under Automobiles, McCleary had circled a picture of a van. Under Churches-Catholic he had circled San Ignacio Church in Belle Glade. Under the Gutters—Hair heading he had starred the listing for "Gymnasiums" and circled the entry for the gym he belonged to, Club Nu. On the "Jewelers" page he had circled the word *pearls*.

For Blue Pearl, Tark thought. His departure from the hospital had to do with the Blue Pearl. He had taken the van and was going to the gym and then to the church. Tark shook his head, not understanding how the gym fit. There had to be more.

In Quin's office the caseboard on the wall above her desk was in complete chaos, papers tacked every which way, some of them curling and yellowing at the corners. Her desk wasn't much better, with stuff strewn from one end to the other, the in and out baskets overflowing, more papers stacked on top of her computer. But on her filing cabinet, held there by a magnetized frog, were several more yellow pages.

Under *U*, for the listing of U.S. government agencies, McCleary had starred the entry for the U.S. Marshal's office in West Palm. On a page from the *L* listings in the yellow pages, Loans—Locks, he had circled a picture of a locker. Under *K*, Kennels—Kitchen, he had circled the entry for "Keys." On the last page he had circled the word *hospital*.

Tark sat on the love seat under the window, lined the sheets up in a row. He arranged and rearranged them, searching for a beginning of the message. He lumped the places in one group: U.S. marshal's office, hospital, gymnasium, church. Next came the objects: van, key, pearls, locker.

Give it to me, Mike.

The rusted gears started moving again and there it was. U.S. marshal's office was Granger, who was looking for the information Blue Pearl had passed to McCleary. The key referred to the key that fit a locker at the gym, where he had stashed the information the night before he was shot. He intended to retrieve it and needed the van to do so, then he would drive out to San Ignacio Church.

What about *hospital*? Tark didn't think McCleary would include it just because it was the place he had escaped from. What seemed more likely was that Granger had come to the hospital, probably threatened him, and that was why he'd taken off. He hadn't gone home for the Miata because it was the first place Granger would check and he hadn't asked Quin for help because he didn't want to jeopardize her or Michelle.

Tark might not have it quite right, but he had enough. The gym had long since closed for the night, but it would open at six tomorrow morning and Tark intended to be there early, waiting for McCleary.

≈

When Quin opened the garage door that morning to let the cats outside, a dark Volvo was parked in the driveway. She recognized it as the car from the migrant camp. It was empty, which meant that Jim Granger or his sidekick or both of them were on their way to the front door.

She ducked back into the utility room, grateful that Michelle was still asleep, and ran into the bedroom. She tore off her robe, pulled on jeans and a bulky sweatshirt, and tucked her Browning into her jeans at the back. Then she heard Flats, wild, frenzied barking that didn't bode well for Granger's longevity if he stepped through the gate.

Since she expected the worst, she swept through the rooms, gathered up items related to the investigation, and dumped everything in the jungle of plants in the atrium.

Flats was still going nuts and apparently the feds had given up trying to get into the yard. They were pounding at the utility-room door and calling her name, making enough racket to keep the neighbors buzzing for a week. She flung open the door and snapped, "Knock it off. You're going to wake my daughter."

"Sorry, ma'am," Granger said, not looking sorry at all. "Your dog wouldn't let us through the gate." His breath smelled of lemons; his silver eyes were badly bloodshot. "Jim Granger, U.S. marshal's office."

"I know who you are, Mr. Granger."

"This is Agent Bob Clarion," he went on, gesturing toward his sidekick.

"Mr. Clarion and I have met." But now Clarion had a swollen lip and a Band-Aid over the bridge of his bruised nose. "What do you want?"

"We'd like to ask you some questions about your husband."

"Ask him. He's in the hospital."

"No, ma'am," Clarion said pleasantly. "He isn't. He left sometime between nine and midnight last night."

What the hell's going on? "Left?"

"Took off," Granger said, and produced a document she recognized. "We have a warrant to search the house, Mrs. McCleary."

"On what basis?"

"We believe your husband has obtained information pertinent to our investigation and that he came here when he escaped from the hospital. Now please step aside, Mrs. McCleary."

"Not before I call my attorney." She started to shut the door, but Granger's arm snapped out, stopping it, and he pushed past her with Clarion right behind him.

"Bob, you take the front rooms, I'll look back here."

Alarmed, enraged, and suddenly afraid for Michelle, Quin charged past them. "My daughter's still sleeping. I'll get her up."

Granger didn't stop her, but he followed her into Michelle's room and waited while Quin picked her up. She stirred but didn't wake. "When was the last time you spoke to your husband, Mrs. McCleary?"

Quin watched him opening drawers in Michelle's desk, poking around inside of them. "He's aphasic. That means we don't speak."

His eyes grabbed hers, a flash of aluminum. "When was the last time you saw him?"

"Last night." She stepped back toward the door. "We celebrated Michelle's birthday in his room. He was supposed to go to a safe house today. He hasn't been here and he sure as hell isn't hidden in that drawer you're poking around in, Mr. Granger."

He jerked a drawer out of the bureau and dumped it upside down on Michelle's bed, a malefic little grin tugging at the corners of his mouth. "This is what a search warrant permits me to do, Mrs. McCleary." He reached up to the Pet Net strung over the foot of the bed and yanked it down. Michelle's toys tumbled over the mattress, a deluge of teddy bears and dolls. "It entitles me to look where I please and as long as I please."

He picked up one toy, tossed it over his shoulder, picked up another and tossed, then another and another, until the floor was strewn with toys. Michelle woke up and cried, "Ba' man! You ba' man!" And Granger just laughed and walked over to the closet, stepping on toys, crushing them, and hurled the door open.

Quin hurried into the hall, trying to quiet Michelle, her mind racing. Clarion was still in the family room, turning it inside out. Quin grabbed the cordless phone and her purse off the kitchen counter, hastened through the garage, and didn't stop until she reached the sidewalk in front of the house.

Michelle had stopped crying, but as soon as Quin put her down, she clung to her leg and kept saying, "Mama, Mama, ba' man."

"I know, Ellie. It'll be okay, they'll leave soon."

Or we will. She called the hospital, but no one answered in McCleary's room. The sheriff's department was her next call; Eastman wasn't in and his secretary didn't have any idea where he was. She called his cellular number, his apartment, and finally his beeper service. Quin stressed that it was urgent, that Eastman should call her immediately. Then she waited there on the sidewalk, in the cold light, her daughter sniffling, her dog still barking, her cats cowering in the bushes, and Eastman didn't call.

Clarion came out of the house, the screen door banging shut behind him, and pulled on the rope that opened the trapdoor to the attic. The wooden stairs unfolded and he started climbing them. She had a wild, powerful urge just then to pull out the Browning and shoot the bastard in the knees.

Instead she called 911, spat out her address, and said two men were breaking into her house. She hung up before the man on the other end could ask her any questions, shoved the phone down inside her purse, picked up Michelle, and cut across the grass to the gate. She stepped inside the yard, Flats barking at her heels, and set Michelle on the grass behind the doghouse. "Stay here with Flats until I come back, Ellie."

Quin hastened back to the garage. Most of Clarion's body was now inside the trapdoor, his feet anchored on the upper step as he dropped things down through the door. Boxes of Christmas decorations, books, an old lamp, a suitcase. A busy, busy man. But as soon as he heard the shriek of sirens, he pulled his head out of the attic to have a look.

"Sounds like company's coming," Quin said.

Clarion hesitated, but not for long. The sirens were nearly on top of them. He scrambled down the ladder, stumbled over the boxes he had tossed down from the attic, and flew for the door just as Granger was coming through it. They collided. Clarion fell back into the garage and landed on a box of Christmas decorations. He yelped, leaped up, and began picking slivers of glass out of the seat of his pants.

She didn't know how Granger had fared until he came out of the house brushing used cat litter from his slacks. He blanched when one cruiser after another shot down the street.

"What the fuck."

"She called the cops," Clarion said.

Granger glared at her. "We *are* the cops, Mrs. McCleary."

"You're hired hands who just trashed my house. Now get the hell off my property."

He moved toward her with those silver eyes narrowed like daggers. She touched the gun at her back but didn't have to pull it out; Granger headed straight for the first police car that screeched to a stop in the driveway, his badge held high.

"U.S. marshal's office," he said loudly as the cops climbed out of their cruisers.

Clarion joined them and the men conferred, speaking too softly for Quin to hear what they said. Now and then they glanced at her, making her feel like a criminal. One of the cops finally strode over to her.

"You call 911, ma'am?"

"Yes. They barged into my house without any explanation."

"They have a search warrant, Mrs. McCleary. They don't have to give you an explanation. There's an APB out on your husband and—"

"For what?"

"He's wanted for questioning in connection with a federal investigation. This came down from the U.S. marshal's office, so that's really all I know."

"Are they finished?"

"Yes, ma'am." His gaze roamed across the mess in the garage, noticed the open attic door. "We'll wait until they leave," he added, then walked back to his cruiser.

Quin didn't know if he was just being polite or if something about all of it had struck him wrong. Whatever, she was grateful for the offer and felt like waving when the Volvo turned out of the driveway. *Don't hurry back, boys.*

21

~~~~~

At 7:30 A.M. Friday McCleary walked into the gym. He scanned his membership tag, which he kept on his key chain, and his name came up on the computer screen. Under it were his address and phone numbers, his social security number, that his wife was also a member and when they had joined.

Nearly every facet of a man's life, he thought, existed somewhere on a computer. How much money he made, his driving record, his health record, his bills, the property he had owned and sold, his marital status, whether he had children and how many, his education, where he shopped and ate, and probably even where he took a shit. Punch a button, type a number, and it was all there. The very details that made his job easier now terrified him.

He expected the computer to beep, to sound an alarm. He had visions of the fireman in *Fahrenheit 451*. He waited for Big Brother to speak from behind the mirror. Every paranoid fantasy Hollywood had ever propagated flitted through his head, quick as a mosquito. But nothing happened. Nothing.

The muscle queen behind the desk didn't glance his way; she was too preoccupied with reading the contents of the amino-acid drink she was holding. One of the trainers, a bear of a fellow with a gold earring and a frizzy ponytail, moaned as he sank into a squat with four hundred pounds resting on his shoulders.

The three plump women on the treadmills usually worked out when he and Quin did. They never sweated, their treadmills poked along while they read magazines, and they wore their gold necklaces, their diamond rings. All glanced up at him, none of them recognized him.

There were other familiar faces: the Ecuadorian doctor and the nurse he was hitting on; the steroid twins, sisters who looked like men; a guy named Theo with long silvery hair who Quin thought was as mysterious as a Greek god; people with whom he had sweated and grunted for nearly three years. Not one of them acknowledged him in any way.

He felt as if he had beaten the system, won the Lotto. He was, finally, a nonentity.

McCleary walked into the men's locker room with considerably more confidence than he'd had when he arrived. It wasn't empty. He had known it wouldn't be. Life at the gym, like life everywhere else, was cyclic. Slow when it opened, peaking between eight and ten, dying completely at eleven, picking up again during the lunch hour and again from four to eight. And when the place was busy, the music blared rock 'n' roll, the weights clattered, the lifters grunted. Sounds, in other words, that would mask blows from a hammer.

Which was why he hadn't been here at six this morning.

He dropped his canvas bag on the floor in front of the lockers. Most of them were open, their padlocks hanging to one side, keys inserted. Locker 20 hadn't been disturbed. And since he didn't have the key, the hammer in his bag would get him in.

But only when the room cleared out.

So he stalled for time. He changed into a warm-up suit, put on a pair of cross-training shoes, and waited for the shower to go off, for the guy in the stall to leave.

And when he was finally alone, he knelt in front of locker 20 and slammed the hammer twice against the padlock. It didn't give. A third blow dented the front of the lock, but it held fast. The locker-room door opened before he managed a fourth blow and he dropped the hammer into his bag and dug around inside, pretending to look for something. Stalling for time again.

"Hurry up and finish, Mike. I'll watch the door."

McCleary's head snapped around and he gaped at Tark, standing guard in jeans and a sweatshirt. Tark, who had pieced things together. "Shoot the horses," he said, laughing, and picked up the hammer again. Two more blows and the lock popped open. He shoved the shoebox, hammer, and broken lock inside his bag, then they left the locker room.

"I'll ride with you," Tark said. "Granger's boys may be watching my apartment, but Estelle's place should be safe. The feds have issued an APB on you. I heard it on the police band while I was waiting for you to show up. You're referred to as armed and dangerous."

It was pretty much how McCleary had expected Granger to react. The local cops would enforce it without question, that was their job. So one way or another, Granger figured he would win.

As they hit the sidewalk, a police cruiser turned into the lot. McCleary resisted the urge to sprint for the van and kept on walking, matching his stride to Tark's. A cop in uniform exited the cruiser and headed for the front door without a glance in their direction.

When they reached the van, McCleary looked back at the gym. Through the picture window he could see the cop talking with the muscle queen, who was studying the computer.

He quickly slid behind the wheel and passed the canvas bag to Tark, who dropped it on the floor at his feet and eyed the side mirror. "I think knucklehead just had an epiphany, Mike. He's running for the door. Step on it and head for the nearest bridge."

McCleary sped out of the lot, the sun in his face. The cruiser charged after them like some enraged beast, siren shrieking. He ran a red light and swerved off Congress Avenue and onto Southern

Boulevard. In the rearview mirror he saw the cruiser swing around oncoming cars and skid onto Southern, hugging the van like a shadow.

Tark turned on the police band radio and the dispatcher's call for backup crackled through the air. Minutes, McCleary thought. In minutes cops from every nook and cranny in the county would converge on Southern Boulevard and he and Tark wouldn't stand a chance.

"Fucker's gaining on us," Tark said, scrambling out of his seat. "Turn south at the next intersection. I'm going to try to slow him down."

McCleary jerked back and forth between lanes, shot through a yellow light, careened around a corner. Air rushed into the van; he glanced in the mirror and saw that Tark had opened the back door and was pushing things out of it. A carton of motor oil, an old playpen, a box of toys that were intended for the Salvation Army, everything was suddenly expendable.

The cruiser dodged this way and that as the cop tried to make it through the obstacle course without slowing or hitting anything. He didn't succeed. He slammed over the playpen and struck a toddler slide that bounced off his bumper and flew over the roof.

McCleary whipped east on Okeechobee Boulevard, which would take them over the bridge.

"I can still hear him," Tark shouted. He slammed the doors and clambered back into the front seat. "But we bought a couple of minutes."

Maybe not, McCleary thought. Just ahead, cars were stacking up at the bridge, waiting for it to open. He could see it all: the guardrails that had descended, halting traffic on both sides of the bridge; the boats idling in the canal; the glimmer of sunlight against the placid waters. He heard the siren closing in, saw the cruiser in the side mirror, charging toward them.

McCleary pulled into the lane for oncoming traffic, empty now, and pressed the accelerator to the floor. The van charged forward with the sleek grace of a stallion. Chrome winked and blurred on his right, the speedometer needle leaped to seventy. He turned the steering wheel slightly to the right, aiming for the empty lane on the other side of the bridge.

The tires struck the bridge as the metal jaws clattered noisily and began to rise. Sky filled the windshield, the van's nose lifted, a burst of sunlight nearly blinded him. They were airborne.

Time screeched to a crawl, then seemed to stop altogether. There was no sensation of movement. It was as if the van were suspended in the soundless blue sky, a ship in a bottle. But when their trajectory broke, the van's nose dipped forward, the ground rushed toward them, and the wind shrieked.

His body strained against the seat belt. He saw the open bridge just behind them, the water, a parade of metal and glass and chrome beneath them. Then his stomach heaved, his skull emptied.

The violence of the impact threw him forward, the seat belt snapped him back, the engine stuttered, died, and the van rolled toward a bank of trees on the right. He jerked up on the emergency brake, stopping the van just short of a drainage ditch, shoved the gearshift into neutral, flicked the key in the ignition. The engine sputtered, the body shuddered; his head pounded from the impact and he tasted blood in his mouth.

He was vaguely aware that people were getting out of their cars, running toward them, and that Tark was shouting, "C'mon, get us out of here!"

The engine caught and McCleary slammed the van into first gear, shifted into second, third, fourth, gaining speed. He raced for the beach road, veered into a right-hand turn on A-1-A, opened the van up as wide as it would go, and hauled ass toward Estelle's place, toward freedom, toward anything but what lay behind them.

≈

Alejandro entered the forensics building through a side door, just as Eastman had instructed. He had called the detective at seven that morning and suggested they meet.

It was warm inside, heat pouring out of the vents to compensate for the chill last night's storm had ushered in. He unzipped his jacket and tightened his grip on the laptop's handle. He took the stairs to the lower level, a twilit corridor that smelled of damp cement and chemicals, the bowels of the building. The second door on the right was open and the plaque on the front read MORGUE.

Eastman was just coming out of an adjoining room and shut the door behind him. "I figure this is the safest place in the county to talk." He got to his feet and gestured at the wall of metal drawers. "The dead can't eavesdrop."

Alejandro set the laptop on the counter next to a TV and plugged it in. "I'm sorry I didn't get back to you sooner, Detective Eastman," he said, and realized he didn't know how to begin.

Eastman saved him the trouble. "I'm not real good at this, Alejandro." He rubbed his unshaven jaw. "Your sister was found in a rock quarry west of town. Buried for two months in the sand doesn't leave much, especially once the vultures have found you. But dental records don't lie. And some of the things forensics can tell nowadays stagger the imagination.

"It's likely, for instance, that your sister's fingerprints were burned off with acid, possibly while she was still alive. Several of her upper molars were pulled, probably to make dental ID more difficult. She was shot in the back, Alejandro, straight through the heart, from a distance of maybe thirty yards. That suggests she may have been running. I have some of her personal effects for you."

Alejandro felt a violent shifting within himself, an upheaval, a tectonic plate surrendering to some deep, internal pressure. It wasn't just grief; he had suspected for weeks that she was dead. This was abject terror that before Holden was finished, his daughter would also be taken from him.

Eastman removed a dark plastic bottle from a drawer under the counter. A container for pills. There were no pills inside, just a small emerald ring and a gold chain with a gold mermaid dangling at the end, his sister's jewelry.

His throat closed up; his fingers tightened around the plastic bottle, and he put it into his jacket pocket.

"There's a tractor moving through that quarry right now looking for your daughter's body, Alejandro. I hope to hell that isn't what it takes for you to tell me what the fuck's going on, why your sister and daughter never made that plane to Chile."

"Who found Francesca?"

"A quarry worker, late yesterday afternoon. I didn't hear about it until two hours or so ago. I've had her dental records on file since Senator Colt and I spoke. She has this wild-ass theory, see, that Barker Holden grabbed your sister and daughter to force you to do something. Or to be a part of something. Experiments, maybe, with Eden White."

"I'd like you to see something," Alejandro said, and booted up the laptop. "There are two encrypted directories on this computer. At least one of them pertains to Eden's research on telekinesis, with me as the focus. Blue Pearl. That was Eden's code name for me. It took me much longer than it should have to figure out the word that got me into the directory."

He accessed the word-processing program, moved the cursor to Blue Pearl, and hit the enter button. The screen cleared and a single word appeared: PASSWORD?

He typed: BARKER. "Because Blue Pearl is really his project. He's the one who has poured four or five million a year into it."

A list appeared of thirty files that covered his entire association with Eden, from the moment Janis had introduced them to the night in the sleep lab when Holden and Eden had had a falling-out. He hadn't read them all, but he had read enough.

"Then there's this one. Beacon. It really had me stumped. I just kept trying words and names until I got lucky." After the password query, he typed: LYDIA.

"Probably because she used to own a private lab called Beacon that tested a clairvoyant named Christine Redman."

"Yes," Eastman said quietly. "I know."

Alejandro followed his gaze across the room, where a corpulent black woman stood in the doorway of the adjoining room. Behind her was Quin McCleary.

Quin smiled at him. Christine Redman strode over to him with her fleshy hand extended. "Christine Redman, Mr. Domingo. I'm here because I have shit for brains. Quin's here because her old man split from the hospital. What's your excuse?"

"Eden is dead," Alejandro blurted out.

She, Quin, and Eastman exchanged glances he had no trouble interpreting. They knew about Eden. "Her assistant found her body yesterday evening," Eastman said, opening a drawer and taking out a videotape. "We thought it best to keep it out of the press until the coroner had a chance to make his report. He says she died of a massive brain aneurysm, which was probably triggered by fear when an intruder broke into her house."

"It was self-defense," Alejandro said, but Eastman ignored the statement and popped the tape into the VCR.

"This tape is courtesy of Noel Unward and has quite a lot to do with Eden White. Frankly, I've been stumped about what to do with the damn thing. Maybe you can tell me." And he started the machine and the tape flickered to life.

≈

They parked the van behind the house, so it wouldn't be visible from the road. Tark was sure the eight-foot-high hedge along the fence would hide the van from the neighbors, if they were inclined to be nosy, which they usually weren't. As they got out, Estelle came through the back door in her terry-cloth robe, Elvis scurrying along behind her. She hugged McCleary hello. "The feds say you're armed and dangerous."

"Fuck the schmucks."

She laughed. "I couldn't agree more. Do they have a make on the van, Gabby?"

"They do now."

"There's a tarp in the shed that should do the trick."

Once they had gotten the tarp over the van, they went inside and settled at the kitchen table. A small black-and-white TV on the counter was tuned to the local news. "They've been flashing your picture every half hour or so, Mike," she said, setting out mugs of coffee and a coffee cake. "Not that it's going to do much good. I hardly recognized you."

Elvis had recognized him, though, a scent he probably associated with old man Boone. McCleary picked him up, fed him a bit of coffee cake, and the raccoon curled in his lap like a cat. "Smack the flies," McCleary said, pointing at the bag on the floor near the door.

Tark retrieved it and pulled out the shoebox. Estelle handed him a pair of scissors to cut through the tape. He emptied the box and arranged the items in a row on the table: a videotape; a pamphlet for San Ignacio Church in Belle Glade with the name Carlos Cardenas penciled in at the bottom; three grainy snapshots of Holden, Eden White, and Jim Granger; a sheet from the sales contract between White and Holden for the property out near Belle Glade that she had sold him. There were also several yellowed newspaper clippings on Christine Redman and a page on psychic healing that had been torn from a book. The words *blue pearl* were circled.

"We already know all this," Tark said, disappointed.

Estelle corrected him. "You didn't know it when Mike was shot, Gabby."

McCleary wagged the tape and pushed away from the table with Elvis draped over his shoulder. While Estelle cleared travel brochures and books off the couch, McCleary popped the tape into the VCR.

At first the image on the screen was so dark, Tark thought the lens cover had been on when the camera started to roll. There was no voice, just the sound of a car, of tires crunching over gravel. Then light washed across the screen. Headlights. The tape had been shot at night.

The car stopped; the camera panned a sugarcane field, lights glimmered through the stalks, and paused on a sign that read BELLE GLADE, 12 MI. Then the car was on the move again, traveling parallel to a canal. Moonlight spilled across the water, the field on the other side of it, and painted the rutted road a pale yellow.

A water tower loomed in the distance, a dark shape against the moonlit sky, a bulbous monster on long, spindly legs. Tark thought it resembled something out of *The War of the Worlds*. He couldn't tell whether it stood at the end of a canal or several miles away; the dark, distorted spatial perspective.

In the next frame the car was approaching a produce sign. Estelle

froze the image and the words were clearly visible: a pound of toma-
tos for a buck, heads of lettuce for a quarter apiece, pick your own
strawberries for fifty cents a pint.

"The Florida sticks for sure," Estelle said. "But twelve miles in
which direction from Belle Glade?"

Tark said, "He's leading us somewhere. The Belle Glade sign, the
canal, the water tower, a produce stand, the sugarcane."

The image faded, and when it reappeared again, the car had
stopped. The cameraman—Unward, Tark thought—was on foot
now, moving down a moonlit road that looked as if it had been cut
through a sugarcane field. The cane was enormous, ten or twelve feet
high, and the road was dirt, rutted with potholes and puddles of
water. He paused for a slow pan, then turned up an even narrower
road. No, a driveway, a gravel driveway that must have twisted into
the cane for a quarter of a mile before it widened.

And there it was, a house on stilts with a ten-foot concrete wall
around the back yard. Parked in the space under the house were two
cars, a pickup and a sedan. With that, the tape ended.

McCleary rewound the tape, then fast-forwarded it to the first
shot of the sugarcane field and froze the image. He tapped the screen
and glanced at Tark. "Yeah," he said. "I see it. A shape, but I can't
make out what it is."

"A plane," Estelle said suddenly, outlining it with her finger, and
McCleary clapped. "You see it, Gabby?"

"I'll take your word for it."

"What's so important about the house?" she asked.

"I don't know," Tark replied. "But it deserves a look, don't you
think, Mike?"

"Vamonos."

"Hey, you can talk!" Estelle exclaimed.

McCleary shook his head and rocked his hand from side to side.

"Sometimes," Tark translated. "When you aren't thinking about
it?"

He nodded, pointed at the tape, then at Estelle.

"No problem," she said. "I know just where to stash it. Look, if
you want to change clothes or shower or anything, make yourselves

at home. Towels are in the linen closet. I'm going to whip up some omelets. I can't think straight without food in my stomach."

A Quin remark, Tark thought, and knew it had struck McCleary the same way. It was in his face as he stared after Estelle and it crouched, shadowlike, in his eyes when he glanced at Tark. Quin suddenly towered between them, her presence as thick and impenetrable as a block of cement.

He knows.

Tark felt a dark, crushing guilt, a kind of corruption. He knew that if McCleary had been able to express himself, he would have said something right then, a blunt question: *"You sleeping with my wife, Tark?"* "I need to get some things together," Tark said, and went into the kitchen.

"You can't drive the van," Estelle said, her back to him. She stood at the counter chopping mushrooms. "The Bug's just had a tune-up. It should do okay."

Tark came up behind her and slipped his arms around her waist, his gratitude as extreme as his guilt had been moments ago. "You interested in driving?"

"Nope. This is your gig, Gabby." She turned in his arms. "Besides, someone should stick around here who knows where you guys are headed." She poked him in the ribs. "Now get out of here so I can get on with my omelet experiment. You'll probably find everything you need in the shed."

≈

They had questioned him, he had questioned them. Now Quin said, "Describe what happens in a typical session in the windowless room, Alex. Start to finish, with as much detail as you can remember."

When he got to the part about the dairy products, she interrupted. "Why would they prohibit you from consuming dairy products for a day before a given session?"

"I don't know. Maybe it's just a way of controlling me."

"Yeah," muttered Christine. "That sounds like Eden."

"But the last time, the night I slept there, they gave me milk to drink," he said.

"Sure. It makes you drowsy," Quin said. "The amino acid in milk does it. Tryptophan."

"Shit, no," said Christine, shaking her head. "Tryptophan synthesizes serotonin, which, like, soothes the brain, makes you less aggressive. That's what puts you into a snooze."

"So they wanted you as hyped up as possible," Quin said to Alejandro.

"Except for the time they monitored my dreams."

"Fitz, can you find out what drug synthesizes serotonin?" Quin asked.

"You bet I can."

While he was on the phone, Quin asked Alejandro if he could distinguish between how he felt when he healed and how this other energy felt. He noticed that she avoided any reference to Eden.

"The first I can control and focus, the other just . . . I don't know, gets away from me. It just happens."

"No way," Christine said, shaking her head and smoothing her hands over her ample belly. "You don't walk around wide open all the time, Alejandro. You tune in and out, turn it on and off. You may not be aware of it, but that's exactly what you do. I been there, you hear what I'm saying? For me it was the white noise, all them voices chattering away in my head until I knew I was goin nuts, huh? So I turned them off. Shut them out. You got to do the same thing and you got to fine-tune, you hear what I'm saying?"

"Lithium," Eastman said as he hung up.

"It's used for manic-depressives, isn't it?" Quin asked.

"Yeah. According to the coroner, it enhances the synthesis of serotonin, which, in turn, stabilizes both the ups and downs that afflict manic-depressives. It doesn't sedate you, it doesn't create dependence, and it doesn't alter normal moods. When it's given as a carbonate salt, it's completely absorbed in an hour and a half. The kidneys get rid of ninety-five percent of it unless you have kidney problems; then it might be toxic." He paused. "You have kidney problems, Alex?"

"Not that I know of. Are there any side effects?"

"Stomach irritation, diarrhea, fine motor tremors. Those disappear as soon as the medication has worked its way through the body, within twenty-four hours."

"So what's it going to be, Alex?" Quin asked. "A dose of lithium or a crash course with Christine?"

You control it or it controls you. He glanced at the big round clock on the wall. The hands stood at 10:17. He reached for the phone. "A call to Jim and then Christine."

22

The farther inland you went, McCleary thought, the less the air smelled of salt and brine. It was filled instead with the odor of fresh water from Lake Okeechobee and the sweet fecundity of the soft, black earth. His old man, a farmer, had once remarked that if you stuck a dead twig into earth like this it would rally and sprout leaves. He believed it.

The scent permeated the air around Belle Glade and drifted like some etheric presence through the stalks of sugarcane. The fields teemed with workers, most of them probably migrants, who were setting up heaters in case the temperature tonight dropped lower than predicted. In some sections of the fields tall sprinklers whipped back and forth, spraying arcs of water.

The eternal battle between man and nature was waged valiantly out here where untold millions of crops were at stake. But nature would have her way one way or the other, McCleary thought. Hurricane Alfred had taught him that much.

Their first stop was San Ignacio Church. McCleary waited in the car while Tark went inside and was surprised when he reappeared five minutes later.

"Cardenas is supposedly out of town and everyone else acts like they've never heard of Alejandro."

As McCleary put the VW in gear, Tark spread open a map on his lap and measured off a twelve-mile circle around Belle Glade. "Even with landmarks, this is going to be like looking for a mite in a cat's ear."

Yes, indeed, McCleary thought. And even if they found the house, they had no guarantee that it harbored any secrets.

They spent the next two hours driving up and down roads so insignificant, they didn't appear on any of the county maps. They saw plenty of canals but no produce signs. They located three water towers but none that looked quite like the one on the tape had looked.

"We need a better map," Tark said. "Pull over for a second."

McCleary did and Tark got out and opened the VW's hood, where the trunk was. He returned with a pack of aviation maps. "I don't know why the hell I didn't think of this before."

Other things on your mind, McCleary thought. Like Quin maybe?

Tark found the map he wanted, smoothed it open on the dashboard. It covered South Florida, a topographical rendering so precise a pilot could fly from point A to point Z by using nothing more than landmarks on the ground. Cities, towns, pastures, fields, power lines, railroad tracks, canals, rivers, lakes, even water towers.

Tark marked off a twelve-mile radius. "With a little luck we'll find this sucker before dark."

McCleary wasn't counting on it. There was less than an hour left of daylight, and once it went, it would be darker than pitch. There were more than a dozen water towers scattered around Lake Okeechobee, and seven of them stood within the circle Tark had drawn. Tark crossed off three of these because they were privately owned and appeared to stand within sugarcane fields; the water tower on the tape had risen from an open field, near or at the end of a canal.

Two of the remaining four towers were close to canals, so they decided to concentrate their search around them.

"But there must be fifty miles between them," Tark said. "By the time we get to one of them, it'll be dark. Produce stand, water tower, the canal, the cane. Those were the landmarks."

He was forgetting the plane on the tape, McCleary thought. He took the map and stabbed a finger at an airstrip, and Tark slapped his thigh. "Yeah, you're right. If there's a plane, there's got to be an airstrip of some sort, especially out in those fields."

They located three airstrips in the twelve-mile radius, probably private strips that were used primarily for planes spraying pesticides. But one of them looked to be two or three miles from the south tower.

"The south tower it is," Tark said. "Let's hit it."

≈

The sky to the east had gone purple, a deepening bruise against which the stalks stood out like black paper cutouts. There were still ridges of color to the west that spilled across the fields and tipped the stalks in gold, but they darkened by the second. Tark figured they had ten minutes at the most before the sun set.

McCleary sped southeast on a dirt road that was barely wider than the VW and angled between the walls of green like a fault line. Leaves and branches slapped the windshield and clawed the sides. Tark had lowered his window and the cold air blew into the Bug, sweet and cold.

The road suddenly widened, feeding into a second, wider road, and an irrigation canal appeared on his left.

McCleary pointed in the distance. The water tower was the color of a silver filling and looked smaller than the one on the tape. It wasn't at the end of the canal, either, but two or three miles to the right.

"Keep driving parallel to the canal," Tark said.

The produce stand appeared moments later, a wooden stand with an aluminum roof at a juncture in the road. "It's not on here," Tark said, studying the map.

McCleary suddenly turned to the right and the airstrip materialized on the left, nothing but a strip of dirt and weeds that cut straight through a field of cane for perhaps twelve hundred feet. There was a fence around it with a No Trespassing sign posted on it. In front of a small hangar were a low-wing single-engine plane and a chopper.

A chopper, for Christ's sakes.

And beyond it, winking through the stalks, were lights.

McCleary plowed through the field and pulled up alongside the fence, where the car wouldn't be seen from the road. They loaded up on extra ammo. "We check it out first, then decide what to do," Tark said. "Sound good to you?"

Thumbs up.

"Then let's go."

A damp chill nipped at Tark's face and neck as he climbed out of the VW. The breeze skipped through the stalks of sugarcane, rustling them until they sounded like sentient beings. He heard a car moving away from him, the crunch of his shoes and McCleary's, then the only sounds were croaks and clicks and animals calls.

As they moved parallel to the fence around the airstrip, the last of the light bled from the air and stars popped out against the black skin of the sky.

≈

I parked on the south side of Las Olas, behind the church. The festival was just getting under way, but I had something to take care of first. Tattoo Gloria must have sensed something was up because as I walked around to the front of the church, she began to hum and strum my comb like a harp.

I slapped my hand against the side of my purse to make her stop and she got mad and pounded back with her blue and red bloated fists. She was a sore loser; I think Eddie had spoiled her.

As I climbed the steps she had a tantrum, making so much racket that I had to take off my jacket and drape it over my purse to muffle the noise. I'd seen old ladies do this with their tiny poodles, yappers no bigger than your hand. It made me laugh, the idea of the tattoo as a hyper poodle, a little pet I could collar and walk on a leash.

It was quiet inside and that made me nervous: I was afraid she would really put up a fuss. I kept my jacket over my purse just in case and glanced through the church. A handful of people sat in the pews, waiting for their turns in the confessionals. The air smelled sweet from the candles burning near the altar.

I'm not Catholic, I'm not anything anymore, but I know what those candles are for. They are lit for the dead, to facilitate their passage through the afterlife. I lit one for Janis and another for Eddie and realized I had nothing to offer them, no blessing, no prayer, not even remorse.

A tap on my shoulder startled me, I don't like to be approached from behind. "I wish you wouldn't do that," I said without turning around.

Her small, coy laugh irritated me just a little. "Don't be such a stick-in-the-mud. C'mon, let's talk outside. It's too hot in here."

We walked out into a tremendous garden at the side of the church, two women who had absolutely nothing in common except Barker. I don't know that either of us ever loved him, love is too gentle a word. He was, instead, the big mistake we each had made in our lives, the decision we most deeply regretted, our private and embarrassing obsession.

Oh, Barker would give you his body readily enough and a taste of his power, but his heart was his own, an undivided country. Except with Janis. I believe he actually loved her, that she had claimed him in a way no other woman had.

Their common history bound him to her, memories of childhood, all that. But I think, too, that he recognized some elusive quality in her that only a man could see. I suppose his feelings for her deepened after she married Alejandro. She was suddenly beyond his grasp, separate and inviolate in her life, in love with a humble fisherman who possessed a power Barker couldn't buy or win. He was seduced by her sudden mystique. So he had to corrupt her marriage, the life she had carved out for herself.

Now here I stood with one of his other women, the two of us

prime examples of the adage about wanting what you can't have. Barker, as unattainable as paradise, drove each of us mad in different ways. I guess you could say we were functional crazies, fooling most of the people most of the time.

"Well," she said as we sat at the edge of a water fountain.

"Well," I echoed.

We were alone out here, the sky strewn with stars, the New River just beyond the fence, close enough to hear the whistle of a tugboat as it passed. I could see the gate from where I sat, covered with bougainvillea vines just like the fence. The padlock on it was a reminder that crime is rampant even in the best of neighborhoods.

Part of the garden was torn up along the fence; it looked as though new pipes were being installed that would carry rainwater to the river. It created a disruption in the visual serenity of this place and for some reason that bothered me.

"A penny for you," she said, handing me one. "And a penny for me."

We turned so we were facing the fountain. The water caught the reflection of light from the church and held the images of our faces, side by side, as though we might be sisters or very old friends. It was like glimpsing another, parallel world down there in the water and I wondered what I had become in that world. Whether Janis had lived. Whether Barker survived.

"If you've got second thoughts, now's the time to voice them," she said.

"The same goes for you."

"No second thoughts from me."

"Me, either."

We tossed our pennies into the water, a silly ritual we had agreed on months ago.

"Let's go over it one more time," she said.

One of us would be on the median strip that ran down Las Olas, the other would be in front of a café on the other side of the street. We would be far enough back from the stage so that we wouldn't be seen, but not so far that Barker would be out of range.

"We shoot as soon as possible after the introductions, at the first thunderous applause," I said.

"That sounds like something Barker would say," she remarked. "So damn sure it's going to be a deafening applause rather than hoots."

She was absolutely right, of course, and I laughed.

"So then we melt away into the crowd," she finished.

I nodded. Even with silencers there would be a noise, but the applause would cover it. "What're you going to do with your gun?" I asked her.

"Get rid of it as soon as possible. What about you?"

"The river."

"That's a long time to hold on to it."

"Only three or four blocks."

"But once people realize someone's been shot, there'll be a stampede. Chaos."

She sounded alarmed and with good reason. We were partners of a sort and if one of us was caught, the other would be in jeopardy. There was no predicting, after all, what you might agree to under duress. A plea bargain, to turn state's evidence for a lesser sentence, it had nothing to do with a breach of trust. It was simply how the system worked and we both knew it.

"Chaos will make it easier," I said. "We play it by ear, do whatever we have to, and meet back here."

She gazed out toward the river, speaking softly. "It's crazy, you know. That we've planned it, that we're standing here talking about it, that we're actually going to do it."

"I don't think it's crazy at all."

It was the essential difference between us. She knew nothing about the world that exists just beneath the surface of this one, the realm of signs and portents, of synchronous junctures. She didn't know that just one day before I intended to shoot McCleary someone else had done it instead. She didn't know about the hard pellet thing the tattoo woman had left inside me through Eddie. She didn't realize that even as we sat here by the fountain I was looking for a sign that would assure me we would succeed.

Her vitriol toward Barker was, in many ways, purer than mine. She hated him. I only wanted to get even.

She glanced at her watch. "I guess we'd better get going."

"You go first," I said.

She looked at me then, really looked at me, searching my face for something. "If you've got something to say, just say it," I said.

That made her smile. "Yeah, we've been pretty blunt with each other all along. What the hell. Did you kill Janis?"

"Did you?" I retorted.

She shrugged. "I thought about it. Then when it actually happened I realized it wasn't Janis I hated, it was Barker. It wasn't Janis I wanted dead, it was Barker. Not too long after that I called you and suggested lunch."

I remembered that lunch last October, every word, every confidence we exchanged. I remembered how strange it was to sit there talking about our individual relationships with Barker, the lies, the deceptions, the sexual games. And of course we talked about Janis.

"So we have Janis to thank for this."

"I guess we do. Janis and Barker." She shook her head. "Ironic."

Not to me. Just the fact that she had asked was the sign I'd hoped for. We stood there a moment longer, a certain awkwardness between us now, a sense of closure. Then she said, "I'd better get going." She stuck out her hand, very formal now. "Good luck."

As if luck had anything to do with it, I thought, and pushed aside the formality by hugging her. It surprised her, but she returned the hug, patting me on the back like a mother comforting a small child. "We'll both get what we want," she said. "What we deserve to have."

With that, she turned quickly and walked off toward the church. I was alone with the sound of the tugboat churning upriver and the promise of the future that was now rushing toward me.

≈

McCleary thought the house looked larger than it had on tape, two stories suspended on eight concrete pillars that lifted it nine feet in the air. Under the house was a space large enough for half a dozen cars; only a blue pickup was parked there.

Stairs climbed the side of the house to a small porch and a front door. Lights burned in the windows. The generator that supplied electricity made a lot of noise and smoke curled out of a chimney, infusing the air with the sweetness of pine. The stalks of cane rustled at his back. Despite the signs of habitation, the place possessed the eerie, waiting stillness of a cemetery.

He and Tark crept out of the field and ducked under the house. Nothing moved here, the gravel driveway was empty. They spread out, checking for another exit; in the Keys many of the houses on stilts had more than one, stairs that unfolded like an accordion from a wall, a trapdoor, a back porch with a pull-up ladder. In the event of a flood, it would provide another means of escape.

This house on stilts, though, was in a league of its own; it had an elevator that was practically invisible, wedged between a work bench and a washing machine. But there was no telling where the door would open inside the house. Until they had some sense of who was inside, how many people, and why it was important enough for Unward to film it, they agreed to scout around some more.

McCleary inspected the laundry chute that protruded between a washer and a dryer. He moved the wicker laundry basket out of the way and listened at the mouth of the chute. Music, too faint to tell what it was. Then he heard a toilet flush, the clatter of pipes, running water. Clothes suddenly flew out of the chute and fluttered to the ground at his feet.

A woman's blouse, bikini panties, a pair of Liz Claiborne jeans, size 6, and a lace bra, size 34C. He gestured at Tark, who hurried over, and they pawed through the laundry in the wicker basket. No men's clothing, just a woman's and a child's.

McCleary plucked up a kid's yellow shirt with Cinderella gracing the front in her evening gown and glass slippers. The tag inside read *4 Small*, and he suddenly understood what Unward had done.

He thrust the shirt at Tark, pointed at Cinderella, then at the tag, but Tark didn't get it. "A kid and a woman," he whispered. "So?"

McCleary stabbed at the size, but Tark still didn't understand. Frustration surged up McCleary's windpipe like indigestion and he spat, *"Hi—hija."*

"Daughter?" Then, when it dawned on him, he whispered, "Sweet Christ. Alejandro's kid is up there."

The pipes clattered again, the sound of running water ceased, he heard splashing. A tub, he thought, the woman was getting into a tub. It wouldn't get much better than this.

He and Tark moved toward the elevator, weapons drawn.

≈

The familiar music drifted through the Lincoln, that haunting melody of flutes, the steady beat of distant drums. In one version or another, this music had played time after time in the windowless room.

Alejandro realized that the music had been part of their conditioning, that even as he sat there the music plucked at his emotions as though they were strings on an instrument. Agitation, anxiety, anger, fear, a black despair. So he ejected the tape and said, "I'm not in the mood for music."

"Then I guess you'll have to listen to me." Granger said.

"I don't think so."

Alejandro dropped his seat back and pulled his baseball cap over his face. The pills Granger had told him to swallow when they'd gotten into the car were still under his tongue and he spat them into the cap. Chemical magic, something that probably enhanced the ancient parts of the brain, the animal brain, something that sharpened his aggression. The music, the drug, and a particular word or phrase to trigger it, that was their plan.

"She'll be in the crowd, Alex," Granger said. "That's where you're going to see her."

Alejandro removed his cap from his face, the partially dissolved pills inside of it, and let them fall between his seat and the door. He looked at Granger, his profile perfectly rendered in the flash of lights on the interstate.

"And she'll be my incentive to be as accurate as possible when I focus, release, and kill the senator."

A beat passed; he had taken Granger by surprise. "Very good, Alex. I'm impressed. Eden didn't think you knew, and since she's been our expert, Barker believed her. The guy Miranda is with has orders to shoot her if he doesn't hear from me by nine-thirty."

And we both know that's the only thing keeping you alive, ass-hole.

"Miranda's actually fond of this guy," Granger went on. "He's been her protector from the big bad wolves who threatened to harm her and Aunt Francesca. That's what she believes, see, that we acted on your request because one of those many nuts out there put you and your family on his list of no-goods."

"How long had Barker been sleeping with my wife?"

The abrupt switch in topic didn't seem to bother Granger. "Years, since she was in high school." He exited the interstate and headed east. "They couldn't live with each other and they couldn't live without each other. I know it sounds corny, but it's true. In one off period Barker married Lydia, in another off period Janis married you. He was an asshole where she was concerned. In all the years I've known Barker, Janis is the only thing I can fault him for."

"So he loved her until she interfered with his political goals, then he decided she was expendable."

"Wrong," Granger said softly, shaking his head as though Alejandro were a young child who didn't know the world was round. "C'mon, Alex. Think about it. Dead, Janis has been a political liability; alive, she was just a pain in the ass. Why would Barker kill her? They both understood the rules. They liked the drama, they enjoyed living out a fucking soap opera."

"And you, Jim? What's the thrill for you?"

Granger just laughed. "I enjoy the game."

23

Music, the distant chatter of the generator. Those were the only noises Tark heard as he and McCleary slipped through the hall. They had removed their shoes outside the elevator and his stocking feet slipped across the redwood floor like skates on ice.

At the end of the hall was a sunken living room, decorated with floor rugs, black leather couches and chairs, coffee tables carved from stone. Everything in its place. Not a sound, not a soul around. They crossed it; McCleary headed up the stairs and Tark followed the sound of water rushing through pipes again.

He entered another hallway. A slice of bedroom was visible at the end, clothes draped over a chair, the face of a bureau. The door closest to him was shut and the noise of water was coming from behind it.

Tark turned the knob and walked in with the 9mm aimed at the woman's pretty face.

Her Oriental face.

Jenny Ming, Holden's secretary, was sitting back against the tub, water to her neck, one leg stretched out above her, the razor frozen at her shin. Surprise didn't begin to describe her expression.

He shut the door with his foot. "Who else is in the house?"

"No one." Her leg came down very slowly. She set the razor carefully on the edge of the tub, kept her hands where he could see them. "I'm here alone."

"Whose house is this?"

"Mine."

"Long commute to work." He stepped forward and without taking his eyes off her whipped a towel from the rack and tossed it at her. Her arms snapped up and she caught the towel in midair. Quick reflexes, lickety-split. "Turn off the water and get out, nice and slow."

She stood, water dripping off her, her lustrous black hair wet at the back, her every movement provocative whether she intended it or not. She wrapped the towel around her body, tucked it in at the front, turned off the faucet, and stepped out. "What now, Mr. Tark?" A cocky little smile crept across her mouth.

"You tell me, Ms. Ming." He grabbed her hair, jerked her head back, and pressed the end of the gun to her throat. The arrogant smile shrank like an island at high tide. "Let's start over again. Whose house is this?"

"Mi . . . mine."

"Barker gave it to you? Sold it to you? What?"

"I . . . I rent it from him."

"For how long?"

"Two years. Since I went to work for him on the campaign."

"And who else is in the house?"

She grimaced. "Jesus, you're hurting me."

"Who else?"

"No one."

"Where's Miranda?"

"I . . . I don't know. Ned picked her up a while ago."

"Who's Ned?"

"He works for Barker."

"What does Holden want with Alejandro?"

"I don't know."

He tightened his grip on her hair and she winced. "Say again?"

"He . . . he wants him to kill Senator Colt."

"Very good." He eased up on her hair. "Where's Francesca?"

"I don't know anything about Francesca."

"Was she ever here?"

"No. Just the girl."

"Then where's Francesca?"

"I . . . I think she might be dead."

"You think."

"Yes." Tears had come into her eyes now; she seemed frightened, but he wasn't entirely convinced that she was. "I woke up one night, I guess I'd heard something outside, and . . . and I saw them out back."

"Saw who?"

"Jim Granger and someone else. They were digging up the grass and flowers at one end of the pool. I . . . I saw them lift a body out of the ground. I decided I'd better not watch and went back to bed."

"How did they get in?"

"Probably the same way you did. The alarm wasn't on."

"When was this?"

"The first week in January, during that warm spell we had."

"And you think the body they lifted out was Francesca's."

"Yes. I . . . I had told Barker about this odor around the pool. He said he'd take care of it."

He let go of her, stepped back. "Who watched Miranda during the day when you were at work?"

She hunched her bare shoulder and rubbed her cheek against it. Her voice cracked when she spoke. "Ned when he was here. Otherwise she pretty much took care of herself. She was happy here, okay? She didn't want to go home."

"And why's that?"

She refused to look at him and her voice was very soft when she spoke. "She thought she was here for her own protection, that someone had threatened to kill her and her aunt."

Tark removed a pair of handcuffs from his jacket, told Jenny Ming to turn around, and cuffed her hands behind her back. He opened the door and gestured toward the hall with the gun. She moved sideways along the wall, like a crab.

"Into the bedroom," he said.

She bit nervously at her lip, then turned her back on him and took small, urgent steps toward the bedroom. "What . . . what're you going to do with me?" she asked.

"Keep moving."

As they entered the bedroom, something changed in her posture, a slight tightening in her shoulders, a sudden tension in her spine, no more than that. He saw it, knew what it meant, but he wasn't fast enough. The man sprang at him from the left, from behind the door, a human torpedo. He struck Tark in the chest, knocking the gun from his hand, and he fell back into Jenny. She screamed as they crashed into a nearby table, toppling a lamp, books, glass objects that shattered when they struck the floor.

The screaming stopped. Tark rolled away from her, his feet scrambling for purchase in the shards of glass. The first shot whizzed past his ear and the second tore into the floor at his feet, freezing him on his ass, his hands behind him, pressed down against the broken glass.

"You're a relentless bastard, aren't you, Tark."

Bob Clarion stepped around the edge of the bed, a Smith & Wesson aimed at Tark's chest. Fresh from a roll in the hay with Jenny Ming, he was wearing just boxer shorts and socks and a Band-Aid across his swollen nose. Under other circumstances Tark would have laughed.

"Nice nose, Bob."

"Move away from her, over to the wall."

"So how do you fit in Holden's new regime?" Tark asked, pushing himself with his feet until his back was up against the wall. "Hangman? Personal bodyguard? Stud service?"

"Shut the fuck up." Clarion crouched next to Jenny and, without looking away from Tark, felt for a pulse at her neck. "C'mon, Jen, wake up." He shook her shoulder. "C'mon."

But she was out cold. Clarion straightened up, pointed the gun at Tark. "If I'd had my way, you'd have been dead five minutes after you left the hospital this morning. Get up."

Tark pushed slowly to his feet, his palms bleeding from the glass, his knapsack a lopsided lump on his back. A pulse drummed wildly at his temple and everything around him was rendered in stark, painful clarity. Clarion in his boxer shorts, his finger twitching against the trigger, and McCleary rushing him from behind, swinging a baseball bat.

It struck Clarion just as his head snapped around, a loud, resounding whack in the ribs and a second quick and savage blow to his wrist that knocked the gun out of his hand and sent him reeling. Clarion's face went completely white; he shrieked and crumpled to the floor clutching his shattered wrist. Then McCleary was on him, a rider straddling a horse, pressing the bat across his throat until he was choking.

Tark suddenly understood that McCleary had his own score to settle with Clarion, that he hadn't shot him because the girl wasn't upstairs. He scooped up his own weapon, knelt next to Clarion. "Ease up a little, Mike, so he can talk." Tark pulled Clarion's arm away from his body; his eyes were bright with pain. "Bet it hurts like a son of a bitch, doesn't it, Bob." He pressed his foot over Clarion's elbow to hold the arm in place. He gasped; sweat erupted on his face. "In fact, I don't think it'll take much to pop that bone right through the skin."

Clarion grimaced and squeezed his eyes shut.

"So where's Miranda, Bob?"

"Gofuckyourself."

"Shame on you, Bob. I expected more from you," he said, and stepped on Clarion's wrist.

He howled, he sobbed, and when Tark lifted his foot, Clarion gasped, "Festival."

"In Lauderdale? On Las Olas? That festival?"

"Y-yes, Jesus, yes."

Music and politics and fifty thousand people. "He's driving her there?"

"He flies to the Boca airport, then drives her someplace to see Alejandro."

"Where?"

"I . . . don't know."

"Not good enough, Bob." Tark rested his foot against Clarion's mangled wrist, no pressure yet, just the promise of pain. "Where?"

"It's the truth," he said quickly. "All I know is it's close to Las Olas, probably a parking lot or something."

In a town of a million parking lots. "And after they see each other, what's supposed to happen?"

"Ned flies her back here."

"And Alejandro? Where's he go?"

"The festival. He and Jim go to the festival. But that may not be right. Sometimes Jim tells me things are going down one way and they go down another."

"And that's where Alejandro is supposed to pop a few blood vessels in the senator's brain."

"You think it's bullshit, but you haven't seen what I have."

"How far away do you have to be not to be affected?"

He was starting to hyperventilate from the pain and his words shot out in short staccato bursts, like erratic gunfire. "It . . . varies. As little as . . . eight feet. As much as thirty."

"Can he direct it?"

"Don't think so. Eden thinks maybe. If he has to."

"Like with his kid as an incentive."

He nodded.

"Then why would Ned fly her back here before they turn Alejandro loose?"

"I . . . I don't know."

"Sounds to me like Granger's lying to you."

He didn't say anything.

"And after this is all over, what happens to Alejandro?"

He had stopped hyperventilating; his eyes were closed. "Jim brings him back here."

"And he and his daughter disappear?"

His eyes opened. "Something like that."

"One last question, Bob. Who shot Mike?"

He didn't reply. He didn't have to. The answer was there in his eyes, a dark, roiling fear. McCleary saw it, whipped the bat up, and slammed the end of it over Clarion's fingers. He didn't scream this time, didn't whimper; he simply passed out.

They moved quickly then, without either of them uttering a word. They tied Clarion's arms and legs and put him and Jenny Ming in the closet. While they searched the house for the keys to the chopper, Tark paused long enough to step into the room where Alejandro's daughter had been living.

It was a tremendous room, bright and cheerful and filled with toys. She had her own TV and VCR, fifty or more videotapes, books and workbooks, even a playhouse equipped with furniture. She had lived there for nearly two months, believing the lies she'd been told, one more of Holden's pawns. He hastened out to find McCleary.

≈

At 9:30 the Lincoln turned into a lot behind a restaurant on Las Olas Boulevard. Quin drove past, searching both sides of the street for a parking space. Cars lined either curb, blocking driveways and fire hydrants, and angled into spaces so tight, their bumpers were up against the trunks of trees. No one gave a shit, a concert was in progress. This was South Florida, after all, the capital of rude and indifferent drivers.

It had taken her an hour and a half to tail the Lincoln as it had hopscotched south through the country, switching from the interstate to roads east and west. She didn't intend to lose Granger and Alejandro now, especially over a goddamn parking place. So she swung into the next unobstructed driveway she saw and stopped on the sidewalk.

No doubt about it, the Miata would be gone in thirty minutes or less, towed to a vehicular hell somewhere in the city's bowels. It would cost her a small fortune to reclaim it. She locked the doors and tucked the keys in the canvas pouch buckled at her waist. They clattered against her gun as she sprinted back down the road to the lot where the Lincoln had turned in.

The music on Las Olas was so loud, she could feel its vibrations under her feet. A sax hit a long, quivering note and she tasted its

metallic resonance against the back of her teeth. The receiver clipped
to her belt kept up its steady beep, indicating that Alejandro was
within its half-mile range. The transmitter was sewn inside his baseball cap, which Granger had neglected to scan before they'd left the
ranch. But Granger, she thought, had had more important things to
dwell on.

Quin reached the lot. The Lincoln occupied a handicapped space,
a police bubble now on its roof. The car was empty, the hood still
hot. She jerked the bubble off as she passed and tossed it into a
nearby garbage can. Let Granger get towed, she thought, and hurried
through the breezeway between the restaurant and the building next
to it.

She emerged on Las Olas, midway between the eight blocks that
had been closed to traffic. It was a wide boulevard bordered on both
sides by shops and restaurants and divided by a median strip shrouded
with black olive trees. The streetlights looked like old-fashioned gas
lamps; even the metal posts had been weathered to suggest the turn
of the century. But Las Olas, for all its charm, had never been intended
for this crushing tide of humanity.

It was impossible to estimate the size of the crowd. People sat on
curbs, in beach chairs on the median, on towels in front of the
shops. They spilled into the street, milling, laughing, talking, dancing,
drinking beer. They had turned out with their kids and their exotic
dogs in their best clothes and their worst: Anglos, Latinos, blacks,
and Orientals; tourists and residents; young and old and middle-
aged; the whole complex face of South Florida.

She anxiously scanned the crowd on the sidewalk, looking for
Granger and Alejandro. They couldn't have gotten too far. No more
than five minutes had elapsed since the Lincoln had parked, and she
knew Alejandro would dally as much as he could without rousing
Granger's suspicion.

The receiver continued to emit a steady beep as she moved west
on the sidewalk, headed for the main soundstage. The closer she got,
the more congested the crowd became, forcing her into the street,
where she hugged the curb and dodged adults, kids, dogs, strollers.
The sax hit a high note, a thunderous applause lifted through the

cool February air. A break appeared in the crowd on the sidewalk and she suddenly spotted them two hundred yards ahead.

Alejandro was leaning against a wall, trying a shoelace, and Granger stood next to him, watchful and tense, a hand-held radio at his mouth. Quin dropped back behind a clutch of people with dogs, waiting until they moved forward again. When they cut into the crowd in the street, she followed.

The music ended and a man's voice boomed from the speakers with the rah-rah enthusiasm of a disc jockey. Everyone feeling good? Everyone having fun? Wasn't this weather great? Roars and more applause, the power of the herd. The ghosts of other mob scenes suddenly haunted her, the Rolling Stones at Altamonte, the Democratic Convention of 1968, race riots in Miami, in L.A., the ubiquitous momentum of the masses.

A terrible tightness burned in the center of her chest and it was difficult to breathe. Her stomach churned; the back of her throat went dry. Quin tried to keep them in sight, elbowing her way through the crowd, the sea of bodies closing up behind her, a gelatinous, sentient mass.

The voice coming over the speaker was now thanking Budweiser for their generous sponsorship, the city of Fort Lauderdale for their cooperation, the police department, the shopkeepers, the musicians, the candidates. Granger and Alejandro reached the median and crossed it, their heads bobbing. Quin was close enough behind them to keep them in sight and just hoped that Granger didn't glance around.

She stopped on the median, where she had a better view of the crowd in the street. Granger and Alejandro were now ten or twelve yards from the front of the stage. Quin didn't see Clarion, but three men in suits hovered at the sides of the stage, all of them equipped with hand-held radios. Eastman was nowhere in sight, which worried her.

Onstage the last of the musicians were packing up instruments and the moderator was introducing the candidates. Neither Holden nor Sasha Colt looked completely at ease. They squinted against the footlights, smiled uneasily at the moderator, at each other, at the crowd.

If they had figured this correctly, then Alejandro's daughter should be somewhere nearby. But there were dozens of kids in the vicinity of the stage, clinging to their parents' hands, riding on their shoulders. It was like looking for the proverbial needle in the haystack.

Holden was speaking to the crowd, his voice flowing from the speakers, smooth as scotch. She glanced back at Granger and Alejandro, hoping for a cue, anxiety clawing through her. That was when she saw the bearded fellow in the denim coveralls working his way through the crowd until he was ten feet or so behind Alejandro. He might have been anyone except that he, like Granger, held a radio close to his mouth and a small girl was riding on his shoulders.

Alejandro's daughter: Quin was sure of it.

She stepped off the median and pushed her way toward them.

≈

"Get closer to the stage," Granger was saying. "Closer, closer." His fingers dug into Alejandro's back, the figures onstage shifted, swayed, blurred. *Closer. Closer.* The words slammed around inside his skull; he felt the pressure building inside of him now, the heat, the racking urgency to release, to release. The memory of Christine Redman's voice drifted through him.

When you feel it building, imagine it as a narrow beam of light that you can direct, brighten, turn off or on.

Yes, he thought, and then he saw her. Miranda.

She straddled the shoulders of a bearded man wearing denim coveralls and a flannel shirt. One of her hands was pressed against the man's forehead, the other was clasped in his hand. She was laughing, Miranda was laughing, her head thrown back, her hair tumbling over her shoulders, a black cascade. *Laughing.* She had believed their lies, she had been sucked into their intricate deceptions. Her name died on his lips and he lunged toward her and away from the stage, away from Granger, the inside of his head on fire.

Miranda saw him. Her arms reached out; she shouted, "Papa!"

Just when it seemed she was within his reach, Granger grabbed the back of Alejandro's jacket and Miranda sank from view, sank into the mob, gone, vanished. Alejandro whipped around and the heat swept through him and out of him with a terrible purity, a beam of energy aimed straight at Granger. He stumbled back, his face skewed with pain, and Alejandro spun again, searching frantically for Miranda, for the bearded man. The inexorable mass gave way to his urgency, thinning here, breaking there.

And in one of those breaks he glimpsed Quin with his daughter draped over her shoulder, Miranda kicking and screaming, and the bearded man pushing through the crowd toward her. Fitz Eastman suddenly appeared out of nowhere and slammed into the man, hurling him to the ground. Alejandro grabbed Miranda and Quin yelled, "Get out of here, just get out of here!"

Alejandro bulldozed through the mob, oblivious to everything but his daughter clinging to him like a spider. He reached the median strip, stumbled across it, and Eastman appeared at his side again, gripping his forearm and shouting, "Down this way!"

They burrowed a path through the herd in the street until the mob thinned and then they ran, ran for the shops, the nearest breeze-way, ran for freedom.

≈

Those moments exhilarated me, I'd be lying to say otherwise. The cold against my cheeks, the heat of the bodies around me, the hard reality of the gun in my hand, and Barker up there onstage with the lights stroking his face. A man with the world literally at his feet.

And I was going to end it.

You can't possibly understand what it's like to play God in this way, to know you possess that kind of power. Zap, you're dead, you're gone, you're fucking history, fella. This man had made love to me with the smell of other women still on him. He had manipulated and cheated me with his lies, his deceptions, his duplicities. But, worse, I had let him do it. There's no forgiving that, an acquiescence that became his sanction.

In the seconds before I squeezed the trigger, I no longer thought about the possible consequences, prison, the electric chair, the end of the life that had fueled my obsession. I thought, instead, about a target, about the bull's-eye that covered a head and torso in a shooting gallery. I took aim.

I was jostled from behind as I fired. The bullet intended for Barker flew wide of its mark and struck someone in the crowd. I fired again and this time Barker toppled back, and although the shots were muffled by the silencer, a woman started shrieking and the PA system picked up her voice and it exploded from the speakers. "Oh my God, my God, he's been shot!"

And the crowd went berserk.

It crashed over me, the screams and the shrieks, the stink of panic as fifty thousand people tried to flee at once. I was literally swept away, no more significant than a pebble in a raging flood. People slammed into me from every direction, a human stampede. Those who fell were trampled.

I somehow managed not to stumble, to falter, to fall. I struggled for space in the crazed and frantic mob and somewhere inside of it the pressure blew and I could breathe again, I could feel the pavement under my feet again. Moments later thousands of bodies spilled into an intersection and I was spat out like undigested food. I fell to my knees, people tripped over me, the ground shook beneath me. I hauled myself up and raced for the safety of the church.

24

~~~~~

Quin wasn't sure how she made it to the sidewalk or how the guy in the coveralls had managed to stay with her. But he was gaining on her, plowing through the hordes behind her, a missile that never deviated from the target. She couldn't get to her car, she was on the wrong side of the street. Even if she hadn't been, the car was no longer an option because her canvas pouch had been torn from her waist during the stampede and the keys were inside it. The keys, the transmitter, her weapon, gone gone gone.

The nearest intersection was still half a block away and she didn't think she would make it before the bearded fellow reached her. But just ahead people were scrambling through the shattered window of a café, leaping toppled tables and chairs, rushing for whatever safety an enclosed space might provide. She dashed for the door and squeezed through the crushing human weight.

Inside, looters were smashing display cases, fighting over money in the open cash register, and hauling away anything that wasn't soldered down. Quin barreled past them to the ruin at the back of the café, where more people scurried like panicked rats across shattered plates and glasses and overturned booths.

She nearly tripped over the huge copper espresso machine that lay on its side, water leaking from its belly, and skidded through puddles of liquid toward the rear door. She glanced back only once, but it was enough. The bastard in the coveralls was pushing into the chaos, his face bright with rage.

Quin leaped over the fallen chair that blocked the door and tore left into the alley. Her shoes slapped the worn cobblestones, her breath erupted from her chest in noisy bursts. People charged past her for the nearest side street. Her head snapped around for another look and there he was, relentless, inexhaustible, closing the gap between them. Never mind that everything had ended when the senator's screams had shot from the speakers. This guy was a maniac on automatic who had decided that she was going to pay for what had gone wrong.

As she flew out of the alley, she heard the shriek of sirens, the chatter of helicopters, and the blaring of horns from the knots of traffic as cars attempted to flee the area. It sounded like the end of the world.

The closest building was the Catholic church on the corner. Its stained-glass windows were lit up and people seeking refuge or looking for trouble were crowded on its steps. She glanced back quickly and when she didn't see the man behind her, she cut through the church parking lot.

It was jammed with cars, horns were honking, frightened faces were pressed to windows. She plunged through the hibiscus hedge on the other side and loped parallel to a wire-mesh fence that enclosed the property behind the church. In there, she thought, and grabbed onto the fence and started climbing.

≈

The chopper swooped east just two hundred feet above the panic on Las Olas. Thousands of people swarmed through the street, a dark, undulating mass that looked aware, McCleary thought, conscious, like some new life-form. A police chopper hovered just above the main stage while injured people were loaded inside. Several other choppers were landing on rooftops and cops in riot gear were pouring out. Spotlights swept through the streets.

The chopper lifted and Tark swung it out over the buildings on the north side of Las Olas, then dipped in low again. Cars choked the roads, the intersections were blocked, and people were scattering across lawns, front yards, sidewalks.

"There!" Tark shouted, stabbing a finger straight down.

Alejandro was racing up the street with a child on his shoulders, Eastman at his back, and Granger was galloping toward them with two other men. Tark dropped another hundred feet and headed for a cul-de-sac outside an apartment complex. McCleary was already out of his seat, at the door.

When the chopper was within half a dozen feet of the road, McCleary slid the door open and the air rushed in, cold, sweet, and clamorous. Alejandro and Eastman raced toward them and Granger suddenly opened fire. People nearby scattered or hit the ground and Eastman faltered, gripping his thigh. He motioned wildly for Alejandro to go on and struggled forward. But Granger was closing fast. Too fast.

McCleary leaped out, dropped to his knees, and sighted down the barrel of the .38, giving Eastman the edge he needed. He felt an almost savage satisfaction when Granger stumbled and sprawled in the road and his two companions decided their future lay elsewhere.

Seconds later Alejandro and his daughter scrambled into the chopper and McCleary reached Eastman and helped him inside. Then he slammed the door and the bird lifted, fast, effortlessly.

≈

Quin dropped to the ground on the other side of the fence and pressed back against it, blood pounding in her ears, and tried to catch her breath. Through the trees she could see perhaps a dozen people. They were coming through a side door in the church, milling around a water fountain, talking to several priests, and huddling in small, tight groups.

They seemed fairly calm and she suspected the front doors had been locked, thus preventing a repeat of what she had seen in the café. She moved unsteadily away from the fence, her legs like rubber, and headed for the nearest group. Standing off to one side, talking on a cellular phone, was Rita.

Quin didn't question what she was doing here, how she had gotten here, or anything else, her relief was too great. She started toward her, then Rita turned and she saw her. In the spill of light from the church's windows, her face looked odd, contorted somehow, as though excess gravity were pulling her skin in opposite directions. Her arm dropped to her side, her hand still gripping the phone, and she glanced quickly at someone exiting the church. A woman. Lydia Holden.

Quin froze, looking between them, trying to piece it together, dimly aware that both women looked as shocked as she felt. Lydia and Rita, here, together. There was only one way it fit.

She lurched to the right and raced for the mango trees that stood beyond where people had congregated. Heads turned her way, one of the priests raised his arm as if to catch her attention, but she didn't stop. Rita shouted, "Quin, wait!"

Low-hanging branches slapped her in the face, weeds scraped against her jeans; she tripped over roots that protruded from the ground. She reached the gate, but it was locked, of course it was, the goddamn thing was locked and she could hear them behind her now, Rita calling her name, Lydia hissing at her to shut up.

She ran deeper into the trees and finally dropped into a ditch alongside the fence. It was partially filled with water that flowed into the opening of a concrete pipe, a drainage pipe large enough to hide in. She ducked inside of it, scurried through several inches of water and gunk, hunkered over until the pipe narrowed and forced her to her hands and knees.

When she couldn't hear Rita anymore, she sank against the side of the pipe, fear consuming her like an acid. It was wet—cold, wet, totally black. Noises echoed in the pipe: drips, splashes, rustlings, other sounds she couldn't identify. It was impossible to gauge distance by sound because every noise echoed. She dropped to her hands and knees again and crawled forward. She heard them again and looked back.

There, a dim glow at the opening. A weak flashlight, maybe the flame of a lighter, she wasn't sure. If she screamed for help, she probably wouldn't be heard and Lydia and Rita would know for sure that she was in there. If she remained as she was, she would be too easy a target. So she sat down in the water and flattened out on her back.

Water rose to her earlobes, mud oozed through her hair.

The echo of Rita's voice reached her first. "I'm telling you, she's not in there, Lydia. Quin wouldn't go in someplace like that. She scaled the fence."

"We would have seen her. Where's the pipe go?"

"How the hell should I know? C'mon, let's get out of here. We've attracted enough attention."

"The river," Lydia said as though Rita hadn't spoken. "I bet it goes to the river."

Something whistled through the air just above her head and she realized one of them had fired a silenced weapon into the pipe. Another shot flew past her, then a third that was too close for comfort. She flipped over, sprang onto her hands and knees again, and dived forward.

A shot pinged against the concrete to her right and she dropped to her stomach and slithered like a snake, propelling herself with her feet, her hands. One or both of the women scrambled into the pipe behind her and now the glow appeared again, definitely a flashlight with weak batteries. Its beam swept around, seeking her.

The curved, damp sides of the pipe reflected enough of the light for Quin to see how it narrowed and seemed to turn or slope downward just ahead. Moving toward her from the darkness was a pair of luminous red dots. *A rat, Jesus, a rat.*

She dived to the side to get out of its way, water splashing into her mouth and eyes, and rolled into another pipe. She scooted back on her buttocks, through a thick slime, and the air filled with the choking stink of sulfur, of rotten eggs. It was colder here and she began to shiver. She pulled her legs up against herself, wrapped her arms around her legs, and pressed her lips together to keep her teeth from chattering.

Think fast. Her stiff, slippery fingers fumbled with the buttons on her leather jacket. She shrugged it off and unzipped an inside pocket. A lighter, a pack of soggy matches, several quarters, a couple of bills, a pack of Kleenex.

She removed the quarters, the lighter, the Kleenex and put everything but the quarters in her shirt pocket. Then she wadded up the jacket and pressed it against her knees. Her eyes were fixed straight ahead, where the light slipped over the side of the pipe she had just left.

"Quin, I know you can hear me."

Rita, her voice echoing through the pipe.

"It's not like you think."

C'mon, keep coming, Rita.

"Barker's the only one I was after. I didn't kill Janis. I didn't shoot Mac. Quin, say something, please. Jesus, I never meant it to go this far. But, my God, Barker was going to kill Sasha. You said as much yourself, Quin, you—"

"You went after Barker because he used you, Rita, and you hated him for it."

Her voice, like Rita's, echoed through the maze of wet pipes. Quin couldn't tell exactly where she was, but the beam of light slipping over the walls gave her a distinct advantage. She estimated Rita was four feet from the juncture of pipes.

"You're right, you're exactly right," Rita said. "But he deserved it, Quin. Look at the things he did, abducting a kid, murdering Janis, the—"

"You've been sitting in judgment on the bench too long, Rita, and Barker didn't kill Janis, you did. Which means you also shot Mac."

The light slid closer. "No, you're wrong. I swear."

"Then let's walk out of here if I'm wrong, Rita."

She had an image of Rita sitting next to her daughter at the picnic table the other night, feeding her. Aunt Ree, who could do no wrong. The thought sickened her.

Now. She hurled the quarters. As they clattered against the concrete, a muffled shot pinged through the pipe, and the noise echoed through this subterranean place. Quin groaned and slapped the water with her hand, quick, frenzied splashes, an injured woman struggling for cover. Rita fell for it and hurried forward, Rita, who couldn't stand to bait a hook but who would do almost anything to preserve her nasty little secret and save herself from prison.

And when the light was almost in front of Quin, flickering weakly against the concrete, she threw her wadded jacket. Rita fired. Quin exploded out of the adjoining pipe and they both went down, rolling through the water and muck, the flashlight gone, the gun gone, and the darkness alive with rats.

They were everywhere, the rats, squealing, scurrying, panicked by the gunshots, their eyes burning red in the blackness. They scampered across Quin's legs, her back, her head. Claws poked through her clothes like nails, teeth sank into her flesh. She reared up, trying to throw them off as Rita screamed and thrashed somewhere nearby, then fell back.

Quin expected to strike the side of the pipe but there was only air, the colder air of the other pipe again. She clambered forward on her hands and knees toward a light that was pale and milky and not quite real. The squeals surrounded her, the squeals and Rita's hideous screams. Then she was lifting up, she was rising, she was shooting through a metal grate with rats clinging to her jeans. She was still kicking and grabbing at them when she collapsed on the grass, in the fresh, cold air, in the chilled sweetness of the night.

And Lydia was there, waiting for her or for Rita or for both of them. As Quin rocked onto her knees, Lydia backed away from her, shaking her head, her arm snapping up as she muttered, "Christ, look what you've done, just look, you've ruined everything, you . . ."

Quin didn't hear her after that, didn't see her gun, didn't see anything but her skinny legs moving backward very quickly. Something inside her snapped, she could almost hear it, a sound like a dry, dead branch struck by lightning. She leaped up screaming, a raw, primal scream wrenched from some pocket of rage so deep inside her she didn't recognize it as her own until she tackled Lydia and the screaming stopped.

They struggled for the gun, and it went off, a deafening explosion.

Lydia ceased moving and Quin rolled away from her, rolled across the cool, soft cushion of grass, her ears ringing, the smell of the earth thick in her nostrils, her body lit up with pain, bleeding where the rats had bitten her.

People rushed toward her. She could see them bobbing in the lights beyond her, but she couldn't hear them through the terrible ringing in her ears. There was only the strange, vast silence of the night, stars winking like portals to other worlds, the full moon rising and setting off on its solitary journey across the February sky.

MAY 16

West Palm Beach

I don't know what else there is to tell you, Alex. I've tried to be truthful about how things were, about why I did what I did, about all of it.

I may not regain the full use of my right arm, did they tell you that? The bullet shattered my elbow and I only see a physical therapist twice a month. It's not nearly enough. My attorneys have to fight for every privilege, it doesn't matter how small it is. But that's how the system works, Rita and I knew that. How is she, anyway, Alex, do you know?

I heard via the grapevine that she had to have plastic surgery on her face. Because of the rats. Rumor also has it that the bar pulled her license. But that's no surprise, is it? She won't be practicing law where she is.

She should've gotten a heavier sentence, three years is nothing.

But in some ways I think I actually got off easier than she did. With gain time and good behavior, I'll be eligible for parole in ten years. It's not all that long, really, you just take it a day at a time. I'll be in my fifties then, not too old to start over.

I expect to lose my appeal about Barker's will, but I've stashed away enough in Caribbean banks to see me through. It was something Janis and I did together, two trips to the Caymans, both of us with money sewn into our clothes, money to hide from the IRS, that's what we told each other.

We were lovers on those two trips, our private experiment, our little adventure. I wanted to know what Barker saw in her and I guess she wanted to know why he had married me. I don't think either of us found answers to those questions.

I don't feel any remorse about Janis, but I do hope that you can find it in your heart to understand why I had to kill her. You do understand, don't you, Alex? Don't you?

≈

Lydia Holden's voice echoed in McCleary's ears long after Eastman had turned off the tape recorder.

"That's it?" Tark asked.

Alejandro shrugged. "It's more than I expected."

Quin popped the tape from the recorder and tossed it to Alejandro. "I figure this sucker is yours, Alex."

He turned it over in his hand, looked at Tark, at Quin and Eastman, then at McCleary. "What do you think?"

"Who needs it?" McCleary replied.

"My thoughts exactly." He proceeded to pull the tape out of the cassette and snipped it into confetti with a pair of scissors from Eastman's desk.

McCleary got up and walked over to the window. It was May outside. The tourists were long gone, the acacia trees were just starting to bloom, the brutal summer heat was around the corner. He had been seeing Alejandro once a week for two months now. He stuttered occasionally, but otherwise he could speak again. His doctor, of course, attributed it to the natural course of aphasia, not to anything the Chilean had done.

With Holden dead, his Harvard buddy had not fared very well. Jim Granger was awaiting trial and, with testimony from Noel Unward and Christine Redman, would probably get eight to fifteen years. Other candidates had rushed into the senatorial race but, despite the publicity about Rita, every poll indicated that Sasha Colt would maintain her seat.

He and Quin still had good days and bad. Although he wondered what had happened between her and Tark, he had never asked and she had never volunteered the information. He no longer thought of the marriage as a possession, as something that would always be there, like furniture, like rooms in a house. Just like Lydia Holden, he took it one day at a time, one foot in front of the other, and hoped for the best.